Wait For You

LIANNE LA BORDE

Matador
Unit E2 Airfield Business Park,
Harrison Road, Market Harborough,
Leicestershire. LE16 7UL
Tel: 0116 2792299
Email: books@troubador.co.uk
Web: www.troubador.co.uk/matador
Twitter: @matadorbooks

ISBN 978 1805140 092

British Library Cataloguing in Publication Data.
A catalogue record for this book is available from the British Library.

Printed and bound by CPI Group (UK) Ltd, Croydon, CR0 4YY
Typeset in 11pt Minion Pro by Troubador Publishing Ltd, Leicester, UK

Matador is an imprint of Troubador Publishing Ltd

For Grandad Ray, who told me to be a writer when I was still scribbling kids' ghost stories.
For Grandad John and his sense of adventure.
For Grandma Marje, a poet and writer who inspired me with her creativity and love of the arts.
For Grandma Ruth who gave me her sparkle (and my dad).
And for Grandma Joan, whom I never met but who gave me my mum.

April's Hospital Room

SUMMER 2022

Dylan

It was taking a lot of noise to keep April alive. If it wasn't for the heart-shaped birthmark on her delicate wrist bone, I wouldn't have recognised my ex-girlfriend underneath the spaghetti mountain of wires and tubes. They snaked in and out of her body like laces looping up a trainer. Plugged into machines hissing and sucking with the ferocity of Darth Vader as they forced oxygen into her lungs.

My gaze moved to the paper-thin slices criss-crossing April's skin. Crimson cuts caused by the smashed fragments of her windscreen. Angry purple splotches swelled across her limbs where she'd rattled around the driver's seat. Nothing broken, all aesthetic and superficial. They'd heal.

It was the cream bandages wound tightly around her head we had to worry about. Surgeons had done what they could. Pieced her fractured skull back together like some morbid jigsaw. Shocked her heart when it gave up on the operating table using those vicious paddles that look more at home in a torture chamber.

Stand clear, boom, wait... beep.

They'd brought her back to life. Twice. The second time, she'd been clinically dead for ten minutes. Nobody knew the extent of the damage to her brain or if my April was still in there at all.

Rubbing my temples and blinking back the dull aching behind my eyes, I wasn't sure what caused me more pain. April vanishing three years ago, her sudden reappearance yesterday or that now she was almost certainly going to die on me.

But this couldn't be how our story ended, could it? Me, slumped over her empty shell with nothing but regrets and a handful of memories.

Like everything always had with April, it turned me into a tremoring wreck whilst simultaneously wanting to scream into a pillow. Mostly because I could no longer deny what I'd been hiding for three years. I was incontrovertibly still in love with her.

Damn it, April.

My emotions fizzed inside me, threatening to explode like a shaken bottle of Coke.

Before April had left without a word, we'd been that sickly in love couple that annoys the hell out of everyone. And she'd certainly picked her moment to show up again. My arms teetering with boxes as I packed the car, ready to move in with my new fiancée.

The second I found her standing on my driveway, the breeze blowing her wavy brown hair in front of those royal blue eyes that had always anchored me, I'd known everything would change. Because April was back.

Still, her sudden reappearance brought on a bout of

that pillow screaming I mentioned. We rowed. She drove off in a state, just as drops of a summer shower splodged onto the tarmac. My stomach lurched just thinking about it. Now she was barely alive, and it was my fault.

Raking through our chequered history, I tried to work out what led us here.

'I kissed her too soon,' I said. I was talking to myself, really. Still, my best mate, Adam, sitting legs splayed on a plastic fold-down chair next to me, wearing his PE teacher joggers and hoody, answered anyway.

'In all honesty, Dylan, pal, ye and April were a car crash from the start. Pun unintended.'

I scowled. Clumsy as Adam was, he was right, and he'd been there at the beginning, when we were still students at The University of Manchester. The very morning April and I met, we set off hurtling down a dangerous road. Spent weeks playing a perverse game of will-they-won't-they chicken. It was me who slammed my foot on the accelerator when I should have braked. Me and my stupid lips.

Yes, it was certainly that stupid bloody first kiss. The moment my mouth pressed against hers, I'd known it was a bad move. Too soon. People would get hurt. But April was so damn intoxicating. Impossible to resist, standing all tiny and dishevelled as the first flecks of dawn light shone in her bay window. She tasted of cheesy Doritos and Pinot Grigio. The rose scent of her perfume lingering on the curve of her neck.

In romcoms, first kisses usually come at the end. The indisputable sign of a happily ever after. Yet, for April and me, it triggered a domino effect of bad decisions. One after another until we smashed headlong into each other,

3

careering into several others. We caused a whole motorway pile-up of broken hearts.

Thinking about that early February morning of our second year, I could almost feel the softness of her lips brushing against mine. The firmness of her thighs as she wrapped them tightly around my waist.

Stop it, Dylan.

'I can't live without her,' I choked. My voice was a hoarse whisper as I experienced a lull between sobs and silent panic.

Adam always had a prickly relationship with April. His reasons were understandable, yet I was grateful for his strong and mostly quiet company now. Adam dominated a room with his springy sandy hair adding three inches to his six feet one. Women struggled to tear their eyes from his symmetrical freckles and hung off the roll of his Rs. Blokes either wanted to be Adam or sink a few beers with him watching the footy, bouncing off his banter. Me, I appreciated a dose of Adam's always candid Scottish honesty. Now, he sat, elbows on his knees, cracking his knuckles as he spoke carefully yet directly in a way only he could.

'Och, Dylan, pal, she left ye. Ye've been living without her three years. Four, if ye count Rome.'

Bloody Rome. Another disastrous, chaos-causing decision. April had to hold her hands up to that one, though. Burying my head in my hands, regrets crashed down again in a torrent. Why hadn't I gone after her three years ago? All that lost time, and for what? Self-preservation? Some blundering miscommunications? Foolish pride?

'I wasn't living, not really,' I told Adam. 'Just existing. Waiting. Waiting for her to come back. And when she finally did...' I nodded towards where April lay in her noisy coma, somehow as beautiful as ever in her stillness.

Nobody blamed me for the accident. April's parents, her best friend Lizzy. But they didn't know how cruel I'd been. I called her selfish. Accused her of abhorrent things. Shouted at her until she fled my house in tears and got in her car. Drove off.

I'd never yelled at her before. Not even back at university when she was slowly and inexpertly chiselling my heart from my chest. I'd done the same to her. For a love that took such an iron grip of us both, we did an impeccable job of destroying each other.

'I'd do anything to go back and change things.' My chest hitched; another influx of grief was on its way. 'But I definitely kissed her too soon.'

'Kissed her too soon?' a twenty-something woman cried in an American accent, almost having to duck under the doorway before filling April's hospital room with her presence. 'What total crap.'

Mouth agape at this new visitor's statuesque beauty and spikey, bleached crop, Adam leapt up and offered her his seat. If it wasn't for the circumstances that had her flying to Manchester from California, I was sure he'd have started drooling.

'You,' she said, pointing a long index finger in my direction, 'should have had the balls to fly to San Francisco two weeks ago when I sent you that ticket.'

'Jen?' I asked, meeting a pair of dark eyes blinking out under the longest black eyelashes and sitting above a chiselled cheekbone shelf. Until a week earlier, Jen had been April's flatmate in San Francisco. I guessed Lizzy had dropped her off straight from the airport. 'So, you're my mystery plane ticket benefactor.'

Jen wrinkled her perfectly sculpted nose as she sheepishly folded her limbs into Adam's seat. 'Thanks for cancelling that, by the way. Turns out I needed the Air Miles.' She sighed, looking over at April and pursing her lips. 'But, I gotta say, I wish you'd gotten on that plane. Then April wouldn't be in this mess.'

We all looked at April now. The tubes wrapped around her like the tentacles of a giant jellyfish. Jen had spent hours in the air not knowing if April would be alive or dead when she landed. Her make-up had slid off her angular features, and her complexion was blotchy under her Californian tan.

'Oh, April, babe.' Jen's eyes pooled. 'This can't be it.'

Jen's arrival made everything more real. After the crash, April had been rushed straight to Salford Royal, a major trauma centre specialising in brain injuries. She'd spent the whole night in surgery. Her parents, and Lizzy after her airport diversion, had only just gone home for some much-needed sleep.

'I'm talking to you too, Dylan,' Jen added. 'All I've heard about for the last three years is your epic love story. The library, the womanising best friend, the kiss. Bloody Rome, the text, the voicemail.'

'Womanising?' Adam's voice squeaked from where he stood leaning against the windowsill. Jen shot him a challenging glare so fierce Adam quickly conceded the point.

This stranger knew so much about me and was so territorial in her protection of April it knocked the wind out of me. It was a testament to how much of April's life I'd missed since our savage break-up.

Grief slammed into me again as my thoughts flicked back through all those critical moments in our relationship. Some had me squirming with shame. Others made me want to physically reach back in time and force myself to make a different choice. Could I have saved April from this? Saved us?

We'd been kids when we met. Both twenty. April was a passionate history of art major who lived in her own colourful dimension. "April World" I used to call it. I was a slightly lazy archaeology student plodding through life, happy with a beer in front of the footy with my mates. Until she looked at me one day and lit my universe on fire.

Her beauty didn't just sit on her face but shone through her like sunlight sprinkling through the leaves of a forest canopy. She didn't see the bad side of humanity, or if she did, she ignored it. Life was an epic adventure. Monday wasn't merely a new round of lectures; it was its own fresh start, filled with boundless possibilities. Her dreams were big, and she burned so brightly it blinded me to the fact she didn't always think her ideas through. Or ever, actually.

But at least she had dreams. For me, lecture timetables and coursework deadlines pulled me from one day to the next. The monotony of it all bogged me down, my average existence dull around the edges. I saw life through a sepia filter, yet April turned it technicolour. Within our little bubble, our love had been perfect.

'I'm all in,' I'd promised her the day we'd got together, holding her close and curling her soft brown hair behind her ear. It was corny, sure, but I knew she was it for me. And I'd give her everything, always, if she did the same.

Only, trying to stay in that utopia became impossible as real life got in the way. In the end it consumed us, until our relationship morphed into a dystopian prison we both needed to escape. April fled before graduation, and I stopped chasing her.

My life moved on, but my heart didn't. No matter how much time passed, the fire April had lit inside me wouldn't burn out.

'April never forgave herself. For hurting you and leaving like she did.' Jen's Californian twang lifted me from my maudlin. She explained April had spent every single day persecuting herself. Channelling her feelings into her art in the gallery workshop where they both worked in San Francisco.

'That's why, after a few glasses of wine, I thought "fuck it" and sent you that plane ticket. Your story wasn't finished, and I hoped, if you saw her sculptures, you'd know she still loved you. If you'd just got on that plane, Dylan, you could have got your happily ever after.'

'So, all I had to do was fly halfway across the world based on a drunken email from a total stranger?'

Jen was obviously a diehard romantic. Just like April.

'Hell yeah!' she cried.

Adam scoffed behind us, and Jen shot him another withering look. April had clearly painted Adam as a panto villain for his part in all this. If chatting Jen up had crossed his mind, which it would have, he didn't stand a chance.

With the urgency of the previous night over, the three of us sat in April's room, flitting between chatter and silence.

The hospital moved around us like a busy beehive. Nurses, physicians and support staff quietly keeping people alive under the hubbub of rowdy equipment.

After a couple of hours, Jen gave into jet lag and Adam offered to drive her back to Lizzy's. She was too tired to refuse. Alone with April for the first time, I pulled my chair close to her bed and curled my fingers around her hand. Her nails were short. She'd always kept them that way, so they didn't get in the way as she sculpted. I smiled at the familiarity of her hand. The pale pink polish on them was chipped and flecked with paint, her skin dry and rough from a variety of art materials and turps.

As I trailed my fingertips over her heart-shaped birthmark, her skin became softer and more delicate. I noticed her tan for the first time. Not as deep as Jen's, but a warm glow had replaced the paleness of her student days.

Blinking heavily, I realised I'd not slept for nearly two days, having spent the previous night sitting with Lizzy and April's parents while surgeons battled to save April's life. They'd warned it could be days, even weeks, before she woke up.

If she woke up.

Those three lost years were a chasm between us. I knew little of her life now, and despite what Jen said, I didn't know for certain if April still had feelings for me. Yet, I couldn't bring myself to leave her side.

'I still love you, April,' I whispered.

The emotional Coke bottle erupted, and suddenly I was sobbing again. Willing her to live. I needed her to live. To come back to me again. I'd barely made it the first time; I wouldn't survive losing her a second time.

My tears finally slowed. Only because the effort of it had sapped my body of energy until my eyelids started drooping. Blinking heavily again, my head dipped forwards.

I'll just close them for a second, I thought, resting my forehead on my arm, not letting go of April's hand. *Just for a second.*

The Coma

SUMMER 2022

April

Was this death?

Darkness pressed on me from every angle, heavy and inescapable, squeezing out any chinks of light. It had the rusty, metallic smell of old blood and was cold, too. Not so much to make me shiver but bracing like icy air filling the corners of your lungs on a winter's day.

I couldn't tell if I was breathing, but I could hear the slow, rhythmic thump of my heartbeat. There was no pain. My body felt suspended in time.

Was that it?

Had I been cryogenically frozen until some point in the future when scientists had discovered how to reverse whatever it was that killed me?

No. It couldn't be. If I focused, I could hear voices around me. One stirring my fractured mind more than the rest.

Dylan.

I pictured his face. His golden flecked brown eyes that always found mine even in the most crowded room. The dark brown hair that he'd get cropped short and then allow to grow until it flopped in front of his face. Whichever way he slicked it, he looked like the boy next door. Until he smiled, bringing his dimples to life and sending the sexiest, most disarming glint to his eyes.

A memory floated in front of me. Dylan, sweeping me into that urgent first kiss, so strong and self-assured, his body rock solid against mine. OK, so the circumstances surrounding the start of our relationship had been… unfortunate. We'd been impetuous at times, naïve even. But there'd been slices of magic, and that kiss was one of those moments in life that's so spectacular, you know little will match it.

Thinking of Dylan's mouth nuzzling my neck flooded me with warmth. For a fraction of a second, the heat of that memory radiated from my centre, making my fingertips tingle.

The sensation jolted me, sending a flash of light into my dark, splintered brain. I held onto the feeling, desperate for it not to burn itself out.

I was alive. Just.

Only, Dylan sounded bereft. I yearned to reach out and grasp his hand in mine. Glue the shards of his heart back together somehow. The heart I'd broken. Yet it was impossible now. This emptiness was holding me prisoner.

Hearing Jen's voice in the far-off distance turned the cold chill to ice. I'd only left San Francisco a week ago, yet she'd travelled all this way to visit. They were talking about an accident, but when I searched for that memory, there was nothing. Just Dylan. Dylan angry, me crying. Running. Driving. A bang.

I still love you, April.

Don't leave me.

His words triggered more streams of light, invading my dark dungeon like a meteor shower. Thousands of shooting stars sprinkled down, each one exploding like a firework into a scene of moving images until I was surrounded. I watched in awe as the blackness was replaced with colourful snippets of my life, springing up around me until I was lost in a hall of mirrors. Only, they weren't mirrors; they were screens, each showing a different moment from my past.

To my left I saw me as a little girl, singing Disney songs as I played with a lump of green plasticine, carefully moulding it into a frog. On my right, teenage April was sprawled across her bed under a Justin Bieber poster and engrossed in a book about Michelangelo. Above that, there I was at twenty, writing my name and number down on a piece of paper to give to Dylan. Thousands of memories filling up the space, playing out like films on a loop.

While I'd been locked in the dark, I'd listened to Dylan picking over the carcass of our doomed relationship. Wondering where we'd gone wrong. Now, while my body was the unwilling hostage of bleeping wires and machines, my mind was suddenly free to roam between screens. Watching it all unfold in excruciating detail.

Was this my life flashing before my eyes?

No. It couldn't be. Because some of Dylan's memories appeared too. One caught my attention because it looked recent, and I heard Adam saying my name as they all sat round a table in the pub. Just in front of that screen, I saw myself in San Francisco, hanging up fliers.

That warm tingle zipped through my fingertips again as Dylan laced his hand around mine in my hospital bed. With a jolt it tugged me forwards and into the first screen, the images springing to life around me. Suddenly, I was inside the memory, a silent, invisible observer.

The Plane Ticket

Two weeks before her sudden reappearance in Dylan's life, April had been standing at the end of San Francisco's Pier 39, pinning a flier to a noticeboard. A mild afternoon chill sent goosebumps up her arms as a salty tang blew in from the North Pacific, yet the sky was clear blue, bathing the city in pale yellow sunshine. Stepping back to admire her handiwork, she wrapped her arms around her bare shoulders.

April Westbury's debut, it read.

Bouncing up and down with a clap, April sprang into an impromptu jig on the wooden boards beneath her feet. Her own show!

Quintessential English sculptor brings the passion, intensity and torment of true love to life.

Her flatmate Jen had written her bio. Why did Americans always use "quintessential" when describing the English? Oh well, it hardly mattered now. Holidaymakers bustled around her as the clunky organ music from the old carousel piped out in the background.

Jen avoided Pier 39. Most San Franciscans did. 'Too tacky and commercial,' she moaned. But April adored it and often went down there when she was feeling homesick. Wandering amongst the arcades, jugglers and souvenir stands, before enjoying the views of Alcatraz and the Golden Gate Bridge, April relished being both a local and visitor. The white rock fortress rose angrily from the choppy waters, a death trap to anyone who dared escape. How many times had she been one of the tourists crawling over it now like ants on an apple core? She'd lost count.

Would any of them come to her exhibition? It'd been three years in the making. Admittedly, she'd been in a bit of a state when she'd arrived in California straight after university finals. Jen, a fellow intern at the gallery whose apartment she'd been sharing, didn't quite know what to make of the inconsolable Brit in her spare room.

But Jen had taken April under her wing. Encouraged her to channel the heartbreak into her art and found an experienced artist to teach her metalwork. It was the only material she'd never used before, and April turned out to be a natural. Copper, brass, bronze and aluminium were all versatile and dramatic, the heat blistering from the blowtorch as she brought her emotions to life.

Her one-year internship turned into two, then three. She carried Dylan with her though. Spending every spare minute in the gallery workshop, singing softly to herself as she created sculptures from the momentous parts of their ill-fated love story. It was therapy, almost. And while Jen was no artist, she had a good eye. By year three, she'd been promoted to Assistant Manager and persuaded the owner to give April her first solo exhibition.

Jen was busy plugging the show on social media. But April couldn't resist hanging fliers up at San Francisco's busiest corners. She'd be leaving the city that had helped her find herself again soon, and she couldn't miss the opportunity to explore it one last time.

Walking back down the boardwalk, April could hear the barks of the basking sea lions alongside the pier. The locals were used to the stench of wet dog and rotten fish, but the tourists scrunched their noses as they marvelled at the hundreds of blubbery bodies chilling on the docks.

Thirty minutes later, April arrived at the gallery. With a sigh, she set about arranging each piece out on the exhibition floor. Putting the finishing touches, positioning their titles and blurbs. Each design a stark reminder of how much she had loved and how much she had lost. Chipping into her excited mood until there was nothing left. By the time it was done, she'd rewound in time to that broken girl who first got off the plane at San Francisco airport.

'Talk about your déjà vu,' Jen cried when April arrived home in floods of tears. Opening the fridge, Jen pulled out a bottle of Pinot Grigio. Gratefully taking a glass, April draped herself on the sofa.

'Why can't I get over him?' She sniffed, throwing her legs over Jen's lap and holding her glass by her chin with both hands. 'Lizzy says I've put Dylan on a pedestal. But seeing my exhibits set up, I know she's wrong. He's real; *we* were real. And I know it's pathetic that I'm still stuck back there, but my exhibition is a screaming reminder of how badly I screwed up.'

Shuffling up the sofa, Jen smothered her in a hug, her long, slender arms almost wrapping round April twice.

When she finally pulled away, Jen's eyes were sprinkling tears.

Jen grew up in Pacific Heights, a neighbourhood in San Francisco that made the Kardashians look poor. Her dad had moved over from Shanghai in the nineties and swept up during Silicon Valley's dot-com boom. Jen and April rode their bikes to her family home once. Rows of immaculate Victorian townhouses stretched down the steep streets in a pastel palette of blues, greys and yellows. Their manicured hedgerows were an impossible shade of rainbow green, like they were cycling through a watercolour painting. But Jen pedalled straight past them all to a mansion with its own white-pillared entrance.

Jen's mum – a tech engineer who'd grown up in Beijing – had the private chef cook everyone fresh sushi, which they ate on the terrace looking out across the bay. Later, April googled Jen's parents and worked out they lived on Billionaires' Row.

Jen was an encyclopaedia of art with an eye for talent; her Ivy League education hadn't gone to waste. Yet, while her parents had bought her apartment in Dogpatch – a chic neighbourhood full of galleries, coffee shops and dive bars that was a magnet to creatives – she didn't take their money. She lived off April's rent and her modest salary from the gallery. Not that Jen had to worry about funds. Knowing the family billions were there should she ever need it wrapped Jen in a cosy security blanket. And she never hesitated to use her parents' accumulated Air Miles when she fancied jetting off somewhere.

With her huge heart and self-assured nature, Jen considered herself an empath. But watching her dab her eyes on the sofa now, April was wondering if perhaps Lizzy was right. Jen's life of relative privilege meant she lived vicariously through – and thrived on – the trauma of others. In this case, April's.

'It's so sad you guys couldn't work things out,' Jen blubbed as April drained her wine glass. 'You should contact him. It's time, April.'

Jerking forward, April almost sprayed Pinot Grigio all over the pile of Vogues on the coffee table. Contact Dylan? Her breathing quickened at the thought. April's instincts screamed at her to put down the wine and run from the conversation. It wouldn't end sensibly. But Jen poured her another glass, while regaling her with all the reasons reaching out to Dylan was a good idea.

'If you feel like this, he must too,' Jen said, tilting her head. 'It wasn't like it was unrequited love. That voicemail he left begging you to stay, you've played it to me a thousand times. It's *the* most heart-rending thing I've ever heard.'

April knew it word for word. She'd never deleted it. It would be playing on a loop as part of one of her exhibition pieces.

'You don't just get over that,' Jen continued. 'You should invite him to opening night. Imagine the press you'll get if he shows up and you fall into each other's arms. It'd make a great follow-up exhibit too.' Assistant Gallery Manager Jen had shouldered in, mercilessly booting aside empath Jen.

'OK, OK, don't get carried away. I can't just launch myself back into his life; it wouldn't be fair,' April objected. 'Besides, I couldn't cope with the rejection.'

But Jen wouldn't let up. As the wine bottle emptied and another opened, things got blurrier round the edges and April started to think Jen's idea wasn't so insane.

'I don't even have Dylan's number anyway,' she slurred. She'd deleted him from her contacts and social media the night she'd arrived on Jen's doorstep, precisely for this reason. So she didn't drunkenly message him or doom scroll through his Instagram page.

'Whose number *do* you have?' Jen asked, grabbing April's phone and scrolling through her contacts. She was relentless once an idea lodged in her brain. Twenty minutes later, fuelled with liquid confidence, April was carefully constructing a text to Adam. Adam, who apart from a few weeks she'd rather forget, had always disliked her. But his was the only of Dylan's friends whose details still languished in an old messaging app.

'Just ask him for Dylan's number,' Jen pushed, reading over her shoulder. She reckoned April owed it to Dylan to let him know about the art show anyway, in case her launch appeared online.

'Someone could TikTok it or put it on the 'gram; it could even go viral,' she said.

April was doubtful. Then again, one of her sculptures *was* called "Meeting Dylan".

'You don't want him getting any nasty shocks,' Jen insisted. April noticed the room was spinning, but Jen sounded logical. Squinting at her phone, she reread the text to Adam, pressing send before she could back out.

Regretting it instantly, April swayed off to bed. 'Before you make me do something else totally idiotic,' she mumbled.

She zonked out quickly, waking up hugging her drool-covered pillow when her 6am alarm chimed. Her tongue felt thick as she snoozed the racket coming from her phone. Then she remembered the message.

Groaning, April pulled the pillow over her face. What had she done? Reading Adam's reply with one eye screwed shut shredded that last piece of hope – and dignity – she had left.

Leave him alone, April. He's engaged.

April's heart shrivelled into nothing, replaced by a black hole sucking the life out of her.

Engaged.

Sinking into the mattress, the hangover throbbing at her temples, she couldn't catch her breath. Whatever she'd expected, it wasn't that. How was she was stuck in a grief-stricken void, dwelling on losing the love of her life, yet Dylan had met someone, fallen in love *and* proposed?

Utterly crushed, April curled up under her duvet and let insanity take over, spending the next hour obsessively googling Dylan. His social media accounts were private, but within minutes of clicking through his old friends, she'd found his fiancée. A blonde Australian named Kelly. Tears poured as she scrolled through photos from their engagement party, at what used to be April and Dylan's local pub.

Dylan was smiling, his arm thrown around his beautiful wife-to-be. Kelly was glowing in every photo, her happiness obvious in her shining eyes. Al, Jonesy and Adam were huddled with Kelly's friends, shoulders, knees and heads touching. A table of half-empties, ice buckets of champagne and open crisp packets showed they were tight-knit.

April scowled, jealousy brewing in her belly. Thanks to Adam's distaste for her – and Lizzy too for that matter – they'd never gelled as a group. Never been a gang.

A cold loneliness crept over April until she could feel it in her bones. She should have known Dylan wasn't single. He was adorably unaware, but girls always had a soft spot for him. He was the shy, considerate boy next door with the face of a Disney prince and a smile that could floor you without warning. Plus, those abs…

Shamelessly picking through Kelly's Instagram, April tracked their relationship. Dylan started appearing two years ago. Every so often at first, then more and more until, apart from her, he was the main character. Two years. Almost twice as long as April dated Dylan. He had more history with Kelly. They'd been on more dates, had more lazy weekends in bed, more kisses, more sex. She quickly did the math. A lot more sex.

Now they were getting married. April couldn't compete; she was resigned to Dylan's dating history. Nothing more than baggage.

Yet, he was still very much her present, which was now all set up for everyone to analyse in an art gallery a few blocks away. Man, did she feel silly.

Engaged!

When April didn't emerge from her room, Jen tentatively knocked.

'Oh, no,' she gasped, her hand flying to her open mouth when April held her phone up to show her Adam's text. 'I shouldn't have pushed it; I'm sorry, April.'

April shrugged, chewing her chipped fingernails from her hiding place under the sheets. 'Not your fault,' she muttered. 'You didn't know.' April had let herself be talked into sending that text. She figured it was going to happen sooner or later. Better now when she had her exhibition to focus on. And once that was done, she could pack up her sculptures and finally move on.

Jen was frantically swiping up and down on her own phone, looking panicked.

'Seriously don't worry about it. It's the kick I need to leave all that behind.' April frowned. She tried to make herself believe it. It'd been so long since she'd felt Dylan's touch or been in the cosy cocoon of his arms. But her heart was crumbling to ash.

After showering April in hugs, Jen propped her in front of the TV with a bowl of Cheetos and a Nicholas Sparks film.

'But the exhibit opens tomorrow.' April was worried. There were still a dozen fliers she wanted to hang up.

'Don't worry. You've already set everything up; I'll just add the final flourishes,' Jen promised. 'And no one goes to an art show they saw on a flier these days, but I'll have an intern put them up for you.'

After lunch, April video called Lizzy hoping for some more sympathy. She should have known she wouldn't get any.

'April, no!' Lizzy roared through gritted teeth, clapping her hand to her forehead. 'Don't pick at old scabs.' If they weren't on FaceTime with thousands of miles between them, April was sure Lizzy would have gone for her jugular.

'I know, I know.' She winced. 'But I'm glad I know. It stops me wondering.'

With a shake of her head, Lizzy took a deep breath, preparing to dish out a lecture. 'Stop looking back, April. This is your own exhibition, your name on the door. Forget about that closure bollocks; this is the start of your dream career.' Lizzy was jabbing a finger at her now. 'You can introduce yourself to strangers as an artist. Not a gallery intern but an actual professional sculptor. That's massive.'

April could always rely on Lizzy to be her biggest critic and biggest champion. She called her out when she was being irrational while always celebrating her successes. 'Don't cry anymore over bloody Dylan. Focus on securing a follow-up show in the UK,' Lizzy ordered. 'And for God's sake, April, put the phone down when you've had a few.'

April laughed. That's why she'd called Lizzy. For a healthy dose of reality delivered with humour. Besides, she was right. Ill-thought-out drunken messages weren't just something to send and regret. April wasn't some lovesick student anymore. She was a grown-up and had no right dredging things up and messing with other people's lives.

Or her own for that matter. That night, she dreamt she was lying in Dylan's arms. Her body tremored as dream Dylan swept the hair from her face and tucked it behind her ear. Smiling that smile. Echoes of the past invading her sleep. When April woke up the morning of her exhibition, she felt empty but for that old, unbearable ache for him. It seemed worse this time, too. Because she knew there was nothing she could do to change things. Diamond rings and proposals made sure of that.

*

Back in Manchester, while April was slumped in front of Netflix with her Cheetos feeling sorry for herself, Dylan was with his mates for the kind of after-work drinks that always turned into a closing-time job.

'Youse will never guess who I woke up to a message from,' Adam smirked. He was five pints in when he decided to launch his conversational grenade.

'April.' He leaned forwards, tilting his pint glass towards Dylan as he rolled over her name.

The smile on Dylan's face vanished and his mouth went dry. It'd been two years since anyone dared mention April. Three since he'd seen her.

'Something about an art exhibition she's doing. Yer in it,' Adam continued, sitting back to watch Dylan squirm. 'Don't worry; I told her yer engaged and te leave ye alone.'

Dylan swallowed, his cold lager scratching down his throat like sand.

'Show me,' he said, biting hard on his bottom lip to keep his expression even. Adam's revelation was having the desired effect. Cartoon barrels of TNT were exploding inside Dylan's head.

Hi Adam, sorry to message after so long. Do you have Dylan's number? He's mentioned in my new art exhibition, and I need to give him a heads-up. April.

Dylan read and reread April's text, his knuckles turning white around Adam's phone. It made no sense. For one thing, she'd messaged Adam, who she hated. And what exhibition? Everyone knew April dreamt of being an artist, and she was incredibly talented. But they'd no friends in common anymore, and April was in America. The chances he'd find out about some indie show she was doing out

25

there were slim. Which led him to one conclusion. She wanted him to know.

Dylan hadn't mentioned April for a long time either. After she'd left for San Francisco, he'd hidden away like an angry unwashed hermit. Once he'd pulled himself together, he'd insisted on a weekly lads' night with Adam and their university housemates, Al and Jonesy. There was no way he wanted them thinking he was still holding on after she'd made her feelings, or lack of them, abundantly clear.

Only, now her name was out there again, making his heart hammer, his palms slick. Drops of sweat trickled down his back, causing his shirt and jeans to cling to his skin.

'Ye OK, pal?' Adam frowned. 'I wasn't gonna tell ye, but I was worried this exhibit might become a thing, and you'd be raging.'

'She sent this yesterday?' Dylan snapped and Adam nodded, realising his attempt at pub banter had misfired. Dylan wasn't just squirming; he was imploding.

Dylan rubbed his forehead with the hand not clutching Adam's phone. April was thinking about him. No, she wanted to talk to him. Last night.

Adam's curt reply made him suck air through his teeth.
Leave him alone, April. He's engaged.

He'd told her about Kel. And that bothered him. Dylan had only proposed the previous week. This was their first lads' night since their engagement party.

'Ye aren't still hung up on her, are ye?' Adam's eyes narrowed as he scrutinised Dylan, chugging the rest of his pint and placing the glass back on the table. 'That lassie ran away and left ye. Kel's far less drama.'

Dylan looked away, unable to answer. Puffing his cheeks out, he put his hand on his leg to stop it jiggling. Jonesy and Al, who'd been watching the exchange, shook their heads.

'Dyl, bro, this ain't good,' Jonesy said. 'If Georgia reacted like this when someone mentioned her ex, I'd be asking serious questions.'

Until recently, Jonesy had been firmly aboard Adam's bachelor train. Then he'd fallen hard for his colleague Georgia, a fiery redhead in Doc Martens who thought he was a Greek God. Dylan often watched Jonesy's face turn puce dead-lifting his own body weight in the gym. Bulking up his biceps to make up for his five feet seven inches. Georgia's adoration boosted his brittle ego and, apparently, also made him a relationship guru.

'You ain't mentioned April in years, not once,' Jonesy said, pointing at Dylan with a beer mat. 'And you and Kel really have something. We all assumed you'd moved on. We were relieved to be honest.'

Dylan moved from nibbling his lip to chewing on the inside of his cheek. He knew he'd spent at least a year driving everyone mad with his April woes. But Jonesy wasn't finished.

'Are you really still thinking about April?'

Dylan folded his arms and looked away. He really didn't want to answer that question.

'How often?' scowled Adam. 'Her birthday? When we reminisce about uni? When ye see a wee lassie that looks like her?'

'Every single day, OK,' Dylan cried, throwing his hands up. 'Every day since the one she left.' He'd been caught out. But he didn't tell them April had taken up residence in his mind the day they met and never left. Or that whenever it got quiet, when he was just sitting in his office at the University of Manchester researching the latest archaeological discovery for his PhD, his thoughts drifted to April. The royal blue of her eyes. The way her wavy dark hair followed the contours of her heart-shaped face. He'd wonder what she was doing, where she was, who she was with. If she was happy.

Then his phone would buzz with a message from Kel triggering a gnawing guilt. Especially as Kel's texts always made him laugh. A snarky comment about a colleague's smelly tuna salad, or a customer's dodgy tan lines. They appreciated the same dry humour.

Dylan knew thinking about his ex wasn't fair to Kel. Yet, he was powerless to stop it. His thoughts of April were intrusive, and he'd hoped if he kept pushing them away, they'd slowly diminish until, one day, they stopped altogether. Only, they hadn't.

Now, one message from April, one mention of her name had reduced him to a puddle in the pub. And his mates had finally seen right through the façade.

'Holy fuck, Dylan,' Jonesy cried. 'Then you've got one giant April-shaped problem coming your way.'

He slid his phone across the table, where he'd googled the exhibit. Seeing April's face for the first time in years, smiling from the screen, made Dylan visibly jolt. Jonesy had pulled up the website of a modern art gallery in San Francisco.

April Westbury makes her debut this Saturday with her raw and unflinching exploration of the greatest love and, ultimately, the most devastating heartbreak. If you've ever loved and lost, April's collection – from the explosively intricate "Meeting Dylan", to the dark and disturbing "Locked Heart" – will reach you in ways you won't be prepared for. This exhibit is on for one week only, after which April will be returning to the UK to showcase her work.

Dylan's stomach lurched. Jonesy's overpowering Burberry aftershave wafting over the stale beer-saturated carpet didn't help the sudden nausea brought on by the deluge of information. Firstly, April had spent the last three years creating art about their relationship. He knew artists did that kind of thing, but an entire exhibition? Christ, she'd named a piece after him. Secondly, "devastating heartbreak"?

If April felt that way, it was the first he'd heard of it. She'd left without a word, he assumed because she no longer loved him. Thirdly – and this was the kicker – April was coming home. Dylan's head spun at the news, forcing his hands to the table to steady himself.

Adam and Al read it on their own phones now too.

'Why didn't she call?' Dylan's question wasn't aimed at anyone. 'If she was heartbroken, then why did she leave without telling me?'

'Oh dear.' Al, who'd been silent until now, was chuckling into his beer. He'd already married his childhood sweetheart, Jodie, a stunning dynamo he'd met in sixth form. They'd done the whole long-distance thing throughout uni, visiting one another once a month. Got engaged the Christmas after graduation. Jodie's slightly pushy parents hadn't wanted her "living in sin", so they'd decided they may as well marry. It wasn't like it wasn't on the cards. They weren't in a rush to have kids though, and Al was often first up for a boys' night. But he was a good husband and Dylan valued his relationship advice above all.

'Personally, Dyl, I had a feeling this day might come,' Al said, his deep baritone booming across the pub. 'It's bad enough you still live in our old student house, but now we know why you've been dragging your heels about moving in with Kel. Oh dear.'

Al was still chuckling when the bartender brought another tray of beers over. Supping fresh pints, the lads launched into a round of opinions and suggestions.

'Fuck April. She can't jump back into ye life like this an' blow it up.' Adam's beer head had taken over – he always became more caustic after a few. 'Kel will get hurt; ye'll get hurt; and she'll inevitably break her own wee heart again. She's a kamikaze pilot, that one. Honestly, pal, ye had a lucky escape three years ago if you ask me.'

But Dylan wasn't asking him. Besides, Adam's recollections of April were never particularly favourable.

Dylan had turned up to freshers' week single, having been dumped while his A level results day hangover still thumped. 'She did ye a favour,' Adam had scoffed, sitting on Dylan's bed in their halls of residence and handing him the first beer of thousands they'd share. Adam had been allocated the room next door, having unashamedly driven his souped-up Mini all the way down from Paisley. Dylan had been a faithful wingman during that first year. Adam's confidence – or was it arrogance? – his Scottish lilt and good looks made it an easy job. Then April happened, and Jonesy had flown into the gap Dylan left by Adam's side with the speed and precision of a Red Arrow.

'Dyl, man, really think about this before you do

anything,' Jonesy warned now. 'Adam ain't wrong – she messed you up big time. Big. Time. Kel picked up the pieces when we couldn't. It's taken you a long time to get to where you are now, and Kel makes you happy, right?'

'Not that simple though.' Al's turn. 'When you've loved like that, nothing compares. You both remember what they were like. Romeo and goddamn Juliet, Antony and Cleopatra, Jack and Rose.'

'Bonnie and Clyde more like,' Adam belched.

Al ignored him. 'Three years down the line, he's engaged to a gorgeous Aussie, then April sends one message – not even directly to him – and it's reduced him to a gibbering wreck? That isn't progress.'

Jonesy sighed, taking another long swig. 'True. And I don't reckon Kel would stick around if she knew you'd spent the last two years thinking about someone else, Dyl. If you do marry her, you've gotta make sure you're choosing her and not just avoiding the heartache April could bring. It's not fair on Kel otherwise.'

Dylan's heart throbbed when he thought of Kel, waiting for him back at his. It'd taken him a while, but he did love her. Yes, he'd made excuses about finishing his PhD before moving out his student house and into her place. But he'd proposed. Stepped up when she needed him to.

'Fellas, we don't even know what April really wants. Maybe she finished her artwork two years ago but took this long to get a gallery to show it? It can't be easy to get your own exhibit,' Dylan said, if only to stop his own mind flying through possibilities. 'Maybe she wants to tell me not to read anything into it. That it helped her process things and move on with some NFL beefcake called Chad. Or she really does just want to warn me on the off-chance I see it on Instagram. She didn't tell Adam she was coming home, and it says the UK – she could be headed to Belfast for all we know.'

'Yeah. I think we all know where she's coming though.' Al was smirking again as he threw his giant hand into a bag of cheese and onion crisps.

Unable to sit listening to the lads speculate, Dylan left them having one last pint and walked the mile home.

His house was quiet when he arrived. The benefit of staying in his old student place, apart from the cheap rent, was that all his housemates disappeared back to their parents' homes for the holidays. Kel's jacket was thrown over a kitchen chair and he knew he'd find her starfished in his bed, so different to April who used to curl into him like a tiny fieldmouse.

Sinking down onto the sofa, the beer causing his thoughts to swirl and skip, Dylan typed April's name into Google. There wasn't much. Her Instagram, which he'd avoided since he met Kel, was full of smiley photos of April in different American cities. Mostly San Francisco. Various friends popped up, with @artyjennifer appearing more than others. A bloke with a serious stare and a paintbrush behind his ear cropped up a lot until a few months earlier. A boyfriend, perhaps? Why did that irk him?

After scrolling through April's social media for longer than he should have done, Dylan absentmindedly clicked into his work emails. He'd been tutoring all day and wondered if he'd missed anything.

Straightaway, a curious email from someone named

Jennifer caught his attention. Its subject was simply "April".

That name again. Sitting with his elbows on his knees, Dylan took a gulp of air and clicked it open. It was only four words. Four words that blew his world apart.

She still loves you.

Jennifer's photo came up alongside her email and he recognised her as @artyjennifer. Opening the single attachment, Dylan assumed it'd be a flier for April's show. It wasn't. It was a plane ticket to San Francisco. For the next morning.

Dylan threw himself back on the settee, his hands tightening around his phone as he stared at the eticket.

'San Francisco?' a voice cried behind him. 'Dylan, why have you got a plane ticket to San Francisco?'

Yanked out his stupor, Dylan jumped up and whirled round to face his fiancée.

'Shit. Kel, you scared me,' he said as her gentle dark eyes bored into his, full of questions.

'Dylan? What the hell is going on?'

Dylan had never lied to Kel. Not once, and he wasn't about to start now. Besides, he was in such shock, the truth was the only ammo he had.

'April, my ex...'

'I know who April is,' Kel barked, making Dylan wince. He wasn't used to hearing an edge to her voice. Steadying himself on the back of the sofa, he started again.

'April's opening an art exhibition. Apparently, some of it's about me. Or our break-up. She messaged Adam to warn me.' It was an enormous effort not to stutter under Kel's scrutiny. 'Honestly, Kel, I found out an hour ago, and

33

now it looks like April's friend has sent me a plane ticket to go to the opening night. I promise I've no idea why.'

'You've no idea why?' Kel scowled, her voice travelling up several octaves at the end. 'I think the "she still loves you" is a pretty obvious explanation.'

Kel's gaze locked on Dylan's as she searched his face for answers. Dylan opened his mouth to reply but came up with nothing.

'Dylan,' Kel said, cocking her head. 'Are you considering going? Because your eyes keep flicking to that draw behind me which has your passport in. And if your first instinct wasn't to click delete and join me – your fiancée – in bed, with absolutely no intention of chasing your ex halfway around the world, then we've got a very serious problem.'

Dylan was still speechless, his thoughts leapfrogging over his options. Kel was right – he *was* wondering where his passport was. He was also thinking he should have followed April to the airport three years earlier and jumped on the next flight to San Francisco back then.

It was only his third thought that told him all that was crazy. That he should delete the email, tell Kel he loved her, wanted to marry her and had no intention of chasing the ghost of an ex.

Jonesy's advice sounded in Dylan's thoughts too. Kel deserved to be his first thought and first choice. Not the safe one.

Closing his eyes, Dylan tried to figure out if it was just shock – and the beer – making him consider boarding that plane and trying to win April back. When he opened them again, Kel's were swimming with tears. His heart lurched.

'I'm sorry,' he said. 'I love you. I do. I meant it when I proposed. I wanted to marry you. I wanted to spend my life making you happy. I was sure.'

Dylan's sentence petered out as Kel's jaw dropped.

'But now you're not sure? You're talking in past tense, Dylan, and because of what, an email?' Kel was already blustering around the room grabbing her handbag and jacket, just to stop herself crying.

'I'm sorry,' Dylan said again, unable to think of anything else as guilt burned through his veins. 'I won't lie to you. But I don't know what I'm going to do.'

Kel stormed out the door still in her pyjamas as Dylan sank back onto the sofa in despair. Then he just sat there, staring at the clock on his phone as it counted down to the flight time on the ticket.

Tick tock, tick tock.

This was it. Crunch time. Did he choose the rollercoaster of true passion or a life of steady contentment? April or Kel?

*

Eight hours later, Dylan tentatively knocked at Kel's door. When he'd sat on his sofa, unable to move as his booked flight no doubt rumbled down the runway of Manchester Airport, he knew he'd made his decision.

'You're not on a plane, then,' Kel said, eyebrows raised.

'No,' Dylan sighed. 'I was never going. OK, Dylan from three years ago thought about it for a nanosecond. But I'm not him anymore, so it doesn't matter if April still loves me or not.' As Dylan spoke, Kel stood in the doorway, hands on her hips.

'She's my first love. It started fast and furiously, then ended horribly. That's my baggage and I can't change it. But now I want a future with you.'

Kel still looked uncertain, but as Dylan reached for her hand, she let him take it.

'Kel, loving April was hard and painful. Loving you has only ever made me happy. I want to be happy. What do you say? Will you marry me still?'

At the second proposal, Kel let a small smile appear, moving aside and beckoning Dylan inside.

'Just tell me this,' she said, as they stood in the hallway, Dylan looping his arms around her back. 'What happens when you think about April?'

Dylan didn't look away as he thought about his reply. 'It makes me feel sad, I guess,' he said finally with a slight shrug. 'Sad that two people who loved each other could hurt each other so much. It leaves a scar.'

'They do say you never forget your first love.' Kel sighed, staring up at him, searching his eyes for the unwavering love she wanted so desperately to be there. 'But I want to be your greatest. I'm just not sure I am.'

'It's all so intense when you're young with hormones raging,' Dylan said. 'Then you grow up and build something stronger, less erratic. Don't walk away because I've got history with someone. I'm right where I want to be. I love you. In fact, I'll move in – next week instead of in six months – I can sublet to another student.'

Kel nodded, tilting her chin to let him kiss her gently. Only, as Dylan squeezed her in a reassuring hug, she noticed his smile hadn't quite reached his dimples.

*

It was almost 7pm in San Francisco. April stood in the middle of the room staring at the gallery clock as it ticked down to opening time. An air of expectation clung in every corner as catering staff waited with trays full of champagne and bottles of sparkling water.

Despite Jen's reassuring smile, April still felt panic rising up her throat.

What was she doing? Putting her deepest, rawest feelings on show. She'd have to answer questions, explain each piece and what it represents.

In one, a beaming post-coital selfie of April and Dylan in bed was set behind a concave lens that made it look far away.

'It represents the physical and metaphorical distance between us,' April had told Jen when she first showed it to her. Happiness just out of reach.

The centrepiece was a human heart blown from glass and set inside a transparent, steel-rimmed box of water. Clunking metal chains snaked around the box centred in the middle of a cold concrete slab. A spotlight shone on the heart, making it shine red through the water. April called it her "Locked Heart". It'd taken months to create and several redesigns to get right.

'It's perfect,' Jen burst when she saw it. 'I mean, it makes me never, ever want to fall for anyone. But isn't it haunting?'

Then there was the football full of vodka. April shuddered, hoping she wouldn't have to field too many questions about that one.

When the doors eventually opened, guests trickled, then gushed, in. Despite April's initial wobble, she was too busy to overthink things as people rushed to meet the artist, ask questions and take selfies.

By closing time, April was stood next to her "Locked Heart", chatting to Jen's teenage cousin Tori and her confused-looking father.

'It's spot on,' Tori sniffed into a damp Kleenex.

Knowing her art had spoken to someone made April feel warm inside. All she wanted was to reach the heartbroken, those who'd experienced any sort of grief. As always, Lizzy was spot on, she thought. This was just the start of something, not the end. Her career as a real-life artist. A dream realised.

Dylan would be so proud of me, she thought, before shoving the image of his face aside and berating herself for letting him creep into her moment.

'April,' a voice said behind her. Startled, April spun around.

'Blake,' she smiled. 'I didn't know you were coming.'

'Wouldn't miss it. I think we can still be friends, don't you?' Blake asked, raising his champagne glass. 'Although I'm starting to understand why I couldn't find a way into your "Locked Heart", Ms Westbury. There really was never any way in, was there?' Blake sighed, his gaze falling on the glass design.

April had dated Blake for six months. Being an artist too – an oil painter – he'd not even bat an eyelid when she told him her current work was an exploration of her past love and heartbreak. He liked the idea of her being a "tortured artist".

'It's important to express your emotions,' he'd said airily. 'Especially for us artists.' But while they'd had fun, when he'd gone on an artists' retreat for two weeks with no outside communication permitted, April barely even noticed he'd gone, never mind felt that longing in her gut. She knew she had to let him go.

'It's not all lightning bolts and butterflies,' Lizzy had despaired over their weekly wine and Zoom, insisting that sometimes love was a slow, simmering burn. Jen had wondered in as she often did and joined in, chastising April for constantly comparing every date and potential boyfriend to Dylan.

'She's made him into an Adonis, and it's impossible for any poor guy to match up,' Jen told Lizzy, who rolled her eyes. 'But it makes her a fabulous artist with all that pain and angst to draw on.'

Blake bounced back quickly, alleviating April's guilt. April noticed he'd even brought a date to her opening night.

'Dylan must have been some guy,' he mused, draining his glass and grabbing another from a passing waiter. 'Jen's arranged drinks at Michelangelo's in your honour, and I've got a bottle of champers with your name on it. You've officially made it, April.'

Locking up with Jen twenty minutes later, she noticed her friend seemed disappointed. Odd, considering there was already buzz on Instagram about the opening.

'Are you checking your Air Miles?' April gasped, spotting the telltale app open on Jen's phone.

'Babe, you're leaving in a week,' Jen said, quickly shoving her phone back in her handbag. 'I'm just making sure I have enough miles to visit. And lucky for you, I've got more than I expected.'

April hugged her. She was grateful to have met such a good friend in Jen. She was the opposite of Lizzy. They could both be the devil and the angel on her shoulder when they wanted to be, and without Lizzy, April wouldn't have made it to San Francisco. But without Jen, she wouldn't be going back to the UK with her own exhibit under her belt.

Checking her own phone as they walked to Michelangelo's bar under the glow of streetlights, April sprung into her happy dance again. She was already being tagged, Tweeted and raved about by local influencers, including one who'd been visiting from New York. The Big Apple.

Dylan's face floated in front of her mind again. Had Adam mentioned her message? she wondered. It was Adam; of course he had. Dylan probably pitied her, still pining after him.

Whatever. She was listening to the advice of her two best friends and thinking about her future. Flying back to the UK clutching a slither of success, hopefully with a gallery lined up to show her work. Art, she decided, would be the new love of her life.

*

'This is a terrible idea, April. Absolutely fucking terrible,' Lizzy cried, holding April's coat hostage. 'You've finally totally lost the plot.'

April had only been back in Manchester a week. Her sculptures were being shipped over to an independent gallery in the city, who'd booked her after an article in the *Manchester Evening News* called her "up and coming".

It'd been a wrench to leave the safety of Jen's apartment, but Lizzy had let her move in for a few months until she found her own place. 'Relive our uni days,' Lizzy had joked, even though her terrace was immaculate compared to their scruffy old uni flat. It looked like it'd been vomited on by a home interiors mag.

April had quickly settled in though. Enjoyed having her parents close by. They'd visited America once a year, but it wasn't enough. Manchester was her home.

It had taken precisely one week and about three hours for April to crack and give in to the urge to visit Dylan. Lizzy, who was the one who'd let slip he still lived in his old student house, looked close to tying her to one of her upcycled shabby-chic dining chairs.

'I've been in the paper, Lizzy. Uni friends are talking about me on social media. Dylan's even been tagged in a few posts about the show.' Dylan hadn't responded, but surely he'd seen them. 'Unless he's living in one of those filthy archaeological excavation sites he loves so much, he knows about my exhibition.'

Lizzy sighed. 'He's engaged, April,' she said through gritted teeth.

April blanched; it was much worse dealing with a Lizzy blast in person.

It'd been a ferocious Lizzy takedown that had led to the pair becoming friends. April had gone to the student union with some of the girls from the art society. It was only the second night of freshers' week, and a suave, bearded guy sauntered over and gave her a glass of wine. Everyone else was downing cheap beer and discount shots, but he acted superior to the chaos of freshers' week around them. Most of the eighteen-year-old first years still struggled to grow any facial hair, so she was both taken and intimidated by this twenty-something manly physio student in his fourth year telling her how attractive she was.

'A beautiful woman like you would be more suited to a fancy cocktail bar than a sticky-floored student union,' he'd purred.

April had lapped up every smooth line, until Lizzy whirled in with the ferocity and speed of the Tasmanian Devil.

'I know who you are, Dave Pickles,' she'd spat. 'The Slam Dunk Hunk. Which, embarrassingly, is what you nicknamed yourself, you loser.' Dave had turned pink, red then purple as Lizzy filled everyone within earshot in on his tried and tested method of picking up younger students, sleeping with them, then leaving straight after.

'To go back to your mam's,' Lizzy cackled.

Lizzy was on Dave's course, just a few years below, so had been given the lowdown when he was spotted lurking around another fresher event the previous night. 'Picking out your prey, weren't you, Dave,' she sneered, accentuating the D. 'And another thing, *Dave*,' interestingly he'd introduced himself to April as David, 'your beard looks more hobo than hipster, and I can smell the Febreze under your Joop! Homme. Now fuck off back to your mam's before I find a science geek to teach me about chemical castration.'

Dave Pickles looked like he'd been through a sandblaster. Which he had, really. Putting his wine down, he'd scurried off, so Lizzy scooped it up and just took up the conversation where he'd left it.

'Did I hear you're on the arts programme?' She'd smiled.

April had been about two more sips of wine from letting the Slam Dunk Hunk come back to her room to talk about their favourite Impressionists. Lizzy, she decided, was just the kind of friend she needed around to stop her making daft decisions. So far, April had been proved right.

But it didn't mean she always listened. Especially when it came to Dylan.

'Just email him then,' Lizzy insisted as April snatched her coat and pulled her car keys from the pocket. 'If you really must. He's doing his PhD at the university. His email address is on the website.'

'I'm not planning on doing anything silly. I just want to explain, that's all,' April insisted. She really believed that too. OK, maybe a small part of her wanted to see the look on his face when he saw her. Just a teeny tiny part.

'I'm warning you, April, this will end badly.' Lizzy shook her head, relenting.

An hour later, April was climbing out of her car in front of Dylan's old place. Looking up at his house, her knees started trembling.

What was she doing?

Feeling ridiculous, April was just contemplating leaving when Dylan opened the door carrying an armful of boxes. Spotting her, he stopped dead, sucked in a breath and held it, the gold in his eyes flashing with panic.

April froze too, and for a few ticks, they just stared at each other. Gulping, April glanced away, noticing his car parked on the street, his boot open and also full of boxes. He was moving, probably to his fiancée's. Today.

Impeccable timing, April, she thought. Now what?

A flashback suddenly flew through April's mind, of

Dylan leaning on the kitchen counter and spotting her creeping out of Adam's room at the crack of dawn.

Standing in front of his house now, she couldn't move, both of them rooted to the spot. As Dylan's mind raced, April's stomach lurched with the familiar dance of butterflies. Just as they had the day she first saw him.

'Hi,' April said, dipping her head so her hair fell in front of her face like a protective curtain. Dylan's hand twitched, the instinct to brush it aside almost kicking in. He glanced up and down the street, looking as sick as she felt.

'April.' He said her name like he was stating an uncomfortable fact. 'What are you doing here?'

'Sorry, I went to your office at the university first and the archaeology department receptionist said they didn't expect you in today. Now I know why. You're moving.'

Dylan bit hard on his bottom lip. 'Yep. To my fiancée's.'

April nodded with a flinch.

'I figured, and I'm sorry to just show up. I wasn't going to. But people kept tagging you in stuff about my exhibition. I wanted to apologise and explain, if I could? It won't take long.'

Dylan walked over and placed the box in his boot, wiping his palms on his jogging bottoms as he nodded towards the front door. Following him into the open-plan room, April was flooded with memories. Boxes were piled everywhere. Some still open, others secured with brown parcel tape. "Living room stuff" and "kitchen junk" were written on two. One just had "misc" on it. Suppressing a chuckle, April noted he'd got no more organised since his uni days.

Her mind was taken back to an afternoon four years

earlier. Dylan packing for Rome and asking if she thought he'd need a jumper.

'Yes,' April had giggled. 'You'll be there all year. I assume at some point you might need a jumper.'

Now Dylan was doing a different kind of packing, and April's presence made him too jittery to sit down. He leaned against the kitchen counter, just as good-looking as always, his eyes pouring into hers.

'I need you to know I'm not trying to drag up the past,' April said. 'With my art show. I was a wreck when I got to San Francisco. It was just my way of working through everything that happened between us, that's all.'

Another nod.

Shrinking back and hiding behind her hair, April wondered if Dylan was going to say anything.

'I get it, April. You're an artist. I'm pleased you're doing well.'

Dylan had said less than thirty words since she'd arrived, each one carefully measured, and he looked determined to say as little as possible. Cheeks burning, April was about to slink away when he finally opened up.

'I was surprised though,' he said. 'I've read some things online, and all that broken-hearted stuff threw me, because you left without telling me. And I called when I found out about San Francisco, begging you to give us another chance, yet you never called back. You didn't even send a text, leaving me to assume I was the only one with the broken heart.'

April shifted from foot to foot. Here it was, the big question. Why did she leave like that?

'I was ashamed. The whole time you were in Rome I'd

behaved horribly. It felt too late to fix it.'

It wasn't a good enough answer. But looking at him now, drumming his fingers on the kitchen counter, surrounded by moving boxes and about to embark on the next chapter of his life, April decided the truth wasn't an option. Why hurt him again, all this time later?

She should've listened to Lizzy. It had been a mistake, stopping by like this. April was just trying to come up with an excuse to leave so they could both pretend it never happened when Dylan blew up.

'That's the reason we're not together?' he cried. 'Because you were *ashamed*? What the fuck does that even mean?' The gold flecks in his irises sparked like fire.

'Me, I was a total fucking mess,' he continued, pushing himself off the counter and gesticulating wildly. 'But poor April was too *ashamed* to call her boyfriend back. So you flew across the world to throw yourself a pity party and make a name for yourself at my expense?'

Dylan usually kept his cool. Only now a vein throbbed in his temple while a stream of vitriol poured from his mouth like white-hot lava. April shrank even smaller at the ferocity of the rant he'd spent three years holding in.

'Now you show up the day I'm moving in with my fiancée. Are you purposefully toying with me? Or are you just looking for material for your next collection of self-indulgent "art"? Here,' he said, kicking a box by his feet, 'take one. You could call it "Fucking with Dylan".'

'Hey,' April cried, crossing her arms in front of her chest. 'I didn't come here to rake over the past, but you asked...'

'Yeah, I asked,' he said, jutting out his chin. 'But I didn't know the answer would be such a big steaming pile of

46

bollocks. That's why I spent a year of my life so miserable I could barely drag myself out the front door? Because you were too ashamed to pick up the phone?'

'I'm sorry.' Tears had started sprinkling down April's cheeks. She'd never seen Dylan like this, and he didn't even know the real reason she'd left so abruptly. If he did, she was sure he'd have hated her even more.

April knew they were having this argument three years too late. The time for the truth had been and gone a long time ago. It didn't stop the tornado of pent-up emotion they'd both been stewing on whipping around them, though.

'I messed up,' April said, pointing at herself before wagging her finger at him. 'But so did you. I went through hell too. I've got a ship container of twisted metal heading across the Atlantic that shows the weight of my misery. You've got a fiancée with a nice shiny new ring on her finger.'

Dylan threw his arms up in disgust. 'Why exactly *are* you here, April? You could have put all this in an email, like your friend Jen did.'

April stopped short, her mouth opening then snapping shut.

'Jen emailed you? When?'

'A couple of days before your show opened. She sent me an invite in the form of a plane ticket. Obviously, I cancelled it.'

April frowned. So, that's what Jen had been checking on launch night. Dylan had returned her Air Miles, ruining her hopes of some romantic reunion. What had she been thinking?

'I'm sorry. I had no idea. That wasn't fair. What did she say?'

'Not much.' Dylan looked at the floor before lifting his gaze and staring questioningly at April. 'Just that you still love me.'

April inhaled sharply. 'Dylan, I… I don't… she shouldn't have…' Unable to find a response, April stumbled clumsily over her words, her eyes darting between Dylan and the door. 'I'm sorry. This was a bad idea. I'll leave.'

She hurried towards the exit, and for a second, Dylan was going to let her go. But unable to help himself, he called after her.

'Is it true? Do you?'

The second the words were out his mouth, she could tell he regretted them. Turning back around and taking in his pained expression, April gulped. What did it matter anyway? He'd chosen Kel; he clearly loved her. What good would this do?

'You can't expect an answer to that. It's not fair on me; it's not fair on you; and it certainly isn't fair on your fiancée,' she said.

Only, just because she didn't say it, didn't mean she didn't feel it.

'Huh.' Dylan forced out a laugh, shaking his head. 'None of this is fair, April. You turn up at my house after three years. I'm engaged; I'm moving in with my fiancée; this is my life; and somehow, you've selfishly burst back into it with as much drama as you fled it.' He glared at her now. 'What did you expect? A handshake and a hearty goodbye, wishing each other well? Or did you really come just to see how I'd react?'

48

As Dylan let the question linger, April took another look around at the boxes and for the first time noticed the footprint of a woman in Dylan's home. Engagement cards on the windowsill, empty champagne bottles that hadn't made it into the recycling bin yet. One box was labelled "Kel's stuff". They'd been together two years, of course she'd left some things at Dylan's.

Snuffling away her tears, April caught the whiff of a plug-in air freshener taking the edge off that rarely vacuumed carpet smell. Fabric softener wafted from the newly washed clothes drying on the radiators, and vanilla-scented candles decorated the coffee table. Touches of a woman who loved him, took care of him.

What little footprints had he already left on the place he was about to move into? A City football shirt perhaps, that Kelly sometimes slept in. A box of Special K in the kitchen cupboard and a spare bottle of Hugo Boss in her bedroom.

What was she doing?

'Well, this is it, April,' Dylan continued, holding his hands out. 'Congratulations. You've managed to whip up all that trauma again just by being you. You can dwell on it and make a career out of it all you like, but I won't look back; I can't go there. Not now. I'm done.'

Dylan turned away, visibly shaking. It was time for her to go.

'You're right. It was selfish,' April said. 'You won't see me again. I'm sorry, Dylan.' The front door banged shut behind her as she hurried back to her car, barely noticing the rain as she climbed in. April had crashed into Dylan's life again like a human wrecking ball, threatening any happiness he'd managed to find.

Needing to put as much distance between them as possible, April sped out his road. Tears blurred her vision as she drove aimlessly, dreading facing Lizzy's "I told you so" or having to admit to anyone the chaos she'd unleashed.

As she hit the outskirts of Manchester, the roads became smaller and twistier. Their fight played on an incessant loop in her head.

I'm done.

More tears replaced the ones she wiped away, until both sleeves were sodden. Struggling to focus, April went to pull over, only there was a corner ahead. And she was going too fast. The steering wheel suddenly felt light as the back wheels skidded out. A high-pitched scream rang out as everything started to tip. Was that her? Or the car? For a moment, April felt weightless. Then nothing, like someone flicked off the lights.

The Coma

SUMMER 2022

April

Blackness enveloped me as the memory I was reliving collapsed, swallowing me whole before spitting me back out into the chilly darkness. Loneliness crushed me.

Baggage. Dylan had told Kelly I was nothing more than baggage. I'd been forced to watch it all unfold, unable to find a way out of the live-action replay, as Dylan chose her for the same reasons I'd spent the last three years hating myself. And he still didn't even know the truth about why I'd left. His gut instinct was to marry Kelly and protect himself from me.

Perhaps he was right to listen to his head over his heart. All I'd ever brought him was drama and pain. Yes, he was beside me at the hospital now, but that was probably just guilt. In the end, sense would take him back to her.

So much for Jen's secret hairbrained scheme to get us back together. What was it she'd said to Dylan?

I wish you'd gotten on that plane.

Me too, I thought. *I wish you'd got on that plane to San Francisco too, Dylan.*

The Plane Ticket

SUMMER 2022

TWO WEEKS BEFORE APRIL'S CRASH

AN ALTERNATIVE REALITY

Dylan

Hunching over April's bed and closing my eyes, I shut out the clinical white hospital room around me. After being awake for so long, I welcomed the quietness of sleep.

It didn't last. With an abrupt, nauseating tug, I looked up and found myself back on my sofa two weeks earlier. Startled, I jumped back. My stomach sloshed with the lads' night beer, thanks to the measly dinner of crisps and nuts we'd scoffed.

I'd gone back in time to that night two weeks earlier. The evening Adam had first brought up April's name in the pub. After hearing the lads' drunken opinions, I'd stormed home to find Jen had sent me that plane ticket.

And now the stench of a pungent air freshener Kel had insisted on plugging in in the living room filled my nostrils, making the churning worse. It was supposed to smell like linen, or cotton or something, but was overpowering and made the place smell like an old bar of soap.

Had I time travelled?

Surely that was impossible. I tried to stand up, but I was frozen in my seat, squinting at the eticket to San Francisco on my phone screen and listening to the pounding of my own heart.

'San Francisco?' Kel cried from behind me. 'Dylan, why have you got a plane ticket to San Francisco?'

Leaping up, I whipped around to see Kel, standing there in her short black pyjamas with her hands on her hips.

'Shit. Kel, you scared me,' I spluttered, gulping at the intense stare of her dark eyes.

'Dylan? What the hell is going on?'

Déjà vu. Time travel. Some sort of quantum leap. I wasn't sure what this was. But that wasn't what Kel was asking. Time wasn't repeating for her. And the last time I'd been here, looking at Jen's eticket, I'd chosen not to fly to San Francisco because I was a coward. And not getting on that plane led to April's accident.

What if?

What if, this time, I did? Jen's words in the hospital echoed.

I wish you'd gotten on that plane, Dylan.

Maybe I was being given a chance to fix things and win April back. Save her life and create a new future for us that didn't involve a coma? And if that were the case, I shouldn't question the why.

Instead, I made a snap decision to do what I should have done all along. With a deep breath, I looked at Kel, determined to make this as quick and painless as possible.

'It's April,' I said, trying not to fumble my words. 'She's opening an art show, and her friend sent me a ticket.'

Kel shook her head, bewildered. 'But surely you're not thinking of going?' she said, her fingers twisting her engagement ring round and round.

'I'm sorry,' I whispered, reaching for her hand but pulling back when she recoiled. 'I love you. I do. And when I proposed, I wanted to marry you. I was sure…'

'Was?' Kel stiffened, interrupting with a gasp and blinking at me with wide eyes.

'I'm sorry,' I said again, wanting to touch her but knowing it'd be unwelcome. 'Kel, I thought it was over, I did. I was grateful when I met you two years ago because it felt like I'd been given a second chance at love. I was happy.'

'And now what? You're not anymore? I'm suddenly not enough?' she shouted, each question scorching her face with hurt and anger.

'No. Not… suddenly.' I bit my bottom lip, hating the sudden brutal delivery but knowing I owed her the truth. And the truth was that my feelings for April had always been there, simmering under the surface.

'I've been lying to myself for a long time,' I said, rubbing my forehead with a rubbery palm. 'Whenever April crossed my mind, I'd push the thoughts away and remind myself I was lucky to have you. I didn't stop to consider that maybe you deserved better than that. But you do, Kel. You deserve better than being a second chance. Better than me.' I stepped towards her again and she jumped back, covering her mouth with her hands.

'How didn't I see this coming?' Kel said, her shoulders juddering at the waver in her voice. 'You told me about April the night we met, but I still thought you'd moved past it.' Squeezing her eyes shut and holding her breath to hold back the tears, Kel doubled over before backing away further.

'I thought that was just heated first love, that we'd built something stronger than the white-knuckle joyride she took you on,' she said, one hand over her mouth now, letting the tears silently trickle down her cheeks.

'That's what I thought too,' I admitted, lifting my shoulders to my ears. 'But it turns out...'

'You want the thrill ride.' Kel's whole body slumped in defeat. 'And I've been living a lie, all this time. Planning a future with someone who was never mine. Who wasn't even close.' Her chest heaved with a loud sob, jerking her into action. While she banged and clattered though drawers gathering her things, I stood limply in the middle of the room knowing nothing I could say would make it better, only worse.

'Here,' she spat, lunging at me and slamming my passport into my chest. 'Good luck. Because if the pathetic mess I met two years ago is anything to go by, you're going to need it.'

When she was gone, I stood in the silence waiting for my heartbeat to slow and my breaths to steady. Hurting Kel had been a horrible inevitability; hindsight taught me that now. I forced my thoughts forwards to April, where they'd always belonged.

*

Buckling my seatbelt on the plane the following morning, I couldn't sit still. I tried to occupy my hands by reading the in-flight magazine, but my focus kept drifting to the insanity of what I was doing. I'd no idea what would happen when I got to San Francisco or what I'd say.

After Kel stormed out, I'd been too restless to sleep, packing and unpacking a backpack several times, drinking endless cups of coffee and thinking of April. The April waiting for me in San Francisco and Coma April, in a hospital bed barely alive. Did she still exist?

It left me an exhausted wreck, and I crashed out by the time the plane was thundering down the runway, only waking briefly for lunch.

It was mid-afternoon when I landed in San Francisco. My phone buzzed alive with messages from the lads' group chat the second I turned it back on. The Adam, Al and Jonesy of this life had no idea about April's accident in my timeline, and word had got round about my ruthless break-up with Kel and rash decision to fly thousands of miles on the off-chance April still loved me. They didn't understand it; they couldn't.

Dylan, pal. WHAT ARE YE DOING?!?! Adam, of course.

He's lost the plot, Ad. Dylan, have you thought this through? Georgia says Kel's in bits. Jonesy.

Thought it through? Adam mentioned April's name twelve hours ago and Dylan has already dumped his fiancée and got on a plane, Al had written. *I think that means he's been on the verge of doing something nuts the whole time. He just hid it well.*

Dylan ye big bawbag. Come home will ye? Adam again.

Come home? He's not nipped to Liverpool, mate. April must give a killer blow job. Jonesy.

Speaking from personal experience, I don't recall her givin' 'em at all. I bristled at that one. Adam couldn't help himself sometimes.

Come on, guys. Dyl's blowing up his entire life on the back of an email from a stranger. Give him a break. Al, as always, trying to be diplomatic.

We're gonna be the ones needing a break when this all goes tits up. Jonesy.

It went on like that, so I stopped reading, firing off a brief reply instead. It was the middle of the night in Manchester now anyway.

Too late now, fellas. I had to give it one last shot. Jonesy was right, Kel deserved more than to be my second choice. See you on the other side...

It was almost evening by the time I got through arrivals. April's exhibit would be opening soon, but in my haste to get there, I'd not thought about where I'd sleep. Finding the nearest Starbucks, I topped up on coffee and used my phone to book a B&B around the corner from April's show, giving me just enough time to dump my bag and get there before it closed.

Walking slowly into the gallery a couple of hours later, my legs were like jelly. I wished I'd found somewhere to have a glug of whisky first, and I still had no idea what I was going to say. I was going to have to wing it. Picturing April showing up on my driveway that day, I wondered if this is how she'd felt. And I hoped the April in this timeline handled it better than I had in mine.

My stomach lurched when my eyes finally found her in the thinning crowd. She was in the middle of the room next to a glowing red metal box. Her hair was shorter than

I remembered, and she'd found her own chic artist style since her uni days. Back then she was either in sloppy joggers and a hoody or her favourite little red dress. This new look was something in-between. It suited her.

The gallery was starting to empty quickly: it was now or never. Steeling myself, I slowly walked over and stood a little way behind her. Watching her a moment, talking to a befuddled-looking man and a tearful teenager, I was transported back to our university days. The way a smile hovered never far away when she talked, the look of concentration as she gave her audience her full attention.

'It represents what it's like when you love someone completely but can't be with them,' April was saying. I followed her gaze back to the glowing red box shrouded in chains. "Locked Heart", the blurb called it.

'Not only is that love trapped inside your heart forever, but there's no way in for anyone else either. One love locked in; the rest locked out. It feels like you're drowning, hence the water,' April continued.

'And the slab?' the teenage girl asked. 'Does that represent how cold and lonely it is?'

April nodded, her smile faltering slightly.

I scratched my forehead. Did that mean she *had* still loved me, all this time? And it'd trapped her in some sort of love purgatory? It resonated. I'd never recovered from our relationship either. Sure, I'd found a way to love again, but only a fraction of what I'd felt for April.

'It's spot on,' the girl said, dabbing her eyes.

The stern man next to her frowned. 'Why are there two padlocks?'

'Because it needs two people to unlock it. The heart's

owner and the one she still hopelessly loves.' The girl nodded knowingly.

'That's right.' April managed a kind smile as the man guided the girl towards the exit.

'Does is get better?' she called back, blinking at April from under smudged, damp eyelashes. 'Will you be doing a sequel?'

'I hope so.' April looked back at the sculpture, turning her back to me, lost in thought.

Now or never.

'April?' I called, stepping closer. Her name was as good an icebreaker as any. April didn't move, and I wondered if she'd heard me. Time slowed as the silence stretched on. Still April didn't move.

'Dylan?' she said eventually. 'Is it really you? Because if I turn around and it's not you...'

'It's me.' Reaching forward, I took hold of her hand, spinning her around to face me. She took a sharp intake of breath as our eyes met, and in an instant, I knew I'd done the right thing. April was here, healthy, beautiful. And I was right where I needed to be.

'Dylan? I don't understand. How are you here?'

'Your friend – Jen – she emailed me a plane ticket.' A nervous smile was still tugging at the corners of my mouth. April shot a look across the room at the tall platinum blonde who looked just like @artyjennifer from Instagram. Jen quickly busied herself talking to some of the last visitors straggling towards the exit, but it was obvious she'd been watching.

'A plane ticket?' April squeaked. 'I had no idea. I'm sorry. Jen can be a bit... well, she shouldn't have done that.'

'It was a bit of a shock.' My eyes searched hers. 'Finding out you'd messaged Adam, of all people, was also a surprise.'

April blushed pink and cringed.

'And I *really* shouldn't have done that. I'm sorry. I guess I lost it a bit the other night. Setting all this up was tough. I had no idea you were engaged when I sent it, I promise.'

I nodded, looking around the room at what looked like a shrine – or maybe a crypt – to our doomed relationship.

'But hey, I'm the one who got on a plane based on four words from a stranger,' I joked. The room was empty now. Even Jen had made herself scarce as April and I continued our awkward exchange. 'And I was engaged. I'm not anymore. As of several hours and a transatlantic flight ago.'

April sucked in a breath. Our conversation was stilted, and I wished I'd prepared a speech after all.

'I feel like I've been on pause for the last few years,' I said, ploughing through the silence. 'When Adam mentioned your name, it switched me back on. A short, sharp shock to the system and I realised I was getting married for all the right reasons but to the wrong person.'

'I'm sorry,' April said, but I waved away her apology. I needed to get this out.

'I can't lie – the last forty-eight hours have been a mindfuck, in more ways than one. And we can talk about everything later. But right now, I just need to know one thing. Jen said… well, she said you still love me, and all that matters to me now is whether that's true. Do you?'

'It's not that simple; there's something I need to…'

I cut her off again. We'd always been good at complicating things, and if I'd miraculously been given a do-over, I was adamant I wouldn't let us make that mistake again.

'It is that simple though,' I said, moving towards her until our noses almost touched. 'That's the only question that needs answering. We both made mistakes last time, but I've spent every day since thinking of you and pretending I wasn't. One tiny inkling of hope and I'm dropping everything to fly here, which should tell you all you need to know. I'm still crazy in love with you.' I stopped to draw breath, gesturing around April's gallery of self-flagellation. 'All of this, if you still feel any of it right now, then it really is straightforward, and everything else is background noise. I'm still all in, April. Are you?'

'Yes,' she whispered. 'I always have been. I just got a bit lost for a second. Just a second, but it was still long enough to ruin everything and I…'

I smiled as she began to ramble, tucking her hair behind her ear and trailing my fingers down her neck.

'April. You can stop talking now.' Then I put my mouth on hers, cupping her face with my other hand as she sank into me. Everything around us faded away as we lost ourselves in each other. This was what I'd come for. The kiss I'd ached for since the moment she'd appeared on my driveway, if only I hadn't been tripped up by fear.

Our lips moved in sync, familiar yet strangers. It was funny – I'd imagined kissing her again would be like that first time. Freeing all that pent-up passion. But this was tender and reserved, both of us unsure. Wanting to take the leap but terrified of opening a painful door to the past.

'Phew,' I said when I finally pulled away. 'My heart is going like crazy.'

'Mine too,' April smiled, her arms looped round me, her fingers teasingly circling the hair that'd grown below the nape of my neck. The intimacy of it sent waves of pleasure down my spine. 'I'm not even sure if this is really happening, that you're actually here.'

'I'm definitely here.' I kissed her forehead. 'Also, we are now literally the only ones who are here.'

April looked around, realising the gallery had completely emptied.

While she closed everything down for the night, stealing glances in my direction as she did, I looked around. The whole exhibit was tinged with this heavy sadness, and I could feel the abyss of loneliness April had fallen into.

It hurt. It was all there. Every stinging moment of our relationship. A cruel text I'd sent her. April's unused plane ticket to Rome, a pleading voicemail playing on a loop. I couldn't stomach putting the headphones on to listen to it.

The trouble was, April had portrayed everything like I was some white knight Prince Charming character who kept swooping in with romantic gestures. On the other hand, she'd painted herself as the villain. The screw-up, undeserving of my love. Pushing me away, building a wall between us, locking her own heart away.

There was a football in one corner. I'd no clue what that was about. And one sculpture was this incredible metal statue contorted into a woman walking away. She was looking over her shoulder, her mouth knitted together with red ribbon and her phone smashed underfoot. I frowned at the title. "The Secrets We Keep".

'April, this is… well, it's a lot.'

'I know,' she said. 'I was trying to work through my emotions and figure out where we went wrong. But I'm not sure I even understand now if I'm honest.'

'That's because my side of the story is missing. I wasn't blameless. You didn't break us up, April, we both did that long before you ran away.'

We were both thoughtful for a second.

'Still, all this, it's incredible. Beautiful but haunting. You're an amazing artist, April. You make falling in love look terrifying though.'

'Well, isn't it?' she shrugged. 'Because you're here, and after all this time, the only thing we both want is to be together. But my palms are sweating just thinking about where this conversation ends, what happens tomorrow, then what happens back in Manchester. I feel like I'm floating on a raincloud that could burst at any moment.'

'Same.' I took her hand and squeezed it. 'But if we face the scary bits together this time, and just keep talking, we'll make it. Hearts intact and unchained.'

We kissed again before stepping outside into the fresh San Francisco night. I'd not seen much of the place, but I could see why April liked it. It smelt fresh, crisp and very un-city like, while the steep glowing streets almost wrapped me in a welcoming embrace.

'My friends are having drinks nearby,' April said as I stifled a yawn.

'You go. I know we still have a lot to talk about, but this jet lag is a killer.' Plus, I wasn't sure either of us could cope with the fuss her friends might make of my sudden appearance.

'Tomorrow, we'll talk properly tomorrow,' I promised,

kissing her tenderly again before watching her walk away. I still felt fragile, but as though a few pieces of me had already been glued back together.

Jet lag knocked me out, but at 5am, I was wide awake and agonising over how things with April would go. Knowing she still loved me made my insides sing, but there was still a lot of stagnant water under the bridge. By 6am, I'd driven myself half mad so went out for a run to clear my head.

My calf muscles were on fire as I pushed myself up the city's hilly streets. Roads so steep it didn't seem possible to walk up, never mind run. The down was just as hard, my thighs burning from the fight against gravity.

The effort proved a great distraction though, and by the time I'd showered and changed ready to meet April in a nearby coffee shop, I'd rehearsed what I wanted to say a million times over. Sod's Law, I didn't say any of it, because when she walked in, it was like being pulled through another time warp, back to those early days of dating.

Her jeans were spotted with paint, and I wasn't sure if it was the design or splashes of her own. Either way, they showed off the curve of her hip all the way to the tuck of her waist. A short black crop top, which I was sure I recognised, was brightened by a rainbow scarf wound round her neck. She was the walking embodiment of a chic San Francisco artist, and I pulled my jacket closed over my dull charcoal polo shirt and tired Levis, wishing I'd put more thought into packing.

April had rediscovered some of the inner sparkle that had disappeared towards the end of our relationship.

'Hey, you,' she said, and all I wanted to do was swap her nervous smile for the one that brightens the universe. Make her laugh again.

'April,' I beamed, standing up and lurching forwards, wrapping her in an inelegant hug that trapped her arms so she couldn't return it. 'I was thinking, I've never been to San Francisco, so before we get into the heavy stuff, why don't we just hang out?'

April agreed, sagging with relief as the tension left her body. I knew I shouldn't avoid the difficult conversation. But I hadn't seen her like this for years. I pictured her hurt, trapped in a coma back in Manchester. What if this attempt to save her didn't work? This could be my only chance to cherish every bit of time I got with her. Wander around a city like we used to, talking and walking aimlessly, at ease in each other's company.

'You can show me what's so magical about the place, give us a chance to get used to each other again?' I suggested.

Nodding, April ordered coffees for us both, and we just sort of stared at each other every so often. Making small talk about my flight, the weather and the slight changes in our hairstyles.

'It suits you a little longer. The stubble does too.' April grinned, reaching out to lightly touch my rough chin. A shudder left goosebumps in its wake, and I laughed.

'The stubble is down to dropping everything and chasing an ex across a few continents, not a fresh look I'm trying.'

'Well, maybe it should be; it's pretty sexy,' April teased, but the atmosphere was charged. With the dramatics of the previous night's reunion over, we suddenly felt like strangers. The canyon of lost years opening between us, making us almost clumsy around each other.

'Jen says sorry by the way.' April had got a grilling when she'd turned up at the bar the previous night, especially as I hadn't tagged along. 'I made her stew a bit before giving her any details. I'm still furious about the plane ticket, even if it is the reason you're here.'

Jen had been horrified when she woke up with a sore head the morning after she'd sent it. Especially when April told her I was engaged. In a flap, she'd kept what she'd done a secret from everyone.

'She almost cancelled the ticket, but the romantic in her couldn't let go of the smidge of hope that you'd come. I'm glad she didn't.'

And despite her contrition, Jen was still adamant she'd done us both a favour. I couldn't disagree, at least not yet.

'So,' April smiled after another silence, 'if you really want to see San Francisco, then we must start with Alcatraz. It's mandatory for tourists. Then I'm taking you to Pier 39, through the city on a cable car and finishing with a walk across the Golden Gate Bridge.'

'OK, let's do it.' I stood up, instinctively taking her hand as we walked out of the coffee shop. After that, with all talk of our sticky history put on hold, we fell into step, and in some moments, it was like no time had passed. We explored the streets of San Francisco like we'd trodden Manchester's waterways, drinking coffee from paper cups, laughing and teasing each other's quirks. Yet, in others, we walked on eggshells. All those things unsaid bubbling under the surface.

'This bridge is definitely orange, not golden,' I said mid-afternoon, as we came to the last stop of our tour. 'But it's even more impressive than Media City Footbridge. I can see why you stayed so long.'

Several afternoons as poor students, we'd got the bus to MediaCity on the banks of the Manchester Ship Canal in Salford Quays and spent hours walking around hand in hand. Scaling the bridge more times than we could count. Stopping to kiss under the glow of the glass architecture. April said she enjoyed being in the hub of creativity and watching the bridge illuminate as night fell. But I knew she was secretly celeb spotting as she once got very overexcited when we saw a gaggle of Corrie stars leaving the soap's set after filming had ended.

'San Francisco was my haven after everything that happened. I'd completely fallen apart, and it felt easier being so far away from Manchester,' April said now, stopping halfway along the bridge to look out over the water.

Back in my living room during that god-awful row, April had said she'd run away out of shame. It was true she'd not handled my year studying abroad well, but watching her now with the breeze in her hair, a dark shadow crossed her face. I knew there was more to it.

The April in a coma hadn't told me the truth. Would this April?

'If you still loved me, why did you just leave like that?' I asked. 'Without even telling me? No call, no text. I've never understood it.' I'd tried calling her the morning she left for the airport. If she'd never stopped loving me, it seemed unfathomable that she didn't call me back.

April went quiet, resting her head on my shoulder as we leant on the steel side of the bridge, breathing in a concoction of exhaust fumes and sea air.

'I wanted to call you,' she sighed sadly, staring down into the choppy, dark water. 'More than anything, I wanted to. But I just… couldn't.'

'OK, well that question has been killing me for three years, so please, make it make sense for me? Put me out of my misery.'

April looked at me sideways, her face darkening further.

'Will you kiss me again, before I answer?' she asked, moving closer and tucking herself close to my chest. 'So you remember how it feels before I say what I have to say? Because there's something I need to tell you, and it's not going to be easy to hear.'

Her words landed in my stomach like the stench of the sea lions on the pier, and I worried I'd throw up over the side of the bridge. What could she possibly be hiding that was this bad?

It's three years of silence bad, I reminded myself. So terrible Coma April had chosen to keep it from me still.

Pushing those thoughts away, I did as she asked, stroking her cheek with my thumb and leaning forwards until our mouths were almost touching.

'I've never forgotten how it feels to kiss you, April.'

My lips were just grazing hers when a squeal of breaks tore through the air. The screeching of rubber on tarmac followed, and my head flew in the direction of the noise in time to spot the pickup truck crashing through the barrier, mounting the pavement and barrelling towards us. On instinct, I shoved April as hard as I could back towards the steel side of the bridge. Our eyes met over the deafening roar, and hers flashed with horror as this immense force crashed into me. Then everything shrunk to nothingness.

April's Hospital Room

Dylan

Waking with a jolt, I emptied my lungs of air.

Had I pushed April out the way in time? What had she been about to tell me?

My breaths rushed in and out. Patting my body down and stretching my toes in my trainers, I made sure that, yes, I was still in one piece. Alive. It hadn't been real.

Had it?

The fright in April's eyes had been horribly realistic. So had the warmth of her mouth on mine in the moments before the truck hit. I looked at the time on my phone. It was just past midnight. I'd nodded off with my head on April's shoulder. My cheek was creased from the starchy white sheets, my palm slick as I released it from hers and wiped it on my jeans.

What was that?

I felt as though days had passed, rather than hours, and I could still feel the heat of April's body pressed against mine. I'd thought I was being given the chance to save her.

Had I wasted it? Changed the wrong thing? Or had it all just been a dream?

No. It had been real. I was sure. The smell of freshly caught crab had lingered on my skin as we meandered past the boats and food shacks on Fisherman's Wharf. I could still hear the clanging bells of the cable cars as they kept the city thronging. Feel the burn as I jogged up the impossibly steep streets, even though I'd never visited the city before.

And the truck…

Shuddering, I tried to remember the last time I ate. Needing a sugar hit to settle my nerves, I wandered out into the corridor in search of a vending machine dinner.

As I walked, a nagging certainty told me there was a Dylan out there in a parallel universe somewhere, who did get on that plane. Somehow, I'd leapt into his life and lived it with him. Yet it had still ended in tragedy, taking me, rather than April.

I was so perturbed, it was several hours before I allowed myself to nod off again, despite the exhaustion pounding at my temples.

*

A nurse jostled me awake just after dawn. By then I'd been at the hospital well over thirty-six hours.

'Dylan, there's someone here to see you,' she whispered. Disorientated, I blinked and looked over towards the door.

'Kel!' I jumped up, suddenly wide awake. 'I should have called. I know. I should have called.'

Kel's lip curled at the sight of me, crumpled into a hospital armchair in the same, but now severely dishevelled,

T-shirt and jeans she'd left me in two days previously. Then she looked at April, knowing.

'Are you April's friend too?' The nurse smiled.

Kel shuffled from foot to foot. 'Actually...' she said, clearing her throat, 'I'm Dylan's fiancée.'

'Oh!' the nurse gasped, looking between us, then at April, her mouth hanging open. 'Oh! Right. Well, perhaps you two should talk outside?' Her voice was high pitched and squeaky.

As I followed Kel out into the corridor, the nurse hurried back to her station, whispering manically to her colleagues. We'd just become the hospital's juiciest slither of gossip.

'Kel, I...'

'No.' Kel held her left hand up to stop me talking, causing her engagement ring to sparkle under the white lights. 'Me first. I've listened to your bullshit too much lately, Dylan.'

I clamped my mouth shut, running my hand through my hair, my eyes flitting to our audience of medical staff and back to Kel's glower.

'About thirty-six hours ago, I arrived home from work with a bottle of champagne expecting to see my fiancé surrounded by moving boxes,' Kel said, arms folded across her chest. 'Exhausted and aching from lugging his stuff over to my house but smiling, wanting a curry to celebrate our first night living together. Only, you weren't there, were you, Dylan? You weren't picking up your phone, answering messages – nothing.' Kel paused, glancing at April's door and touching her forehead.

'I was worried,' she choked, her voice faltering. 'I went

over to your place and all your moving boxes were still in the house. You and your car had vanished, then by late evening your phone stopped even ringing.'

I tried to interrupt to explain that my battery died, but she stopped me again.

'None of your friends knew where you were, so I started ringing around the hospitals. Hospitals, Dylan,' she hissed. 'Including this one, although apparently, I was looking for the wrong person. After a sleepless night, I phoned your office where, finally, things started falling into place. The receptionist told me a woman came looking for you. April, I presume.' Kel's voice cracked saying April's name.

'Then, when I called your mates back to tell them I thought April might have shown up, they became evasive, like they knew something I didn't. Mostly, they told me to give you space; they were sure it was nothing and you'd call when you were ready. Only, that really isn't good enough when your fiancé does a vanishing act instead of moving in with you.'

Grimacing, I stared at the floor.

'So, I started looking for April instead. Her friends on social media were all posting thoughts and prayers, and I knew you'd be here. I convinced myself you were just a concerned ex, but when another night crept by with radio silence, there was only one possible reason why. I had to see it for myself though, and here you are, curled up at April's bedside like a forlorn, lost puppy with the audacity to be shocked by the sudden appearance of your forgotten fiancée.'

Finding the courage to look at her, I saw she'd started crying.

'I'm sorry April got injured, but do you have any idea what you put me through the last two nights? You discarded me. Left me to figure out you weren't coming back all on my own, just two weeks after feeding me some bullshit about choosing me. Insisting April was nothing more than baggage. Have I even occurred to you in the last thirty-six hours? Tell me the truth, Dylan – it's the least I deserve.'

She finished in a crescendo of sobs, her chin quivering as she fought to get them under control. Exposed in the hospital corridor, I felt like a gnat she'd just swatted. And I deserved it. Because I hadn't thought about anything but April since her crash.

'I'm sorry, Kel. I am. Endlessly sorry.' I leant forwards to close the gap between us. 'I should have called but April was in surgery, and I lost all sense of time and reality. It's my fault she's in here, you see. We argued and April, well... she was upset.'

Kel shook her head and looked away with a sneer. She didn't want excuses, just the truth. If only to help her let go.

'I lied to everyone two weeks ago, myself included,' I said, slumping at the shoulders. 'Because for me, April is inevitable. And the truth is, even though we'd rowed, I was unpacking my boxes from the car two minutes after she'd driven off. I was on my way over to tell you everything when Lizzy called about the accident. Blind panic took over and ever since I've been incapable of thinking about anything beyond needing April to survive.'

Kel sniffed, trying to hide that she was in desperate need of a tissue as the nurses covertly watched our excruciating exchange.

'I never had a chance, did I? You just strung me along until your precious April came back. A stopgap.'

'No!' I cried, rushing forwards to put my arms around her, but she jumped back. 'I thought a future with you was my second chance. But you deserve more than that, Kel. Much more.'

'See, that doesn't really help me, because I still love you.' Her tears had stopped, leaving her cheeks damp and blotchy. She closed her eyes, and when she opened them again, her glare had turned icy. 'But in three years' time, I certainly won't still be hanging around, hoping you'll walk back through the door, Dylan.'

Spotting the nurses peeking over, Kel pulled her shoulders back and smoothed her long hair. 'You should have found a second to call me,' she sniffed. 'I shouldn't have had to come here and humiliate myself like this. I hope April makes it. I even hope you make each other happy this time. But I also hope I never see you again.' Tugging off her engagement ring, she pushed it into my palm. 'Goodbye, Dylan.'

As Kel strode off, I rubbed the back of my neck, staring down at the ring sparkling under the bright hospital lights.

One of the nurses who hadn't been obviously gossiping tentatively tapped me on the elbow.

'Let me get you a cup of tea,' she said with a small but kind smile. 'Life can get away from us sometimes. But April, she needs you now. And that's why you're here, right?'

'Right.' Stuffing the ring in my pocket, I slunk back to April's side with Kel's hurt face still at the forefront of my mind. It was odd, but it almost felt like I'd broken her heart twice in one night.

*

'Lizzy's picking up April's parents so they only have to park one car in the lot. Something about extortionate prices,' Jen said, breezing in an hour later looking slightly less weary. As she took a seat, chatting about needing to fill the room with positivity, one of the hospital staff brought another tray of tea in. Everyone was being extra attentive that morning, trying to eavesdrop for more scandalous titbits of gossip.

Jen crossed one long leg over the other before looking over at me with her eyes narrowed. 'What's up, Dylan? Something's bothering you.'

I couldn't face telling her about Kel, so I told her about my overnight disappearance into the past.

'It was like I'd been dragged back in time and given a do-over. More than a dream. I was living it. And, by the way, using that plane ticket you sent didn't end well. Not for me.' I could almost hear the screeching tyres and twisting steel, sending a chill down my spine.

Jen tilted her head. 'You know that teenage girl you saw April talking to in the gallery? She was there, I'm certain. It sounds like my cousin Tori.'

Tori was eighteen, and her high school boyfriend had broken up with her before going to college in New York.

'My uncle's a single dad with zero idea how to deal with this teenage girl sobbing on the couch watching *Five Feet Apart* on Netflix every night. I suggested he bring her to April's exhibition. I thought it'd help him understand Tori a bit more and inspire Tori to do something other than wallow.'

She pulled up a photo on her phone. 'Was this them?'

I squinted at the picture, but it was impossible to tell as I'd been too focused on April. Shrugging it off as a coincidence, I was relieved when Jen changed the subject.

'I googled you by the way. To get your email address when I sent that plane ticket. Saw your bio on the college website. You're a bit of an Indiana Jones these days, aren't you?'

I laughed. 'Why does everyone think I have this fantasy of becoming Indiana Jones? Always saw myself as a Benjamin Gates type.'

'The *National Treasure* guy? Nick Cage? Jeez, Dylan, he has like, no sex appeal. Besides, we both know April's the one with the Indie fantasy.' She winked, and heat rushed to my cheeks as I had a flashback of April in nothing but a fedora.

'What I'm trying to say is, maybe these last few years have been good for both of you. You're about to get your sexy PhD, travelling the world searching for mysterious ancient artifacts.'

It wasn't anywhere near that glamorous. I was mostly buried under books rather than raiding temples of doom. I didn't shatter her illusion though.

'April found the tortured artist inside her. Without all that heartbreak, she'd still be making sculptures of sunshine and flowers. And parachuting teenage girls. As an art critic, I promise you, no one would give her an exhibition for those.' For a diehard romantic, Jen talked sense.

For the next hour, she regaled me all about April's life in San Francisco. Their close circle of creative-type friends from Dogpatch making weekly trips to Ghirardelli Square because April was obsessed with their chocolate brownies.

'Honestly, you'd have thought they were hash brownies the way she went wild for them.' Jen giggled. 'Then there's the time she fell off a cable car at the Powell and Hyde turnabout after one too many margaritas. Blake had to give her a piggyback home.'

Jen rested her chin on her hand and looked over at me. 'There was no one else though, only you,' she said with a sigh. 'Obviously, I nagged her to date, and she had a few flings. Eduardo, Owen and the adorable Blake who was besotted with her before she called it all off.'

I groaned, not wanting to hear about April's sex life, yet Jen seemed determined to fill every silence with banal chit-chat to stop the worry worming its way back in.

'April genuinely couldn't fall in love again. Whether that was on purpose or not, I don't know. You did though?' Her voice went up an octave at the end.

I'd wondered when she'd bring up Kel. I gave her a brief outline of Kel's dawn ambush and how we were now the hospital's hot gossip.

'Even with Kel it took me a while. Plus, the way April left… I had to assume she didn't love me anymore. I guess that made it easier to let someone else in. Eventually.'

Jen nodded. 'April did love you, though. And when she wasn't wallowing, she loved talking about the good bits. The meet-cute, that first kiss and the grand declarations. Plus, the hot Indiana Jones sex.'

Jen sniggered as she watched my cheeks turn crimson again.

'Your love story played like a romcom in her head, and when it turned out not to be quite the perfect fairy tale, she assumed it was ruined forever. So she left.' My gaze fell on April's heart-shaped birthmark as I considered Jen's oversimplified version.

'I tried to make it perfect for her,' I said, watching the involuntary rise and fall of April's chest in time to the Darth Vader ventilator. 'Things get hard sometimes; it doesn't mean you give up or run away.'

Jen finally went quiet before replying. 'But she came back. And I know it may seem like she waited too long, but our girl grew up. She's not the floundering, naïve girl she was when she turned up at my door three summers ago. I like to think I helped, being the quirky best friend. Rather than that sarcastic, judgemental Lizzy. Don't tell her I said that,' she added behind her hand.

I laughed. 'Lizzy *is* terrifying.'

Just then, Lizzy arrived with April's parents. April's mum, Sarah, looked like she'd aged ten years overnight, swaying feebly like a robin on a washing line. April's dad, Ian, had an arm hooked round her waist to steady her wobbling legs.

'Dylan,' Sarah said, as I stood up to greet her. 'I say this with love, and I'm thankful you're here for my daughter, but you need a shower; you need to sleep horizontally; and you need a proper meal. Please, go home for a few hours.' Sarah felt tiny and brittle in my arms as she gave me a hug I didn't deserve.

April's mum had always been kind to me. Even when I'd raced into the waiting room just after the accident, blubbing about needing to see April with great big body-jerking sobs. Weeping herself, she'd taken my hand and told me to sit with them while we waited for news from the surgeons, none of us knowing if she'd make it off the operating table.

And now, when I was hanging around the hospital despite not being April's boyfriend for years, and being the reason she was here, she welcomed me with grace.

Just then, a nurse came in, announcing April was being taken for an MRI scan. Ganging up on me, she and April's parents insisted I go home for a short break while she was gone. In the end, I relented.

Pressing the button for the ground floor and leaning against the back of the lift, my whole body ached. It struck me that the previous night's vivid out-of-body journey to the past was probably an exhaustion-induced hallucination.

The Coma

April

What just happened?

I'd been right there, watching myself spin off the road. Just as my car flipped and crunched into a wall, the memory had ejected me back into my dark, miserable mind prison.

But I'd only been back a few seconds when the art gallery in San Francisco pixelated into existence around me. My sculptures were all set out just like they had been on launch night two weeks ago. Jen's cousin Tori was asking me questions, her eyes pleading for an end to her teenage heartache.

Only this one wasn't a memory; it was something different. Because I wasn't just an invisible observer, I was me. And I heard his voice.

April.

I turned around to find those golden eyes fixed on mine. Dylan had come to San Francisco for me. Kissed me, squeezed my hand in his as we walked along the Golden Gate Bridge. I'd been about to tell him... but then he'd...

gone. Ripped away with the sickening crunch of metal on bone and smashing glass. Then the rush of wind in the truck's wake whooshed my soul out of the body I was in, and I floated back down to this mind prison again.

For a few seconds, I thought it was real. It'd felt real. I thought I'd lost him, and a lifetime of grief crushed my very existence. I never wanted to experience such emptiness again.

Was that what would have happened to Dylan if he'd boarded that plane? Was there an April out there in some point in time and space who'd lost her Dylan so brutally? How would she ever recover?

She wouldn't.

That harrowing thought ricocheted around my damaged brain, and I knew then I had to fight. Find my way back to Dylan to save us both that suffering.

As my nerves steadied, the darkness lifted until, one by one, the screens returned around me, like pop-ups on a virus-riddled laptop. Some like dots in the distance, others right in front of me. Each playing a different episode of the Dylan and April show.

The rolling images were of me, but they weren't *me*. They weren't all from my own life. Some belonged to other Aprils, like the one I'd just come from. There was an April standing at the top of the Eiffel Tower with Lizzy, yet I'd never been to Paris. One cuddling up to Dylan for a photo, both of us wearing a cap and gown and clutching our degrees. The *me* me had left Manchester before graduation. In one I'd rather not dwell on, I was wearing a cheap wedding dress stood across from Adam in what looked like a Las Vegas wedding chapel.

Parallel universes that deviated off course every time Dylan or I made a choice. Something as simple as eggs for breakfast over cereal would nudge us onto a new trajectory.

Not many, but a few, showed events so far removed from those I knew, I barely recognised Dylan in them. Dylan, the personal assistant to an eccentric millionaire attempting to build a spaceship for the first manned mission to Mars. Dylan caring for his sick father, working three jobs to pay the bills.

In this cinema of Dylans and Aprils, I could see our past and every possible future. Including some which ended shortly after now in that coma room of dwindling hope.

April's Hospital Room

SUMMER 2022

Dylan

'She flipped her car,' Ian sighed, rubbing his temples as I put a bag of sausage rolls from the hospital canteen on April's table and took my jacket off. When I'd arrived back at Salford Royal mid-afternoon, showered and changed but no less exhausted, I'd guessed no one had managed to eat anything.

The police had stopped by with news while I was gone. Road accident investigators had established no other vehicles were involved. I'd not seen Ian cry, but I could tell from his watery gaze he had been. He was just trying to put on a strong front for his family.

'Investigators believe she skidded, lost control and smashed into a wall,' he said with the slightest shake of his head.

Mercifully, April had been unconscious when firefighters cut her out the driver's seat. Yet she'd suffered a traumatic brain injury, her skull fractured in several places. There'd been bleeding, swelling on her brain. After saving her life, surgeons had put her in the medically induced coma.

'Doctors keep insisting it's just a waiting game to see if she wakes up. There's nothing any of us can do.' Ian's brow was furrowed, while new crinkles were appearing around his eyes by the hour. That, and the book of half-finished crosswords on his lap, told me he wasn't good at sitting and being patient, especially when the stakes were so high.

The doctors were also testing April for any brain activity. 'Prepare yourselves,' they'd told Ian and Sarah. For what, they didn't specify, but we all knew what it meant. For April to die.

'We'll have some tricky decisions to make if scans show she's...' Ian's bottom lip wobbled, and he struggled to finish the sentence, '...brain dead.'

Sarah let out a fresh sob and buried her face in a hanky. They'd also been advised that April, if she did pull through and wake up, would likely suffer brain damage due to the head trauma. But again...

'Wait and see,' I finished Ian's sentence.

The possibilities for bad news were endless. Lizzy coped by keeping busy. Ferrying people about, sorting meals and supplies, running errands. Popping home to get some of April's things. At dinnertime she arrived back with armfuls of books, April's favourite lotions, some photos and art magazines.

'The nurses say it's important to make the room homely for her as she'll be here a while, even when she wakes up,' she said, Blu-tacking a sunny photo to the wall of the two of them smiling by the Hollywood sign. The room did look less clinical with the Labrador-sized purple Care Bear April had had since she was a little girl perched on the end of the bed.

It was decided Ian would drive Sarah home in Lizzy's car, before coming back to spend the night by April's side. When they left, Lizzy finally sat down.

'No immediate plans to go to work, or home, for you then?' She looked me up and down, scrutinising. We'd barely spoken since she'd phoned to tell me about the crash. She'd also been the one to call Adam after I'd spent that first night snivelling and pacing corridors.

'Figured you needed a mate to talk to,' she'd said.

It'd surprised me, because while Adam and April had tried to rub along eventually, Lizzy had actively loathed Adam at uni. Unlike the rest of the female student population, she'd thought he was a lech, charming women until he'd got what he wanted, before moving seamlessly onto the next. Lizzy had never been one to hide her feelings either, so there was no mistaking her tongue lashings for pub banter. "The walking STD" had been her favourite insult, and she didn't even know about his bout of chlamydia in the second semester of first year.

'I've got to be here when she wakes up. I need to tell her I still love her and I'm sorry for losing my temper.'

Lizzy burst into tears, an abrupt diversion from her stoicism.

'I'm sorry,' she sniffed, drying her cheeks with her open palm and gathering herself back together as quickly as she'd fallen apart. 'When April first mentioned visiting you, I told her to leave you alone and move on. Maybe if I'd talked to her properly instead of being so Lizzy-like and abrupt, she would have gone about things less impetuously April-like. It wasn't fair for her to ambush you like she did, but I let her do it anyway.'

It was reassuring to know I wasn't the only one scrutinising every action or inaction. But Lizzy had always been a much-needed voice of reason in April World. I didn't want her to doubt herself now. There was no denying April needed Lizzy's blunt honesty sometimes.

'You keep her grounded and stop her doing daft things. Usually. It's why she listens to you. That new friend Jen on the other hand drunkenly sends plane tickets to ex-boyfriends.'

I filled Lizzy in about Jen's invite to April's launch night in San Francisco. Whilst she threw her head back, clutching her belly as she guffawed, she was horrified by the whole debacle.

'Wait until I see her,' she said, and I didn't doubt Jen had a Lizzy rant coming her way. Luckily, she'd already gone back for a nap to stave off the jet lag. Although, I sensed Jen was one of the few people who could hold her own against Lizzy. April sure chose some feisty friends. They'd probably bond over their mutual intolerance for Adam.

The atmosphere turned solemn once more, our silence drowned out by Darth Vader and his bleeping minions. My thoughts were tumbling over the past in an unstoppable avalanche of memories.

It had been that dreamworld April existed in that had made me first fall in love with her. It was enticing. The young woman studying history of art to keep her parents happy but who had big ambitions to become an artist and every faith she wouldn't need a boring backup plan. The girl who could wander around a city for hours lost in conversation. Who scribbled her name and phone number on a piece of paper and kept it in her purse just in case she spotted the love of her life.

Pulling out my wallet, I dug out that very scrap of paper and turned it over in my hand. April had given it to me right after our first kiss and I'd never been able to throw it away.

I'd always felt happier when I was around her. The fairy lights of April World danced over my boring life, like someone had installed a disco ball.

'Everything just got so complicated towards the end,' I told Lizzy now. She'd been a witness to the carnage, of course. 'When she just showed up again, even though I was mad, it was like those fairy lights had all flickered back on.'

April's reappearance had dazzled me, when I hadn't even realised I'd been living in the dark.

'I don't even know why I lost my temper.' My body sagged with a sigh, and Lizzy leaned over and put her hand on mine.

'I do. First, she left you, even though she loved you. Then she came back like nothing had changed, and you got angry because it hadn't. You still wanted her. Which meant a difficult conversation with your fiancée *and* risking having your heart ripped out all over again.'

Lizzy shook her head in April's direction.

'It's the most head-bangingly frustrating, rage-inducing situation, even for those of us on the outside. And an awful lot to process with this hot-headed bundle of brunette waves staring at you under those enormous blue eyes.'

I could see why April adored Lizzy. Abrupt she may be, but her advice was fail-safe.

'You and Jen are both wrong by the way.' Her smile turned wicked as she handed me a cup of dishwater-like liquid from the machine in the corridor.

'You kissing April when you did was unavoidable. There was no stopping you two idiots at the beginning. Believe me, I tried talking sense into April twenty-five zillion times a day. Do you really think you could have confessed your undying love then pulled out an emergency stop? Not. A. Chance.'

She had a point.

'Jen's wrong too, though,' Lizzy added. 'About you using that blasted plane ticket she sent. You could have sorted this mess out three years ago, before graduation, if only you'd gone to the airport when *I* told you to. Not Air Miles Jen.'

Lizzy was chuckling, her hands linked behind her head, relishing the opportunity to broadcast her opinion.

'You reckon I should have stopped her going to San Francisco?' I frowned.

Lizzy shook her head.

'Nah, April needed San Francisco as much as you needed Rome, but you could have chased her through the departure lounge and promised to wait for her to come back. Done the whole long-distance thing – properly, not like the Italy mess. April didn't visit home for three years because she couldn't face the misery she left behind. But she would have if you'd gone after her.'

For the first time in days, I heard myself laughing.

'Seriously? You, sceptical, cynical Lizzy is suggesting an airport scene straight out of *Love Actually* would've fixed everything?'

She shrugged.

'Not the way I'd do it, obviously. Your love story, however, has been so cheesy, why not an airport chase to round it off? Everything would've been different if you'd just gone after her, but you chickened out and let her run away.'

I wasn't sure chickened out was accurate. Things had already unravelled so much by then, but I nodded anyway.

'Maybe,' I said.

Shortly after, Lizzy wandered up to the canteen for some dinner before it closed, leaving me alone with April.

'April, I'm sorry,' I began, my voice louder than I expected in the strange square room. 'For lashing out. When you turned up like that, I panicked. I'd been lying to everyone for so long.'

The nurses had encouraged us to talk to her and it seemed better than silence, but I fidgeted in my seat as I spoke.

'I'd convinced myself I was happy,' I continued. 'The lads thought I'd moved on. I told Kel loving you had brought too much pain. But none of it was true.'

Loving her had been easy. The only thing that ever made me truly happy.

'The losing you part was what killed me,' I told her now. 'Knowing you were coming home made pretending harder, until suddenly there you were. It petrified me and I lost it. Now you're in here, and I'd swap places with you if I could.'

A salty droplet trickled down my face and onto April's hand. The tears had crept up on me this time. Taking her hand in both of mine, I squeezed, willing her to squeeze back. For a second, I was sure I felt something.

A twitch? A flicker in her fingertips?

The Airport

MAY 2019

AN ALTERNATIVE REALITY

Dylan

With a blink, I was standing outside April's front door at university, my fist raised to knock.

Not again. I'd leapt back into the past. This time, by three whole years, all the way back to May of my third year at university when I was twenty-one. I remembered this moment well. How could I not? My final exams were done; I'd flown back from Rome to Manchester, hoping for an emotional reunion with April.

An anxious knot wrapped around my stomach, and I recognised the pounding of my heart at the expectation of seeing her. I'd only got off the plane an hour earlier, making April's place my first stop. I'd promised that no matter what happened during our time apart, I'd come back for her after our exams.

Only, things had got tricky. April and I hadn't spoken for months. To cope, I'd thrown myself into coursework. Immersing myself in Rome, finding the most intricate little historical corners and avoiding anything that resembled a student party. It'd helped take my mind off my relationship woes. But that ache for April had refused to subside. I'd become bloody-minded that we were still meant to be together, sure she felt the same.

Now, here I was – again – standing at her door, full of gallant determination to keep my promise. Picturing April running into my arms the second she saw me. Imagining the feel of her against my chest, breathing in the smell of her hair as I buried my face in her neck and told her I loved her.

Only, this time, I knew that wasn't going to happen.

Just as she had three years ago, Lizzy opened the door. I knew what she was going to say before she said it. April was gone.

'Gone? Gone where?' I gasped, playing along until I'd figured out why I was here. Like last time, I felt the hope I'd been clinging to dissipate into the late spring warmth, leaving a sheen of sticky sweat behind my neck.

'San Francisco.' Lizzy looked puzzled. 'She got an internship at some fancy art gallery. An exchange programme. She left this morning.'

When I'd first stood here, getting this news, all the wind had been knocked out of me until I barely had enough air to speak. The same happened now as I wondered what I was supposed to do. Had I been sent back in time and given another chance to save April? But what was I supposed to change?

'Dylan,' Lizzy said, folding her arms in the doorway, oblivious that this was the second time I'd had this conversation. 'She fell apart when you guys stopped talking. She needed something – anything – to cling to, and this was it. She didn't tell you? Or better yet, why didn't you call her?' Lizzy flashed me her familiar infuriated look. My mind raced. I desperately wanted to make the right change this time, save April and avoid ending up under the wheels of a truck myself. Biding my time, I carried on the conversation as I remembered it.

'Call? I didn't think… we said May. We said whatever happened, we'd still be there for each other after exams. We promised.'

'That was before Valentine's Day.' Lizzy glared at me, before rolling her eyes, no stranger to our drama.

'Look, her flight isn't for a couple of hours – go straight back to the airport and talk to her. Fix whatever it is that broke between you and then tell her to get on that plane. Don't let her sacrifice anything else for you, Dylan.'

I nodded, walking away from the door deep in thought. The first time I'd lived through this, I'd been thinking about San Francisco and how much further that was than Rome. Now I was thinking how much I'd always regretted letting her leave so easily.

In my timeline, I'd phoned April, leaving a measly voicemail. And isn't that what Lizzy said in the hospital?

You should have gone to the airport when I told you to, not Air Miles Jen.

She was right. A phone call hadn't been good enough. This was my second chance to create an alternative future for us. A do-over. I needed to do what I should have done the first time. Pulling my phone from my pocket, I googled the next flight from Manchester to San Francisco. It was in three hours. Typically organised of April to go to the airport so early, but plenty of time for me to get there before she boarded.

Fired up, I turned on the engine and retraced my drive back to Manchester Airport. Pulling up in the short stay car park and racing to the terminal, I expected to be searching the airport crowds, desperately hoping to find her. Yet I spotted April straightaway. The check-in desk had only just opened, and she was right at the front of the queue. While she checked in, I went over what I wanted to say. Sure this was how to save her.

Turning to walk away from the desk, April caught sight of me as she tucked her passport back in her bag.

'Dylan,' she cried, stopping short. 'What are you doing here?'

She looked beautiful, if a little pale and tired. But there was no running into anyone's arms.

'I'm not here to stop you getting on the plane,' I promised. 'It's just... can we talk?'

April nodded, still looking shocked to see me, and we found the nearest quiet corner.

'Lizzy told me about the internship, and I know you've got to go. But however long it is – six months, a year, two – I'll wait. You're worth the wait, April. We're worth the wait. Because I love you even more now I know how fucking miserable my life is without you.'

I wondered what had stopped me doing this the first time. Why hadn't I gone after her? It seemed so obvious now.

'I'm sorry about Rome, New Year, Valentine's Day. All of it. Just don't give up on us. I'm lost without you, and I should have called sooner but I'm here now telling you I will wait. I'll be whatever you need me to be in the meantime. I'll spend the summer in America, message every day or just phone to check in every so often.'

Hell, I'd be her pen pal if that's what she needed.

'Just give us another chance to make this work,' I pleaded. 'Because when we work, April, we are everything, and nothing is ever going to match up to everything. Please, I love you, and I'm still all in. Don't run.'

'I slept with someone,' April blurted. Each word penetrated like a bullet, the shock forcing me backwards. I don't know what I'd expected, but that wasn't it.

All the blood rushed to my head, and I sank into a cold metal airport seat behind me, burying my face in my hands. The room started spinning. Time slowed down around me, whilst the holidaymakers and businessmen pulling suitcases behind them sped up. The sensation made me queasy, and I worried I was going to throw up or tip off my chair.

I didn't know which Dylan was real now. The one in the hospital holding her hand, or the one here, not wanting to hear what April had to say but hanging on every word anyway. It didn't matter. Everything I'd thought I'd known about our relationship was being destroyed.

'On Valentine's Day. I got your text message in the middle of the student union, and I crumbled. It was the first night I'd let Lizzy drag me out. It's no excuse, but I was devastated and already in a dark place.' She spoke quietly, rubbing her arms like she was cold and staring at the scuffed airport floor.

'I propped up the bar doing shots, until eventually this fresher from the football team joined me. I got very drunk and went back to his room. I barely even remember it, but I can't lie and say nothing happened, because it did, and it's the single biggest regret of my life. I woke up hating myself, and I've hated myself a little bit more every day after.'

She was sobbing by the end, but it barely registered as I pictured some spotty fresher fawning all over my girlfriend.

'I broke every promise we made, and I knew come May – now – I'd have to tell you the truth. I couldn't bear to hurt you more or see the look on your face that you've got now. I'm so ashamed and disgusted with myself.'

'Stop with the pity party, April, I can't take it,' I snapped. It didn't matter which Dylan I was, this conversation was suddenly my reality, and I was close to falling apart in the middle of the airport, my ears ringing as I tried to think straight. Did I ever really know April? I'd never thought she was capable of this. I'd trusted her without question, but this blew our entire relationship into meaningless little pieces.

'That's why you're running away without so much as a goodbye text?' I was barely able to look at her in case it opened the floodgates.

'I spent my time in Rome agonising over how to make *you* feel better. Make *you* believe that I loved you no matter what. And the first thing you did when things got rough is jump into bed with a fucking teenager. It's like when you slept with Adam all over again.' I was yelling and throwing my arms around wildly by the end and people were looking.

'That's not fair. Adam was totally different; I didn't know you then,' April said, shrinking into herself.

'But it had the same outcome. Poor, heartbroken April doing the walk of shame. Asking everyone to feel sorry for her.' I gulped back the pain, but everything hurt.

'All I wanted was to be with you.' Her voice was thick, but I still couldn't bring myself to look at her. 'I still do. But I won't ask you to forgive me when I can't forgive myself. I have to go, Dylan, and we both know you can't wait for me, not now you know the truth. But I'll hate myself forever wondering how I messed this up so badly.'

The dam inside me was cracking and I needed to be alone. For this gut-wrenching moment to be over. Because this was it. There was no going back, then, now, or whatever fucking timeline I was in. I didn't have it in me to forgive her.

The crushing end to the April and Dylan saga: a blurry, alcohol-fuelled fumble in the dark.

'So much for all in.' I sucked in a breath, flicking away an escaping drop that'd rolled down my cheek. I finally looked at her. Her whole face was red and puffy, yet I was out of sympathy. She'd done this to us.

'At least I can say I tried. I fucking tried. And while you may have broken my heart, April, I didn't break yours. You did that all by yourself.' Turning, I walked away without looking back. Trying to hide my leaking face, I left April weeping in the middle of Manchester Airport.

The second I closed my car door back in the short stay car park, I lost it. Punching the steering wheel and pounding the horn until my knuckles drew blood. It was an hour before I was together enough to start the engine. Driving straight to my mum's and unashamedly crying in her arms.

Back in my real world, I'd been too nervous to call Mum about Kel, or April's crash. All of it poured out of me now; the sheer agony was suffocating.

'First loves are tough,' Mum soothed. But this was different. No one understood that April hadn't just been my first love. She was *the* love. Nothing would ever measure up to that.

That afternoon my mates came over to check on me. They blamed the long distance, but I knew it was more than that. April and I had almost loved each other too much until both of us cracked under the intensity. April self-sabotaged, while I'd relentlessly chased her.

And now what?

Was I trapped here, forced to live this new life where April was a cheat? I couldn't do anything to change her infidelity.

Only then, as I was lying on teenage Dylan's Man City covers in my childhood bedroom, time started skipping ahead, like someone had pressed fast forward on the remote. With another blink I found myself in the pub, I guessed around a year in the future, drunkenly moaning about April.

The more time that flew by, the more immersed I became in this alternative version of my existence. Coma April of my real life faded under the glare of Airport April whose revelation was still red raw.

'She wasn't even going to tell me,' I slurred, noticing Jonesy roll his eyes in Adam's direction.

'Dylan, pal, it's time ye changed the record. This is the second April rant this week, and it's been a year.' Adam's voice was unusually tentative, but my fury boiled over. Swearing at him, I stood up and stormed out.

Something told me he was right, though, and I made a private vow never to mention her name again. Fast-forwarding in time once more, in a flash I was back in the pub sat across from Kel.

Our first date.

We'd met the same way, in my old universe and this new one. In the local pub when our teams shared the quiz winnings. As we worked through the £50 bar tab, she'd asked if I wanted to grab a drink that weekend. I'd tried to say no.

'I'm not always the best company,' I'd warned, swilling my pint round. 'Bad break-up. The worst, actually. Women around here usually actively avoid me.'

'Then I'll go easy on you.'

She did, too, and I lived through it all again until this new Dylan's life was the only life I remembered.

Kel was patient when I held back, afraid of getting so badly hurt again. Didn't get jealous when she saw a flash of residual pain when someone mentioned uni or Rome. Listened when I was ready to tell her the whole story.

And because she was only over from Australia on a two-year visa, there was no pressure. Kel didn't get bogged down in my romantic history or overthink where things were going.

She slowly brought me back to life, and I learnt to open myself up again. We had fun, and somewhere along the way, fell in love. We were content, so when her visa was almost up, I solved the problem by asking her to marry me. Again.

Not particularly romantically. I didn't get down on one knee, or even get her a ring until after. I blurted it out one evening as she was sat on her laptop at the kitchen table, looking for a job that'd come with a visa. Kel didn't care; she just laughed.

'Yeah, OK,' she said. 'Let's do it.'

'And soon,' I insisted. 'Why wait?'

Kel, swept up in the excitement of it all, agreed. 'As long as we move in together first, and I get a big white dress and a honeymoon, I'm all in.' She grinned, moving to sit on my knee, linking her arms around my neck and kissing me.

My stomach did an involuntary lurch when she used those two words. *All in.* But I shook it off. In this new, alternative timeline at least, I knew April wouldn't be showing up out the blue two weeks later. This April had been unfaithful; there was no waiting around for her to come back. My future here was with Kel.

Still, as she fell asleep in my arms later, my thoughts floated back to those royal blue eyes that read mine so astutely. I wondered where she was, what she was doing. Had she found happiness in America?

When I broke my engagement news to the lads the next day, they were all surprisingly pleased for me. Even Adam, who said I'd never been much of a wingman anyway. Mum worried though.

'Kel can get a job here easily enough,' she said, her forehead crinkling. 'You know I adore her, but I don't see what the rush is. Three years ago, you were sobbing in my arms telling me no one would ever come close to—'

'Mum,' I snapped, before she could say April's name. 'I know what I'm doing. I can't live in the past, and Kel makes me happy. I promise.'

Life sped up again after that, like skipping through the boring bits. Kel and I were married within a few months. Honeymooning in Ireland. Introducing her as my wife sounded odd, and the wedding band on my left hand felt heavy and alien. I'd twist and play with it subconsciously. But being Kel's husband was easy.

My mind filled up with fresh memories as I weaved through time. Coma April only existed in my nightmares. Almost a figment of my imagination.

Absorbed in this new version of my life, I heard through the grapevine of old Manchester students that April was busy touring the US with some big exhibition. I'd resisted googling her. It didn't seem fair to Kel to be looking up my ex. But I was pleased for her. She was working as an artist; I'd got my PhD and worked in the field as an archaeologist. Whatever damage we'd done to each other, we'd rebuilt into something, maybe not better but different. We'd both found a way to be happy, which was more than I'd thought possible when April had made her revelation in the airport.

Then, one day, April finally came home. She was a big deal by then, in the art world at least. There was a lot of buzz about her latest show in Manchester.

I'd been married contentedly five years, so I didn't see the harm in a quick internet search. One of the top results was a blurb for her first ever art show.

April Westbury makes her debut this Saturday with her raw and unflinching exploration of how even the greatest love story can end in the most devastating heartbreak. With all the self-sabotage of a modern-day Romeo and Juliet, if you've ever loved and lost, April's collection, from the explosively intricate "Amore a Prima Vista", to the dark and disturbing "Locked Heart", will reach you in ways you won't be prepared for. This exhibit is on for one week only, after which April will tour the US showcasing her work.

"Amore A Prima Vista". Love at first sight. April had dedicated the beginning of her career to our tragic love story. A shockwave rippled through me, followed by the faintest sense of déjà vu. Looking at images online, I could see her pain had mirrored my own. Only, it was even darker because she'd punished herself for what she'd done.

For the first time, I could clearly see my own mistakes glaring out at me from her sculptures. After the Rome debacle, I'd behaved terribly, punishing April with silence. Was it any wonder she'd ended up boozed up under a sweaty fresher?

Sitting in front of my laptop, I chewed my bottom lip. April had blamed herself all these years, and the guilt of that sat in my gut. She'd not abandoned me; I'd let her down, right when she'd needed me most.

A bio on another art website told me that after her US tour she'd sold most of the pieces and started working on new material. One well-known art critic had named April in his thirty under thirty artists to watch, so it was a coup when she agreed to join the line-up of artists showcasing at Manchester's MediaCity over the summer. When I heard where it was, curiosity got the better of me, and the day it opened, I went to look around.

I didn't tell anyone. They'd tell me not to be such a fucking idiot and leave the past in the past. But April's show was an irresistible tug. That day at the airport had been so ugly; I wanted to replace it with a more peaceful ending. At least, that's what I told myself.

I figured she knew I was married. A few years earlier, Al and I had bumped into Lizzy at a Manchester alumni reunion. But it didn't stop me rubbing my wedding ring with my thumb as I walked across the footbridge and through The Piazza.

The exhibiting hall was vast, each of April's designs given space to breathe and tell their story. I didn't know where to start, until my eyes fell on one I recognised. The clay model of a girl, cutting the strings of her own silk parachute. Despite being tiny in comparison to some of April's other work, it was on its own plinth, and she'd somehow bathed it in a pale-yellow sunlight.

Smiling, I recalled April telling me about her clay creation the day we met. She'd designed it at eighteen, firing it in her first kiln, a university gift from her parents. She'd said the girl signified her journey alone into the big bad world.

'It's silly.' She'd shrugged. 'In reality, she'd just plummet to the ground. But it's a start. I'm an artist in progress.'

I'd made some corny remark about the girl perhaps learning to fly, and April had laughed.

Now, it was part of her latest collection, depicting different key moments throughout her life. I noticed she'd included that brutal "Locked Heart" from her first show. But the centrepiece here was a plane weaved from wire, with a figure of whom I took to be April as the pilot. Only, instead of passengers, it was just full of baggage as she flew home over a sea of memories. "Memory Soup" she'd called it.

April's adult life, in one big loop.

Poetic, I thought. It was then I felt a stare burning into my back, and I turned to see April across the room. As our eyes locked, she broke from a trance before tentatively walking over and standing beside me, back at the parachuting girl.

"'Fall or Fly?'," I commented. 'Interesting title.'

'A throwback to something somebody said once. It stayed with me,' she said, tilting her head as she admired her own work.

Turning my head, I studied her properly for the first time. She'd lightened her hair and had a natural tan. The America effect I guessed. I'd forgotten what being in her presence did to me. My insides were sloshing like a washing machine on a spin cycle.

'You really did it. I'd heard you were touring with your art, but… this is incredible, April. *Exhibiting artist of international renown*,' I read from her bio on the wall.

'You're not doing badly yourself, Dr Heritage Consultant.' Her smile was electrifying. Even her teeth were whiter. 'You popped up as a suggested connection on LinkedIn a while back. I snooped,' she admitted.

'Yeah, I surprised even myself. Never miss a deadline these days,' I joked. 'After Rome I worked at the uni while I got my Master's, then my PhD. After that I was a field archaeologist, but the travelling… I was away too much. So now I manage restoration projects across the north-west.' I nodded back towards the clay model. 'I'm glad Ms Parachuter is getting her moment to shine. Everything else looks phenomenal, but this is the April I remember. So excited about the future, she took a leap of faith. It's simple, a little naïve and dreamlike. Before life gets tangled up in itself.'

'That's very deep and philosophical, Dylan.' April giggled, and it set a firework off inside me. I'd forgotten how much I loved that sound. Genuine and uninhibited.

'Yeah, well, I'm a doctor now, didn't you hear? Plus, I went through some tricky emotional stuff in my early twenties. It can do that to you.'

April fell silent and we just stood there before I broke the spell.

'When I heard you were coming to MediaCity, I googled you and ended up reading an old interview you did for some online art mag during your first exhibition in San Francisco. You said you thought our biggest mistake was thinking love was enough, when in the end, it wasn't. Do you really believe that?' I kept my gaze steady, trying to read the expression on her face.

'I don't know. I overanalysed everything in San Francisco, and my art, it helped me process stuff.' She gave a huge sigh. 'I do know that those two people in the airport that day, they did really love each other. But in that moment, it wasn't enough.'

'It should have been though,' I replied wistfully. As I looked at her again, a thoughtful sadness had fallen across her face. 'Shall we have this conversation somewhere else? A walk maybe. I could do with some air.'

Strolling into The Piazza, we stopped to grab a coffee before continuing back over the bridge. The atmosphere between us was more relaxed than I expected. Like we were nothing more than old friends catching up. It made it easier to say what I'd come to say.

'I didn't turn up to reopen old wounds,' I said, falling easily into step as we meandered along the old familiar paths we'd walked in our uni days. 'The opposite. Just seeing online photos of those sculptures from your first exhibition was a gut punch, especially that "Locked Heart" one. I don't know how you spent so long travelling around carrying all that old angst with you. But it was also the first time I'd really looked at things from your point of view.' I looked across at her as we walked.

'You've really been blaming yourself all this time? Because you were persecuting yourself for things that weren't all your fault, April. That one with the old iPhone that had my Valentine's Day text on? Ouch. Was that your real phone from back then? With the original message I sent? Not a replica?' I asked.

Seeing those three shameful words permanently pasted across the internet, almost a decade after I'd drunkenly sent them, I could physically feel the hangover.

'Yep, real phone, real message. I chose to take it halfway around the world just to torture myself more,' April said, and for the first time I noticed a few frown lines on her forehead. Otherwise, she'd hardly aged.

'And you're still tormenting yourself. I could see it in some of your work back there. That plane with all that baggage? Anyway, what I'm trying to say is, I owe you an apology.' Gulping, I felt a short, sharp ice blast of adrenaline flood my veins as I broached the subject of that day in the airport.

'My outburst was misdirected, and I let anger end something I didn't want to end. Love *should* have been enough. It should have won over my hurt, your regret, our dumb lack of communication.' I noticed paint splattered on April's trainers as I kept my eyes fixed on the ground in front of us.

'If we'd had one honest conversation, I would have

been able to understand why you did what you did and you might have forgiven me for how I behaved after New Year. Who knows, maybe we'd even have laughed at how stupid we'd both been.'

April looked up at me with one eyebrow raised and I laughed.

'In a sane environment, not five minutes at airport check-in,' I added. 'Then maybe that crazy love we had for each other would have come out stronger than all that background noise.'

'But I ran away.' April exhaled.

'Then I ambushed you in a departure lounge. Typical April and Dylan. Dramatics over sense.'

'Sounds so simple now,' April said with a taut smile. 'But don't forget you're thinking with hindsight. Being so young and in the thick of it, we were incapable of being that rational. I remember really trying. To be rational. But in the war between head and heart, insanity won out.'

'Well, we did always have a way of complicating things. It suited the narrative of our great love story, I guess. And don't all the great love stories turn into tragedies?' I half smiled, while April broke into a laugh, sipping her coffee as we strolled along the canal.

'I've missed that sardonic sense of humour,' she said. My heart skipped a beat, but I was careful not to tell her how much I missed making her giggle.

'See. One sensible conversation and we're already laughing at our idiocy,' I joked instead.

'Pity it's a decade too late,' she said, stopping my laugh in its tracks.

'It is though. Too late.'

I stared seriously into her shining blue eyes. They still dazzled me, yet the atmosphere tensed again, and I couldn't help twisting my wedding ring round and round.

'Oh, I know,' she said, waving her hand in the air. 'The sculptures back there all represent moments in my life that changed me, but I refused to spend any more time raking over our old heartache. I'd worked through all that in San Francisco. The only piece I'd hung onto and not sold – sentimentality I guess – was "Locked Heart", and it seemed the perfect representation of that part of my life, which is why it's included now. I'm happy with my life, honestly, Dylan.'

We stopped to watch a bearded old man navigate his rickety canal boat through a lock, the water lapping at the concrete banks, before we looped back up to the road.

'The premise behind "Locked Heart" does still stand though. I experienced the ultimate love and heartbreak with you, and I can't do it again. It's like my heart is frozen back there. I'll always love you, Dylan, or my version of you from ten years ago. I've made peace with that and moved on, in my own way.'

April had been quite vocal in interviews about her determination to stay single, calling art the love of her life.

'I hate the idea of you feeling trapped, especially if I'm part of the reason why. It's a lot to be responsible for,' I told her. 'I came here because the last time we saw each other was so awful, and I suppose I needed some closure too. But I also wanted to make sure you knew that love can be enough, if you let it be.'

'Daddy,' a voice suddenly called. April looked around in confusion, clocking that we'd stopped outside a primary school. A little girl raced over, and I scooped her up, swinging her around.

'Hello, kiddo, ready for our date?'

'Can I have an ice cream milkshake?' she asked, sticking her tongue out the corner of her mouth. A mannerism she'd picked up from her mum. Everyone said she had my eyes though, and my smile.

'Sure. First, I want you to meet Daddy's old friend, April. April, this is Missy.'

'Hi,' Missy chirped. 'Are you coming for milkshake?'

'Sadly not,' April said, her expression unreadable. 'I've got to go back to work. But you have a lovely date with your daddy.'

'Wednesdays are Missy and Daddy afternoons,' I explained. 'Just the two of us, while Kel – my wife – is on maternity leave. Alfie's eight months now.'

April nodded, but her smile didn't quite reach her eyes and she focused all her attention on Missy to avoid looking at me. She'd had no idea I had a family. I'd switched jobs because I missed the kids while travelling for work.

'It suits you, fatherhood,' April said finally, watching Missy reach out for a butterfly fluttering by before looking at me. 'I'm happy for you. You know, you could have just told me...'

'I know. Couldn't quite work out how though, so I thought I'd introduce you to my best girl.' From her tight smile, ambushing her hadn't been the answer.

'Sometimes,' I continued, 'no matter how hard you try, you can't stop loving someone. But I learned it can co-exist alongside something else, something different. Love is complicated and messy. This, though,' I said, kissing

Missy on the nose, 'loving this one and her baby brother is easy. You've always been this unstoppable force, April, and you've made all your other dreams come true. Don't be the pilot of that weighed-down plane. Ditch the baggage and be the girl with the parachute again. Take a leap of faith.'

April laughed and brushed away a tear before Missy could see it.

'You know, I did always like her. Parachute girl. April World was far brighter when she was at the helm.'

'She's still there; I can see her waiting to spread her wings,' I said. I needed April to feel free and strong enough to fall in love again. I needed someone to love her. Because I couldn't.

'So, this is me, giving you your key back to that locked heart. Don't let my mistakes stop you finding love again. I believe you have the other key, and I think it's time you forgive yourself enough to use it.'

'Come on, Daddy, I'm hungry,' Missy moaned, wriggling to the floor and tugging at my hand.

'Yes, go. You have far more important places to be,' April smiled. 'Perhaps I'll see you both around.'

'Bye, April.' Before turning to walk away, I took out my wallet and handed her a scrap of paper. It was my baggage, and until then I hadn't realised how heavy it'd been. When I looked back, April was smiling, reading her name and phone number in her own curly handwriting.

April's Hospital Room

SUMMER 2022

Dylan

'Well, that were gross,' Lizzy announced, flouncing back into the room and flopping into a chair. Jerking my head up from April's bed, my mind felt thick and foggy. For a minute I didn't have a clue what was going on or even which Dylan I was.

Was I Missy and Alfie's dad? A thirty-something husband and father finally letting go of the past?

Or was real life here, in hospital, my body aching from where I'd slept hunched over April's bed? I shook my head to shuffle the muddled memories into separate piles.

That hadn't been a dream. It was too vivid, too exacting. Barely an hour had gone by, yet it felt years to me. This time it was like I'd lived through an entire decade of another Dylan's life. In an alternative timeline where I'd saved April's life but not our relationship.

That airport fight.

It'd been much worse than the one in my living room.

And I'd been a father. My heart tightened with the

whispers of unconditional love I'd had for "my" two children just seconds before. I could still feel the weight of Missy in my arms as she leant into me with unfailing trust. Fading quickly now, but it'd been powerful and all-consuming.

'You OK, Dylan? You've gone pale,' Lizzy said. 'I asked if you'd tried the food in that awful excuse for a canteen?'

'The sausage rolls are alright,' I muttered, as chunks of that other Dylan's life scurried into a new corner of my mind.

What was happening to me?

Somehow, I was being given the chance to undo the regrets I'd held onto all these years. Seeing the difference it could have made to my life. Slipping into an alternative reality. Only, in the one I'd just left, April had...

Cheated on me?

I didn't know which pieces were from my reality and which bits had been different. Had *my* April cheated? The timeline only changed after I chased her to the airport on the day she left for San Francisco. Everything before that had been the same. Did that mean...

I shook the thought away as April's dad arrived. Battling the magnetic pull to stay by April's bedside, I left to give him time with his daughter.

'I'll call if anything happens,' Ian promised as I said goodbye and went home.

By morning, after a fitful night's sleep, I'd come to only one conclusion. Whenever I held April's hand in hospital, I was somehow slipping through my own Sliding Door and into another life. But if it happened again, and I changed the right thing, saving April *and* our relationship, would I stay there?

'It's still touch and go,' the consultant warned with a serious expression, watching Ian embrace Sarah until she almost disappeared in his arms, while Jen and Lizzy bounced into me for a group hug. We all nodded enthusiastically, digesting the first piece of good news we'd had since the accident.

April's latest test results showed she wasn't brain dead. Ian and Sarah were saved the agony of making the harrowing decision to turn off life support and let their daughter go.

We tried to heed the consultant's warning that there'd still been little change in April's condition. There were no guarantees she was going to wake up or of the extent of her brain damage when she did. But we needed that good news. It gave us renewed hope, and hope did for us what April's ventilator did for her; it kept us going.

She's in there, I thought. *She must be.*

Visibly buoyed, Ian and Sarah went home for lunch and a rest, leaving me sitting between Jen and Lizzy. I was still struggling to unpick my reality from the other Dylans' lives I'd visited, and one particular question was eating away at me.

'Lizzy,' I asked, tapping a trainered heel on the floor. 'In uni, did April cheat on me?' Airport April's departure lounge bombshell still felt raw, and I grimaced, waiting for a reply.

'God no,' Lizzy cried, sitting back and looking at me with a furrowed brow. Relief washed away the lead weight pressing on my chest, and I felt my muscles untense. Only, Jen flushed pink and couldn't meet my eye.

'Actually...'

She spoke quietly, sending the room tipping as that nauseating spinning sensation hit me again.

'No!' Lizzy gasped, staring open-mouthed at Jen. 'April? She wouldn't. She couldn't.'

I didn't know whether it was a consolation or not that Lizzy hadn't known either.

'Valentine's Day,' I croaked, swallowing back bile.

'Yes,' Jen squeaked. 'A footballer in the first year. But you'd just sent her that horrible message, and you hadn't even spoken since New Year...'

I tuned Jen out. My head was whirring so fast it felt like centrifugal force was squashing my brain into the sides of my skull. I was seeing spots and fighting to keep my breaths even.

That parallel reality was my reality too. April had slept with someone. She'd upped and left without a word because of a sleazy five-minute fumble with some opportunistic fresher.

The room was closing in on me, the walls pulsating. I needed to leave. I couldn't look at April, lying broken under a mountain of noisy machinery, when I was working up to a frenzy inside. All these questions I needed to demand answers for blistered my insides.

'I've got to get out of here,' I said, striding from my chair and through the maze of pale blue corridors, down the lift and out the front doors into the warm summer breeze.

Jen and Lizzy both called after me, but I couldn't talk to them. Not about this. Not now.

*

The lads found me a few hours later, hunched over and staring into the bottom of my pint glass in our local.

Lizzy. She must've called them.

Adam and Jonesy sat down while Al got a round in.

'You don't have to talk about it, mate. We'll just sit here and chill,' Jonesy said.

Al came back with four lagers and chucked a few bags of nuts in the middle of the table. For an hour or so they made small talk about work, football and Adam's latest friend with benefits.

I was grateful for them. We'd grown up a lot since rocking up at uni, released from parental tethers for the first time. Four lads from different backgrounds with polar dreams and goals but one thing in common. Make the most of our new freedom. I was the only one from Manchester and expected them to drift off home, or to various other parts of the world, after graduation. But Adam had five siblings back in Paisley and living here was the first time he'd felt like an individual with space to call his own. Jonesy was desperate to hold onto the uni days, so he stuck around. Al disappeared to London for a couple of years while his girlfriend Jodie did her barrister training but boomeranged back with her in toe when she got a job offer at a legal chambers. Taking those first steps on the career ladder, putting down roots and learning the ropes of life bonded us like brothers.

'It's all been for nothing. The last few years, waiting, hoping she'd come back. Breaking it off with Kel. And for what? Someone who jumped into bed with a footballer at the first sign of trouble?' I said, when I eventually opened up.

Why hadn't she told me? I'd deserved to know. Knowing could have set me free, rather than secretly pining for someone who'd already betrayed me.

April cheated on me.

I still couldn't believe it. The guys all exchanged loaded glances. Jonesy nodded at Adam to go first.

'Thing is, Dyl...' Adam's Scottish tome was more hesitant than usual. 'Did she cheat on ye? Because ye called me on Hogmanay and told me it was over, six weeks before she slept with that fella. Ye hadn't even spoken to her that entire time.'

I blinked, totally thrown. I was sure they'd be on my side.

'Adam's right,' Al said. 'Mate, we know you're hurting right now. It feels like April cheated on you yesterday, not three years ago. But did she actually do anything wrong? She was arguably single by then, and heartbroken. Isn't having a one-night stand with someone unsuitable after a break-up almost even a... right of passage?'

I scowled, looking away as I gulped down my drink. They'd obviously colluded about this little intervention with Jen and Lizzy.

'I suppose you agree with them?' I barked at Jonesy, who shrank into his chair, shrugging.

They were forgetting one major thing. April considered it cheating. It's why she ran off to San Francisco. She knew if she called, she'd have to tell me and that I'd never forgive her.

'If she thinks she cheated, and I think she cheated, then she cheated.'

I was several beers down and it was doing the opposite of helping my mood.

'Ye don't know what she thinks though, pal. She's in a coma. Doesn't she deserve a chance to be heard out?' Adam looked at me carefully from across the table. His gaze made me falter. Adam wasn't usually the one on April's side.

Was I being unreasonable? Finding out now did make April's betrayal fresh and raw. But if I'd found out back then, and a second chance with April came around now, would I care about a drunken indiscretion during what was already the middle of an excruciating and drawn-out break-up three years ago?

When did April and I officially break up? It was hard to put a date on it. I hadn't considered seeing anyone else between January and May of third year. And yet, I'd not picked the phone up to April either. I chose to throw everything at my degree and finals, believing I'd be able to save our relationship that summer. Like we'd promised we would.

I'd arrived back from Rome planning to beg to try again, so part of me must have considered us sort-of over. But it was her getting on that plane without telling me that really ended things in my mind.

'Why are things so fucking complicated?' I sighed, washing back the dregs of my pint and signalling to Adam that I wanted another.

I looked at Al, so self-assured and settled, his thick platinum band proudly on his left hand.

'I don't know how you and Jodie did it, Al, man.'

Childhood sweethearts who'd met at fifteen. From day one they'd known where they were headed. Even at eighteen, when they'd gone to separate universities, they'd been solid.

'You made a long-distance relationship look a breeze. It's partly why I was convinced I could go to Rome, and it'd all be OK. But I fucked up at every turn.'

Al sat up straight, looking riled.

'Dylan, stop putting me on a pedestal of relationship goals. I hate it.' His whole body stiffened as he lashed out, smearing a thumb down the condensation on his pint glass. Al was normally so mellow. Raising my eyebrows, I noticed Jonesy elbow Al in the ribs.

'Tell him, Al. It's time.'

'I'm going to, alright,' Al snapped, putting his elbows on the table and picking at his nails.

'It wasn't easy. It was tough as hell. And… I cheated on Jodie.' He paused as his revelation landed.

'In third year. You were in Italy, and when you came back, April had left, so I told the guys not to tell you. These two…' he nodded at Adam and Jonesy, 'were working their way through the netball team and constantly taking the piss out of my commitment to Jodie. But you respected – even admired – our relationship. I wanted there to be one person left who wasn't disappointed in me, because it was the worst thing I have done.'

I struggled to keep my jaw grazing the floor as Al started shredding a beer mat. While he spoke, I could almost feel the shame emanating from him.

Like April and I, Al and Jodie had started seeing less of each other as the reality of our final year kicked in. Then Al had joined a revision group, and one of his study buddies was a girl he'd only previously known in passing.

'Megan was the opposite of Jodie. Jodie was a high achiever who'd meticulously planned our life out and would accept nothing except success. Yet, bar passing her degree, Megan had zero intention of deciding what she wanted to do or where she wanted to end up.'

Al sighed, his eyes flicking to the ceiling as he took himself back in time.

'She was like this untethered, roving butterfly, excited by every new flower she came across but never feeling obliged to stick around longer than she needed. Untamed, I guess.'

That didn't sound exciting to me; it sounded like trouble. How had he kept this from me?

Al continued.

'For three years I'd listened to Adam and Jonesy's wild stories of flings and al fresco one-night stands. Adam's bedroom was a revolving door of beautiful women, and somewhere along the way, I'd become envious, fretting if I'd missed out on an important part of my life.'

I wished I'd been around to tell him how little he was missing. How unfulfilling it was to wake up next to someone whose name you barely remember.

'I loved Jodie, no question,' Al insisted. 'My fiery, unstoppable goddess who'd known when she was just ten years old that she'd become a lawyer. But the thought that I'd never be young, free and single, well, ever, it scared me. Then there was sexy Megan with her blonde Afro, retro denim dungarees and hand-painted Converse.'

Al sat back, letting a shower of shredded beer mat drop to the table.

'Having this building attraction towards her was a thrill. By then, Jodie hardly ever picked up the phone unless I'd scheduled a call in advance. Not that I'm blaming her.'

I could see by the whites of Al's knuckles on his balled fists that he'd forever punish himself.

'It wasn't even some stupid one-night thing either. It was an affair. For a month.'

A month? I tried not to gasp. I'd assumed he was about to tell me about a weekend fling at most.

'The first time I just went over to "study", but we both knew what was going to happen. I wanted it to, that's the worst thing.' Al shrugged. 'We'd go on dates, or she'd sneak over between lectures. Megan was different in every way. I think that's what attracted me most. I wanted to see if what I had with Jodie was real, if it was as good as I thought.'

Al fell silent as he mulled over his multiple indiscretions.

'So how did it end? Did Jodie find out?' I was trying my hardest not to judge him even though I felt let down. I'd always held Al in higher regard; he seemed more grown up than the rest of us. Even at university.

'One afternoon I noticed Megan hanging back to flirt with the guest lecturer. Her Afro was braided, and her rainbow eyeshadow had been replaced with dark, demure eyeliner. A glow-up for a new phase, and I realised she was moving onto the next petal.'

Untethered. Bored of Al.

'In that one crushing moment, I realised Jodie never tired of me. Even if I had to schedule myself in, she gave me every slice of her attention. She listened, she cared and, without fail, made everything better.'

Jodie had only regimented their relationship to keep them going while she was in Oxford, and he was in Manchester.

'She was only trying to stop us drifting apart which,

as you found out, Dylan, is nearly impossible in a long-distance relationship. Sure, she was ambitious, but when we were together, Jodie was also spontaneous and exciting; I'd just allowed myself to forget that.'

I certainly understood the drifting apart but could never have cheated on April. Then again, I'd had my time as a young, free and single student learning I liked monogamy.

'Megan never asked me anything serious about my life; she didn't know my sister's name or that my parents divorced when I was twelve. We were nothing more than a distraction for each other during the last slog that was finals. Only it wasn't fun, because I'd risked everything for it, and it hadn't been worth it.'

Al had ended it, without a flicker of emotion from Megan.

'When I called Jodie to confess, she'd already guessed – nothing gets by Jodie. She didn't bother grilling me or even particularly care who Megan was. But she did refuse to talk to me for weeks, telling me to leave her alone while she got through her exams.'

It was Al's turn to drain his pint, searching for some solace at the bottom but finding only emptiness.

'I obeyed her wishes,' he said. 'But missing her was like missing a lung. I needed Jodie to breathe.'

'So how did you convince her to forgive you?' I asked. And could I find the same grace she had?

'Honesty, maybe. Persistence. I told her everything like I've told you, and when she wouldn't listen, I emailed. I never considered giving up because life didn't make sense without her.'

Jodie had said Al's cheating made her feel like he

couldn't possibly love her as much as he claimed. Which is exactly how I felt.

'But that wasn't true,' Al said. 'The thing with Megan was only ever about me and my stupid shit. Eventually, Jodie was able to understand that and found it in her to take me back.'

Even now, he was deeply ashamed.

'I'll forever be making it up to Jodie. I'm the only man she's ever been with, yet I can't say the same, and it wasn't worth it. For a month of vanilla sex with someone unremarkable, I irreparably damaged something sacred. I can even see it in your eyes, Dylan. The disappointment.'

Seeing them together over the last few years, Al and Jodie had a secure marriage. They were crazy in love.

'We are,' Al agreed. 'I just made a mistake as an idiotic, hormonal student, and it forced me to grow into a better man, a better husband. I don't belong on your pedestal, Dylan, but I do know mistakes are part of life.'

He'd always suspected April and I would find our way back to each other eventually.

'Just because things went wrong once doesn't mean you're not soulmates,' he said, now piecing the beer mat back together like a jigsaw. 'But it still takes work to love someone that hard. The only thing you can really do is never give up. Jodie didn't give up on me, and I'll never give up trying to be the man she deserves.'

It jarred that it'd taken until now for me to find out this massive event in Al's life.

'I must've been a mess if you managed to hide all that from me,' I said. The three of them shot each other sidelong glances. 'OK, still a mess. Al, mate, I'm sorry. If it helps, you're still the best couple I know.'

My bunched muscles started to soften as my nerves settled. Between them, they'd managed to calm me down. Find perspective.

Did I really want some misunderstanding about our relationship status three years ago to stop us being together now?

'I'm just so mad at her though.' I couldn't help it.

Suddenly, Jonesy was laughing, his head thrown back. We all looked at him in surprise as he shook his head and took a swig of his pint. 'Mad at April, mad about April. Has there ever been a difference?'

'What's that supposed to mean?' I asked.

Jonesy was still chuckling. 'She infuriated the hell out of you every single day and, Dyl, I hate to tell you this, but you loved it. That's what love is, right? Being crazy about someone for the very thing that would drive everyone else crazy.'

Jonesy had only been with Georgia a year, but he seemed to have become some form of love guru.

'I'm not Georgia's manager, but I *am* senior, and she pulls all sorts of shit at the office. Bumping up her expenses, long boozy lunches when she's meeting clients, clocking off early when the boss is out. Drives me nuts.'

It was true. Georgia had recently encouraged the whole office to stage a coup until they got free snacks on a Friday.

'She's a troublemaker, and I'm constantly covering for her. But if I don't leave it at the photocopier when we finish for the day, we wouldn't make it. She drives me to distraction, and you know what? It really turns me on.'

'Did she shag a footballer?' I still couldn't understand why they thought I should forgive April so easily.

'No, but by the time April shagged a footballer, you'd all

but cut her out your life. Don't let something meaningless and forgettable she did eons ago stop you being there for her now.'

Like Adam, he thought I should hear April out once she woke up.

'And,' he added, gesticulating with his chest puffed out like he was presenting a TED talk on relationships, 'in the future she'll do something else daft and impetuous you'll have to forgive her for. Then there'll be a time you push too hard because you've got tunnel vision when it comes to April and neglect to look at the bigger picture. But for now, please go hold her hand and stop drowning your sorrows with us bozos.'

His TED talk was spot on. I pictured April in the hospital, fighting for life. Then I pulled out a memory belonging to the Dylan who'd chased April to the airport. What was it he said?

I let anger end something I didn't want to end.

He'd found his way to a content life, but he also wished he'd forgiven April back then. Not driven her further away. With hindsight, he understood. Isn't that what I had now? Hindsight. His and mine.

'Love should have been enough,' I muttered under my breath. I didn't want it to be over. Loving April was so deeply embedded in me it had become part of who I was.

What the hell was I doing in the pub?

My reasons, which had seemed giant that morning, suddenly seemed tiny and insignificant.

'You're right. Boys, I've got to get back to the hospital.' Standing up quickly, I swayed, using the table to keep from collapsing back into my seat.

'Woah, Dyl lad. How many bevvies have ye had?' Adam grabbed my arm to steady me.

'No idea,' I slurred, squinting my eyes together to stop myself seeing double.

As desperate as I was to get back to April, I couldn't show up in that state. Adam called us an Uber and took me home to sleep it off.

'When ye are awake, I'll drive ye over,' he promised, putting a large glass of water on my bedside table while I wobbled out my jeans.

*

Clinking in the kitchen woke me up hours later. Crawling out of bed and staggering out my room with one eye screwed shut, I found my mum making a pot of coffee.

'When I couldn't get hold of you, I worried and called Adam,' she explained, thrusting a steaming Manchester City mug into my hand.

I'd been avoiding her calls since April's accident. Partly because she'd always been angry at April for leaving me the way she did. Mostly because she'd already told my whole family about the wedding. Even talked Kel into letting her help plan it. I hated disappointing her.

'I bet he didn't spare any of the details. Why does everyone always call Adam? Why not Al or even Jonesy?'

Mum chuckled.

'Because, while he may like the ladies a little too much, and too often, for my liking, he's your most loyal – and straight-thinking – friend who'll drop everything for you, love.'

Adam had assured her they'd talked some sense into me, but Mum had needed to see me for herself.

'I knew you'd be angry. About Kel and how I ended things.'

'Sit down.' Mum ushered me into a seat at the kitchen table. 'I'm not angry about anything, love. But I do have a story to tell you. About your father.'

I groaned, not sure my hangover could cope with this, but Mum rarely brought him up, so I knew to shut up and listen.

'I remember the first day I kissed your dad. I was the age you are now, so mid-twenties. He was a close friend of my housemate and always coming over, for the parties or just to watch *Friends*.'

Mum had told me this part of the story before. After several snake bites in the pub watching England lose on penalties at Euro '96, my dad had leaned in for a commissary peck which turned into a full-on snog in the corner booth of The Rose and Crown.

'Didn't he chuck his football shirt in a hedge?' I asked.

'I think it was a flower bed.' Mum grinned, slurping her coffee.

'Anyway, after consoling each other over the result, life stayed the same, only we were a couple at those parties and nights in watching TV. Your lazy father got away without taking me on a proper dinner date or even so much as asking me out. We just… were.'

Dad had moved in a year later when mum's housemate joined a touring cast of *STOMP*. I remembered her taking me to see the show when I was about six and being made a fuss of backstage. Drove Mum and our neighbours mad for weeks after, banging around with the bin lids.

'I thought fate had made falling in love easy,' Mum continued. 'Looking back, for your dad it was simply convenient. He did love me though, because – and this is the part I've never told you – I found an engagement ring in his pants drawer.'

I stopped, my mug halfway to my lips. My dad had bought a ring?

'Nothing fancy, a modest diamond. Very sparkly.' Mum looked wistful as she pictured it. Wherever this story went, she was choosing to let the memory be a happy one. She was like that, my mum. Refused to hold grudges.

'I think the night he was planning to ask me – because he made a big show of taking me to the pub – was the night I found out I was pregnant. I wasn't going to tell him until after he'd asked, wanting to prove to people it wasn't some shotgun proposal. Only, he barged in the bathroom to grab his hair gel as I was waiting for the test result.'

They'd not gone to the pub, spending all night talking about the future. Back then they'd still lived in a house share, my dad job-hopping while he tried to make it as an actor. A dream he'd only recently given up on after a failed turn as a stand-up comic.

'We bought a little house we could make into a family home. Your dad came to every scan, and I kept waiting for that proposal. But it never came.'

Mum smoothed down her dress, brushing off some stray fluff as she picked over her words. 'I looked, but the ring had gone. I guessed he'd returned it to help pay for the house deposit. I convinced myself it was a good sign that he was investing in our future.'

My dad hadn't invested in anything, ever, as far as I could tell from our annual father-son bonding session. Even his acting attempts were half-arsed, and he stole all his comic jokes from YouTube.

Mum smiled at me now. 'Then you arrived, and while having a baby was wonderful, it was hard. We were young, sleep deprived and had little patience for each other. Your dad started working longer hours in a restaurant, picking up extra bar shifts, then going out "job hunting" every morning.'

Mum had guessed what was happening but was still blindsided when she came home from my nan's one day to find all dad's stuff in suitcases.

'You were ten months old. He said he wasn't mature enough to be a dad and you were better off without him. I agreed, even though I wanted to rain down hell. It was pointless to fight because it wouldn't make him stay, and I didn't want him to anyway. He didn't deserve us.'

My nan had helped Mum out lots after that. I'd stay over for pizza and chips every Monday to give Mum a night off, and we'd walk Sinatra, Nan's Jack Russell. Nan would pick me up from school when Mum was at work, and I'd watch cartoons while she batch cooked a stew for us.

Mum sighed. 'He'll never know the joy of watching you become the considerate, funny and accomplished young man you are. I kept the engagement-that-never-was a secret because walking out was on him, not you, and I didn't want you thinking otherwise.'

I'd still always assumed it was my fault Dad left. Nan once said I'd scream whenever he held me. But I didn't tell Mum that.

'Your dad gave me you, and I'll always be thankful for that,' she said. I admired her unwavering ability to hold onto the good.

'For a long time after, I told myself I didn't need love. I already had it in buckets from this tiny tyrant who woke me up at 5am and, when he was eight, made me learn the names of Manchester City's first eleven so we could chat about the match,' Mum said.

I was ten when she met my stepdad at work. Mum was in her late thirties.

'Bryan took me by surprise. Asked me out for dinner on his first day, sweeping me off my feet like an old-fashioned gentleman and a horny teenager all wrapped up in a slightly balding middle-aged package. He slotted into our lives like he'd always been there.'

'Mum,' I groaned, even though she was right about Bryan slotting in. At first, he acted like a goofy uncle, teasing me about buying a Galaxy bar for the girl I had a crush on at school. Then about the Michelle Keegan poster I put up above my bed when I was a teenager. Gradually, he became more disciplinarian. Backing Mum when I sneaked a bottle of brandy from Nan's liquor cabinet to drink in the park with my mates or moaned about dragging the stinking rubbish bin to the top of the drive every Wednesday evening.

I never called him Dad, because by the time the twins came along, I was fifteen and considered myself too grown up. Plus, my real dad had started showing up once a year around my birthday, and it was a delicate relationship. I didn't want to give him a reason to disappear again.

But Bryan was solid, and I showed him respect. Partly

because he showed it to me, partly because, after he arrived, Mum was different. Humming while she cooked, less strict over how much screen time I could have.

Mum continued with her story.

'I'd been happy us two, then us three, but as a girl, I'd wanted a big family. A house bustling with mess and laughter, cuddling up with my husband after wrestling our kids to bed, pulling crackers round the Christmas dinner table. Your dad took that dream when he left.'

That's why they'd had my sisters. I was thirteen when they'd told me over a bucket of Kentucky Fried Chicken one teatime that they were going to try. I probably grunted a reply. But underneath the adolescent nonchalance, I just wanted Mum to be happy. She'd been selfless in the sacrifices she'd made when I was little.

'I know you struggled during the IVF, not knowing what to expect with younger siblings and seeing us go through fertility treatment,' Mum said.

It'd been a rough two years while I was doing my GCSEs. Mum would get her hopes up constantly, then sob through several failed cycles. Being a teenage boy, I left her to Bryan, making myself scarce playing Xbox upstairs when I sensed they'd had bad news. Probably why I always needed to fix things for April.

'Mum, I love the crazy, loud family the twins turned us into. Let's face it, those rascals run the show.' I smiled.

'Run me ragged more like. And I wouldn't change any of it.' She chuckled. 'Perhaps proposing to Kel was a mistake if your heart wasn't truly in it. Ending things now doesn't make you your father, and eventually she'll be better for it. I certainly was.'

Mum reached across the table and put her hand on mine, patting it with motherly reassurance. 'You can make mistakes when you're young, so long as you learn from them, and if you love April, let everything else go. I've seen you fall in love twice, and while Kel could raise a smile in you, April made you shine. I want you to shine again.'

'Thanks, Mum,' I mumbled. I meant it. I hadn't realised how terrified I'd been of becoming my dad. Of letting people down. Plus, her pep talk helped me see that bigger picture Jonesy was TED talking about. I had to forgive April, but I had to forgive myself too, to be the man she needed.

Getting up, Mum took my empty mug and put her arms around me before ushering me towards the bathroom.

'Brush your teeth, love. We better get you back to that hospital.'

The Coma

April

Can you have a panic attack in a coma? Because if you can, I was definitely having one. My breathing wasn't rapid; I wasn't conscious of my chest heaving up and down; some magic machine was doing that for me. I couldn't feel my hands shaking. But my thoughts were zipping from one thing to another, unable to settle.

Dylan knew.

He'd figured out what I'd buried deep inside for three years. The secret that'd tormented me, manifesting into a whole exhibition of self-torturing art. He'd found out about the footballer. The reason I'd fled with no explanation. And now he was gone.

But how? In this strange place of real memories mixed up with alternative lives, I'd been exploring a world where Dylan chased me to the airport the day I left for San Francisco. In that different version of my life, I'd confessed right there by the check-in desk, using one of a thousand speeches I'd rehearsed in the bathroom mirror.

That Dylan had stormed off, and it'd been a decade before we'd spoken again. But now, somehow, my Dylan, in my real life, knew too. Had he been there, living that alternative reality with me? Listening to that awful, fumbled confession too? Surely that wasn't possible. But how else had he suspected enough to ask my friends the truth?

My questions were drowned out by Jen and Lizzy talking. Or arguing. I couldn't tell; they sniped at each other a lot. But it didn't matter; Dylan had left me.

The picture of Dylan walking away in Manchester Airport during that parallel life was still vivid. He'd not looked back. Then, in a flash, we'd been standing on a Manchester street, both ten years older, and he was introducing me to his daughter. I could still feel the loss I'd experienced when it dawned on me he'd become a dad. That somewhere, in some time or place, Dylan had a family with someone who wasn't me. His future wasn't mine, but this beautiful bundle of brown curls with his gold-flecked eyes.

I'd always known the thing with the footballer would be a deal-breaker. Dylan would never have done anything like that. No matter how many dark clouds took up space in his head, he'd never have stumbled home with some exotic leggy Italian girl who pouted at him across the bar.

I'd always hoped to tell him the truth one day. But in none of my imagined scenarios did Dylan find out while I was in a coma unable to explain or beg forgiveness. I wondered where he was, what he was thinking. Did he hate me? I hated me.

From the depths of my coma, I heard Lizzy calling Adam, asking him to go and find him.

Bloody great. Of all the people I wanted to talk Dylan round and get him to come back, it was not anti-relationship, anti-April, "I'll show you what's under my kilt" Adam.

Unable to react physically, my consciousness span like someone had pulled the plug out the bath until I was circling the drain. I imagined Dylan sitting in his car somewhere in our world, taking his anger out on his steering wheel or, more likely, the amber contents of a pint glass.

The morning after that awful one-night stand, I'd been too ashamed to even tell Lizzy, not that she'd ever judge. Chastise, yes. Judge, never. She'd have been pragmatic, instantly working out a way to break it to Dylan, which she'd insist without question I had to do. Probably why I chose not to confess. Much easier to tell Jen, a sympathetic stranger thousands of miles away who neither knew Dylan nor witnessed our disastrous relationship crumble.

Back in May of my third year, Lizzy had been mad enough that I'd not told Dylan I was going to San Francisco. She'd called to give me a mouthful after he'd turned up at her door straight from Rome.

As I recalled that 2019 spring morning, my swirling consciousness plopped down the drain and straight into the real memory of the day I left for San Francisco. Suddenly, it was three years earlier, and I was stood in the cool, stale airport check-in hall, watching myself grimace as I answered the phone to an irate Lizzy.

The Airport

MAY 2019

Patiently standing at the front of the check-in queue, April heard her phone ringing in her handbag. She jumped at the trill, her nerves on edge, even though her passport, tickets and visa had been organised and quadruple checked. It wasn't her many immigration documents that worried her. It was the enormity of what she was leaving behind that had her chewing her fingernails to the quick.

Pulling her phone from her bag, she was surprised to see Lizzy's name flashing up. They'd only said goodbye an hour earlier and she definitely hadn't forgotten anything. Had she?

'April. Why the fuckety fuck didn't you tell Dylan about San Francisco?' Lizzy raged before April could even say hello. April's heart quickened at the mention of his name, heat rushing to her cheeks.

'You spoke to Dylan?' she gasped.

Lizzy let out an infuriated sigh. 'Yes. He showed up here straight off the plane from bloody Rome. Poor guy went pale when I told him where you were. Honestly, I thought he was going to cry on my doorstep.'

April started pacing back and forth from her suitcases, her mind in overdrive.

'For God's sake, April,' Lizzy ranted. 'You didn't even *tell* him? Thanks for letting me break that nugget. It was like telling him you were dead. You made out to me that it was definitely over after Valentine's Day, but he didn't look like a bloke who knew it was over. What's going on?'

For a second, April opened her mouth, wondering if this was her window to tell Lizzy the truth. Only, it felt too late for that, and what good would it do?

'I didn't tell him because I didn't think he'd care. He wasn't speaking to me,' April lied. 'Anyway, it's too late. I've got to go; check-in is finally opening.' Hanging up, April switched her phone off and didn't turn it back on until she was sat on the plane, having drowned her sorrows in several gin and tonics in the departure lounge.

Lizzy hadn't called back. But Dylan had. April's heart almost flatlined when she saw his missed call, only to be jolted back into rapid beating when she realised he'd left a voicemail. They'd not spoken for five months, despite all those promises they'd made. 'We'll fix it all when I'm back,' Dylan had said. But that was before Valentine's Day. So, she'd left.

Securing a place on a US internship had been the one little piece of happiness she'd had in the last few months. Her chance for a fresh start. She couldn't give it up. But now, after all this time, Dylan's voice was waiting in her mailbox.

Hands shaking, April dialled her voicemail, pressed her phone to her ear and held her breath.

April, it's me. I'm not phoning to stop you leaving; we both know you've got to go. I only want to tell you that I'll wait. I'll wait because I love you. Even more now I know how unbearable it is to live without you.

Hearing Dylan's voice brought a tidal wave of pain crashing back over April and she shrank back into her seat, staring out onto the grey airport tarmac.

Just don't give up on us, please. I'm sorry about New Year, then sending that shitty text on Valentine's Day. I was lost without you, and I should have called sooner. I should have shown up at your door sooner. I'm kicking myself for being too proud and dumb. But I'm telling you now – I will wait. I'll be whatever you need in the meantime. I'll visit; I'll message every day or just phone you every so often. Fuck, I'll be your pen pal if that's what you need. Just give us another chance to make this work, because when we work April, we are everything, and nothing is ever going to match up to everything. Please, just call me. I love you, and I'm still all in.

April listened for a second, then a third time, feeling as though her heart would rupture. Dylan still loved her. He wanted to be with her. He was still all in.

But he was too late. If she called him back now, she'd have to tell him her secret, and it'd tear him apart.

As the plane's engines fired up, April turned her phone off again. By the time the aircraft lifted off the ground, she was curled up against the window, a blanket pulled over her head to hide her sobs. She stayed like that for most of the flight, knowing she was leaving part of herself behind forever.

Stepping off the plane in San Francisco, April felt that dark cloud step off with her. She knew then she'd been naïve thinking there was a fresh start waiting in California. The reality was, she'd just dragged her misery halfway across the world instead.

The Coma

April

Watching myself disembark the plane in San Francisco three years earlier, I chose not to follow, and the memory disappeared into nothing. Now the secret that had taken me there was out, and a faceless footballer whose name I barely remembered had driven Dylan away. The delayed wreckage of that horrible Valentine's Day night unfolding in the present while I was stuck in a wall-less prison of memories and regrets.

I was probably the only person in any universe who could break someone's heart from a coma. But I needed Dylan to come back. Without him, I worried I'd never find the strength to wake up.

The agony of that single thought manifested into a real, searing hot pain scorching its way through my head. A deafening shriek rang out alongside the burning, and I couldn't tell if it was me screaming or some audible interpretation of my suffering. I needed it to stop. It had to stop.

Shutting my thoughts off altogether, I plunged into the clutches of darkness.

April's Hospital Room

Dylan

Chaos had broken out in April's room when I got back shortly before 9am. I'd hurried back after Mum's pep talk to find Sarah sobbing on her husband. Lizzy was pacing the room, her fingers flying over her phone's keypad. Jen was sat quietly in the corner, her hands clasped in prayer.

'What happened, where is she?' I demanded, trying to keep the nausea sloshing in my stomach at bay.

'Surgery. They rushed her back in first thing this morning when her machines started blaring. She's suffered a secondary bleed on her brain. A clot, they think.' Lizzy's lip curled into a snarl as she turned to me, chest puffed out. 'I would have called but Adam said you were sleeping off a heavy night.'

My head spun as I walked back and forth between the window and the door, panic chasing off any remnants of a hangover.

Nobody knew anything else; updates weren't forthcoming. Time crawled by.

None of us ate; we barely touched the rounds of tea

the nursing staff kindly brought. Helplessly waiting while someone you love is in peril is the devil's torture.

Staring out across the car park from April's window, I remembered how soft her hair felt on the tips of my fingers when I brushed it out her eyes. I thought of April World and worried it was crumbling as surgeons poked around her damaged brain with sharp, shiny implements all lined up on a tray. Was the magic that made April who she was draining away? That light dimming to nothing?

I remembered the way her kisses could switch back and forth between passionately wanton, to gently loving in a way that made every part of me quiver. Always craving more. I'd do anything for just one more of those kisses.

Late morning, one of the doctors came in. He didn't bother asking to speak to Sarah and Ian in private. April had suffered a ruptured aneurism. There was only fifty per cent chance she'd make it. Fifty-fifty. The toss of a coin. Roulette. Red or black. Odds you wouldn't bet a drink on, never mind your life.

'It might be a good idea to call any loved ones that aren't already here,' he said. 'Just in case.'

Preparing us. *To say goodbye.*

Sarah crumpled. Ian caught her, guiding her to a chair. But there were no sobs. She was pale and silent, her whole body trembling like a phone on vibrate, staring at the empty space where April's bed should be. Lizzy and Jen were holding each other up, while I couldn't take anything in. Only the previous morning we'd been on a high after getting good news. Now this? A low so crushing the antiseptic bleach smell I thought I'd acclimatised to made my head pound. Reminding me where we were, the horrors ready to floor you just as hope resurfaced.

Ian found his phone and started making calls. Lizzy did the same. Yet I had no one to call. I felt useless, observing the terrified turmoil around me like an imposter in the corner.

April's aunts and cousins flew into the ward with a flurry of tears and hugs. Chairs were brought in, but few people could sit still as we waited. I hardly uttered a word to anyone. Like Sarah, shock froze me in place. Not daring to move until I knew for sure which way it was going to go.

Fifty-fifty. The toss of a coin. Heads April lives; tails she dies.

It was 3pm when a surgeon came to tell us April had pulled through.

'She's lucky,' she said. They'd caught it quickly. If she'd been anywhere other than the hospital, it would have been fatal. Now she was stable and on her way back to critical care. Sarah finally let the tears fall, and there was a collective release of air from us all.

'But we don't know what, if any, further damage it's caused,' the surgeon added. 'It's still the long waiting game I'm afraid.'

We shared small smiles, relieved hugs. We'd not lost her yet.

A fresh, cream wrapping of bandages wound around April's head, and I was sure she was disappearing under the wires snaking round her like triffid roots. But just having her physically back in the room strengthened us all. April's relatives trickled home from the hospital, and around teatime, when Sarah nodded off holding her hand, we finally convinced her to go home to rest. Lizzy, Jen and

I stayed, each of us exhausted but not daring leave just yet.

'Feel better after your pub session then, Dylan?' Lizzy sneered, her sharp bob swishing as she jerked her head in my direction, eyes ablaze.

Jen looked awkward.

'Lizzy, let's go for a coffee. Give Dylan a minute with April,' she said, her hand on Lizzy's shoulder. Still glaring at me, Lizzy stood up, sending her chair screeching across the floor.

But I could deal with Lizzy later. As they disappeared to the canteen, I shuffled my chair up to April's bed. I hesitated to take her hand, in case I lost my grip on this reality again. Instead, I settled for brushing her cheek with my fingertips.

'Don't do that to us again, April. Keep fighting. I'm sorry I ran off, but in my defence, I was back within twenty-four hours. It took you three years to come back.' Making a joke made me feel less vulnerable and exposed.

'I hate what happened. What you did. Finding out now makes it feel like it happened yesterday. I want to punch things. Footballers, mostly.'

I sighed deeply, caressing the soft skin between the tubes on her face again. 'Three years though. That's a lifetime in your twenties. I proposed to someone a month ago for fuck's sake, even though I still loved you.'

There'd been a Kel, an Eduardo, an Owen and a Blake in-between then and now.

'If I'm honest with myself, we were broken up by Valentine's Day. Not overtly, but we hadn't spoken for weeks, and that's on me. I was far from innocent. It's time to let all that stupid stuff from back then go,' I said.

April's coma had shown everything else for what it was. Insignificant melodrama.

'Nothing before right now matters; I just want you back and to be what we were in those first six months. Which is why you've got to wake up. We owe it to the Dylan and April who immediately fell madly in love to get it right.'

'Quite frankly, Dylan, you were even more insufferable then.' Snarky Lizzy was back, marching into the room and plonking down next to me.

'Jen thought you needed more time, but... well, I wanted to apologise,' she said, eyes fixed on April.

I raised my eyebrows. I'd never known Lizzy to apologise and wondered if Jen had something to do with it.

'I didn't know,' she continued, 'about the footballer. I'm angry at her too, for not telling me. Then we almost lost her again and I felt guilty, but I shouldn't have taken it out on you.'

She finally looked at me, and I took the coffee she held out as a peace offering. It was in a paper cup from the canteen too, not a plastic one from the dishwater machine on the ward, proving her apology was sincere. I didn't want to hold a grudge against Lizzy; she'd verbally castrate me. Plus, there was no need; we both loved April.

To fill the time, I told Lizzy about my slips into an alternative reality.

'It's happened twice. One minute I'm in the hospital and the next I'm reliving the past, only it's not quite the same. I change one thing, and life veers off in a different direction,' I explained, cradling my hot coffee.

Lizzy cackled.

'Stress. Bound to be. I hardly think April's coma is dragging you into your own version of *The Butterfly Effect*.'

She reckoned I must have known, at least on some subconscious level, that April had cheated on me.

'Looking back, it really was the only explanation for her vanishing act.'

I nibbled my cheek, unconvinced, and we both watched April for a while. The steady beep and whoosh of life support oddly calming after the day's drama.

'Weird though,' Lizzy said, leaning back in her chair and stretching. 'You discovering her cheating, then her brain rupturing. Coincidence, I'm sure. It's just odd. Almost like somewhere in there, she knew you'd found out.'

As Lizzy chattered, I stared out the window, thinking.

'Anyway, if April *had* told me about the fresher, I'd have told her it wasn't cheating. You can't cheat on someone who hasn't spoken to you in six weeks. You ghosted your own girlfriend, Dylan. Who does that?'

She was still whittering on about that footballer. It all seemed so trivial now. I was glad when two nurses interrupted, bustling in to take April for some post-surgery scans. I needed space to think.

Perhaps April really could hear us. Or was she trapped too, slipping between alternative realities with me?

*

Over the next two weeks, we fell into a pattern of shifts sitting with April. Talking to her, holding her hand. Or in my case, resting my hand on her forearm. I didn't dare let our palms intertwine just in case it opened another portal to the past. I couldn't risk the damage it might be doing to April's brain. Doctors didn't think she'd survive a third surgery.

We left the sponge baths to the nurses, but Jen and Sarah would do her nails or rub a selection of doctor-approved beauty products onto her skin. Lizzy read her classics. Her dad played her old rock songs or sat in silence half doing crosswords. Adam, Jonesy and Al took turns sitting with me, usually bringing a pizza and a pack of playing cards.

Sometimes we'd forget where we were, why we were there. Then a machine would change its bleeping pattern, or a nurse would come in, and we'd be pulled back to reality. That initial horror we'd all felt after April's crash settled into a constant state of agitation. Whiling away the long hours, then leaping out our seats whenever a doctor appeared with an update.

Alone with April, I'd talk about the good memories, the possibilities for our future. Even though I didn't know if she'd want one with me when she woke up.

'I just hope April and I get a chance to make it right,' I told Jen and Lizzy one afternoon as we sat in a triangle around the bed, telling our favourite April stories. They both had more of them than I did. It made me feel an odd mixture of jealous and sad.

'What are the chances of that?' Jen asked. Doctors had given us the whole "wait and see" speech and told us not to look up brain trauma online. 'But I'm guessing you've looked up every possibility, Dylan. So, what does Dr Google say?'

I exhaled loudly. She was right. I had caved to temptation one night, dived into a rabbit hole of brain trauma information online.

'Are you sure you want to know?' I asked, and Jen nodded fervently. 'OK. Well, there's no miracle scenario where she wakes up one day fully recovered and ready to get on with her life. It's just not going to happen.'

Jen's face fell, and I knew that's what she'd been praying for.

'Most likely, she'll have some post-traumatic amnesia. It'll take a while for her to understand where she is or that she's been in an accident. It's unlikely she'll ever remember the crash. She'll probably be confused and scared, struggle with her short-term memory, which may or may not be permanent.'

Jen's pupils widened as I spoke, while Lizzy stared straight at me, her mouth a tight line. I guessed I wasn't telling her anything she hadn't already looked up herself.

'April might not remember other recent stuff too, or recognise people at first, although that shouldn't last. Mostly she'll be tired, agitated, frustrated. And that's just in the first week. Or so I've read.'

Jen gulped and Lizzy stayed stony-faced as I moved on to the longer-term problems.

'Her muscles will have atrophied. That, and any potential brain damage, means she'll have to relearn to walk, maybe talk. Damage to her frontal or temporal lobe might cause some not particularly nice changes to her personality.'

Jen's hand flew to her mouth.

'Like what?' she gasped.

'She might be constantly angry,' I said, scratching my head. 'Unempathetic, self-centred, unable to make simple decisions or look after herself. She might not be the April we knew.'

Jen started weeping, which is probably why doctors didn't want us looking up worst-case scenarios.

'But it's a whole lot of maybes and what ifs,' Lizzy cut in, putting a hand on Jen's knee. 'So, the docs were right. It's better to wait and see rather than terrify ourselves.'

'Oh, April.' Jen sniffed.

'Sorry, Lizzy's right. I shouldn't have laid all my biggest fears at your feet,' I told her.

'I asked. I wanted to know. But what about best case? We should know those too, right? I need to know what to pray for.' Hope replaced despair on Jen's face.

Praying wasn't something I thought would do any good, and I'd been trying not to get my own expectations up. Yet, if it helped Jen.

'Best case?' I continued, looking back at April. 'Once the confusion and amnesia start to fade, April will show some understanding of what's going on, answer questions, follow conversations. In an ideal world, after a few weeks, she'll be well enough to go home for physio and occupational therapy. And she'll mostly be our April. But she has to wake up first.' For now, that was all I cared about.

Jen reached over and took my hand, and the three of us sat quietly until April's parents arrived.

'Still stable,' Lizzy told them. The same thing we said every time we changed watch. Sarah took my seat and clasped April's hand in hers. She was looking more exhausted and drawn by the day. My mind drifted to those families whose loved ones never woke up, who remained unchanged for months, then years. I wondered how they coped. How they got through each day, and if they ever stopped spending every hour they could by their bed. When they finally gave up.

'Actually, we do have an update.'

All five of us turned to look at the doctor who'd come in just behind April's parents. 'Sarah, Ian, could you come with me?'

Exchanging scared but optimistic looks, April's parents hurried after the doctor and into a private room. Jen, Lizzy and I gave each other similar looks as we loitered in April's room. I couldn't sit still, pacing from the door to the window again, while Jen nibbled her fingernails and Lizzy sat jiggling her leg.

After what felt like hours, they came back in.

'They're going to start trying to bring her out of the coma,' Ian said, not smiling, but buoyed. 'Tomorrow. They'll start lowering the sedatives, and gradually she should – we hope – start to wake up.'

Jen, Lizzy and I collectively exhaled. Ian strode over to April's side and started talking to her in muted whispers. This was it, after weeks of waiting, we were about to find out what we were dealing with.

*

She looks awake, but she's not, not really. Not yet.' April's mum spoke quickly, looking less drawn but more wired than two days previously. 'She's in there; I know she is. Once, she even looked straight at me.'

I'd arrived to take my overnight shift. So far, April had blinked her eyes open every so often and stared blankly around the room. It wasn't much, but we clung to it, especially Sarah. Ever since, her demeanour had brightened, and she was more animated when she spoke.

I couldn't yet find the same enthusiasm, but I was careful not to show any doubt that might take that hope from her. April was going to need her mum's unwavering belief.

'I wanted to thank you, Dylan,' Sarah said, as Ian topped up the jug of water for me. 'For being here. I know it hasn't been easy, given everything that happened between you. But if April can hear us, and I think she can, I know your voice will help bring her back to us.'

'I'm not going anywhere. Until April says otherwise, at least.' It had occurred to me that she might wake up and tell me to do one.

'Something tells me she'll want you around for a long time to come,' Sarah reassured, looking at her husband. 'The last time we saw you – before this – was—'

'Christmas of third year.' I grimaced as Sarah nodded.

'Lizzy tells me you've been beating yourself up about all that. I've been doing the same. And I aways circle back to that Christmas. Well, New Year really. I should have banged your heads together. But I told myself you were adults; you had to find your own way; and I couldn't make everything better for April.'

'You can't protect your kids forever,' Ian said.

I agreed with him. It wasn't her job to stop me and April acting like fools.

'Doesn't stop you trying though.' Sarah sighed. 'Maybe a bit of motherly interfering was what was needed, and I could have saved you both some heartache. I wish I'd called you, Dylan, after April spent that New Year unable to drag herself out of bed. But I worried about you too. Rome wasn't your fault, and I didn't want you to do anything silly and jeopardise your own future. You had your degree to think about.' Sarah paused a second. 'I just wish I'd done more.'

Knowing we all had regrets put my own in perspective. Later, as I sat with April, the last of the summer evening light fading, I thought about how insistent I'd been when I'd left Manchester after that Christmas. I'd been so sure if I could just get April to visit me in Rome, I could make it all OK. I always wanted to fix things.

As my thoughts wandered to the past once more, April's fingers jolted. I gasped, lurching forwards to take her hand. For a second, I paused. Was April strong enough for this?

Was I?

It'd been two weeks since her last surgery. I hadn't visited the past since, but those journeys into an alternative life, where I could undo my regrets, had felt so real.

The urge to see April again – awake, healthy, maybe even smiling – was irresistible. I could talk to her, maybe even kiss her again. So, I gave in to temptation, grasping her hand and feeling her fingers curl around mine. This time, as I was lifted from my reality and into the past, I was ready for it.

Christmas

DECEMBER 2018

AN ALTERNATIVE REALITY

Dylan

It took me a while to realise where I was. Then I recognised the faded, worn beige of April's university sofa. April was sitting at the other end from me, and there were fairy lights hung around the bay window behind her. I felt this urge to reach out and wipe the tears sliding down her cheeks.

Only, I was picking my nails with annoyance, and this frustrated feeling crept up inside me until I wasn't Dylan in the hospital, needing April to survive. I'd slid through a door into the body of Dylan from three and a half years earlier. The one who'd come back from Rome for Christmas in our third year of university, furious at her.

This time, I sank into the experience. Knowing I'd at least be able to change something in this parallel world. Maybe this was the time we could get everything right.

In front of me, April was dabbing her eyes on a screwed-up piece of toilet roll, her tears dampening the fire that'd raged inside me the whole flight home.

'Can't we just spend Christmas together, like we planned?' she pleaded. Just like the first time, April wanted us to forget about Rome for the Christmas holidays, while I was back. Pretend nothing had gone horribly wrong.

It was a bad idea then, and it was a bad idea now. We had to deal with what'd happened. But I could still hear the whoosh of Coma April's ventilator and see her shrinking under the wire monster keeping her alive. In this past life, I only had two weeks before I went back to Italy. Both parts of me – past and present – missed my girlfriend. So, like I had the first time, I nodded. I could change something later. For now, five minutes after our first big fight, April and I retreated into our utopic bubble.

'Two weeks in April World is exactly what I need,' I relented, pulling her into my arms and smelling the familiar rose scent of her hair.

After, I made sure to do everything the same, enjoying the bliss of waking up with April in my arms. Touching her soft skin and relishing the feel of her body as it curled into mine.

Christmas Day arrived quickly, and we spent it with my mum, Bryan and twin sisters, Ivy and Lola. The girls were only six, so it was a day full of fun and endless piles of presents. Boxing Day we did it all again at April's parents' an hour-long drive away, yet, with April being an only child, it was boozier.

Still, Rome, and my return there, hung over us like a date of execution. At night, April clung to me. I could feel how much she wanted everything to go away. Passion and playfulness had given way to this gripping sadness. Every time we made love, it was tactile and tender, that sorrow consuming us. I'd stroke her hair and kiss her head as she nodded off, wondering how I could change things to make it better.

Christmas flew by. Then the night I dreaded arrived, my last one before I flew back to Italy for New Year. We spent it in the pub with my mum and Bryan, arriving home slightly worse for wear. After everyone else had gone to bed, April sat on my lap on the sofa as we kissed tipsily.

I didn't want the night to end, but my thoughts kept flitting to the plane ticket burning a hole in my inbox. I'd bought April a ticket to Rome for New Year's Eve. In my real life, I remembered springing it on her this very night. I'd bought it well before our Big Fight. Before I'd found out why Rome was such a mammoth hurdle I wasn't sure we could clear.

'April,' I swallowed, unlocking my lips from hers. 'I have something for you, and I need you to hear me out, please.'

She froze, a worried look momentarily flitting across her face. I hadn't noticed it the first time round, blustering through to give her what I thought was a magic plaster for our wound. Only, now it made me pause, giving April an opening to interrupt.

'Dylan, don't,' she blurted. 'Hear me out first. I know I've been avoiding the whole subject of Rome, and that's selfish. But I can't visit you there again, I just can't. Not after last term, it's too difficult.'

My whole body sagged, my face crumpling while April pushed through a pre-prepared speech I'd not let her get to last time.

'But you know what wasn't hard? Being with you, here, these last two weeks. We've just been us and it's been perfect.

Well, almost, if you forget the bit about you leaving again tomorrow.' Holding my face in her hands, April touched her forehead to mine. 'Can't we just have that? We can make it work, even if you only come back one weekend in the next twenty. That'll be enough for me – just. If I know we'll be together again by summer.'

Hearing the desperation in her voice, I knew this was it. My moment to make a change. In my original timeline, I'd naïvely imagined us watching the midnight fireworks from some romantic sangria-soaked Italian piazza, toasting the New Year and pledging a fresh start. But I knew now that didn't happen. It had been cruel to try and make her face Rome again. The city was too loaded with all the never-to-be-made memories April was grieving for.

And wasn't that what Sarah regretted most? Not opening her eyes to how much April was suffering during this Christmas? She thought she could have done more. I realised we all could have.

'OK, April,' I surrendered. 'If that's what it takes to get us through this, then I'll do it.'

I loved her more than I thought it possible to love someone. It left me teetering on the brink of insanity. So maybe letting her dictate the terms of our separation would stop her feeling pressured. Stop her seeking solace from my anger in the bed of a sweaty footballer. And what was five months? In my real life, it'd turned into more than three years.

'If there's a lifetime with you at the end of it, I'll do it,' I told her now.

'And it will be a lifetime,' she promised. 'All in, remember.'

April started kissing me again, and I let it consume me, hoping in this world, I'd finally put us on the right track. I knew I still faced five months without her though, so taking April's hand, I led her to my bedroom. She'd bought me a brown fedora for Christmas. I'd visibly blushed opening it in front of my mum, even though she obviously wasn't in on the joke. Grabbing it now, I plonked it on my head, needing to see laughter replace the worry on April's face.

'Snakes. Why'd it have to be snakes?' I smouldered, giving my best Indiana impression. Giggling, April took my hat and put it on herself, pushing me down onto the bed. Laughing, we devoured each other like it was the first time. After, falling into a deep sleep, I hoped this change was the one that made everything right. And that it stuck.

*

Dropping April home the next morning, unease crept in. It was even harder than the first time I'd done this, because then I'd assumed she'd be flying out to visit me in a few days. Now I'd not forced that plane ticket on her, we didn't even know when we'd see each other next.

To keep my thoughts off April, I called Al on the way to the airport.

'It'd be too much pressure for her.' I sighed over hands-free, telling him about the cancelled plane ticket.

'At least if you're back in Manchester more, we'll get to hang out. We miss you, mate,' he said. I felt another tug, this one for the friends I was missing whilst spending my final year studying abroad. I didn't tell Al that I was already too deep into my student loan to afford multiple trips back.

Then there was the not-so-small issue of my final exams, plus all the weekends I'd need to spend at different dig sites.

I'd almost got to the airport when April's mum phoned.

'Sorry to call, Dylan, it's just, April got home and went straight to bed, and it's not the first time since all this Rome stuff.' Sarah's voice was hushed, but she sounded beside herself.

'Last term April would come home and spend entire weekends in her room. She told us she was coming back to study. She aced all her exams, got a first on her coursework, so I thought she was coping. Only, I just called Lizzy.' I heard Sarah close a door behind her as she wove through the house. 'Apparently, April barely left her room at uni either, except to go to lectures. And now she's in there, just sobbing. I'm so worried. Maybe if you could talk to her?'

My mouth went dry, and I stared at my phone handset on the dashboard, unable to focus on the road. Being apart the previous term had been rough. But I'd always assumed she'd focused on studying, spent her free time drinking wine or watching Netflix with her friends. Not sat in a dark room by herself.

'I'd no idea it was that bad.' I gulped. 'I knew she was sad; we both were. But I didn't know... I'm coming back.'

'I'm sorry, I didn't mean for you to miss your flight; I just can't seem to help her.' Sarah was close to tears, but I'd already turned the car around. Making sure April was OK was the only thing I cared about. I could catch the earliest flight to Rome on New Year's Day and put it on my mum's emergency credit card.

Walking into April's room an hour later was a fierce dose of reality. Her curtains were drawn, and she was curled up in a ball under her duvet. Sarah had already told me she expected April to spend the next several days there before she had to go back to uni.

The first time I'd lived through this, I'd thought I'd seen through the happy smiles April plastered on. Now I was learning I'd only got a glimpse. The light hadn't just dimmed in April World; it'd gone out completely.

'Mum, please just leave me alone,' she muttered, not bothering to look up. Seeing April's blotchy, tear-stained face, curled up in a scratty old pair of PJs and scrolling through photos of us on her phone ripped my heart out. Had I done this to her?

I was out of my depth. Unable to find any words that could make it better. I just climbed in bed behind her and pulled her to me. She felt impossibly small in my arms. For the first time, I clocked how much weight she'd lost. She was almost skeletal. April didn't resist or protest, instead curling in as tightly as possible. I held her silently like that for hours.

At one point, I snuck out to speak to Sarah and Ian. Between the three of us and Lizzy, we pieced together what April had been hiding.

At uni, she'd told Lizzy she was studying and saving up to visit me. Going home every other weekend to disguise the fact she was avoiding socialising. Then she'd told her parents she was visiting them to avoid parties and study. Between us, we also figured out she was only showering and putting make-up on before our video calls.

'She's depressed,' Sarah said. We exchanged frightened nods. This was bigger than the pressure of third year doubled up by a long-distance relationship. April was ill.

It scared me.

This is what I'd missed the first time. But I still didn't know how to make it better. Thankfully, Sarah took my hand.

'You just need to be there for her, Dylan. Let us do the rest. We're her parents.'

Torn, I considered giving up Rome. But all my projects were out there, my dissertation subject approved. Leaving was impossible without redoing the whole year. Also, April would never let me.

Climbing back into her bed, I entwined my body back around hers. Wishing I could absorb her pain.

'April,' I whispered after she woke from a fitful sleep. 'Don't hide this from me. If April World isn't always bright and excitable, that's OK. When things get dark and a little scary, or you feel lost, I'll be here to lie with you until it passes, or we find a way out together. That's what all in means. You can shut out the world if you need, but don't shut me out.'

She didn't answer but reached for my hand and squeezed it tightly.

'I don't know what's wrong with me,' April said later in a monotonous whisper. I was sure it was past midnight by then. 'I don't feel like myself. It's like I'm grieving. I lost everything all at once, especially you, and it was my own fault. Now I feel adrift, like I'm stranded in the middle of an ocean, freezing and drowning.'

'Do you feel like you're drowning now?' I asked.

'Not when you're here with me. But we both know you've got to get on a plane at some point.'

'I do,' I admitted, drawing her into me again and kissing the top of her head. 'But I can still be your life raft, April.

I'm here now until the very last moment I have to leave. And then, whatever time of day you need to call me, you pick up the phone. If you're hiding under your duvet, I'll climb under mine, and it'll be almost like I'm here.' I put my mouth to her ear and whispered, 'You're not alone in this; we will get through it. But you have to let me in.'

April rolled over and put her arms around me too. 'I love you. So much. It's why I've been trying so hard to be OK. I want to be the person you fell in love with,' she said, her head pressing against my chest.

'But you are. I love all of you, every single piece.'

'Even this part?'

'Especially this part,' I promised.

After, we both fell asleep and, when I woke up, she was still curled up in my arms. But there were telling red rings circling her closed eyes. I ached because I couldn't fix things for her, and for the first time, it occurred to me that perhaps I never could.

For four days, April stayed cocooned in my arms. I mostly just held her, promising to always be there. On New Year's Eve, we watched the fireworks on my iPad. Her mum would bring us food, throwing furtive looks my way, wanting to know if there was more she could do.

April felt guilty I was missing the big New Year party in Rome. I reassured her I was exactly where I wanted to be. Each day she seemed a little stronger, and when I couldn't put off leaving any longer, I could only hope I'd done enough.

'I can't pretend the next five months are going to be easy,' I said. 'But while I'm physically in Rome, I'm not going anywhere. I'll swim the ocean to get back to you the second you need me.'

Despite more tears flooding when we said goodbye, I was reassured that April's mum had booked her to see both the university counsellor and a doctor. 'You've already made a world of difference,' Sarah promised, even though it didn't feel like I had.

*

By Valentine's Day, we were doing OK. Ish. My life in Rome followed the same path it had the first time I lived it, only instead of staring at my phone willing April to call, we spoke every day. The trouble was, we'd started running out of things to say. I avoided mentioning Rome, the elephant in the room. Stuck to chatting about my course, how thrilled I was to be part of a real research team.

April still spent her time going from lectures to home, but she was doing better. Watching endless boxsets on the sofa rather than hiding in her room. She'd refused the doctor's suggestion of anti-depressants but had seen the university counsellor. We all agreed it was progress.

'Lizzy's convinced me to go out tonight,' she sighed down the phone that evening. 'Some hideous Valentine's-themed student party.'

Once again, the more time that passed, the more this new life took over residency in my mind. Eventually, memories of comas and crashes faded until I was so preoccupied with this alternative reality, it seemed like my only reality. But I still went cold at the thought of April going out that night. A distant Valentine's memory niggling in the far reaches of my mind.

'Try and have fun,' I said, keeping the edge from my

voice. Because despite the nagging unease, I was also relieved she'd agreed to socialise again. Besides, Adam, Al and Jonesy were sure to be going. I'd ask Al to keep an eye out for her.

With my Rome friends mostly coupled up and spending the evening indulging in some typical Italian romance, I'd bought a few beers for a night in alone.

Only, I'd been so focused on April, I'd not paid attention to my own isolation. Feeling sorry for myself, that few turned into several. Boredom kicked in too, and I couldn't help but scroll through my phone.

Al had Instagrammed some selfies he'd taken with April, both smiling. I was surprised not to see Jodie somewhere. She and April had always got on, and I was sure she must be visiting Al for Valentine's Day.

Adam sent a photo of a girl in a bodycon dress sitting in front of a line of purple shots, following it up with an aubergine emoji. Honestly, I sometimes wondered how we were friends. I'd enjoyed the single life as a fresher, but it'd soon got boring trawling student bars as Adam's wingman. Trying out his cheesiest chat-up lines.

Sat on a battered old computer chair, my tiny room squeezed around me as the loneliness closed in. After extending my stay at New Year, I still hadn't planned a weekend to visit Manchester. Flights were expensive on a student loan. And while Rome was incredible, I hated missing so much back home. Unable to help myself, I picked up my phone to message April.

Miss you. Wish we were spending Valentine's Day together, I wrote.

The woozy cogs in my brain told me it was a nice message, reassuring her I was thinking of her. But I got no reply. Irked, I sat on the end of my bed and bashed out another without thinking.

It's so romantic in Rome.

Still no reply. Two ticks told me she'd read it though. Obviously having too much fun to think about me, I sulked in my drunken grump.

Who knows when I'll see you next, I wrote. The beer thumbs were now in control, flying over my keypad, conveniently forgetting my girlfriend was suffering from depression. Eventually, I gave up and passed out in my sad single bed under a duvet which I had no reason to wash.

Blinking awake the next morning, phone still in my hand, I squinted to block out the invading sunshine. My head screamed with a hangover, and when I saw the messages, I felt even sicker. Groaning, I buried my face in my hands. Sending loaded messages, purely designed to give April a guilt trip, despite witnessing first hand how much she was struggling, was repugnant.

After chugging a litre of water, I crawled back in bed to call her. No answer. In the end, I laid on my sheets, which were starting to omit a rather sour odour, and spent an hour composing an apology message.

I'm sorry. Those messages were mean and insensitive. I was drunk. I just miss you more than words can say. Can we talk?

For the next few excruciating hours, I checked my phone every few minutes. Finally, she called back.

'April,' I answered. 'Man, I've been so worried. I'm sorry. I was just pissed and sad that I was all alone, I guess. How can I make it up to you?'

I heard April sniff, and when she spoke, she was quiet. 'I know I'm oversensitive about it, and I know you've been avoiding mentioning all the wonderful things about your Rome life. But I already felt like the worst girlfriend in the world; I didn't need the reminder.' She sounded muffled.

'Where are you?' I frowned.

'Hiding from the world,' she said from under her duvet. Because it sounded like a good place to be right then, and because I'd promised I'd always join her when she needed to hide, I climbed underneath my own, wincing at the smell. It really did need a wash.

'I'm sad too,' she continued as my eyes adjusted to the darkness. 'But your messages pushed me over the edge and, well, something happened. I did something stupid.'

My stomach, already sloshing and queasy from all the beer I'd thrown down my neck, churned.

Not again, I thought, before immediately wondering where that thought had come from. Then, I listened as April told me in excruciating detail about her night. How she'd cried in the toilets for twenty minutes as my chain of awful messages landed one after another. Then she'd made a beeline to the bar where an opportunistic fresher from the football team plied her with shots.

'Things got foggy, and I woke up this morning with no idea where I was. Luckily, I was in Lizzy's bed, and we were both fully dressed,' she said.

For a brief second, I thought she was going to tell me she'd gone home with the footballer, and my hands shook with relief.

Together, April and Lizzy had pieced together the rest of the night. They'd got an Uber home from outside the student union at 2am, after running away from this footballer.

'The thing is, he kissed me,' she said, still muffled. 'At least he tried to. I vaguely remember him shoving his tongue in my mouth and pushing him off. Then he got angry and demanded money for the drinks he'd bought me. That's when Lizzy arrived, gave him an earful, and we legged it. Lizzy says I cried in the Uber home then made her spoon me like you do when I'm upset.'

That image at least made me laugh a little. I didn't imagine that request went down well with Lizzy.

'She said it was preposterous but did it anyway. She's making me a bacon sandwich now,' April said.

'How *is* your hangover?' If mine was raging, I imagined hers was worse.

'Head-splitting. You?'

'Never drinking again,' I said.

I couldn't decide how I felt about the whole thing. Guilty, for putting her in such a state. Mad that some expectant fresher took advantage of the situation and frustrated she'd gone along with it until the stage his tongue got involved.

'But you're OK though?' I asked eventually.

'I'm OK. Don't think I can stand missing you much longer though. And I'm upset at myself for misjudging the situation last night. I feel sick, because I know I'd be distraught if you let another woman get anywhere close to kissing you.' April was rambling now.

'But I swear I told him a million times I had a boyfriend. I don't think I stopped going on about you and Rome.'

I could hear the lump in her throat and knew she'd punish herself enough for both of us. Mostly, I didn't want her to end up back where she started: in bed at her parents' every weekend.

'You were vulnerable, and he took advantage,' I said, burying my anger as deeply as possible. 'I can't lie and tell you I'm not gutted, but you didn't do anything wrong really. Just don't replace me with Lizzy permanently. I'm your big spoon.'

Lizzy delivered April's bacon sandwich to her duvet hideout, making it clear providing breakfast in bed was a one-off. Then we spent hours on video call. Sometimes chatting, often just lying in silence enjoying each other's company. But the distance between us seemed bigger. April had started to feel just out of my reach.

*

'I'm looking for a new art placement,' April said during a call a few weeks later. She'd had several sessions with a counsellor, and it was refreshing to hear her voice alive with some of that old April determination. 'I need to do something for me, to get my oomph back.'

'Oomph?' I laughed. 'I'm sure I could help give you some oomph back.'

'Very funny.' April giggled, before sighing. 'Third year was supposed to be the year I found my artistic inspiration, but that's never going to happen stuck in rainy Manchester. Plus, a post-graduation internship means I can focus on getting experience in the art world and working on my sculptures without having to juggle it with lectures and coursework. There's a whole world of art out there for me to see.'

'Great idea.' I smiled. Once that April spark was set on something, she was guaranteed to find what she wanted. 'I want you to be happy.'

'I will. Especially when we're together again too.'

April stopped asking when I was visiting. We both knew it was impossible. My own workload aside, she had her own finals to think of, and April was determined on graduating with first-class honours.

I kept telling myself that no matter how stilted our phone calls became, how little we had to say to each other these days or how infrequent our messages were becoming, our love transcended it all. And in May, when I was home for good, we'd fix it. Be us again.

We almost made it to Easter when April called, babbling away like a runaway train about all the plans she'd made. Her sentences all joined together, giving me no chance to ask a single question. She made it sound like the opportunity of a lifetime, and it was. For her.

The first red flag was that she originally told me her news in an email.

I've got an internship in sunny California! San Francisco, America's capital of art and culture.

I could almost hear her voice all high and excited as I read it mid-lecture.

Not as historic as Europe but modern, progressive and fast-paced. Instead of immersing myself in the Renaissance or Baroque periods, I'll be focusing on modern art, which is what I should have been doing all along. Art history was always the backup plan. The creative scene in San Francisco is young and inclusive rather than stuffy and pretentious. It's perfect!

April's internship was part of an exchange programme and she'd be working in an independent gallery, gaining experience curating with time to work on her own art. She was right; it was ideal for her. I just couldn't see where I fitted into it all. Of course, April being April had planned it all out.

Lizzy says it's not easy to get a US visa, but I'm sure you can find a course or internship or job sponsorship in San Francisco. And if you don't, you can alternate working three months in the UK, then visit on a three-month holiday visa until my internship year is up. Then we can travel wherever you want to go. Imagine – we can wander around San Francisco and cycle across the Golden Gate Bridge...

I pictured April's face, her blue eyes dancing, all the lights of April World flashing as she planned our future. Without so much as running it by me first.

I desperately wanted to go on that journey with her. To watch her blossom into the artist I knew she could be. Only, there was no way I could. When I finally pinned her down to a video call to discuss her grand plan, I knew my reaction wasn't going to be the one she wanted.

'April, it's like Rome all over again. You've made all these decisions and plans without me and just slotted me in without even asking. I can't just drop everything and go to San Francisco with you. Even if I could miraculously get a visa, which is almost impossible. Lizzy was right.'

April's smile vanished and I saw the shadow of uncertainty nudge its way back in. The lights dimming.

'But you'll have graduated. We can do whatever we want,' she said petulantly. I didn't want to pop the bubble of happiness she'd finally found, but I had no choice.

'And I want to do my Master's in archaeology. Then my PhD. I've already got a place in September and a job with the university to help me pay for it all. It'll take five years, and I don't want to waste a year in America first.' I was pissed off that it hadn't occurred to her I might have plans too.

April scowled. 'A year with me would be a waste?' she cried. 'I've spent a year waiting for you while you're in Rome, but a year with me somewhere as amazing as California would be a waste?'

'It's not my fault I'm in Rome, though, is it? It's yours. Again, a decision you made without running it by me. San Francisco sounds incredible, it really does. And I'd love nothing more than to go with you, but I can't put my Master's on hold.' I'd waited to tell April this when we spoke, rather than in an email, but my stomach sloshed with nerves.

'My tutor out here has offered me a placement while I study in Manchester. It's a one-time offer, not one I can defer a year. And I can't spend all summer in America, not paying off my student overdraft.'

'But I have to go,' she said, her face unreadable.

'I know you do. I can't be the reason you're stuck in Manchester again.' I chewed my cheek, unable to find an answer.

'What does this mean? We do another long-distance year?' April sounded as helpless as I felt. Flying to America wasn't like jumping on a plane to Rome, and we'd barely managed that. It was ten times the price, ten times the distance, ten times the time difference. And there was no guarantee April would want to come back in a year. I had every faith she'd make something of herself; more opportunities would come her way. Ones that didn't involve the north of England.

'I can't do another year of feeling you slip away from me. It's too painful. Not when I don't even know if I'll get you at the end of it.' I was incapable of disguising the despair in my voice.

'So, what do we do? Are we breaking up?' April started to squirm and fidget on her kitchen chair, and I could see the panic in her eyes.

'No. I can't do that, either. All I want is you, but I need to know there's an end to the long distance. Let's just put this conversation on pause. Just to think and find a way through all this.' Really, I just needed to end the conversation.

Neither of us could face another year apart. April wanted to see the world, and I couldn't be the reason she didn't. She'd resent me. And Rome, however damaging to us as a couple, had changed me from directionless layabout to promising archaeologist.

Our relationship wasn't compatible with our ambitions, but choosing between them was paralysing. So, we did nothing. The months rolled on while we avoided talk of the future, all references to Rome or San Francisco.

Taking the topic off the table made it easier to get through finals, but we were in denial. Delaying the inevitable, Adam called it.

*

It seemed like eons, and yet no time at all, until I finally arrived back from Rome for good. Standing in Manchester

Airport arrivals, I breathed in the scent of April's hair as she nestled into my chest.

'I've been dreaming of this moment.' I sighed. It'd been too long since we'd seen each other, and I'd flown home hours after my last exam.

Back at April's, I tried to ignore the packed suitcases and empty shelves in her bedroom. Focusing instead on being with her. It was strange, knowing what was coming. Our kisses were soft and tender, as we savoured each one. We weren't in a rush; at times we took it agonisingly slowly. We fell asleep after, and when I woke up, I saw April had been crying. She turned to face me in bed, and I curled her hair behind her ear.

'Now what?' she whispered, intertwining her legs with mine. We couldn't delay this conversation any longer.

'Loving you is part of me,' I said, tipping her chin up to look at me. 'Nothing else is ever going to come close. Nothing. But not being able to hold you in my arms, kiss you, it makes me physically hurt. Video calls, messages and social media updates aren't enough. I need you, April, not the idea of you.'

'I *am* coming back,' she said. 'I choose you; I'll always choose you.'

'No, April. For now, you have to choose *you*. Otherwise, you could get sick again. I'm not going anywhere. But we can't put ourselves through the pain of this endlessly. I can't spend every day constantly checking my phone for a snippet of your life or wondering where you are, what you're up to and if you're thinking of me.' I hated every word coming out my mouth, but I had to keep going.

'I can't walk around with this constant longing for you.

It's killer. Ending us hurts like hell too, and I'm not sure how I'm going to get up every day, but I need to let you go so I can get on with living my life here. Just promise you'll come back. Because when you do, I'll be here. There'll never be anyone else.'

'I know you're right.' April wasn't even trying to wipe the tears away. 'Whenever I hung up the phone these last months, I cried. But I'm not convinced this way will hurt any less. My heart is breaking.'

'Mine too,' I choked. 'But it's inevitable, whatever we decide. Hopefully this way, we can both heal a little quicker and not drag it out. It's not the end, April – it's not over. We're just taking time for ourselves so when our time comes, there's no resentment or regret. I need you to be happy.'

I scooped her closer, holding her head to my chest. 'Nothing will shake my love for you, and I'm not saying we can't pick up the phone when we just need to hear the other's voice over the next year or so. We just can't be waiting by it.'

'How am I going to say goodbye to you?' she murmured.

'You won't have to,' I breathed, kissing her, my palms holding her back and head as I pressed my mouth on hers. Losing myself in April as she melted into me. I forced my brain to memorise each moment, taking my time, not leaving an inch untouched or unkissed. Remembering the feel of her dewy soft skin on my fingertips, the way her body entwined in mine and the sound of her rhythmic steady breaths as she moaned gently at my touch.

At first light, I crept out her bed and dressed. April was right – I couldn't put either of us through a goodbye.

Watching her sleep for a few minutes, I wasn't sure how I was going to walk out the door. But if I didn't go now, I never would. Just one look into her eyes and I'd cave.

Grabbing a piece of paper, I scribbled her a note, leaving it on the pillow to find when she woke up. My name and phone number, identical to the one she'd once given me. I pictured her tucking it into her purse, knowing I still carried hers.

Then, I don't know how, but I left. Walking away from April was like defying a gravitational pull. My feet lead weights as I closed the front door and walked to my car. Sitting in the driver's seat, I sent her a message.

I'll wait for you.

*

The weeks and months skipped by, with April constantly on my mind. Yet, as I was going to bed in Manchester, I'd think of her having lunch in San Francisco, knowing we'd done the right thing. Planning video calls and messages around that time difference, fighting to keep a relationship alive indefinitely? Impossible. Things would have died a slow, agonising death. I feared, if April stayed, or we tried to hold onto each other, the depression would creep back until it devoured her.

This way, our love could burn in the background. It was ours, untouchable and constant. And it'd be there when we were both ready. Knowing that eased the agony of losing her.

There were reminders of April everywhere though. The café where the waitress knew our regular two lattes with a shot of vanilla, the canals we walked for miles, talking and holding hands. The pub we drank in, kissing in the corner booth. The library, my car, April's old flat, the student union, the university I'd committed to spending the next several years at. All April-less yet haunted by her presence.

I wondered how April was coping. Exploring a new city. Probably calling Lizzy every time she yearned to phone me. Lizzy would threaten to fly across the Atlantic to give her a shake. Once the initial shock of our break-up had worn off, April would no doubt throw herself into work, her art.

Digging deep, I found some April World enthusiasm of my own and did the same. And meanwhile, I waited.

*

Life, somehow, went on. A year skipped by without a word from April. I hadn't called either, not wanting to pile pressure on her. That hope she'd arrive home and fall back into my arms started slipping further away.

We'd never discussed whether we'd date or not, although I hadn't. Only, then I met Kel. I was honest, told her my heart belonged elsewhere.

'Well, I'm going back home in two years; *my* heart belongs in Aus. I guess we're both unavailable long-term. Doesn't mean we can't have some fun, right?'

Kel's logic was faultless. I'd spent a long time watching other people date, have flings, casual sex and fall in love. It was lonely. We started spending time together. As friends first, but it gradually became more than that. Eventually, I realised I'd stopped mentioning April.

I'd not stopped thinking about her though. Assuming she'd come home eventually and we'd be together. But I'd cobbled together some sort of life in the meantime. That's how I saw it.

Only, two years after we met, Kel dropped a bombshell. She'd got a new job and extended her visa. 'We can move in together now.' She beamed, bouncing on the sofa in excitement. I blinked back, blindsided.

'Ye not bein' fair to that lassie, pal,' Adam warned when I met the guys at the pub a few days later. 'You know she's in love wi ye, right?'

Groaning, I dropped my head in my hands.

'Ye know I'm right,' he added, swigging his pint.

How had I ended up in such a mess?

'I never promised Kel anything,' I protested. 'We've never said the L word, never talked about anything further in the future than the following weekend.'

Adam laughed. 'Youse have been together two years. Ye seriously think that's just some extended casual fling? Course she assumed it'd got serious.'

I groaned again.

'You need to have a conversation with April, mate,' Al piped up. 'See if there's even a choice for you to make.'

April and I hadn't spoken for three years. It'd been nearly four since we were living in the same country. Maybe time had healed, and she'd moved on.

'Ummm, don't think she has,' Jonesy smirked, handing me his phone. After a couple of years of us all avoiding the topic, he'd googled April and found a website about her debut art exhibition. 'It's called "Lovestuck". And it's all about you, my friend.'

I'd seen April's picture on Instagram a lot over the years, but seeing her now, smiling in a professional headshot, my insides did their old flip. And Jonesy was spot on – she'd created an entire collection of sculptures about our relationship and the circumstances forcing us apart.

'Very Taylor Swift,' Adam joked. I shot him a warning look and told him to shut up.

'Mate, it says she's coming home,' Al read from the long blurb. 'After her show closes in San Francisco, she's heading back to the UK.'

I frowned, adrenaline suddenly pumping, palms sweaty.

April was coming home. Why hadn't she told me? My heart was thumping so hard I could hear the blood rushing in my ears.

'What you going to do?' Jonesy asked, bringing over another round of beers.

'Look at his face,' Al laughed. 'We all know what he's going to do. If April is coming back for him, which we all know she will be, Dyl will be waiting at the airport before he's even remembered to tell Kel.'

'Just let Kel down gently, will ye,' Adam said. That old friction he had with April had him firmly on team Kel. Head still pounding, I made my excuses and went home, too confused to listen to their idle banter.

The idea of April coming home churned me up inside. That single thought brought back a tidal wave of feelings I'd kept at bay. Obviously, I'd choose April. I'd hate hurting Kel, but it'd always been April.

Would she still want me, though? Why was I reading about her imminent arrival online?

Back home I sat on the sofa, mind whirring. I had to speak to April, and it couldn't wait. Looking at the time, I calculated it was mid-afternoon in San Francisco, so I nervously dialled her number.

'Dylan,' she answered after enough rings to tell me my name flashing up had sent her spinning. Her voice was quiet, unsure.

'I wondered if you'd know it was me,' I said. 'It's been a long time.'

'Too long.' I heard a door shutting as April found somewhere private. 'It's funny. I spent a year desperately trying not to call you and the last two trying to find the courage to.'

I chuckled, even though it wasn't a joke. More the depressing reality of loving someone far away.

'Yeah, me too. And now I'm calling I don't really know where to start.' I sighed. The awkwardness crackled between us. April could always read me, and she could tell I was upset. Angry, even. 'You're coming home.'

It was a statement not a question, and saying it made my stomach churn. 'I wish you'd let me know. I found out from Jonesy, who read it online. *Online*, April. You didn't think I'd want to know?'

I was twisting the knife, but I was hurt. It didn't quite have the effect I'd intended, though.

'Dylan, are you even single?' April snapped, throwing me into silence. She knew about Kel. Of course she did. She'd have seen photos of us on Instagram. I didn't post much myself, but Kel was always tagging me in stuff. My arm thrown around her, our faces pushed together in some silly selfie. Or Kel perched on my knee in the pub. Our pub.

How had it made April feel? I'd thought little of it. But she'd probably assumed I was in love with someone else, not just whiling the time away, waiting for her.

'I didn't expect you to stay celibate, Dylan. But it wasn't hard to work out you had a fully fledged long-term girlfriend, and those promises you made to wait for me had evaporated. I was crushed.'

Closing my eyes, I bowed my head. I'd hurt her first.

'It was like finding that note on my pillow all over again,' she continued. 'You've been with her for, what, two years now? That isn't waiting, Dylan; that's moving on. Everyone told me I had to do the same, which is why I stayed out here so long. I didn't call because I didn't want to put either of us through the trauma of you telling me about her. And I didn't think you'd want to see me when I got back.'

April explained she'd originally only extended her stay in America for six months to finish her collection. But when she'd seen photos of me with Kel, she'd decided not to come back at all.

'I did wait,' I said, forcing my voice through gritted teeth. 'For a whole year, technically two if you include Rome. You stayed in San Francisco, and you didn't even have the decency to call and let me know, even if it was only another six months. Not a "hey, Dylan, I've got some things to finish and I'm staying a while – mind hanging on a bit longer?".'

Again, she'd made decisions that affect me without talking to me first.

'After that, yes, I started dating someone. Neither of us wanted anything serious. Hell, I didn't even think it *was* serious until she announced she wanted to move in together last week. Then tonight I find out you're coming home, and I don't know what that means or if it even means anything to you at all. So yeah, perhaps a phone call would have been nice.'

April's sharp laugh sounded so alien I had to pull the handset from my ear.

'So you could weigh up your options?' she cried. 'What am I supposed to say to someone about to move in with their girlfriend of two years? "Pick me, pick me"? Should I have swooped in and told her to move aside, honey, because I'm back? I know I should have called when I decided to stay a few extra months, and I'm sorry. But I was scared you'd tell me you couldn't wait anymore. Which obviously, you couldn't.'

As the conversation unravelled, I walked over to the kitchen and rested my elbows on the cold stone counter. We'd been talking all of two minutes, and we were arguing worse than ever before.

'April, I didn't call to fight. All I've had from you for three years is silence and a few Instagram likes. That wasn't enough to hang around for. I phoned tonight because an hour ago I learned you were coming home, and everything shifted. I needed to know what that means for you. For us.'

The L word was lingering in my throat, but I couldn't bring myself to say it. Or tell her that even if it didn't look like it, I had been waiting for her. I wasn't brave enough to put all that out there and have it drop into emptiness.

Besides, April wouldn't let the Kel thing go, and I couldn't blame her.

'What did you say?' she demanded. 'When your girlfriend asked you to move in with her, what was your answer, Dylan?'

I closed my eyes under my hand, knowing I couldn't lie. 'What was I supposed to tell her? Can we keep it casual because I'm still hanging on in case my ex comes back? I said yes, April. I couldn't keep my life permanently on hold. I said yes because I do love her. She makes me happy, and when you left, I thought I never would be again.'

'Then what good was my calling going to do?' April snapped.

'I guess I always thought we were worth fighting for,' I said. 'I was obviously wrong.' Unable to bear arguing anymore, I ended the call with such ferocity I bent my thumb back. Hissing in pain, I straightened up, casting my phone aside. Only, as I shook my hand it dawned on me it didn't matter that we'd rowed or that she'd not said anything I'd wanted to hear. Me picking up the phone to April in the first place told me all I needed to know. I'd still drop everything if I thought she was coming back to me, and that wasn't fair to Kel.

I didn't try to sleep, lying on my bed fully dressed, agonising over what to do next. The moment the sunlight hit the asphalt, I drove to Kel's to tell her the truth.

'For our entire relationship, you've just been waiting for her?' Kel cried, her indignation pinging off the walls. 'It all makes sense now. Why you never told me you loved me, even though I was sure you did. Why you always insisted on booking everything last minute, and why, when I asked you to move in, you didn't look excited. You looked frightened.'

Kel was pacing her living room as she ranted, crying and shouting at me in equal parts. I sat in the armchair, not because I felt casual about breaking her heart but to bring stillness to the room. Following her round would only make the situation more frantic, and I needed her to calm down.

'When we got together, we both said we were just hanging out, having fun,' I said, following her with my eyes. 'But I did love you. I do. I was just always holding back. This is why.'

My excuses were lame. It didn't matter how many times I told her I was sorry, or that April and I hadn't plotted some romantic reunion, Kel still flew between fury and distraught sobbing. Taking me round in circles, unpicking every significant moment in our relationship. Agonising over the reasons she hadn't been able to fill the void April left in my heart.

I didn't know what to tell her as she accused me of being stubborn, refusing to let anyone else in. Of living off the fantasy of me and April.

'It's not real, you know. You've created this crazy love story in your head. But it's not real. This, you and me in a grown-up, steady relationship, that's real. And when it all goes wrong with April again, you'll realise what you've given up for make-believe,' she seethed in a moment when the anger took over. 'It'll end in disaster and tears again, just like last time.'

She was lashing out, but her words stung. April and I had been torn apart by circumstance and I'd already made myself a private vow that if I managed to win her back, I'd never lose her again.

When my phone rang from an unknown number, I almost didn't answer. Only Kel and I had been looping back over old ground for hours. I wanted to ease her pain, but I wasn't sure there was anything else to say.

'I've got to get this; it could be the university.' I'd gone to Kel's early, but the time I was due at work had come and gone.

'Hello?' I answered, standing up and walking a few metres away as she shook her head in disgust.

'Is this Dylan Rose?' The caller had a strong American twang.

'Yes, who's this please?'

The man said he was an officer from the San Francisco Police Department, but after that, things stopped making sense. I asked him to repeat himself several times before his words sank in.

'This must be a mistake,' I stuttered. 'You've got the wrong person.'

'No,' he insisted. Her photo ID matched; it was April. With her being British, they had no record of her next of kin. All she'd had in her purse was her American driving licence and a folded scrap of paper with my name and number on. My mind flashed back to the day I'd written it, hoping it'd be a constant reminder I was back home waiting for her.

'There's a birthmark on her wrist that looks like a heart,' he added.

A roaring white noise filled my ears as the phone slipped from my hand and I sank back down onto Kel's sofa. I was vaguely aware of Kel picking it up, getting the same news from the officer on the other end and turning to look at me in shock. I could see her talking as she wrote something down. Then she was sitting next to me. I could see her lips moving, saying my name, but I was paralysed. The world was moving forwards in time, yet I was frozen.

Unable to function other than stare blankly, wordlessly. Was I even still breathing? I wasn't sure.

I've no clue how long passed, but suddenly I was aware of Adam putting a glass of water in my hand and forcing it to my lips.

'Dylan? Dyl? Pal, ye need to snap out of it. Dylan?' I could hear him, yet I was catatonic. If I moved it'd all become real. April would really be dead.

'Should I call a doctor?' Kel asked Adam, standing in front of me, her forehead crinkled. Her words brought me out of my trance.

'He said he was a police officer,' I stuttered. 'But he could have been anyone. Just some idiot who found her purse and thought he'd play a joke.'

Kel, her own heartache on pause, threw Adam a concerned look.

'They've got the wrong person, they must have, right? She wouldn't do that. We need to call them back.' I tried to grab my phone from Kel. 'Please, we need to call them and tell them they've made a mistake. Or call April. She needs to know what's happened.'

Before either of them could reply, my mum blustered into the room, suffocating me with a hug. Kel had called her too. The feel of Mum's wet tears on my collar brought me further out of my stupor and it started to dawn on me that this was all horribly real.

'I need to call April's parents.' My voice was barely audible. And what was I going to say? All I knew was they'd found her handbag after fishing her body out the water.

'You're in no fit state to do that, darling,' Mum said, sniffing as she held me closer. 'Adam's spoken to the hospital

184

in America, and he's got hold of that friend of hers, Lizzy. We just need to get you home.'

Adam helped bundle me into the car and they drove me to Mum's where my stepdad was also waiting. Thankfully, the twins were at school as my parents helped me into the bed in my childhood room.

Things got hazy after that. I don't remember crying. A string of people took turns to sit by my bed. Adam, Jonesy, Al, Mum. The twins would come in, snuggle under my duvet and put on our old favourite films. When they were there, I tried to muster the odd reply, but otherwise I withdrew into a silent world of grief.

At some point, Lizzy came over. She sat on my bed for hours, in pieces as she explained what'd happened. April had been OK when she first got to America. Focused on her art and the promise of us at the end of her stay. But as we'd drifted apart, the darkness took hold. She'd spent more and more of her time locked in her room or the studio, dwelling on the past.

'She thought you'd moved on. And honestly, she pretended she was fine with it. We all thought she was coping, what with her big art show and everything.'

I stared at my hands as Lizzy spoke. History had repeated itself, and just like in third year, April had retreated from life. Only, I'd not been there to catch it. None of us had.

'She hid it, Dylan. The depression. She told her parents and me she was having therapy online, but she only saw her counsellor twice. By the end she was so ill, she didn't think she had a place in the world anymore.'

April had taken her life the same afternoon as our phone call. That was the excruciating thought boomeranging round my brain as I pictured her, alone and distraught by thoughts of me moving in with Kel.

She didn't know, I thought. *She had no idea I'd been waiting for her all this time. That I loved her.*

'We spoke. Argued,' I croaked, my voice hoarse from lack of use. 'I told her it was too late. But it wasn't too late. I always loved her. It's my fault.'

Lizzy shook her head. Told me April had been too poorly to make proper decisions and that I couldn't shoulder blame. The burden would destroy me. But I did, and I knew I always would.

April's mental health struggles went much deeper than lost love. It was an iceberg, and I was merely the tip. But April had died thinking I'd chosen another life. One without her. She'd let the darkness back in, and this time it had swallowed her whole.

It took a couple of weeks for April's parents to have her body repatriated. Visiting her in the Chapel of Rest at least got me out of bed. She'd been found quickly, after just an hour in the water, and there wasn't a mark on her body. But she still didn't look like my April. The sparkle that had shone from every pore when we'd first met was gone. There was no trace of any of the joy she'd once been full of. She was impossibly still and empty. April really was just… gone.

Her mum asked for her to be dressed in a beautiful long red dress. I sat, stroking April's cold forehead, curling her washed and carefully blow-dried hair behind her right ear.

'I have a million things to say, and yet nothing at all,' I told her. 'The thought of you coming back one day kept me going these last few years. I just didn't for one second imagine it'd be like this. I'd picture our future, especially on the many nights I couldn't sleep.'

Those imagined lives sprung in front of my eyes before fading to whisps.

'A big house with a garage studio for you to sculpt in and an attic full of smelly old artefacts for me. A couple of kids who think we're the biggest geeks ever but still love hearing the story of how we fell in love. Especially our little girl, who looks just like you. We were always off on adventures, whether I was dragging you all to a new dig site in the middle of Guatemala or you were taking us to some fancy art show in Florence or Singapore.'

I'd pictured it all a million times over, almost to the point I didn't know what was real anymore.

'When we were home, we spent whole days curled under blankets watching films and eating pizza. I'd have a midlife crisis, probably start dressing as Indiana Jones again, maybe buy some futuristic drone. You'd just laugh and go along with it until the phase was over. Then we'd get old, see the grandkids at weekends and spend our days sitting in the garden talking about the zillions of memories we'd made. Listening to old playlists – you'd still be making fun of my taste in music or lack of it.'

Sitting there, it struck me that a lifetime of loneliness was all that lay ahead.

'I planned it all, April,' I said. 'Sometimes in my imagination, we retired by the sea in Greece; other times we travelled endlessly. Graduating to old people cruises when life on the road got too strenuous. I dunno, maybe it was all a fantasy. None of those scenarios involved this. You always came back to me, April. Always. I don't know what my life looks like without you.'

I was quiet for a long while, just holding April's hand in mine, wondering how the hell I was ever going to let go. Walk out that room knowing all I had left were one solitary year of memories and a few stupid Instagram selfies. Robbed of a lifetime together, all because I was too proud to tell her during that last phone call that I was unequivocally hers and always had been. That I would be waiting – if she'd have me – when she got home.

'I'm sorry. I'm so fucking sorry.' Finally, the tears came in torrents, making my whole body convulse.

Adam and Al, who'd been waiting outside, finally managed to get me out of there.

'They're closing, pal, come on.' Adam put his arm around me and almost carried me out the door. I hated the thought of her there all alone. But of course, she wasn't really there. She wasn't anywhere anymore.

'You can say goodbye properly tomorrow,' Al soothed. April's funeral. Her parents had chosen to have her cremated.

'I don't want some shrine-like place pulling me to it like a magnet. I don't want to spend my days drawn to the cemetery, unable to tear myself from April's graveside. I want to scatter her ashes in the wind, for April to be free and to feel her all around me,' Sarah had said, her face gaunt and blotchy. It sounded perfect, if it was possible for there to be such a thing in circumstances like this.

I reverted to grieving zombie for April's funeral. Her parents generously allowed me to sit with them, though I felt like an intruder. People hugged me and gave me condolences I didn't deserve. After all, I hadn't been her boyfriend for three years. I hadn't been there to get her help. Jen had flown from America and, through uncontrollable tears, told me how much April had loved me. She invited me over to see April's show, which her parents had agreed could go ahead posthumously.

'April would've wanted people to see her art,' I said, although I knew I'd never find the strength to see it myself.

Sarah let me put something in April's coffin before the cremation. Once again, I found a scrap of paper and clumsily wrote down my name and phone number in biro. *Wait for me*, I wrote. *Wherever you are, wait for me.*

After the wake, I went back to my own place rather than my mum's. But I'd still only get out of bed to go to the university when I needed to. Everyone told me I had to live my life, and I was determined to finish my PhD. Otherwise, staying behind while April went to San Francisco and losing all that time together would have been for nothing. I had little enthusiasm for it – or anything – anymore though.

Most nights, I crawled under my duvet, closed my eyes and, in the darkness, played the fantasy of my future with April over and again in my head like a film. Immersing myself in the fairy tale like some tragic Walter Mitty.

Until Kel showed up around three months after the funeral. Letting herself in, she found me in my usual spot slumped in bed, surrounded by takeaway containers and empty beer bottles.

'Oh… Dylan.' She sighed. 'Dylan, you have to snap out of it.'

'No. I don't,' I groaned, as she started picking up rubbish before giving up and sitting down on the end of my bed.

'Yes, you do,' she said. 'Because I'm pregnant…'

April's Hospital Room

SUMMER 2022

Dylan

My eyes flew open, and for a second, I couldn't move a single muscle. I could see the white sheets and the tubes shrouding April's body. My hand was still curled round hers.

Warm.

Her fingers were soft, entwined in mine. Her skin rough but supple. Not cold, stiff and chalky like they had been moments previously. My chest was rising and falling heavily as I sucked in air.

Closing my eyes again, I steeled myself, before lifting my head to look at April's face. Her eyes were closed, but her lips were plump, her cheeks pasty yet with swatches of pink.

She was alive.

In this life at least, April remained in a machine-forced stasis but alive. My body still shook from the shock of being told she was dead. I could still feel my life stretching out in front of me like a black hole, knowing she was gone. And that she'd taken her own life.

But it hadn't been real. Or if it had, it was in a different time, or some far-off parallel universe.

I can't lose her. It was my only thought.

She had to live.

'Dylan! You look terrible.' Sarah and Ian had tiptoed into the room, and I looked at my watch in surprise. It was morning already. My eyes throbbed like I hadn't slept. Had I been to sleep? It was hard to tell. Leaping through years of an alternative reality had seemed so frighteningly – and exhaustingly – real.

'The nurses said you slept right through; they hadn't wanted to disturb you. But are you OK?' There was an extra layer of worry on Sarah's face.

Using my sleeve, I dried my cheeks and turned over the wet pillow I'd slept on. 'Bad dream,' I croaked. 'April... well, she didn't make it.'

Sarah gave me a hug. It was just what I needed. Her motherly warmth soothed the cold feeling that'd crept over me. Or was it because I'd been slumped over April's bed all night without a blanket?

'She's going to be OK; I know it.' Sarah seemed so sure.

'Sarah, we don't—' Ian started, trying to keep his wife's hopes in check until she cut him off.

'I know, Ian, she's only opened her eyes a few times. But she's in there; I'm certain. Call it mother's instinct, but she's going to come back to us.'

*

'Tell me about this dream,' Sarah said later, as we all tucked into ham salad sandwiches she'd brought from home. I kept the details vague. Leaving Sarah with visions of her daughter's suicide would have been cruel.

'Looking back, all that stuff with Rome. The way April was acting. It was more than her missing her boyfriend. She was depressed.' To me, it was a revelation I'd discovered during my trip back in time, but when I finished, Sarah was nodding.

'I'm certain of it,' she said. 'I'm ashamed I didn't catch it then. I should have. Yet I just thought she was so hopelessly in love she was operating with her heart rather than her head. When she told me about Rome, I kept wishing I'd done something. But I hadn't wanted to be that busybody of a mother.'

'Pah.' Ian was finally laughing. 'You called the university unsuccessfully ten times to try and sort out that Rome debacle for her.'

I wasn't sure April knew her mum had done that. Looking over at her husband, Sarah gave a sheepish smile, before turning back to me with a glint in her eye.

'You know, Dylan, I dumped April's dad when we first started dating.'

April always spoke of her family as this solid unit of three. They'd been content having one child, and April had been happy being an "only". She'd revelled in the attention lavished on her. Mocked me for being a mummy's boy, although I couldn't have been anything else given my dad did a bunk before I was one. But April wasn't a daddy's girl or a mummy's girl. She was both.

'Really? April always said you guys had the perfect marriage,' I replied.

'Perfect? Certainly not. It's pretty close, but I was a bit

like April when I was young.' Ian was still chuckling as Sarah talked, his salt and pepper hair shaking from side to side.

'A bit? She's a carbon copy. You *are* where she gets her dreamy nature from,' he said.

Sarah beamed and looked fondly at her daughter, who had her bouncy brown hair but not her hazel eyes.

'I was a head in the clouds type, and I'd watched far too many romcoms,' she confessed. 'I kept expecting to be swept off my feet and into the arms of a man who solved all my problems. Who was muscle-bound protector and champion of my independence at the same time. A man who declared he loved me after a series of dramatic trysts and encounters. I thought when true love found me it would bowl me over and all that romantic jazz.' Sarah's whole body jiggled as she laughed.

'I didn't think it'd be the quiet boy from college whose idea of wooing me was buying me half a cider in the pub and telling me how the internet was about to change the world. I expected love to be instant and mind blowing, so when it wasn't, I dumped him.'

'Ah, always my favourite story,' Ian joked, taking Sarah's hand and holding it tightly.

'So how did you end up getting married?' I asked.

Gazing adoringly at her husband, Sarah shrugged. 'I missed him. Listening to his stories, the cute way he always asked about my day, the gentle habit he had of placing his hand on the middle of my back as we walked. Love hadn't hit me over the head, but it had certainly crept up on me.' She rested her head on Ian's shoulder.

'So, I called him and invited him to meet my parents.

He was over in twenty minutes flat, and we were married the following year. Our love got stronger every day and still does. There's no one else who could get me through this. Whenever I'm about to fall apart, Ian holds me together.'

I'd watched them deal with April's injuries as a team.

'Now, I know for you and April it was different,' Sarah said. 'Love really did come at you full pelt, like you'd got caught in a stampede of your own emotions. April got trampled by it while you rode the wave right off a cliff. Either way, the whole experience spat you both out, leaving you shell-shocked. Maybe even a little traumatised.'

I shifted in my seat. Seeing our story from the perspective of others was enlightening.

'But for April, it was more than heartache. She had other demons making her ill, and while perhaps we all could have done more, none of us are responsible for her depression.' Sarah sighed.

'You can't blame yourself for what happened back then, Dylan. Life has a way of giving you what you need, and in this instance, maybe it was space, perspective. Some growing up time. You're here now, and that's what matters. Learn from the past; don't agonise over it. Believe me, I'll be watching her like a hawk from now on. Getting her to the doctor the second I see any sign of depression.'

Ian was nodding. They'd clearly talked a lot about this.

'Just promise you'll keep loving my fanciful, passionate, if sometimes impetuous, daughter, because at the end of it all, that's all she really wants.' Sarah smiled.

'I couldn't stop if I tried. I did try, actually. It failed spectacularly,' I admitted, looking over at April. 'She's opening her eyes again,' I gasped.

Ian jumped up to fetch a doctor while Sarah clasped April's hand tighter, talking to her in soothing tones, trying to coax her mind out its medicated fog.

I was watching, pleading for a sign of progress. Then April looked straight at me and for a second my heart leapt at the glistening in her blue eyes. Only then I realised they were tears as April started silently crying.

The Coma

April

Bright white lights were drowning me. Voices I recognised murmured low and constant all around, accompanied by the rhythmic hissing of machines. But my thoughts remained trapped inside my mind, unable to make my body obey commands.

How much time had passed?

After shutting out that unbearable searing pain, I hadn't been able to hear my loved ones talking anymore. Instead, I drifted through time, exploring the memories of a hundred different Aprils, including my own, and the thousands of possible futures ahead. Sometimes I watched from the sidelines; other times I'd be in my own body, or some version of it, taking part like an actor in a TV show.

The last parallel universe had been the worst though. Hopelessness slithered around me like the coils of a boa constrictor, squeezing until I had nothing left to give. I'd experienced something similar in my third year of uni after Dylan left for Rome. Only this had been a thousand times worse.

Alone in San Francisco, my mental self-harm had spun out of control. Every little misstep, mistake and faux pas I'd ever committed fired from my past and into my present like missiles tearing giant holes in my self-esteem. The wide-eyed innocence that once made me a target of the more sophisticated girls at school suddenly seemed deserved. With each heaving breath after that last phone call with Dylan had come a new reason to hate myself. I'd lurched between terror and a loneliness so unbearable, throwing myself off a bridge seemed the only way to find release. Then it'd all gone blacker than black again.

Yet, the shock of it threw my consciousness into my hospital room, and I woke, blinking up at those blinding lights. Now, using every ounce of effort, I managed a slight turn of my head. Only a fraction, but enough for my eyes to meet his. My Dylan.

Not the angry Dylan in Manchester Airport or the one barrelled down by a truck. Not the one who left me sleeping, with just a note to wake up to. Real Dylan. Who must love me because he was here. He'd come back.

One solitary tear slid down my cheek. A few more salty drops followed, and then he was gone. My mind jerked back down into the cold, where I was nothing more than a disembodied jigsaw of memories piecing themselves back together.

A new sensation of warmth came back with me though. Because, despite everything, Dylan was waiting for me.

Just then, I realised I hadn't landed back down in the dark after all. I'd leapt back into a memory. A real one this time. One of my own. It slowly came into focus, and I saw Dylan and I, entwined on his parents' sofa.

Almost New Year, I realised. It was 2019, my third year at uni, just after the only Christmas I'd ever spent with Dylan. He'd come back from Rome utterly dejected after discovering what I'd done. We'd rowed, and I'd begged him to put it on the backburner so we could enjoy Christmas.

Only, watching us together now, I knew this moment had been the beginning of the end. That those were some of the last kisses we'd ever share.

Christmas

DECEMBER 2019

Dylan's lips were on hers, his right hand in her hair while the fingertips of his left edged past the hem of her thigh-high red sequined dress. But as she pressed her body against his, April could tell his mind was elsewhere. Eventually, whatever was bothering him couldn't wait any longer and he pulled away.

'April, I have something for you, and I need you to hear me out before you say anything,' Dylan said, tucking her hair behind her ear.

April's heart raced. She desperately wanted to jump in and give Dylan her well-rehearsed speech. Yet there was a longing in his eyes she couldn't bear to disappoint.

'Before I knew the truth about Rome, I bought you a plane ticket,' Dylan continued, linking his fingers behind her back. 'For the 31st of December. Please, can you just come and celebrate New Year's Eve with me? We'll make our own Italian memories, make the city ours, not mine.' Pausing, he bit his bottom lip, trying to gauge her reaction.

'After, if you still hate it there, you never have to go back. And whatever happens over the next five months, we'll sort it in May after our finals. Go travelling, see the world together. Just don't let me get on a plane tomorrow not knowing if I'll see you next term.'

April flinched at the desperation in his voice. How could she say no? How could she tell him that no matter how much he wanted to fix it, he couldn't? A party in Rome wasn't going to cure her of the crushing depression that had crept up on her since Dylan announced he'd be leaving Manchester. It flowed through her veins like liquid despair.

'It's not that simple,' she started. But Dylan's ingrained desire to make everything OK railroaded through.

'I know it's not,' he insisted, stroking her hair and kissing her softly. 'Believe me,' he breathed. 'I know.'

But he didn't know, not really. No one did. She was incapable of finding the words to explain some days her emotions suffocated her until she almost couldn't breathe. Hopelessness and sadness reached so deep inside her it was like an anchor holding her down. The exhaustion of it all made it difficult to set foot outside her bedroom door. Some days it was difficult to even move. Yet shame rendered April mute.

Spending the last two weeks with Dylan had lifted it temporarily, but only because she forced him to play make-believe, which had been just as exhausting. Now the reality of Rome was back, and Dylan wanted her to run headlong into it.

'Don't decide anything now,' he said, seeing her hesitate. 'Just promise you'll think about it. Please.'

Unable to bear hearing Dylan beg, April agreed to consider it. The following morning, he stood in her parents' driveway after dropping her off and emailed her the ticket.

'Please, April. I love you. Just come to Rome one more time, for me,' he said, kissing her through her tears.

April nodded. 'I love you too,' she choked, standing forlornly by the front door, watching him walk back to his car. But she already knew she wasn't going to use that ticket.

Inside, April fell into her mum's arms, the pressure of the plane ticket spilling over. 'I haven't been coping very well,' she confessed. 'I can't go to Rome and pretend. But I don't want to lose him.'

Sarah was shocked but relieved her daughter was finally opening up, rather than hiding away. 'We'll get you through this,' she promised. 'Focus on finishing your degree and think of all the things you're both free to do after that. It's only five months.'

April nodded, drying her eyes with her palm. But if she thought talking to her mum would help, she was wrong. The thought of letting Dylan down ate away at her. She barely replied to his messages over the next couple of days, still choosing the solace of her duvet to block out what was happening.

'I just need space,' she insisted when her mum fretted.

Worrying sucked all the energy from April's body until it was easier to disconnect from everyone. Even Dylan, whose heartfelt texts were becoming fewer the longer she left between replies.

On the morning of New Year's Eve, April opened her inbox and stared at the plane ticket for the millionth time.

Come on, April, she urged. Willing for the strength to drag herself out of bed, pack a bag and fly to Dylan. Instead, she watched the clock tick slowly until the hands crawled past the flight time. Dylan called several times, but April turned her phone on silent and put it in her bedside drawer. Just before the plane was due to land, she retrieved it and sent one solitary message.

I'm sorry.

She knew it was cruel, yet it was all she could muster. The second those two telling ticks popped up, assuring April he'd read it, she turned her phone off, unable to face his disappointment.

April didn't turn her phone back on until the day her dad dropped her back at uni.

'Dylan hasn't replied since,' she told Lizzy, refreshing her messages on repeat. 'I don't blame him though.'

Lizzy rolled her eyes and handed April a glass of wine. 'You're your own worst enemy. Poor Dylan, waiting at the airport for someone who was never coming.'

April expected more of a tongue lashing from Lizzy. Yet, instead her best friend eyed her curiously, sipping her drink. 'Are you OK, April? Most people put weight on at Christmas. You look like a pale little waif.'

Shaking her lank hair, April tried to find a smile. 'I just need to concentrate on finals. Everything will be OK after that. Dylan promised.' Lizzy didn't look convinced but didn't push it. She knew April could crack under pressure.

Over the next few weeks, Lizzy doubled up on her food shop to make sure April ate. Brought her endless cups of tea and her favourite custard creams as she sat in front of her laptop studying endlessly.

Dylan still didn't call, and April ached for him. But while she desperately wanted to hear his voice, the thought of physically picking up the phone made her want to shrivel up inside herself. Her skin crawled with shame when she thought of him waiting at the airport for her on New Year's Eve.

She imagined Dylan reading her pathetic message, shouting, 'Dammit April,' before shoving it in his pocket and storming back to his room. He'd begged her to go, and now she'd abandoned him.

'We'll work it out when Dylan's back for graduation,' she told Lizzy again one evening as she sank into the permanent crevice she'd created on their battered beige sofa.

'Perhaps you should visit the uni counsellor,' Lizzy suggested, when April once again refused to join her at the student union. 'I'm serious, April, you're going to have a breakdown. You're swinging from utter certainty that it's over, to telling me it'll all be perfect again by graduation. It's rather hard to keep up. Not to mention disturbing.'

April insisted she was fine. Yet at night she'd lie across her bed, twiddling her hair while staring at the last message Dylan sent her. Sometimes, as she dug for the courage to write something, three dots would appear. Dylan was finally replying, or at least trying too. But it'd always disappear after a few minutes with no message arriving.

Until Valentine's Day, when a reply finally landed as April was walking up the stairs into the brightly decorated red and pink student union. Lizzy had finally persuaded her to go out, and they'd had several pornstar martinis as they got ready, preparing April to face the outside world.

It was the first night since the start of term she'd agreed to leave the house for anything remotely sociable.

Dazzling lights from the retro disco ball bounced off the staircase walls, blurring April's vision as she reread the message, trying to convince herself she'd seen the words wrong.

You broke us.

It was brutal. April blinked vigorously, willing Dylan's words to swim into something kinder. The pendulum that'd been swinging between hope and despair stopped abruptly on the latter like a missile that'd found its target. It knocked the wind out of her. For a few moments, she couldn't breathe. Her lungs burned as though on fire. Then the tears came. Gushing torrents of them, washing April's mascara down her face and taking her highlighter somewhere south of her chin.

'This is when he decides to reply,' Lizzy fumed, dragging her to the loos and locking the cubical door. 'Bloody Valentine's Day when you're half cut? I'm gonna kill him.'

Lizzy's rage rubbed off on April and just thinking of those three cruel words made her temples throb.

'I broke us? Me?' she blubbed. She'd spent the last weeks piling the blame on herself, but what about Dylan? Forcing her to make a decision she didn't have the emotional capacity to make with that blasted plane ticket? Putting something so huge on her shoulders when she was at her lowest point?

'Maybe *he* broke us,' April spluttered, her face a mess of snot and tears. Those three little words had reached her all the way from Rome and ripped her heart out. Her head may have been swirling from too many cocktails, but she was suddenly aware that there was no fixing things. No giving each other space to get their heads straight. It was over.

'Otherwise, he'd have said he still loved me, right?' April wept as Lizzy tried to mop her tears with cheap toilet roll that broke off a sheet at a time. 'Or told me he'd still wait.'

'I dunno, April.' Lizzy sighed. 'He's probably a few pints deep too. Just… screw him. Screw the whole maddening situation; get your hot arse to that bar and have a night off from being the CEO of self-pity.' She pulled out her red lippy and slicked it on April's lips. 'We're students for sanity's sake not tragic Shakespearean tropes. I want to get drunk, dance to trashy love songs and see if any of the boys, girls or anyone else on that sickeningly pink dance floor can twerk their way to the top of my Tinder deck.'

Lizzy's harsh pep talk was effective. Within five minutes, she'd wiped off the make-up smears, confiscated April's phone and packed her off to the bar where the football team were playing drinking games. April swiftly ordered a Jägerbomb, then some horrible blue concoction. Every time she thought of Dylan's text, she stopped her eyes prickling by downing another shot.

Seeing her one-woman mission to drink the bar dry, one of the football team sidled over, buying her another cocktail to go with the shot. He was a fresher who'd managed to get a place in the first team, and April noticed he'd overused the Paul Smith aftershave. That's where her memory ended.

It restarted when she woke up. In his bed. Naked. It was 5am; her head still span from all the booze; and she rolled off the mattress, lurching across the pokey room to his loo to throw up. After, April sat on the footballer's bathroom floor with her back to the radiator, grateful he had an en-suite as she sobbed as quietly as possible.

If she'd hated herself before, it had nothing on this moment. Make-up clogged her pores and stuck her eyelashes together; her forehead was clammy from convulsing over the loo; and her hair felt frizzy and irritating on the back of her slick neck.

What have I done? she thought. Right then, she knew she'd lost Dylan for good. She'd done something they could never, ever come back from. She didn't deserve him, and he certainly didn't deserve what she'd done to them.

Going back to a fresher's dingy, smelly room in halls of residence too. April flashed back to Dylan making a joke about that being his biggest worry just before he'd left for Rome. April shrank into herself thinking how she'd fulfilled his prophecy.

Water started shooting furiously into her mouth, her stomach contracting violently as she vomited in the toilet again. This time she wasn't sure it was simply from all the shots.

By 6am, April managed to pick herself up off the floor, make herself presentable enough to sneak out and grab an Uber home. She couldn't face the sticky bus and its judgemental passengers.

Back home, she peeled her cocktail-stained dress off and replaced it with some fresh PJs before throwing herself under the covers, where she read Dylan's message, over and over. Hating that, after last night, he didn't even know how true his words were.

You broke us.

And now she'd made Manchester as uninhabitable for herself as Rome. Thoughts of escaping occupied every thought. Getting as far away as possible where she couldn't hurt anyone anymore.

Lizzy stumbled into April's room around midday. 'I've no idea how I got home,' she said, squinting as she climbed into April's bed, her face still thick with last night's make-up. 'Where did you disappear to? I lost you around 1am when you refused to leave the bar to dance.'

Lizzy had no clue she'd not slept in her own bed. For the first time, she couldn't even bring herself to tell Lizzy what she'd done. That's when she knew Dylan was right. She had broken them. *She* was broken.

'Dunno, it's all a bit of a blur,' April lied, passing Lizzy a make-up remover wipe for her face. 'Shall we order McDonalds and have a Netflix day?'

Lizzy nodded. 'Pretty sure I had my tongue in one of the netball team's mouth last night.'

Finding a smirk, April tilted her head for more info, relieved Lizzy had a drunken story to distract from hers. 'And? Could it turn into a "thing" do you think?' she asked.

'Don't think I got her number.' Lizzy frowned. 'But I definitely thought she was hot.'

'You said that about the guy from your anatomy and physiology course,' April reminded her. 'And he's gay.'

'Well, I guess I'm still the Q in the LGBTQI+ then.' Lizzy's thick black bob shook with laughter as she chucked a pillow at April before ordering McDonald's on her phone. But as they consoled their hangovers with junk food, the icy despair crawled its way from the tips of April's toes up, until it gripped her whole body.

*

A silent coldness sat between Dylan and April after that dreadful Valentine's Day. April felt in a constant state of panic. Wanting Dylan to call, thinking he was cruel not to, but dreading the day he swallowed his pride and picked up the phone all the same. What would she say?

Immersing herself in finals and coursework wasn't enough to help her cope this time. Blurry flashbacks of the footballer with his sticky, nail-bitten hands on her bare skin left her cold.

The truth doubled the weight of the iron anchor around her neck until she longed for release. A morning when she didn't wake up at all.

Scared by the dark thoughts creeping in, yet not wanting to worry anyone, April went to the doctor, who suggested a course of anti-depressants. She refused at first, but as the outside world became a more terrifying place to be, April accepted she needed a bit of extra help.

'It's likely just a temporary measure,' the doctor reassured. April was diagnosed with depression. A type that had a trigger, a root cause: that moment Dylan told her he was leaving for Rome, and she realised she'd lost everything. She was put on a low dose of anti-depressant to get her out the hole and advised longer term talking therapy could help her understand how it crept in to start with. Teach her coping mechanisms.

April waited a few weeks for the pills to kick in. But, slowly, she felt braver and brighter. Then one morning, she got up and got dressed for a lecture without even thinking about it. Walking down the sunny street, she had a spring in her step. Being outside felt wonderful. She felt driven.

Yes, her heart hurt whenever she thought of Dylan. But she got used to the pain rather than succumbed to it. Boxed off the shame she felt about the fresher and vowed to leave it behind by graduating and getting away from it all.

Whenever April wasn't furiously finishing essays or revising, she was applying for art internships across the world, or firing off emails on spec. America, Australia, New Zealand, Singapore, Hong Kong, Dubai, Egypt. It didn't matter so long as it was a different continent. Thousands of miles from Rome and Manchester.

She had several promising replies.

'No surprise there, you're obviously still getting a first, even though you barely bother washing these days,' Lizzy quipped as they both revised for finals.

'My non-washing days are behind me,' April pouted. It was true. Lizzy had noticed April had turned a corner and had stopped insisting she see the university counsellor.

April still didn't tell anyone she'd been diagnosed with depression though. She was embarrassed. Instead, April claimed she needed to get away because she simply felt trapped, like a parrot in a cage.

By mid-spring, she'd been offered a San Francisco internship. Getting that email was the first time since Dylan left that she'd felt any actual excitement zip through her body. Taking a sharp intake of breath, she felt something unfamiliar on her lips. A smile.

It didn't cross her mind to tell Dylan. What would be the point?

'Erm, because you still love him?' Lizzy's lips were pulled into a tight line. 'Because you've been pining after him so much even the postman actively avoids you.'

Ignoring her pithy comments, April promised Lizzy she'd tell Dylan when she was ready. It was a lie. But there was no way of explaining without telling Lizzy about the sordid one-night stand with the smelly footballer. Besides, Dylan hadn't been in touch for months either. He wouldn't care that she was leaving. At least, that's what she told herself.

Dylan's Place

Dylan

'They actually told ye to leave?' Adam asked, eyebrows raised. The four of us were lounging around my living room with a conciliatory curry.

'Yep,' I sighed, watching Al opening foil trays and discarding the lids back in the paper bag. 'Ordered, really.'

It'd only been a few hours since April's parents asked me to go home. And not just to sleep this time either. Indefinitely. I already missed her so much my soul ached. My hands were cramped from clenching and unclenching my fists. I was checking my phone for updates every other second, which hadn't gone unnoticed by the lads. Not that I didn't agree kicking me out was the right thing do. For April.

She'd woken up several times over the last few days. There was a lot of staring and blinking, but she didn't appear to understand when we told her about the accident or her injuries. Doctors assured us it was perfectly normal, she was still heavily medicated, and was otherwise responding well.

It was her reaction to me that was the problem. That first time she looked at me and cried silently. The next time she was so focused on my face she didn't take in anything anyone told her. Earlier today was most alarming. She all out panicked, thrashing in her bed, yanking on the tubes snaking into her skin and down her throat. The fear on her face was shattering. Everyone knew our story; we were the talk of the hospital still. So, after a hushed meeting between April's parents and the doctors, it was suggested I retreat for a while. I was obviously a negative trigger for her.

'When she's more herself again, I'm sure she'll ask for you,' Sarah implored, patting my hand as she held it. She looked so anxious that I nodded and left. She was still fraught about getting all the pieces of her daughter back. I couldn't tell her this was one of my biggest fears coming true. That April couldn't cope with seeing me.

'I get it, I do,' I sighed now, rubbing my forehead. Adam, Al and Jonesy had come over, so I wasn't alone. 'But being banished from the hospital because the woman you love – who's fighting for her life – can't handle seeing you is a total mindfuck.'

'Mate, once April understands what happened, she'll ask to see you; you know she will,' Al assured. He was always one of the champions for a Dylan and April happily ever after. Probably because he'd got his.

'Och, her parents love ye for some reason. They'll tell her all about the forlorn little puppy dog who hasn't left her side, don't ye worry.' Adam, surprising us all with his compassion, as usual.

'Thanks. I think,' I said, throwing my head back on the sofa and staring at the ceiling. More waiting, only now it was from a distance. Lizzy had promised to send regular updates, but I felt useless. Worse than useless. An inconvenience.

'Aye, like I said before, this could all have been avoided if ye'd not kissed her when ye did,' Adam said, wandering to the kitchen for four more bottles of beer.

Jonesy and Al laughed, chucking their twist tops on the pile on the coffee table.

'Five years ago, if you'd shown some restraint and talked to me first, I'd have let ye mop up ma sloppy seconds,' Adam continued, perching on the arm of the sofa.

'Here we go.' Al rolled his eyes so far into the back of his head they nearly didn't come back. Adam had circled back to this a lot over the years. He liked to hold a grudge, even if just to slowly torture me under the guise of banter.

'Wait, hear us out,' he said, his sandy hair springing back into place as he raked his fingers through it. 'April was dating me. They started their relationship by going behind ma back. Which sparked all that drama and theatrics. It all went wrong from there.'

Adam had a point. Right after April's accident, when I'd said I kissed her too soon, that's exactly what I meant. That was the crux point. The moment everything went to hell.

The Coma

SUMMER 2022

April

Waking up was terrifying. I couldn't keep track of how many times I'd fought my way back to consciousness, but every time I arrived in that bright white room, my mind inexplicably went blank.

For the first few seconds, my brain would be an encyclopaedia of memories, all categorised and filed into different sections. My real ones, those of alternative Aprils and the possible futures yet to be made. My eyes would find Dylan's or my mum's.

Until doctors rushed in shining torches in my pupils. Then the name of the handsome man with the gold flecks in his eyes looking at me so intently would fade until it slipped away altogether. I'd reach for a memory of him, sure I'd had one a moment ago, but there'd be nothing.

Just like that, I'd have no idea where I was or why. Overwhelmed, I'd panic, shut out the glare and sink back into the darkness.

It was like existing in two completely different worlds. This one, where I was a jumble of disembodied thoughts, my mind bouncing through cinematic memories and parallel universes. Then the blindingly bright one out there where I was a broken shell. At least here, I knew who I was.

And now, whenever I made it back into that bright room, Dylan wasn't there anymore. He'd gone. Feeling Mum's hand in mine was a comfort; Dad's calm voice helped me feel safe while Lizzy and Jen's idle chit-chat gave me a taste of normality. But it was Dylan I needed. Remembering him, remembering us – it was the only thing bringing me back.

I pictured his face. Not the soft, boyish Dylan from uni, with the grin that played on his lips as he lounged, manspreading on a pub chair. The slightly older, more serious Dylan whose chiselled jaw held a smattering of stubble. The man I'd ambushed on his driveway. I'd never seen that Dylan smile, and I very much wanted to.

I wanted another first kiss. A replay of that dewy Sunday morning when Dylan's soft lips crashed onto mine. Had it really been almost five years ago? I let the memories flood in, until I was back there, looking at Dylan on the opposite end of his and Adam's sofa. The living room clock read 5am, and the cloak of a loaded silence shrouded us.

The Kiss

FEBRUARY 2018

'It's late. Well, early. Better call that taxi,' April said. Unable to put leaving off any longer, she pulled out her phone and opened the Uber app. A few hours earlier, Adam had brusquely offered to order one for her, but she'd tactfully declined, clinging to the last few moments she could spend with Dylan.

Everyone else had trickled off to bed, leaving the two of them up chatting into the early morning, a habit she and Dylan had fallen into the day they'd met. Only, as she tapped on the app, Dylan stood up and started putting on his jacket.

'I'll drive you. I haven't had a drink since closing time,' he said, looking towards Adam's bedroom door.

April paused, her finger hovering over the button. It was a terrible idea for Dylan to take her home. Not because they'd been drinking; he'd sobered up since they left the pub six hours ago. But because of how she felt about him. Still, she nodded her agreement, put her phone back in her clutch bag and found her shoes strewn by the front door.

Pulling her seatbelt on, she looked at Dylan, who flashed her a nervous smile. Yes, she thought. This was definitely a bad idea. The group of them had all ended up back at the boys' house on Dylan's closing time invitation. Shortly after they'd arrived, Adam had proceeded to dump her in front of everyone with his offer to book her a cab home. It was clear she was no longer welcome in their student house. Their toxic fling was over.

April wasn't fussed. She'd spent more time with Dylan anyway, and Adam hadn't even noticed. But Dylan was Adam's best friend. Whatever had been brewing between them, they were in the danger zone.

They drove in silence, but April was sure she could hear Dylan's heart pounding as he pulled up outside the flat she shared with Lizzy. Hers was hammering too, as Dylan stole glimpses at her, and by the time he'd walked her right to the front door, the blood was roaring in her ears.

'Thank you.' She smiled with the slightest head tilt that sent her hair draping over her face like a curtain.

'You're welcome,' Dylan nodded, hovering on the porch as April stepped inside. Their exchange was strangely formal. 'Bye then,' he added, turning to leave. April had almost closed the door when something in Dylan gave in, and he span back, stopping it with his hand.

'Wait...'

Sucking in a breath, April opened it again, staring up at him expectantly. Dylan followed her in, kicking the door shut behind him.

'April, I can't leave without knowing when I'll see you

next. I know things are impossible because you're dating Adam, or you were until a few hours ago.'

As words rushed from him, April was vaguely aware of the mess behind her. Eyeshadow palettes and contour brushes spilled out over the coffee table alongside the dregs of two vodka Cokes where she and Lizzy had got ready the previous evening. A strapless bra and cherry jumpsuit were discarded by the TV from April's last-minute outfit change. Zoning back in on Dylan, April reminded herself he wouldn't notice. He was the messiest of the boys, his books, gadgets and sports bottles staying wherever he dumped them.

'I should go home and talk to Adam first,' Dylan continued, and she noticed his hands starting to shake. 'But before I do I need to know it's not just me that's been driving myself crazy these last few weeks. Because I *am* crazy. About you, April.'

Standing in the living room, April felt like everything around her was slowing down while her insides sped up.

'The first second I saw you, my life got inexplicably brighter. I saw my future play out, and it was with you. Ever since, I've wished I'd finished that damn essay and gone out with the lads instead of having to pull an all-nighter,' Dylan said, barely stopping for breath. 'Then it would've been me, not Adam, chatting up the beautiful girl at the bar who was pining over some undeserving loser. And it wouldn't have been some meaningless fling. You'd have woken in my arms and stayed there, knowing how special you were. How much I needed you in my life. Because I do, April.'

Dylan began chewing on his bottom lip as he finished. For a few beats, April couldn't find her voice. Only Lizzy knew how long she'd ached to hear Dylan say all this. To know the intensity of his feelings mirrored the madness of her own. She could feel it now, rushing off him in waves. They were on the precipice. The danger zone.

April's head told her to be rational and pull Dylan back. But she couldn't find the willpower, so she dived off the edge with him.

'I wouldn't have been sad,' she said, dropping her head and looking up at him through her hair curtain.

Dylan looked confused as she babbled, taking over his monologue. 'If it had been you at the bar instead of Adam, I wouldn't have been the sad girl. Because the guy I was pining over, well, the strange thing is... it *was* you.'

Dylan's brow furrowed. 'Me? How could it have been me?'

The sun had started to rise, shining through the bay window and making the gold in Dylan's eyes glitter. April swallowed, feeling her bones ache with tiredness and the effects of last night's Pinot Grigio throb behind her eyes. Too exhausted to continue her daft charade, she launched into the real reason she and Dylan were in this tangle. Because it hadn't started with her meeting Adam at a bar a few weeks ago. The event that truly sparked the complicated chain of events had taken place several months earlier.

'I saw you,' April said, starting to tremble herself now too. 'In the library one evening after reading week last October. You were in a rush, late with an essay probably, which by the way is a terrible habit. You were bolting through the foyer towards the stairs when you ran slap bang into me.'

Busying herself to disguise her embarrassment, April kicked her heels off by the back of the sofa. 'I dropped my coffee cup, my bag and would've fallen on my arse if you hadn't caught me. You scooped me up, pushed my cup back in my hand and looked straight into my eyes. And I just knew. I was supposed to be with you.'

The kitchen clock echoed in the background as April paused, meeting Dylan's gaze again. The rhythmic tick-tick mimicking the thump of her heart.

'Your mouth was so close to mine, I could smell the spearmint chewing gum on your breath. You tucked my hair out my face, your fingers stroking my cheek, and every part of my body woke up. You asked if I was OK; I nodded; and then you were gone, racing up the stairs for whatever book you were looking for.'

Tick, tick, tick. The second hand rang louder now.

'It took five minutes standing in the foyer to compose myself. My skin prickled; I was breathless, but the fluttering in my chest wasn't just the shock of nearly stacking it. I was overwhelmed by you.'

Dylan's face was unreadable as April's revelations tumbled out.

'I started searching for you wherever I went. Pubs, lecture halls, the student union, coffee shops in town. It drove my friends crazy, especially Lizzy, who loved pointing out there were forty thousand students in Manchester. I even wrote down my number in case I saw you in a hurry.'

She knew she should stop there, she already sounded like an unhinged stalker. She still had the scrap of paper with her phone number on it tucked in her purse.

'I knew I needed to see you again though. Even if it was to check what I'd felt was real or if I was insane. When I was still hunting bars for you after Christmas, Lizzy snapped.'

Noticing April scouring the smokers crowded under the old railway arches while they queued for Ark nightclub in Deansgate, Lizzy had lost it, ranting about her chasing a fantasy.

'This library guy you're searching for isn't real,' she'd roared. Blustering about it being some "nutjob fairy tale" Princess April conjured up after the briefest of encounters. 'You need to start looking at all the guys that do exist. Maybe even shag one of them,' she'd ordered.

April had always appreciated Lizzy's blunt honesty. Lizzy was her voice of reason. Still, her harsh words left April reeling, and once the bouncer let them in, she'd stropped off through the luminescent lighting to the bar.

'I was sitting on a bar stool feeling like a miserable loser when Adam appeared with his confident Scots charm. You know the rest. But, Dylan, if it'd been *you* offering to buy me a drink, I'd have thought it was fate and been terrified of messing up my chance with the guy from the library I was destined to be with.'

April took a tentative step closer to shorten the distance between them.

Tick, tick, tick.

'When I did finally meet you, I was screaming inside, wanting to tear my hair out. And I ruined everything anyway, by making everything confusing and messy. Adam was oblivious to our late-night deep and meaningfuls, but I still couldn't tell if you felt the same or if it was wishful thinking. Until now.'

April's mouth was unstoppable, spilling every secret she'd hidden. Including that she'd only slept with Adam once, on that first night. She needed Dylan to know that.

'I couldn't.' She shrugged. 'He assumed we did, whenever he was too drunk to remember otherwise. Or I'd make some excuse. I was surprised Adam put up with it for as long as he did.'

Dylan stayed silent for a long moment, staring at her in bewilderment.

Tick, tick, tick, tick.

'So, the last few weeks...' A flurry of thoughts danced behind his eyes. 'None of it was about Adam?'

Tick. The clock slowed again as Dylan spoke carefully.

'Never. It was always about you, Dylan. All of it. Meeting Adam was unlucky, I guess. But it got me to you.'

A blundering confession, but the truth all the same. There was nothing else she could add to make it less preposterous. She'd fallen totally and crazily in love with Dylan months before he – or Adam – even knew she existed.

Dylan took a step back, raking a hand through his hair, leaving it sticking up. His eyes flew to the ceiling, his expression unreadable. His jaw clenched as April's revelation sunk in. He was nodding to himself as everything finally clanked into place.

The silence stretching between them was timed by the ticking of the clock, the room crackling with anticipation.

'I'm guessing Adam didn't admit I was the worst fling ever, who wasn't even putting out.' April's joke broke the tension, and Dylan flashed a playful grin.

'Adam tells me when he *is* getting laid, not when he isn't.'

As they shared a smile, the clock sped up again.

Tick, Tick, tick.

Then Dylan let out a breath, linking his hands behind his head, every muscle tensed.

'Fuck. Just… fuck,' Dylan said to himself. Looking at April, then away again, he took several paces back towards her front door, muttering under his breath. April was sure he was going to leave. But then he turned back towards her, dropping his arms and shaking his head in defeat. With two giant strides, he almost knocked her off her feet, sweeping her into a kiss.

One hand lifted her chin while his other curled through her hair. April gasped as his lips softly met hers, nudging her mouth open with his tongue. Wrapping her arms around him, April pulled herself into his solid chest. His body enveloped hers, the feelings they'd battled to keep inside escaping. April was dizzy from the rush of it, her heart beating so fast she felt faint. She knew he wasn't going to be able to stop there; neither of them could.

Suddenly, Dylan broke off, his forehead pressed against April's, slightly breathless as he looked into her eyes.

'Bedroom?' His voice was gruff, and she nodded as he lifted her off her feet, her legs wrapping round his waist as their mouths crashed back together. April was thankful her room was only ten feet behind her.

Dylan carried her in, whirling her around and putting her down with her back pressed against the door. They became more intertwined with the surging intensity, hands roving further, pulling at zips and clasps. Every touch giving April's body the release she'd been aching for, fantasying about, since that day in the library.

'Are we rushing this?' she gasped between kisses.

'Definitely,' Dylan muttered in her ear, his fingers teasing down the shoulder strap of her bra.

'Should we slow down?'

'Probably.' His lips were grazing past her chin, leaving her covered in goosebumps.

'Maybe talk some more?' she asked.

'April?' Dylan paused, his mouth hovering over her collarbone, but she could hear the smile in his voice. 'Do you want me to stop?'

His lips were heading south agonisingly slowly as his fingertips trailed up her thigh.

'Definitely not,' she gasped, a shiver rippling out until her whole body trembled as his warm mouth continued its journey. Then everything went hazy again.

*

It was dark when April stirred, woken by Dylan moving his arm from under her naked form, tangled up in the duvet with his. Her back was warm, curled against his chest. Dylan's stomach growled with hunger as he shook his right arm back to life.

'Hey.' He smiled, and April shifted from under him, until she was sat with her legs hooked under her bum.

'Dylan,' she whispered, needing to say his name to confirm he really was there. That it'd all happened. They'd only slept a few hours after spending most the day exploring each other over and again. April was drained yet energised, not ready for him to leave yet.

Neither of them had thought things would go this far when Dylan offered to drive her home. His impromptu confession replayed in April's mind.

I'm crazy about you.

Her tummy barrel rolled at the memory, and she

pulled the duvet tighter to her chest. The last few weeks of sneaking smiles, sharing life stories and creating inside jokes. It'd all been leading here.

But now what?

She wasn't Adam's ex-girlfriend, but she was his ex-something. And she had a feeling it wouldn't take him long to piece together where Dylan had disappeared off to.

'Do you remember running into someone in the library that night?' April asked, looking down at Dylan. Frowning, he rested his head on his bent elbow.

'No.' He sighed guiltily. 'I was distracted. My essay was already so late I could barely think straight.'

April was disappointed. It'd been a real-life Romeo and Juliet thunderbolt moment for her, and she'd always hoped they'd shared it.

'I wish I did. But that morning when you walked into our kitchen all tiny and dishevelled, I felt it then. And if I thought I was in trouble at that point, well...' Dylan reached up and curled her hair behind her ear. 'Well, now I'm done for.'

He paused, worrying about Adam waiting back home. But as she traced her fingers down his chest, across the smattering of hair between his smooth pecs, the heat between them sizzled. Leaning forwards, Dylan kissed her deeply, lowering her head back down to the pillow, all thoughts of Adam dismissed. As they made love once again, April felt like her body was erupting, the electricity between them exacerbated by finally knowing they both felt the same. They were falling uncontrollably in love. Nothing else mattered but that.

After, as they lay in each other's arms, Dylan's stomach

growled again.

'Shall we order pizza?' April giggled.

'You read my mind.' Laughing, Dylan left a series of butterfly kisses across her nose and forehead. 'There's a tricky conversation waiting for me back home, and I'd like to delay it as long as possible. Not that I could tear myself away from you right now.'

Knowing Adam, chances were he wasn't going to be reasonable. There were lines you didn't cross and your best mate's former – by mere hours – fling was probably up there under ex-girlfriend and sister.

Yet, while April hated the idea of coming between friends, the feeling firmly lodged in the pit of her stomach also told her Dylan couldn't give this up for anyone. She certainly couldn't.

*

The next time April woke up, it was Monday morning. Dylan was sprawled on his back, and her neck ached from sleeping with her head on his chest. She didn't move for a while, taking comfort from her skin on his, the gentle rise and fall of his chest.

'Hey. Again.' He smiled when she eventually moved.

'Hey.' April's tummy fluttered with a fuzzy mixture of euphoria and nerves. Waking up next to Dylan was a dream come true, but she was terrified it'd all implode, Dylan would change his mind, or she'd somehow mess it up. And now Dylan was nibbling his bottom lip anxiously.

'I wish you didn't have to go,' she said. Being together

the past two days, talking and laughing without having to pretend they were just friends, or fear she'd let her gaze linger too long, had been bliss. Effortless but exciting.

Dylan pulled her to him, brushed the hair off her face and kissed her nose.

'I wish we could stay in our bubble. But the real world calls. And I'm pretty sure we both stink.'

April screwed her nose up. 'My shower's only across the hall?' Thoughts of Dylan, water cascading down his solid, silky skin like lashing rain on a marble statue sent a quiver down her spine. 'Twenty more minutes in the bubble?'

After, as they dressed, April felt a pang in her chest. It'd been less than thirty-six hours but saying goodbye to Dylan was going to be a wrench.

Lizzy was in the kitchen when they finally emerged, her eyebrows almost hitting the ceiling. April had dodged her all weekend, only replying to a text asking who she was "entertaining".

Lizzy was the only one who knew the whole story. The library, Adam, the secret late-night chats with Dylan. She'd despaired, watching April dig herself deeper into a hole.

'Dump Adam, wait a few weeks and then call Dylan – it's simple,' she'd said. 'Adam will be several shags down the line; he won't even remember your name; and I've seen how Dylan looks at you. He'll wait.' It hadn't felt that simple at the time, though.

'Morning, you two,' Lizzy said. April couldn't hide her sheepish smiles as Lizzy's eyes bored into hers.

'Morning, Lizzy.' Dylan squeezed April's hand nervously. They both had some explaining to do, and they knew it.

'I'm leaving in five if you want a lift. Just let me clean my teeth,' Lizzy said. April nodded and Lizzy headed into the bathroom. Monday lectures called.

Walking Dylan out into the grey February morning, every nerve tightened, and it wasn't just the cold. April worried what'd happen between now and next time she saw him or when that would even be. Would she be able to kiss him as easily as she had the last day, or would things rewind as though they'd never happened?

Dylan sighed, turning to her as they arrived at his car.

'I wish I could see you later, but I've got to talk to Adam,' he said, his stomach churning at the thought.

'What will you tell him?'

'Everything. It's the least he deserves. I only hope he doesn't punch me.'

'I'm sorry. I never meant to come between you. Or cause such a mess.' April stared at the concrete pavement as Dylan shook his head. Little dark splats started to drip haphazardly onto the slabs.

'I'm the one who went behind his back,' Dylan said. 'This fight I'm about to have isn't going to be about you, April; I've had plenty of chances to be honest with him. Funny thing is, if I'd told Adam how I was feeling, he'd have probably told me to go for it. We've both made some stupid decisions these past few weeks.' Dylan sighed, looking up at the grey sky. 'We both knew what we were doing. What we were getting ourselves into. If we're honest with ourselves.'

April flinched. 'I guess so. I just...'

'I know.' Dylan lifted her chin and kissed her lips softy.

They'd both been selfish; they knew that. But the deeper they'd got, the harder it'd been to see a way out. And now it was too late.

'But here we are. Cold light of day. It's time to tell the truth,' Dylan said, the smile on his lips replaced with a taut line.

April's throat felt tight. Her thick tears splashed down alongside the drizzle and her wet cheeks felt cold as the wind picked up.

'Hey,' Dylan said, stepping forwards and wrapping his arms around her. 'I'm sorry. I'm just dreading this conversation with Adam; I've been a crap best mate. But whatever happens, I'm not walking away from us. I couldn't. This has been the most incredible weekend of my life.'

A gust blew April's hair back as she looked up into Dylan's golden eyes. They shone with warmth, a stark contrast against the dull grey skies. Her tears disappeared with another of Dylan's kisses, and while the words stuck in her throat, she hoped he knew she felt the same.

'Call me,' she managed. 'When you can.'

As Dylan drove away, Lizzy appeared under an umbrella eating a slice of peanut butter on toast.

'I think you better catch me up,' she said with her mouth full, climbing behind the wheel and buckling up her belt one-handed. 'Things seem to have escalated rather quickly with library boy since your date with his best mate on Friday.'

*

Adam had left by the time Dylan arrived home that

morning. April was so worked up, she could barely focus all day, doodling on her notepad at the back of the lecture hall. Time crawled by. She imagined all sorts of scenarios. Adam telling Dylan not to see her again. Dylan refusing. What if they did end up fighting? What if Adam, Al and Jonesy kicked him out?

The responsibility of it all weighed heavily on April until she couldn't take any more. Unable to help herself, she got the bus to Dylan's. Lurking outside in the winter evening darkness, she called Adam.

'Can we talk? Please,' she said when he answered. Ten seconds later, Adam strode out the front door, his freckles dark and thunderous.

'*April*. What do ye have to say for yeself?' His vitriol alarmed her, as he forcefully rolled over the R in her name.

Leaping off the neighbouring wall she'd been perched on and stuttering a reply, it occurred to April how little they knew each other. They'd rarely spoken in any depth since first hooking up three weeks earlier.

Adam leaned over April, blocking the beam of the streetlight, making her feel tiny and insignificant. A silly girl bringing melodrama into his life.

'This isn't Dylan's fault; I was the one with secrets. It was me who stuck around even though I had feelings for your best friend. Please don't blame him for my mess.'

Distain poured out of Adam as he stared her down. 'Aye,' he said. 'This *is* all mostly your fault. Ye used me, from day one. Everything ye did was a lie. Ye manipulated us both.'

April shrunk even smaller, feeling worse because he was right. She'd done exactly that. Used Adam to spend time with Dylan.

'It seems ye've got under Dylan's skin though. He's made it pretty clear who he'd choose. Reckons he's in love wi ye.'

April choked on air as Adam spat the L word at her.

'He didn't tell ye that part?'

April shook her head. Adam knew what he was doing. Stealing a moment from her and Dylan they could never get back. But it didn't matter; they didn't need to say what they already knew.

'I love him too,' she said. 'And I *am* sorry.'

Adam's sneer twisted until it was almost upside down. Chilled, April pulled her coat further around herself to shield from the icy air.

'Then I'll just have to watch while ye screw him over too. Lassies like ye always do. Just do me a favour, and don't come around here again, especially if ye want me to forgive Dylan.'

He span around and stormed back inside, his sandy hair flattening and springing as he went. April was still stood there, stunned and trembling, when Dylan appeared, a tense smile on his lips.

'Adam's rather furious.'

'Yes,' she squeaked. She couldn't blame him, and she was used to Adam's acerbic banter. But she still hadn't expected this level of anger. 'His ego's bruised. And I did use him, which was mean and thoughtless. This isn't about us getting together; he's mad about how we've treated him.' And Adam had a point. 'If you want to sort things out with him, I should make myself scarce. For a while at least,' April added.

Dylan stepped closer and wrapped his arms around

her. Sinking into him, for the first time all day, April's nerves steadied. His body was warm against hers and she closed her eyes as his lips brushed her forehead.

'Thinking about you, then Adam, then you again all day was dizzying. We've gone from zero to a million miles an hour in one weekend, and while Adam will calm down eventually, we have to put the brakes on. For now,' he said.

His words, while reassuring, did nothing to dissolve the lump in her throat. Dylan pulled his head back to look at her, his face lit up by his lightning smile. And those dimples. Only, as soon as they'd appeared, they were gone, and April was swallowed whole by the intensity of his gaze.

'I'll smooth everything over. Probably not tonight, but I will, I promise. In the meantime, maybe I can take you on an actual date? Tomorrow?'

April nodded, frustrated that a tear had sprung and was now trickling down her cheek. Dylan wiped it away, brushing her hair off her face in a way that had quickly come to feel familiar. Then she was melting into one of his kisses, already slightly breathless and light-headed when he pulled away a flash later.

'I'll text you later.' He hung onto her hand until their palms slipped apart as she walked towards the bus stop. The telltale twitch of the living room curtain was proof Adam, Al and Jonesy had been watching from the window.

Later, Dylan messaged.

Whatever you said to Adam, it helped.

He'd made Dylan pay for the beer, order everyone pizza and dished out plenty of barbed comments about sloppy seconds. Adam had also made it clear April wasn't welcome in their house. But he'd not kicked Dylan out or broken his nose.

Hope so. Sorry for just showing up. Miss you.

He just needs time. Miss you too. Promise it'll be OK and whatever happens, I'm all in with you.

April understood the meaning behind those two words.

All in, she replied.

*

After that, despite trying to slow things down for Adam's benefit, April and Dylan went full throttle. Neither of them had ever considered it was possible to love someone that much. Just seeing Dylan made April's heart throb. He had a smile that he saved just for her. It warmed his whole face up, softening the brown in his eyes so they swam with golden. It was like he was reaching into her soul and breathing fresh life into it. All day, she'd count down the seconds until she could see that smile.

And April was effervescent. Making her laugh became Dylan's entire reason for existing. At least, it felt that way to him.

Within weeks, it was like they'd always been Dylan and April. Even imagining her life without him made her palms sweat and her heart rate quicken. Dylan spent most nights at April's, at Adam's behest. Being together was so intoxicating April felt lost and frighteningly alone the nights she had to go home without him.

'Honeymoon phase,' Lizzy insisted. But April couldn't see it ever fading.

For several weeks, they obeyed Adam's orders for April

to stay away from the house. Adam would occasionally chuck an insult Dylan's way about mopping up his cast-offs.

'I know wa ye girlfriend looks like naked,' was his favourite. April wasn't sure that was even true given they'd been plastered, and the lights stayed off the one and only night she'd had sex with Adam. Still, Dylan bit his tongue, waiting for Adam to get bored of taunting him. Plus, part of him believed he deserved it.

Until one night at the pub, after a few too many, Adam started bragging that he'd only kept April around to pull other women. Feeding his future conquests some sob story that she was about to dump him, flashing his charming smile and stockpiling their phone numbers. While Dylan and April were enjoying the throes of their new relationship, Adam had been working his way through his list. Or so he said.

'Well, we all know I wasn't getting laid, so I figured I had te get something out of her,' Adam smirked.

Dylan flew at Adam, accusing him of using April like bait. Al swiftly pulled him back, while Al's girlfriend, Jodie, calmed everyone down. Made everyone agree that they'd all acted badly, and it was time to put it behind them. Jodie could be very persuasive; it was easy to see why Al was besotted.

That night, Adam agreed April could go round for post-pub drinks and, after that, he tolerated her existence.

*

All too soon, their second year came to an end. Everyone

was scattering home for the summer holidays. Dylan's family only lived an hour away from April's, yet it might as well have been Mars. They'd both got full-time summer jobs, too, and April dreaded spending so much time apart after waking up every morning to his butterfly kisses or his solid form curved round hers. Dylan's presence was a comfort blanket. An incredibly sexy one at that.

On their last night together, April lay in his arms across her sofa, his body rigid under hers. She thought he was building up to tell her he loved her. Something they'd not said, thanks to Adam's successful steamrolling over of that romantic milestone. Turning to kiss Dylan, she hoped to calm his nerves. Skimming by her lips, he buried his face in her hair, linking his fingers through hers.

'I love you,' he whispered in her ear, relaxing as he released the words. Then he kissed April again, brushing her cheek with his thumb. 'I love you, April,' he said again. 'I'm sorry I waited until now to tell you that. But I love you. An insane amount.'

'Me too,' April said, resting her head on his chest and breathing in his woody aftershave. 'I loved you that first day in the library and even more now.'

They laid in silence for a few minutes, absorbing the moment, then April kissed him again. A deep, charged kiss that was intended to head only one way.

Only, Dylan pulled away.

'Wait, there's something else,' he said, his muscles tensing again. April suddenly felt anxious as he launched into his "something else".

'I only found out today,' he said carefully. 'But I've been given a last-minute place on the study abroad programme next year. In Rome.'

Horrified, April's hand flew to her mouth as Dylan explained.

'I hadn't even applied,' he said, scrutinising her face. 'But a place unexpectedly opened up. And it's Rome. One of the most historic cities in Europe.'

Dylan started talking quickly about how he'd be working with some of the finest historians and field specialists at the Crypta Balbi, the archaeology branch of the National Museum of Rome.

'I can't turn it down, April, I can't.' He'd noticed her stunned silence. But the less she said, the more he rambled. 'The idea of being so far away from you kills me. But I'll never forgive myself if I don't go. It could change my entire future.'

April tried to squeeze back the tears springing in her eyes, hardly able to look at Dylan as she focused on breathing in and out.

How could this be happening? she thought.

'April,' Dylan said, leaning forwards, taking her hands again and touching his forehead to hers. He'd known she'd be upset but was still shocked at how she was taking the news. 'I love you more than anything and I know you feel the same. Which is why we can make this work. You can come over for half-term, and we can visit each other every month. If we book now, it's dead cheap.' He felt his own panic start to match the look on her face.

'Then I'll be back for Christmas, and Easter, and by then it's finals. After we graduate, we can plan the rest of our lives together. We won't go two weeks without seeing each other, I promise. Can you just say something? Please.'

He'd thought it'd be so simple, broken down into a few weeks per term. But April looked as though she were made of glass, about to shatter into a million pieces.

'You've really thought of everything,' she said, her voice weak as she fought to stop it cracking.

'If you don't think we can do it, then I won't go,' he said, becoming desperate. 'I'd choose you over Rome. You're the most important thing in the world to me.'

April took in Dylan's strained, puzzled expression, struggling to find anything to say. She felt the same. Being with Dylan was the most important thing to her too. It was why she'd just signed the lease to live with Lizzy again next year, taking her best friend completely by surprise. Shaking her head though, she knew she couldn't ask him not to go.

'You'd resent me, eventually.' Her voice was barely a whisper, and one by one, the tears she'd been holding in started falling as gulping sobs overwhelmed her.

'You have to go. I just... I just...' She didn't know what else to say, so she threw herself into him, blubbing into his chest. Alarmed and racked with guilt, Dylan held her, stroking her hair before eventually lifting her up and carrying her to bed. They slept in their clothes on top of the covers, April crying herself to sleep while Dylan just said he was sorry over and over. Wondering why on earth him spending a year studying abroad was the end of the world.

But it was. Her heart was in shreds. She'd planned their third year together, in Manchester, and it was all gone. She couldn't see how they'd survive this.

*

April's eyes were red raw when she woke up. Dylan looked at her, a pained look in his eyes. She spoke before he could.

'You have to go,' she said, her voice flat. 'Turning Rome down would be crazy. I'm just sad. And scared, because you'll be out there experiencing all those new things, having the time of your life, while I'll be here. In Manchester. Going to the same places with the same people. Not working in some of the most culturally stunning museums in the world.'

Dylan frowned. 'Well, it'll just be one museum. But, April, we can do this, I promise. Every morning you'll be the first thing I think of, and I'll never go to bed without saying goodnight. We have summer together first and I'll spend every second I'm not working with you. I'm all in, now more than ever. Loving you is part of me.'

Dylan was desperate to make it work, and April wanted it to. She really did.

'All in,' she said, digging deep to find a small smile. 'It's disconcerting, trying a long-distance relationship. I'm scared of how hard it's going to get.'

Dylan pulled her tighter into him on top of the duvet. He'd been so thrilled to be picked by his course tutor, despite his casual approach to deadlines, that he'd convinced himself it'd be easy. They loved each other; they'd see each other every few weeks; what could possibly go wrong? he'd thought. Only now he saw it wouldn't be quite that simple.

'I'll be strong, for both of us,' he promised. April worried that was a lot of pressure to put on one person but gave into him as his fingers lightly brushed down the curve of her spine and his lips found hers.

April sobbed again as they packed her belongings into her mum's boot. Saying goodbye as the car pulled away felt impossible, even though she was seeing Dylan later that night.

During the hour-long drive, April told her mum everything.

'Oh, April, no,' Sarah despaired, taking her eyes off the road to stare at her daughter in disbelief. But there was nothing her mum could do other than watch her daughter cry in the passenger seat.

April felt something shift inside her too. For the first time since they'd got together, they'd left their cosy bubble, and their relationship was no longer warm or safe. Underneath her heartbreak, April felt cold and angry at the world.

*

Dylan was excited about Rome. April wasn't. It was a difficult dynamic to juggle that summer. Still, they both worked nine-to-five temp jobs so Dylan could drive over every Friday night and stay until Monday morning. With no coursework, exams or house parties to distract them, and Dylan's departure imminent, their relationship intensified.

They'd talk into the night, laughing. Spend whole days in bed. Thankfully, April's parents were understanding.

When they were at Dylan's, they'd take his twin sisters out. April's heart ached watching Dylan dote on Ivy and Lola. His protective big brother role quickly became one of the sexiest things about him. They were the life and soul of his family.

Yet that invisible but deafening countdown to Dylan

leaving ticked. They tried to gloss over it, but the time to say goodbye loomed.

'I just want to skip ahead to graduation,' April told Lizzy on the phone. 'Fast forward through it all so it can just be me and Dylan again, without worrying about Rome.'

Lizzy sighed. 'April, tell Dylan the truth. For your sake as well as the rest of us. Please? Just start being more honest and tell him how you're feeling. Keeping secrets keeps getting you in a mess.'

'But—' she started, knowing another Lizzy lecture was coming.

'No buts, April. It's not his fault he's going to Rome. Don't ruin this for Dylan now. You love him, right? Then start communicating better. This fantasy land you live in, where everything must be perfect, isn't sustainable,' she said, hitting full rant mode. 'Life isn't perfect. But Dylan, he pretty much is. That gorgeous boy would stay if you asked; he'd go to the bloody moon if you wanted him too. For some reason, he loves you down to your silly little daydreaming knobbly knees. So, give him all the gory details, then you can deal with it together. Don't hold him hostage in April World, because trying to stay in that utopian hellhole will end up hurting you both.'

Lizzy rounded off her harsh words with promises to spend third year being April's sounding board whenever she needed to rage, or cry.

'Or just get ridiculously pissed,' she added. 'But I will not be your secret keeper, or your enabler, April.'

Lizzy twisted the knife, pointing out that Dylan was already torturing himself about leaving. 'You both know he has to go. So give him a break and talk to him properly.'

April promised to try, wondering how she'd got so lucky having a friend like Lizzy. Unafraid to call her on her crap, painfully honest, but always, always in her corner. It was what April needed, and she repaid the favour by forcing Lizzy to lighten up when her constant mockery of the world became too vicious.

*

'How have you got everything into one suitcase?' April asked, looking at Dylan's bag in his boot, surrounded by her mountain of things.

Dylan shrugged. 'Because the only thing I really need, I have to leave behind,' he said, slamming the boot shut and kissing her on the nose. April sniggered at his corny line. Humour only got them so far though, as Dylan pulled onto the motorway to drop April at university before heading to the airport.

'I'm scared we won't make it,' April blurted. It was her biggest fear and she'd spent all summer plucking up the courage to raise it. 'What if you're having so much fun in Rome, seeing me becomes an inconvenience?'

April stopped there, unable to explain the envy building inside her. It was too toxic to admit.

Dylan looked over at her while he was driving. Then he burst out laughing.

'That's what you've been bottling up all summer? April, do you not think that's exactly how I'll feel, but in reverse? I'm terrified you'll move on with some eager fresher who follows you around like a puppy dog.' He looked at the road then back at April.

'You'll be here partying with all our friends, while I'm over there on my own. I'm scared it'll be *you* who'll be too busy to miss *me*.'

Shaking his head, Dylan turned off the motorway. 'April, when you're in my arms, everything gets quiet and calm. Seeing you at the end of a bad day, this relief sweeps over me. I don't know how I'm going to get through a year without that, but I will if I know that in nine months – because that's all it is really – I'll never have to go a day without seeing you ever again.'

April looked at him now. Most people made her feel silly for being dreamy. For living on her own planet. Not Dylan. He wanted to move in and measure for curtains.

'I love you,' she said, staring out the window at the blanket of cloud mirroring the grey road. 'You make me feel like my flaws are my superpowers. How do you do that?'

'Just promise me one thing.' Dylan smiled. 'Wait for me. Whatever happens while I'm in Rome, promise you'll be here after. I'm planning on seeing you so often you'll barely know I'm gone. I'll be a constant ding on your phone, the first face you see when you wake up. But, if things do get difficult, if we do lose our way, promise me you'll be here. Because I'll wait for you.'

It seemed such an easy promise to make. 'I'll be here. I'll wait,' April said.

They spent the rest of the drive in silence, their thoughts moving to how they were going to say goodbye.

*

An hour later, they parted at April's. It was more private than the airport and April was scared she'd fall apart.

'I'm back in two weeks. It's already booked. Pretend I'm just going on holiday,' Dylan said, trying to be positive. But he hated that moment every bit as much as April did. He could still taste her tears as he turned to walk away, blaming himself for causing her that pain.

And the moment she closed the front door, April crawled into bed to cry. It was only Rome. But it may as well have been the moon. Over the next weeks, April came to understand what it felt like to just exist. She'd planned to take it day by day, but she considered it a success just making it to the next breath.

Waking up was the worst. Remembering where Dylan was crushed her, and it didn't matter what photo or message was waiting on her phone from him. She was alone. Not that she didn't put on a good show for Dylan. Doing her make-up and smiling when he called. They exchanged thousands of messages, from declarations of love to what they had for lunch.

But April barely left the house. Telling Lizzy she needed to stay home and study. Visiting her parents every other weekend and telling them the same. No one clocked that she was living in her PJs most of the time.

During Dylan's first visit, she showered, put on her favourite dress and leapt into his arms. Running on that euphoric feeling his kisses gave her for forty-eight hours. She was alive again.

And yet, the countdown until he had to leave left her feeling cold. Saying goodbye that time was ten times harder. Neither of them knew why. It just was.

A sadness rose inside April and swallowed her heart. The heaviness on her chest making it hard to breathe until it was easier to spend most of her time in bed.

Dylan struggled too, but the reality of studying abroad kept him afloat. His course was hands-on, forcing him from his room to experience the ancient relics of Rome and work amongst his team of peers. Missing April became a constant ache he carried around with him.

*

'Welcome to Rome by night.' Dylan grinned, meeting April off the plane when her turn to visit arrived. 'I've got a tour all organised,' he said, picking up her bags like an overenthusiastic puppy bouncing around her feet. He'd put hours of effort into their weekend plans, but April couldn't face it.

'I just want to be with you tonight,' she whispered, sinking into his arms. 'Please?'

Dylan's shoulders drooped and his smile faltered, but he pushed aside his disappointment and took April back to his room. Zoning out their surroundings, they focused on only each other – and the authentic Italian pizza Dylan ordered.

But in the morning, it was still there haunting April. Rome, the city that'd taken everything from her.

Picking up on her resistance, Dylan was on edge by the time they hit the city streets. Nibbling his lip and talking too quickly as he pointed out his favourite bar and spilled secret historical snippets he'd found out from his tutors.

'This is the oldest café in Rome. I come here because it makes me think of you,' he said, as they sat having a morning coffee in a cosy nook of Caffè Greco. Dylan was telling April about the famous artists who'd frequented there for nearly three centuries to chat about art and politics.

April listened, laughed and smiled. But it never quite reached her eyes. Her thoughts kept drifting, and she pictured herself sneaking off to this café to enjoy a quiet cappuccino while doodling in her sketch book. Drawing on the energy of some of history's most important artists. A couple of centuries too early for Michelangelo, but very impressive none the less. Dylan knew her well. The café was perfect and definitely would've been her favourite place if she were the one studying in Rome.

Next, they made fleeting visits to the Colosseum, the Pantheon and the Roman Forum before Dylan whisked April to Vatican City. For a brief moment, she was allowed to be transfixed by Michelangelo's "Pietà" sculpture inside St Peter's Basilica. Looking up in the Sistine Chapel brought tears to her eyes. Dylan squeezed her hand, assuming she was moved by the beauty of it, which she was. Yet April was also mourning. The ceiling eclipsed Manchester's cathedral a million times over, and it wasn't lost on her that one of their biggest landmarks was the Etihad football stadium.

Rome was a dream. Beautiful. Old yet modern, romantic but bustling and exciting. Everything April knew it'd be and more. If only being there didn't make her insides churn with longing.

Later, as Dylan took her to his favourite student pasta place, he was almost glowing with pride.

'So that's our whistle-stop tour. Next time we can see the bits we missed and revisit your favourites.' His cheeks were adorably red from being outside all day, and he'd splattered spaghetti on his T-shirt eating too fast. But still, April couldn't muster a real smile. She wasn't sure there'd be a next time.

Dylan's intentions were sweet and thoughtful. Everything Dylan was. But she didn't want to be dragged around some of the world's most historical architecture at a hundred miles an hour. She wanted to explore every ruin, relic and piece of art individually, in her own time, over weeks and months. Memorising every brush stroke and flawless chunk of chiselled marble.

Rome had given Dylan something special. A spark that wasn't there before, like he could see his potential in the ancient ruins he was helping dig up.

I used to give him that fire, April thought.

Dylan had taken her to all the places he knew she'd love. But Rome wasn't hers; it was his. And it was giving her boyfriend everything he needed, while she felt like she was just dragging him down. Making him anxious. No matter how hard April tried, she couldn't shake the awful reality that she'd be going home the following day, leaving Dylan and Rome behind.

After dinner, Dylan took her to a bar to introduce April to his new friends. He'd talked so much about April they felt like they knew her, making their excited welcome genuine and heart-warming.

'*Ancora più bella della tua foto, April*,' a feisty Monica Bellucci lookalike named Giana beamed, brushing both cheeks with a kiss. 'Dylan does not stop talking about the girl who brings the sunshine.'

'*Sei troppo gentile. È bello conoscerti*,' April replied.

Dylan's jaw dropped and he looked at her in shock. 'You speak Italian? Why didn't I know that?'

April shrugged. 'I taught myself using an app, but I've never put it into practice. I'm actually understanding it better than I thought.'

Dylan eyed her curiously, before grinning and kissing her. To him it was just another part of April to marvel. 'You never stop surprising me. But you could have helped translate when I got us lost earlier.'

Lively chatter buzzed around the table, jumping between Italian and English. April could only follow the Italian when spoken slowly, but she adored the European atmosphere the dual languages brought, and Dylan looked at home amongst the melee. Giana translated anything important they missed.

April tried to join in, laughing when they explained their private jokes and told stories about Dylan constantly getting lost on the metro. But secretly she felt like she'd brought nothing but the UK's grey, cloudy sky over to Dylan's Italian haven.

'I'm tired,' she announced after a couple of hours. It was only 10pm, and his friends were just getting going. Disheartened once again, Dylan took her home.

'Have fun, Romeo and Giulietta,' Giana called after them. They were both relieved his friends assumed they were sneaking off to tear each other's clothes off and not because April was sucking all the joy out of the weekend. She knew it was far less than Dylan deserved. She felt less than Dylan deserved.

'This is just so much harder than I even imagined,' she told him later. Her excuse for ruining one of their only weekends together for nine months was weak. But Dylan nodded.

'I know,' he agreed, curling his hand through her hair and kissing her deeply. April got lost in his kiss until Rome faded away and all that mattered was how much she loved him. For a second, the nagging sorrow disappeared. Yet, as she boarded the plane home, it returned with a vengeance. And she knew she could never visit him there again.

*

'You're fading before my eyes, April,' Dylan said one night as they curled up together in her bed. It was reading week, and as promised, Dylan had spent it in Manchester. They'd gone to parties, seen their friends, but mostly they'd spent it naked in her room. April had developed a carnal need for Dylan. He loved it, but he also could see that there was something deeply wrong.

'You used to radiate light, and now, it's like you're disappearing,' he said, peering into her eyes. 'I'm trying to grab hold of you, but I'm flailing in the dark. Help me out. How can I make things better?' He was desperate to close the gap between them before flying back to Italy.

'It's just hard, that's all,' April said. 'I'm trying to take it a day at a time.'

Dylan told himself Christmas was round the corner; they'd have three whole weeks together. And by then, they'd almost be halfway through, which he hoped would buoy his girlfriend. So, he didn't push it, flying back to Rome with that same ache in his chest.

Then, the day before he was due home for Christmas, he found out the truth.

April spotted Dylan from her living room window, pulling up outside her flat to drive them both to his mum's. He was pale, his forehead furrowed. He was chewing his bottom lip too, with no sign whatsoever of his happy dimples. She knew he'd found out her secret.

Opening the door before he could knock, April looked up at him. Instead of diving straight for her lips, he pursed his more, looking defeated with his hands buried in his jeans' pockets. His hair had grown a lot, and it was sticking out all over the place where he'd been raking his hand through it.

I should have told him, April thought.

Lizzy had been right. She was always right. April should have confessed the second he told her he was going to Rome.

'Why?' Dylan pulled his hands out his pockets, gesticulating wildly. 'Why, April? And before you answer, I already called Lizzy. I knew she'd tell me the truth. But you should have told me. Why didn't you? God, April, what are we supposed to do now? I can't fix this.'

Inside, he paced across the hall and into the kitchen, turning to lean on the counter. April opened her mouth and closed it again. She didn't know what to say. She'd been terrified of having this conversation and where it'd end.

'How did you find out?' she asked.

Dylan rubbed his face with his hands. 'I bumped into Shaun at the end-of-term party last night.'

Bloody Shaun, April thought. He was on her course and also spending his third year studying in Rome. Dylan and

Shaun didn't know each other, but they'd got chatting over a beer.

'Imagine his surprise when I told him who my girlfriend was. "History of Art April?" he asked. The History of Art April who'd been desperate to win a spot in Rome since the day she arrived at university. The April who told everyone who would listen – except me – she'd only chosen the University of Manchester specifically for the opportunity to study in Rome. The April who then dramatically pulled out of the study abroad programme at the last minute because she didn't want to leave her boyfriend. *That* April?'

Dylan was trying not to shout, but it was hard. April had put them in an impossible, irreparable situation.

'The April who decided studying art abroad could wait because she'd fallen in love. Do you know what it was like, hearing that from some stranger?'

Listening to Shaun's revelation, Dylan had gone pale. It'd felt like the walls of the bar were closing in on him.

And hearing the truth from Dylan's mouth like that made April feel so small. So ludicrously stupid.

'If I've got this straight, you sacrificed Rome for me – without even letting me know – and then because life is just one big fucking cruel joke, I get offered your place instead. Which I snapped up. How does that even happen, April?' Dylan shook his head in disbelief. He'd spent the flight home going over and over it in his head.

When April finally spoke, her voice sounded like it was someone else's. 'The art programme starts in the summer. I was supposed to leave that week. There was no time to replace me, so they decided to send an archaeology student to start in the September instead. Believe me, it was the last thing I expected.'

April sank to the floor, overcome with exhaustion. Her legs felt weak as she sat cross-legged with her back against the plate cupboard. The gold in Dylan's eyes flashed with anguish and he sat down next to her with his knees bent.

'I didn't tell you about my placement in Rome at first because I didn't want to jinx it,' she said. 'Then I didn't tell you because I was scared what it meant for us. But Shaun's right – I only chose Manchester uni because of the Italy programme.' April picked some fluff from her sock as she spoke. 'I read about it when I was fourteen, and it became my single ambition. But it was competitive; I needed to ace all my exams. By the time I found out I'd got the last spot, I'd met you, which was like this fairy tale romance.'

Dylan bowed his head and closed his eyes as everything started making more sense.

'I was so torn I ignored it for months, until the deadline passed when I was supposed to provide all my travel documents. I'm never late with anything, and I realised it was because I wanted to stay with you more than I wanted to go. The arts programme started in June, so we wouldn't even have had the summer together.'

April looked at Dylan now. 'I couldn't bear the thought of leaving you. I told myself that after graduation we could go to Rome together, maybe even tour Europe, visiting historical sites you've read about, the best galleries and museums. You know what I'm like, with my stupid daydreaming. I convinced myself that was my new dream, and I'd spend third year here, with you.'

She'd been utterly floored when Dylan told her he'd been offered her spot that same evening. It'd been a brutal blow. She'd given up everything, and then the reason she'd done it was whipped out from under her. The memory of it alone made her nauseous. As Dylan had told her he was going, she'd had to battle hard not to throw up.

'I wouldn't have let you give it up,' Dylan said. 'Never. I could have spent the summer in Rome with you, waited tables, got a bar job. We'd have made it work. Being a dreamer isn't silly; it's one of the most beautiful things about you. I love that you have hopes and make all these plans, especially when they include me. But you need to loop me in.'

Seeing her shivering, he pulled her to standing, led her to the sofa and handed her a blanket.

'I feel like I stole your dream, April,' he said, his voice shaky and quiet. 'How do I make up for that? I don't know what to do.'

He started picking his nails in frustration while April grabbed a tissue and wiped her eyes. She'd made a mountain of Everest proportions for them to climb.

'I know this is all my fault and I feel unbelievably stupid. When you told me you'd been given my place, it wouldn't sink in. It was like having my heart smashed twice. First, because you'd be gone, and second, because I'd lost Rome when it's all I'd thought about for six years,' April said.

'This is killing me. I've taken something from you, something you can never get back. I'd never, ever want to hurt you like that,' Dylan said, before groaning with despair. 'Then when you visited, I raced you through all those places you'd been dreaming of in about five minutes flat, thinking you'd love seeing so much in one day. Of course you were despondent. And no wonder you don't want to visit again. I've ruined an entire city for you.'

'I ruined it.' April shrugged. 'But yes, spending forty-eight hours with the two things I wanted most in the world – you and Rome – then having to leave again, was torture. My heart broke when I arrived and saw how perfect the place was, then shattered again when I left you there.' She hated that she was ruining it for him too.

'You're doing incredible, and I'm so proud of you, Dylan.' She sniffed, meaning every word. 'I'm destroying something that's clearly changing your life. It's not fair on you.'

'If you'd told me all this in the summer, I could have done something,' Dylan huffed, his frustration boiling over. He always wanted to mend things for her and hated it when he couldn't.

'It was too late for me; I'd turned it down. And I couldn't ask you to give it up too. You were so excited; it would have been selfish.'

They talked, argued, then talked some more. April was sick of faking smiles, sick of crying. She wondered how she could be so in love yet so desolate at the same time.

'Now what?' Dylan asked. 'I can't lose you. You mean more to me than fucking Rome. I almost hate the place.'

'But we both know you have to go back,' April told him.

'Then I'll visit every other weekend. I'll increase my loan to cover it. April, I'll do anything to make this OK, just, don't make any more rash decisions. And don't keep anything else from me. Please.'

It was an impossible situation though.

'Dylan, it's third year. There's your dissertation, finals. My finals. Be realistic. I love you, and I want to get through this; I just don't know how yet. Can we just spend Christmas together, like we planned? Please?' April was pleading but she didn't care. For now, she needed to pretend.

The Coma

SUMMER 2022

April

Sucked from the memory and back into the cold emptiness of my coma with that gut-wrenching argument fresh in my mind, I felt this immense compulsion to tell Dylan I was sorry. For Rome. That's what had killed us. It'd turned our relationship into a pressure cooker.

The urge was so strong I mentally pulled myself towards those bright lights. With every ounce of energy, I connected my mind and body to fling my eyes open. Only, when I tried to speak, no sound came out. Frantic, I started tugging at the tube going into my mouth and down my throat, almost choking and gagging as I flailed.

I needed to tell them to bring Dylan back. Before I forgot everything again.

Blinking rapidly round the room, I searched for a familiar face. In seconds, Mum and Dad were standing over me, saying my name.

'Calm down, April,' Dad soothed. His voice stayed even, but panic reached his eyes.

Doctors arrived, and I felt my limbs being held as the offending tube was gently pulled from my throat. With a wheeze and a splutter, my chest rose, and fresh, cold air not pumped by a machine flooded into my lungs.

'Dylan,' I rasped. 'I need Dylan.'

Dylan's Place

SUMMER 2022

Dylan

'Do you boys remember Dylan coming home after that weekend with April?' Al let out a deep laugh.

'Yeah, man. Crept in like a dead man walking.' Jonesy snickered.

'Alright, alright.' I managed a laugh too. It felt like yesterday and another lifetime simultaneously. Al and Jonesy had rumbled me straightaway, but it'd taken Adam almost an entire day to figure out where I'd disappeared to. He'd made me stew, before finally confronting me on the Monday evening. I'd arrived home to find him sipping a beer at the kitchen table.

'The wanderer returns.' He'd smiled. 'So, tell me, pal, how many times did ye screw ma lassie over the weekend?'

I'd sat peeling the label off my beer bottle as I confessed everything. But as much as I'd tried to take the blame, he'd accused April of using him to get what she wanted and told me never to see her again.

257

'I can't do that, Ad. I love her. I'm in love with her,' I'd told him.

We could laugh, looking back. But it'd been a tense evening for all of us.

'And like I told you back then,' Al said now, nudging Adam's knee with his foot, 'Adam may be a womanising man whore with the emotional maturity of an armchair, but he's not an arsehole. He wouldn't have stood in your way.'

'Aye,' Adam agreed, chucking a leftover piece of naan bread at my head. 'Take the piss, sure. But I had that hot barmaid waiting in the wings. Remember her? Boudoir photographer on the side.'

Jonesy leaned forwards to grab the last samosa before anyone could use it as a weapon. 'Perhaps,' he said, shoving the whole thing in his mouth, 'everything would've all worked out better if April hadn't slept with Adam in the first place.'

'Maybe. But he was on a mission to sleep with the entire student population.'

Adam took a swipe at me, laughing. We were still sat talking about uni days an hour later when my phone rang. I jumped for it, seeing Lizzy's name flashing.

'She's awake. April's awake,' she blurted. 'And she's asking for you…'

April's Hospital Room

SUMMER 2022

Dylan

Twenty minutes later, I tore into April's hospital room, half expecting to see her sat up in bed, smiling. Only, she was unconscious again.

'I'm sorry, Dylan,' Sarah said. 'But it is good news.'

I suddenly noticed the silence. The Darth Vader ventilator was gone, and a few less tubes weaved into her body. Standing at the end of her bed, I watched April's chest noiselessly rise and fall independently. She was breathing.

'Can I stay?' I asked, noticing Sarah and Ian had both put their coats on to leave. I'd been gone from April's side less than twenty-four hours, but it felt like a week.

'We thought you might say that.' Ian nodded. 'Lizzy's coming back for us once she's dropped Jen off.'

Feeling guilty for their temporary banishment, he offered to give me his nightshift. Other than asking for me, April hadn't said anything else, and doctors didn't expect her to wake up again until at least the morning. A good opportunity for her parents to get some much-needed sleep.

Finally, we were alone.

'I missed you,' I told her. I'd missed her like those early days when she'd first left the country. So much it burned. Being back by her side now, April wasn't the only one who could breathe again. And I needed to see her. Not watch over her in a coma but really see her.

As the hospital emptied of visitors and the nurses dimmed the lights for the night, I pulled a chair as close as possible to her bed. Then I laced my fingers through hers, rested my head on her arm and closed my eyes.

Please work, I thought. Hoping that whatever weird time warp I'd been experiencing would quantum leap me to April. Any April, from any point in time.

The Kiss

FEBRUARY 2022

AN ALTERNATIVE REALITY

Dylan

It worked. When my eyes flicked open, I was in April's university living room. Rays of dawn light were twinkling through her bay window, and from the way my heart was pounding and the look on April's face, I knew I'd just unloaded my undying feelings for her. Now, she was about to tell me about our library encounter. And once she'd done that, I'd be powerless to do anything but kiss her.

That kiss. I could have it again.

The mere thought made the blood fizz through my veins until all I could feel was adrenaline. And nerves. But I couldn't let it happen.

I kissed her too soon.

Those had been my words. I'd told everyone who'd listen – Adam, Al, Jonesy, Jen – that the first time I kissed April was exactly when it all started to go wrong. This ill-advised moment of passion had cursed us.

And, as much as I wanted to feel the warmth of April in

my arms, I had to stop it. Stop us. One last-ditch attempt to force our lives onto a different course. Get it right now, and maybe this new life would become our only life. I'd save April, and we'd be together.

Or, if everything still went wrong, if we didn't survive, at least then I'd know my regrets were wasted before time kicked me back to the future again.

'I'm sorry,' I blurted, interrupting April before she could speak. 'I shouldn't ambush you with my feelings at 6am. You were just on a date with my best mate. I'm going to go.'

'Wait, Dylan, don't go,' April cried as I turned to leave. 'Just, give me a second. That was a lot to take in.'

I watched her mull everything over, marvelling at how beautiful she was. Even after no sleep, she radiated joy. I missed that.

'Things have got a bit… complicated, haven't they,' she said, looking at me and tucking her own hair behind her ear. 'But I've wanted to be with you since the day we first met. I just didn't know what to do about it and ended up making a mess.'

I felt myself smile, and it struck me for the first time that it wasn't complicated at all. It never had been. Adam was already planning his move on the pub barmaid. In the nicest possible sense, he didn't give a shit about April.

'You know what, I'm going to go home and talk to Adam,' I said, shoving my hands in my pockets and backing away. 'Because if I don't leave now, I'm going to give into the urge to kiss you, which will lead to other things I've been thinking about way too much.'

April blushed, making my desire to kiss her even stronger.

'Yep, definitely leaving.' I fumbled for the door handle behind me. 'And then I'm going to take you out on a date.'

'Sounds perfect.' April smiled as I shut the door and jogged back to my car.

*

Back in my old university room, I dived straight into bed, not waking until 2pm when I heard Jonesy shouting outside my door.

'Dylan, mate, it's beer o'clock. Adam wants to go to the pub, something about a barmaid.'

Rolling my eyes, I crawled out of bed and into the shower. Twenty minutes later, Adam handed me a bottle of Stella as we stood around the kitchen.

'They're playing the City game at 3pm. Plus, I've been messaging that barmaid lassie all morning. She's proper keen.'

Predictable. I chuckled, my anxiety easing. Adam was far from thinking about April, already resigned to his history books.

'Ah, yes, April got the Uber dumping last night,' Al bellowed, shooting me a pointed look.

This was my window. Adam reckoned his savage method of dumping conquests wasn't a tactic. But we'd all seen it before. Whenever things fizzled out, he'd order them a cab home from whatever pub or club they were in. Or, in April's case, our living room.

'That lassie was as interested in me as I was in her. Barely even took her clothes off. Handy to have around though. The numbers I got pretending my girlfriend was about to ditch me.'

My eyes narrowed as Adam boasted of his sleazy genius, but I swallowed my anger.

'About April, mate.' I cleared my throat.

Al and Jonesy's heads whipped up before they both scarpered, making excuses about shoes and aftershave. Watching them disappear, Adam turned to me, puzzled.

'Do they know something I don't?'

Swallowing, I launched into it, glad I'd had four years to consider what I should have said in this moment.

'They *might* have clocked that I like April. Not that I've mentioned it to them. I swear you're the first person I'm telling.'

'Ye like April?' Adam's frown deepened, his mind ticking. 'Hhmmm. Seems obvious now.' He swigged his beer as I told him the truth in as little detail as possible.

'Mate, I promise, nothing has happened. But I can't deny that I've developed feelings for her.'

Adam folded his arms, still holding his beer.

'Right,' he said. 'And what does April think about that? Assuming ye told her?' Frowning, he scrutinised my face.

'She feels the same. Look, Ad, I only told her last night. After your Uber dumping. I just want to ask her on a date. But if you have a problem with it, I won't; I'll walk away.' I flinched internally at the lie. I couldn't walk away if I had a gun to my head.

Adam silently downed the rest of his beer, before walking over to the fridge and cracking open another.

'Mate, you said yourself, she was just convenient to have around.' I was trying to keep the desperation out my voice. 'You're not interested in April, are you?'

Adam paused, and suddenly I wasn't so sure. Had I misread him all this time?

'No,' he replied, shuffling his feet.

'Then just let me take her out, see how it goes...' My sentence petered out as I realised I was begging.

'Ye went behind ma back just by telling her,' he said. 'And why do Al and Jonesy seem to know about it? What else has been going on?'

So much for keeping things simple. Adam was stubborn and the more he dug, the more he unravelled my story. Wheedling details out about our late-night chats.

'Nothing happened,' I insisted again.

'Nothing happened, apart from secret late-night liaisons and ye both having feelings for each other.' Adam's lips curled into a snarl and I wondered how this could possibly be worse than what I'd done the first time.

'OK, well, that happened, and I should've come to you sooner. But I'm telling you now, and anyway, you're about to chat up some blue-haired barmaid. One date, let me take April on one date.'

Adam nodded to the clock. 'It's almost kick-off; we've gotta go,' he said, heading off to round up Al and Jonesy.

'Just think about it,' I called after him. He was pissed off. Adam would much rather his former flings exited stage left never to be seen again. But pissed-off Adam I could handle. Last time he'd been furiously humiliated Adam, who was much trickier.

For the rest of the day, he threw relentless sloppy seconds jokes my way. Again. I got a brief reprieve whenever the barmaid had a break and Adam took his chance to schmooze her.

'I'll break, ye like taking the next shot, don't ye, Dylan?' he quipped as we played doubles at pool. It was worse when he told me to take his turn at the bar, because that one he meant. I bought at least half his rounds as Al and Jonesy exchanged amused smirks. Mostly banter, but Adam kept me on edge.

At one point I spotted Al having a word in his ear. Still, the persecution only ended as we waited for Adam's barmaid to lock up.

'Aye, alright. Ask April out, I couldn't give a fuck,' he slurred. 'But don't come crying to me when yer stuck in a sexless relationship. She's a bonnie lassie, but she hardly lights the bedroom on fire.'

I was too relived to argue.

*

The following Monday evening, I showed up at April's door.

'I brought food.' I grinned, holding up a box. 'Can I interest you in a night of pizza and Netflix?'

Beaming, she invited me in, leading me straight past where Lizzy was watching us from the sofa and into her bedroom. An arty poster hung above her bed that I'd not paid attention to before. The Rome Colosseum all lit up from the inside. But I did recognise the gallery wall of photos of her friends and family, pale gold fairy lights looped around the frames. Her inexplicable number of brightly coloured cushions were thrown in the corner, and I had a flashback of buying her a purple one that coming Christmas.

'So… Adam?' April sat casually on her bed, with no idea how nervous I was being in her room again.

'Spent the weekend torturing me and rinsing me for beer.' I shrugged. 'But he won't stand in the way. So, this is me, asking you, April, out on a date. Or in, I guess, if this counts?'

'It definitely counts.' Her eyes shone with a thousand smiles, each one just for me.

She gestured for me to sit next to her. My heart pounded as I sat on her fluffy duvet. I yearned to kiss her but couldn't rush in and ruin things.

'If it's OK, can we take things slowly? Adam seems fine, but I don't want to give him ammo by moving too quickly. As much as I want to.' It was my turn to blush. Was it obvious that slowly peeling her clothes off and kissing every inch of her was all I could think about?

'Ah, this is a Netflix and actually chill date?' April joked. 'I can do that.'

We spent all night watching films, mocking each other's dodgy taste. My Ben Stiller obsession fuelled much of April's teasing, yet I had to suffer through her Nicholas Sparks choices. We talked through most of them anyway.

'This has been a perfect first date. My best ever.' April was lying across the bed on her tummy as the credits to some Netflix romcom rolled.

'Not bad for a poor student. I'm sorry – after Adam squeezed my loan for beer last night, there isn't much left. But for date two, I'll take you out for dinner? Although I can't promise I won't use a voucher. And for date three, there's a Valentine's Day party at the student union next weekend?'

'Will we be counting all our dates?' I loved hearing April laugh. Especially when she teased me, her lips forming a sexy pout. I propped up on my hands, considering my reply.

'Actually, I thought we'd count to at least date five before we, you know… take things further.'

April scrunched her nose up. 'Dylan, are you putting us on a sex ban?' She was really laughing now, making the whole bed shake.

'I guess I am,' I said, laughing too. When she finally composed herself, she fixed her eyes on me.

'Does that include kissing?'

'Definitely not.' Unable to resist her any longer, I pulled her across the bed and pressed my mouth on hers. She sank into my arms as I curled her hair behind her ears and kissed her deeper. I was dizzy and breathless as our bodies crushed together, limbs intertwining.

It was a battle to stop my hands wandering further than her back. But hers had stopped at feeling my abs over my T-shirt. I couldn't be the one to break my own rule.

There was an incredible intimacy in just kissing, with no pressure about where it was headed. We'd switch from tender and slow to more passionate and urgent as we worked ourselves up before dialling it back. When we finally parted, I opened my eyes and looked into April's before softly kissing her one last time.

'Five dates.' I exhaled, chewing my bottom lip. 'That won't be as easy as I thought.'

'Only four dates left…'

'Phew. But you need to take my mind off sex for a minute before I get carried away. Tell me about that picture.' I nodded towards her poster. This could be another chance to change something big. Make sure it was April who went to Italy.

'Why the Colosseum?'

Smiling, April told me about her application to study in Rome the following year.

'It's the dream,' she admitted coyly. 'Studying all the art and exploring the ancient ruins. Historical sculptures on every corner.'

It worked – I wasn't thinking about sex anymore. My heart was breaking for my April again. Seeing this past April speaking of Rome with such joy and excitement reminded me what I took from her. Or, what she'd sacrificed for me. Plus, it was a cold, harsh reminder that, even in this new life, April and I were destined to spend our third year apart.

*

What a dumb, idiotic thing this five-date rule was. I'd been trying to be chivalrous, whilst placating Adam. Proving a point by dating April rather than jumping into bed with her. Yet I came close to breaking it every time I was with her. And what happened on date five? Now it was loaded with expectation.

By date three, Valentine's night, I'd morphed completely into the Dylan of four years previous. The kid who could physically feel himself falling more in love with April with every minute that passed. It was one big, terrifying adrenaline rush, sending the memories of my real life into the dusty and forgotten archives of my brain.

Spotting April as I walked around the corner with Adam, Jonesy, Al and his girlfriend Jodie in toe, I couldn't believe how lucky I'd got. Her curls grazed the contours of her face, and her red dress clung to her like a silk siren call.

'Hello, April,' Adam said with a pointed leer. But while I'd been on edge about their first meeting since their vague break-up, that was the extent of his acrimony. Plus, Lizzy diffused any awkwardness by suggesting we headed to the bar.

'At least that's over with,' April said later, sitting close to me in a dark corner of the student union. 'I was dreading seeing Adam.'

'Trust me, I'm the one he's enjoying torturing. But he's too busy with his barmaid for now to dwell on us,' I shouted over the music, putting my arm around her shoulders. By the time we left at 2am, we were very tipsy.

'Come back to mine,' April slurred while we waited for Ubers. 'Go on. Coffee in your kitchen, last Friday night when you dropped me home, Netflix and actual chill, dinner and then tonight. That's fiiiiivvvvve dates.' She grinned, holding up her spread hand, her blue eyes sparkling.

I could still feel the heat of her body pressed against mine as we slow danced to the last cheesy love song. The whisps of her silk dress, barely a barrier between my fingertips and her soft skin. It made my body shiver as we kissed drunkenly in the cold. April's warm hands running up my back under my shirt almost had me giving in. Almost.

'You've no idea how hard it is to say no,' I muttered, my forehead touching hers. 'But I'm pretty stubborn about this five-date thing. Plus, I accidentally told Lizzy and she's watching closely. I owe her a drink if I cave, and if I even come within twenty metres of your bedroom, I'm going to want to take your clothes off.'

Just then, her Uber pulled up and she and Lizzy climbed in. 'You don't know what you're missing.' She pouted. But as I watched them pull away, I had a fair idea.

*

Walking down by the canal on date four, April's hand felt comfortable in mine. Date five was still this looming high-pressure deadline. But for now, I just enjoyed learning everything there was to know about April.

'I picked Manchester so I wasn't too far from my family,' I admitted. 'My mum likes to tell people it's so I can take my laundry home. But really, I'd miss my little sisters too much if I couldn't nip back to visit.'

'Cute.' April grinned, sipping her coffee. 'I'd love to meet them.'

April told me about Rome. She'd already devoured endless books about the city, worked out the best arty nooks. Mapped out her entire year there.

'I just need to get a 2:1 this year to secure my spot.'

I'd seen April's coursework marks. Most were firsts. There was no question – she was going to Rome. I was happy for her, but thinking of her leaving gave me this uneasy pang.

'So, date five,' I said, changing the subject.

'Oh, I've had an idea about that.' April's eyes sparked as she spoke. 'Breakfast.'

'Breakfast?'

'Breakfast,' she said with a firm nod. 'One day next week we go out for breakfast. No one has sex after breakfast. After that we just put it back on the table, without the pressure.'

'Apart from one thing,' I said. 'I'm pretty sure I'd be up for sex after breakfast. I'm twenty.'

*

'It's like the whole pineapple on a pizza debate,' April said, sloshing a third helping of syrup over her pancakes and bacon. 'Some people think that's a monstrosity; others love it. I for one think pineapple and jalapeños are the perfect pizza combination.'

'Pineapple on a pizza? They'll throw you out of Italy.' I laughed between forkfuls of my full English. April was refreshingly lively in the morning, without being overbearingly cheery. It perked me up even better than the two coffees I'd already managed.

'You were right.' I smiled, walking her to her lecture after breakfast in the student café. 'That was an excellent fifth date idea.'

'See, and neither of us feels like sex.' She grinned.

'Not actually true. Twenty, male, insanely beautiful girlfriend.' I laughed, pointing to myself. 'But sadly, we don't have time.' Leaning in, I kissed her softly on the lips, relishing the taste of coffee and syrup.

'Or anywhere to go.' April giggled.

'I dunno, I could improvise,' I said, kissing her again before watching her bounce into the lecture hall.

Another coffee date later, I went to April's one evening to pick her up for a house party. Lizzy let me in, nodding to April's bedroom where I found her still doing her hair. Sitting on her bed, I watched, fascinated as she twisted the last lock of hair around her curling tongs.

'Women have so many decisions.' I frowned. 'Curly or straight, flats or heels, what colour lipstick, dress or trousers. I just picked the only clean shirt that wasn't on the floor.'

Carefully putting away the terrifying hot poker things, she walked over and looped her hands round my neck.

'Don't tell me you didn't spend at least twenty minutes sculpting that manicured mop of yours,' she teased. 'But I'll let you in on a secret. We like the getting ready bit. We could probably do it quicker, but we enjoy the transformation.'

She kissed me playfully and I put my arms around her waist to pull her closer.

'Tell me more secrets of your kind.' Laughing, I threw her onto the bed next to me. Careful not to tousle her perfect curls, I gently put my mouth on hers. It was meant to be brief, but as I teased her tongue with mine, she pressed herself into me. My lips automatically moved to the curve of her neck while my hands grazed her bare midriff where her crop top didn't quite meet her jeans. The warmth of her skin and feeling her fingers tugging at my shirt unleashed the desire we'd been bottling up.

We weren't going to make it to the party.

'I can't wait any longer,' I whispered, nuzzling her neck and running my hand down her spine.

'Me neither.' Her back arched and I could feel her body come alive under my lips, aching for more. More of me. Or us, and everything we were together.

After, as we laid snaked under the duvet, I enjoyed the feel of her bare flesh against mine.

'Well, that was...'

'Worth the wait,' April breathed.

Pulling her on top of me, I started kissing her again.

'Actually, I was going to say it was a good start.'

I woke the next morning, April's head on my chest, exhausted but in a dreamlike bliss. We'd snatched sleep a couple of hours at a time throughout the night, both of us feeding our insatiable appetite for each other.

Fuck, was I in trouble. I'd thought I was in love with April before; now I was enraptured by her. She was everything, and nothing else mattered. And yet, uneasy thoughts began worming their way in. April would leave for Rome soon, and something told me it was going to be tough.

It'd only been five weeks since I first laid eyes on April, but her existence wound around mine like ivy over a trellis. I couldn't get through a single day without seeing her – how would I cope for weeks at a time?

All too soon, reality crashed upon us.

'I'm in,' April said, meeting me in our favourite coffee shop after seeing her tutor. 'I leave in three weeks.'

'That's incredible.' I grinned, swinging her round before ordering her a latte. That night, we celebrated, because this was April's dream. But the next morning, as we lay in bed nibbling toast, we both fretted about the long-distance stuff.

'I won't go,' April said. 'We can go to Italy together after graduation. Or somewhere else. We could travel the world.'

I shook my head. Something told me it'd eat her up from the inside out if she gave up Rome.

'You're going, no question. I'd never forgive myself otherwise. I'll defer third year and come with you. Wait tables or something.'

April looked sad. 'I don't think you should do that, Dylan.'

She was right. If I put my degree on pause, I might never finish it. And as she pointed out, I didn't speak Italian, while she'd spent the last few years teaching herself.

April looked pained as we accepted the truth. We'd be spending our final year apart. Pushing the hair from her face, I cupped her chin.

'Hey, we knew this was coming. It's a once-in-a-lifetime chance for you, and I've got to stay here and graduate. I'm literally not going anywhere. We'll make this work; I promise.'

Still, watching April walk away from me in Manchester Airport three weeks later was heart-rending. We tried to be realistic. Promising one of us would fly over every month, split the holidays between us.

'I'm all in,' I whispered as she wept silently on my shoulder, trying not to make a scene. 'All in, all the time. I love you; never forget it.'

'All in.' She smiled, her chest hitching at the effort of holding back sobs. 'Just promise me, however hard it gets, we'll tough it out.'

'I promise,' I said. 'I'll be right here waiting.' Then I kissed her until it made me dizzy. Her knees weakened as she leaned into me. It was intense. It was wrenching. And then, she was gone.

Back home, I went straight into my room, shelved all my manly pride and cried quietly. Sitting with my back to the door so none of the guys could get in and see me a snivelling wreck. A visceral reaction, but it hurt more than I thought possible. I physically felt her absence as though she'd taken my heart with her in her hand luggage. Then, I realised there was only one thing I could do.

*

Seven days later, I stepped off the plane in Rome with a flurry of nerves.

Am I insane? Or a hopeless romantic, I wondered. Adam reckoned insane; Al thought my grand gesture was the right play. I flitted between the two.

April planned to spend the summer like she had her first week out here. Hopping between museums, working long shifts until well after closing. But today was her day off.

Having a coffee in Caffè Greco, she messaged as I boarded a bus outside the airport. The little ancient coffee shop had quickly become her favourite place in the city. After a short bus ride and getting lost on the metro, I found it. Through the window, I saw April sketching while sipping a cappuccino. Calling her, I watched her face light up as she saw my name flash up.

'Dylan?' She smiled.

'Hey,' I replied. 'Just calling to see how you're enjoying your cappuccino?'

Enjoying her puzzled look, I walked inside. Hearing the door open, her head whipped round.

'Dylan,' she gasped again, almost dropping her phone. Her face was expressionless for a second, then she laughed. 'Dylan?' Racing over, she slammed into me, covering my face in kisses.

'You're here.' Her kisses turned into one long, fervent

one. April wiped away a tear as we finally broke apart. 'This is the best surprise. How long are you here for?'

Suddenly, I felt nervous again.

'Actually, if I'm not intruding on your big Italian adventure, I'll stick around all summer.' April threw herself on me again. Eventually, she realised everyone was watching and ushered me onto the stool opposite hers.

I'd managed to get a job for the University of Manchester creating an online archive of some newly digitised ancient research papers that'd been discovered in a forgotten cabinet in the basement. It was boring and tedious, but I could do it from my laptop in Rome.

'I'd have paid off my overdraft waiting tables, but my Italian isn't up to scratch.' I grinned, as April ordered me a coffee and sandwich in perfect Italian. I'd also talked my way into a room in student halls, not far from April's.

'I've missed you. You've no idea how much,' April said, talking a mile a minute. 'I wake up reaching for you, and it's just horrible when I realise you're not there.' She'd made a few friends on the programme, but campus was mostly empty over the summer, so she'd spent her spare time exploring using her museum pass.

'I've spent hours staring up at the Sistine Chapel ceiling already. And I could sculpt a clay model of the Colosseum from memory. There's a whole museum dedicated to excavation and archaeology. I've been saving it for your visit.'

'Can't wait.' I grinned, taking her hand across the table and kissing her fingertips. Being back with her again was like walking on air. We had another three months together. Three months in this beautiful city.

Waking up in Rome the next morning, with April stirring in my arms, I knew I was exactly where I was supposed to be.

'Morning.' April beamed. 'I still can't believe you're here. Have I said thank you yet? I never thought anyone would do something so romantic for me.'

'I'd follow you anywhere, April. All in, remember? Besides, you thanked me enough last night.' My lips found hers in the dingy student room and I sensed her body spring awake as I grazed my hand down her waist and over her hip.

I quickly became part of April's new friendship group. A history student named Giana nicknamed me Romeo, while the rest were fascinated by my grand romantic gesture.

'L'amore a prima vista,' a Brit named Shaun, who wasn't from Rome like Giana but from April's course in Manchester, called it. Love at first sight.

We spent our days studying, working and exploring. Our nights drinking cheap Italian wine in the student dive bars or in some hidden piazza. Then, in a flash, summer was over.

'Goodbye, Romeo.' Giana winked as I boarded a bus to the airport. It was difficult to believe I was leaving April and our new friends already.

Adam promised – well threatened – endless parties to help me with the "transition". Most of which involved freshers' week and shots. Not something I was enthusiastic about compared to the glamorous evenings in the late Italian sunshine. Talking about art, history and politics, laughing as our discussions became boozy and heated.

Still, as my heart tore in two once more, I was glad I'd have third year, a dissertation, and the lads to keep me busy. I felt better about April too. Leaving her with a hub of friends and more students arriving on campus every day. She had people watching out for her.

Memories of walks around Rome's ancient monuments and spending every night squashed into a single bed next to April would get me through the next months.

'Best summer of my life,' I'd told her, kissing her goodbye and wiping her tears away with my sleeve. I'd be back in Rome for reading week, then she'd be home for Christmas. Our friends had pitched in to buy me a ticket for New Year. In between that, we'd make it work.

*

Somewhere in my mind, in a dark recess covered in cobwebs, I was aware this alternative life wasn't really mine. That my April hadn't gone to Rome, I had. In her place. But time sped on nonetheless, until I was back in Italy watching the sky light up with New Year fireworks.

'Almost halfway,' April said, sinking into me at midnight. Goosebumps sprang up over her skin as I skimmed my mouth over her ear.

Almost.

'We're going to be OK,' I promised. Each of the three weeks we'd managed to spend together that autumn term had been more intensified than the last. Passion exploding whenever we were back in each other's arms.

There was no denying the in-between times were getting harder, though. And that January, a few days after

New Year, was the toughest goodbye yet. For the first time, neither of us had a visit booked. Plus, coursework was ramping up; there was my dissertation and finals to think about.

'I'm coming back,' I promised. But as January turned to February, our video call schedule disintegrated. Our WhatsApp messages misaligned so conversations dragged out across several days. Until one morning I woke up and there wasn't a single notification on my phone. No message, DM or missed call. No tag or mention. Dread sat in the pit of my stomach. We swore we'd never miss a goodnight or good morning.

Even if April *was* mad at me.

'I thought I had until next month,' I'd told her the previous afternoon. My tutor had sent an email reminder just as I was booking a last-minute flight to Rome. A chunk of my dissertation was due. Reading it, I'd almost punched a hole in my wall before calling April to tell her I couldn't come.

I wanted to reach through my phone screen and hold her. I'm not sure she'd have wanted me to, though. It wasn't the first time my forgotten deadlines had got in the way of our relationship.

April had been putting in so many extra hours at the museums on top of her studies she'd not been able to visit me either. I felt like crap. All I wanted was to see her. Only, now, being behind on my dissertation meant I had to double down on research. Recheck the timetable, focus on catching up.

'I know I fucked up,' I confided in Al. We'd found an hour to escape to the pub to let off some steam. 'It's not like

I wanted to cancel. And she's prioritising her course too. It just leaves little time for us.'

Al sympathised. He'd been moping lately too.

'Jodie has me scheduled in on an Excel spreadsheet. She won't answer the phone if it's not timetabled in. I'm like a box on her to-do list.'

Al understood how difficult a long-distance relationship was. Jodie was studying law and fiercely ambitious. She wasn't as far away as April, but even her and Al's visits had got fewer since we started third year.

'I'm starting to wonder what we're putting ourselves through it for.' Al sighed. 'And between you and me, there's this girl in my revision group. Megan. She's just so sexy and intriguing...'

'Al, stop,' I blurted, almost spitting out my beer to cut him off. The name Megan triggered something deep within me. 'Mate, listen to yourself. Have you lost the plot? Some girl? Don't do it. Don't even think it. You love Jodie; I know you do.'

Al shook his head and pushed his empty pint glass away. 'I do. But how do I know Jodie's the right person for me, when I've never known anything else? Right now I just feel like an inconvenience.'

The conversation shook me. This was Al and Jodie, who'd cruised through first and second year at different unis and still been stronger than ever. If they couldn't make it, how could me and April a thousand miles away in Rome?

'Al, this isn't like you. Text Jodie, now. Tell her it's urgent and that you need to talk. Get on her schedule. Tell her you're struggling.'

Chances were, she was too.

'Don't drift off to some girl you've just met because Jodie can't give you the time you want right now. You'll regret it. Carry on in this direction and you'll damage your relationship with Jodie forever.'

Al nodded. 'God, you're right. I've just never been single. I can't help but wonder what I've missed out on.'

'Nothing. Trust me. It works for Adam and Jonesy, but for guys like you and me, the novelty wears off.'

Sleeping around in first year had been fun for about five seconds, before I realised I needed more.

'Waking up with someone you want to stick around and have a conversation with is way better than waking up to an awkward exchange and hoping they'll scarper home soon,' I said, desperate to save Al from making the biggest mistake of his life. 'And if you guys need to take a break to work that out for yourself, take one. But agree to the terms, don't start something without telling Jodie you need some time. It's the worst kind of cheating.'

Al promised to talk to Jodie before he did anything rash. As for me, April was the one sulking. Ignoring me felt cruel. The distance between us had never seemed greater.

'You should take your own advice. Jodie and me, I'm worried we've gone stale, but you and April barely got out the gate before she left for Rome. Talk to her. You'll see nothing's changed between you,' he said.

*

I was still waiting for April to call when I bumped into Lizzy in the campus café. She let slip April wasn't coming home for Easter anymore.

'It's a shame, but she's thrilled to be working such an important art exhibit. Easter's the busiest time for the Vatican,' Lizzy said, assuming I already knew.

Not wanting to let on that I'd been left in the dark, I smiled. Told Lizzy I was happy for April.

'She's counting the days down until May.' Lizzy smiled, with a reassuring pat to my arm that only came off as patronising. 'We should throw her a welcome home party. I'll message you.'

Having Easter pulled out from under me like that stung. Walking out the café, I found a bench and sat with my head in my hands. Had April known about Easter when I'd cancelled? Was that why she'd been so upset?

When she finally did call, I could hear the nerves in her voice. I hated that. The last thing I wanted was to put her under pressure, and I couldn't face an argument. So, I let her off the hook.

'About Easter,' I said, 'it must be busy over there, being the Vatican, and after my dissertation I'll have finals to study for. We're both so slammed, maybe your visit isn't such a good idea. It's only an extra six weeks until the end of term, then we'll have the whole summer together.'

April went quiet. When she spoke, I could hear the lump in her throat.

'You're right,' she whispered. 'I hate it. But you're right. If we see each other, we'll end up ignoring revision. Plus, there's a big art exhibit at the Vatican Museums my tutor has asked me to help with.'

'That's amazing, April,' I said, trying to muster some enthusiasm. 'You can't pass that up. And it's only six extra weeks. I promise, the moment you land back in Manchester, we'll make up for everything.'

I could hear her sniffing as she agreed. 'It's nearly eleven weeks in total though,' she said. 'Easter's still a month away.'

Three months. It suddenly felt like eternity. Before I could say anything else, April made an excuse about meeting Giana and hung up. I had a feeling she was going to bed to cry, though.

It killed me, leaving it like that. I was just trying to give her Rome. To make her last few months out there easier. And I wasn't lying when I said I needed to focus too. But this dark mist enshrouded my heart. I suddenly felt like I'd done the wrong thing.

After that, our messages became sporadic. April was rushed off her feet, getting back to her room late. I spent most nights in the library, as I got more work done there than at home.

I missed her more than ever. My heart felt heavy in my chest. And yet I felt nervous and unsure whenever we did manage to speak. Our conversations became stilted, unsure. Awkward. Then one day the messages and calls stopped altogether.

We'd always chatted simultaneously over Instagram, SnapChat, WhatsApp, text and email, so I couldn't work out which of us failed to reply first. All I knew was weeks passed and I didn't hear from her. Several times I picked up my phone to message her. Yet, I'd no idea what to say to my own girlfriend. Was she even still my girlfriend?

'It doesn't matter.' Al shrugged. 'You've told her you'll wait, so just wait. When you see her in May, you'll know pretty quickly if there's something there to salvage.'

Since his deep and meaningful with Jodie, where they'd recommitted to each other, Al had been in a much better place.

Ignoring Adam's advice to download some sordid hook-up app he'd discovered, I waited. It hurt like hell. I was just grateful for the pile of uni work to distract me.

By the time I put the last full stop on my final exam, April and I had communicated solely in Instagram likes. She seemed to spend most of her time in some museum or other. But having only that small window into April's world wasn't enough to sustain me. I needed living, breathing April. Then, one morning, she posted a photo of her plane ticket home.

'Yes, I'm going to the airport,' I told Adam when I left the morning she was due home. It was never in question. Seeing the ticket only meant I didn't need to wheedle the details from Lizzy.

Standing in arrivals, I was a nervous wreck. I didn't even know if April wanted to see me. But I needed to see her. Tell her I planned to keep my promise. That I still loved her. I couldn't let April and I drift apart so meaninglessly without trying.

When I spotted her walking out, dragging two suitcases behind her, she was searching the waiting crowd. Looking for me, the hopeful but anxious look in her eyes matching mine. When she finally saw me, she stopped. Then she broke into this smile that caused the fire inside me to roar back to life.

Instead of running into my arms, she walked over and stopped in front of me.

'Hey, you.' I smiled. With that, April melted into me until we were almost one. 'You came. And you smell like you.'

'I promised I would. And I hope I smell good.' I laughed, holding her tightly. I couldn't let go. This calm settled over me, like my heart had finally found its normal rhythm again. April's head was on my chest, listening to it steadily thump.

Eventually, I tore myself away, took one of her suitcases, and we walked hand in hand to the car. We drove mostly in silence. There was too much to say to know where to start.

'I'm staying with Lizzy for the last week of term,' April said. 'Her flatmate went home after exams.'

We made small talk until we'd lugged April's bags into her old room. Then, suddenly, we were tangled in a kiss. I don't know which of us dove in first. But as our lips joined, I felt whole again. April was back.

Her hair felt silky and familiar as I brushed by fingers through it, my lips finding the soft spot under her jaw.

'We should probably talk,' I gasped, not quite pulling away.

'Uh-huh,' April breathed, finding my mouth with hers again. 'But let's do this first.'

I wasn't going to disagree. By then her back was against the door and I lifted her up as her legs wrapped around my waist.

*

'I missed this.' I kissed April's hair as her head rested on my chest. 'I missed you. Relentlessly. But…'

'We can't avoid this conversation any longer.' April gave a small smile, but she pulled the duvet up around herself and I sensed a shift in her. Like she was angry.

'You dumped me,' she blurted.

Dumped her? I sat back, frowning.

'That phone call about Easter. You told me not to visit and I thought you were done. It'd got too hard. So, you cut me off with the "wait until you're back" stuff.' April pulled the duvet tighter around herself. 'What did that even mean? Were we on a break? Was it over? I felt so alone and lost. I was heartbroken, Dylan.'

'I don't understand…' I was stuttering, taking in the betrayal in April's eyes. How had things got so turned around? 'That's not what happened. I was trying to give you space. You were too busy to visit; Lizzy had already let that secret slip. You knew you weren't coming home for Easter for weeks. Don't deny that.'

April looked down, unable to meet my eye.

'Exactly. You knew when I cancelled my visit, and you didn't tell me. Instead, you let me feel like shit.'

I'd almost flown to Rome anyway, risking my entire degree.

'That's how much I wanted to see you,' I said. 'And I guessed you were struggling to break the news about Easter, so I thought I'd save you the trouble.'

'Give me space? Save me the trouble? Dylan, I never asked you to do any of that. I'd planned this crazy romantic weekend, and two days before, you announced you weren't coming. Yes, I knew about Easter, but I wanted to tell you in person so we could plan a way to get through it. Together.'

April looked away to hide her tears.

'Things were suddenly falling apart, and I freaked out,' she said. 'I could feel you slipping further away. When I did finally call, I was going to tell you how devastated I was. I wanted us to go back to messaging every morning and night, daily video calls, phone sex. Anything to get us through those horrible months.' Sniffing, she looked back at me. 'But you were too proud to let me. Then you stopped talking to me altogether.'

'April, you hung up on me and never called back,' I gasped. 'I was trying to let you enjoy Rome without worrying about me – about us. It was your dream and I wanted you to live it. That's why I promised I'd be there in May. I didn't want to keep hounding you.'

I'd already followed her to Rome for the summer, visited at reading week and New Year. 'I was scared if I tried any harder, I'd suffocate you and you'd end things altogether,' I shouted.

'Enjoy Rome? Dylan, I was miserable.'

She'd spent the last three months holed up in her room every night. Barely gone out unless it was to work or a lecture. I hadn't given her space to enjoy Rome. I'd ruined it for her.

'I skipped out on my own leaving drinks after an hour because all I could think about was you and whether you'd show up at the airport or not.' She was twisting the knife, and it was working. I'd never felt worse.

'I need some air.' I stood up, gathering my scattered clothes and hurriedly pulling them back on. 'I can't think straight. Your version of things… it's not how it was for me.'

Everything seemed upside down and turned around. I couldn't work out how to make it all the right way again. Where had I gone wrong? The guilt was stifling, I had to get out of there.

'I need to think.' I walked out her room, past Lizzy in the living room, out the door, past my car and just kept going.

Meandering blindly, I ended up by the canal. Our canal. Memories of getting to know April in those early days flooded me. Had I given up on us too soon? Stepped back when I should have stepped up? How had I got it so wrong? What had I missed?

Just as I was torturing myself, a message from April arrived asking me to meet her in the library.

It's important.

I frowned. Yet something about the library rang a distant bell. Twenty minutes later, I walked through the revolving door to find April already sat in the foyer, her legs jiggling.

'I thought I'd finally seen the back of this place,' I joked, sitting down next to her. 'I'm a little confused about why we're here. I'm sorry for running away...'

'Please stop talking.' April had a serious look on her face that told me she meant it. 'And stop apologising. It's about time I did some of that. There's also something you need to know.'

I nodded, trying to place the library amongst my memories of April.

'After you walked out, I was on the end of a rather scary Lizzy lecture. She stormed out too, after pointing out you still didn't quite know everything, and that I didn't deserve you. She said it was my turn to make some grand romantic gesture. She was right.'

April handed me a piece of paper with her name and number on it.

'Your phone number?' I asked, puzzled. 'I already have this.'

'Obviously.' She laughed, before looking serious again. 'But I wrote this to give to you nearly two years ago. In October 2017 at the beginning of our second year. I've been carrying it around ever since, as a reminder.'

I was even more confused. 'A reminder? Of what? You didn't know me that October. We met in January 2018.'

'Actually, we had met before. Briefly. For just a few seconds. I know you don't remember; there's no reason you would. But it was right here, in the library foyer.'

I looked around the grand entrance. Not a single part of my brain recalled meeting anyone in the foyer, in all my three years of coming here. But something was familiar about this story. I just couldn't place it.

'I've been keeping a pretty big secret from you, Dylan,' April continued. 'I don't even know why. I was embarrassed, I guess. But the truth is I saw you. In the library three whole months before I ended up drinking coffee in your kitchen. You were rushing, obviously late with an essay.'

Instantly, I knew when she was talking about and smiled wryly. My research paper on Pompeii. I'd already been given an extension but still left it until the last weekend.

'You were hurrying through the foyer towards the stairs when you almost sent me flying. Somehow, you caught me before I hit the floor. For a brief second, you looked intently into my eyes. Your nose was almost touching mine and your hand was in my hair, gently pushing it off my face. Just like you do now.' April smiled shyly at the memory.

'As you tucked it behind my ear, your fingers stroked my cheek. It was only a second, but it was all it took. You asked if I was OK, and then you were gone, racing up the stairs two at a time.'

I looked towards the staircase, echoes of old memories beginning to stir.

'The whole experience left me breathless. And I also knew, whoever you were, that I would love you, and I needed to find you. I looked for you everywhere, driving Lizzy crazy.' She tapped the piece of paper in my hand. 'This is the piece of paper I wrote my number down on, just in case I saw you in a hurry again. I've kept it in my purse ever since.'

April took a deep breath before continuing. 'By January, Lizzy snapped, told me I was acting crazy, and about ten minutes later, feeling well and truly pathetic, I met Adam at the bar. The next morning, who should I run into sneaking out his bedroom?'

'Me.' I realised I'd been holding my breath as April told her story.

'You. If I could've screamed, I would. Have you ever heard of anything so absurdly unfair? Because I haven't. Things got messy after that. Then we started dating, and I knew everything I'd felt in the library that day had been real. I almost told you about it once. The morning you said you had feelings for me. But then you ran off to talk to Adam.'

Her mention of that dawn conversation in her living room unlocked a floodgate in my mind. Everything rushed back. This wasn't my real life. My real life was three years in the future, sitting next to Coma April's hospital bed. And I'd stopped this April telling me the library story that morning because it was what originally triggered our first kiss. I'd blamed that kiss for everything that went wrong after, and I'd wanted to change it all.

Had it worked? I wasn't sure. We'd both still lost our way somehow. And Coma April – my April – was still in hospital fighting for her life somewhere in another reality. Any minute I'd be pulled back there; I could already feel my real life tugging on the edges of my soul.

Meanwhile, the April in front of me was still talking.

'I loved you before you even knew I existed. Even tried to hunt you down like a deranged lovesick fool. Perhaps if you'd known that, you wouldn't have worried about giving me space, or suffocating me, because you'd have known you never could. I was always yours, Dylan. Always.'

Sitting with my elbows on my knees and staring across the foyer, a cacophony of thoughts torpedoed through my mind. My ears rang with the chaos of them.

'I needed to know,' I said finally, turning to look at her. 'About the library. I needed to know earlier than this.'

Knowing she'd had the same crazy thunderbolt moment I had, albeit three months earlier, was what had made me so sure. It'd driven our passion for each other. But in this alternative life, not knowing had made me hesitant. We were still together, but something was missing. Our fire didn't roar; it simmered.

Getting up, I strode into the middle of the foyer.

'I still don't remember the library,' I said, looking over at where she sat, tapping her feet and chewing her fingernails as she watched me.

'You were too distracted for lightning strikes.' She shrugged, elegantly rising and joining me in the centre of the room. She looked desperate and lost. Kind of how I'd felt sometimes this last year. 'But now you do know. You're everything to me and always have been. I'm sorry you questioned that. Can you forgive me?'

Facing this April now, I tucked her hair behind her ear.

'There's nothing to forgive,' I whispered, touching my forehead to hers. She had no idea this wasn't her fault. That I'd been the one to stop her telling me this secret. 'Just keep loving me like that.'

She nodded, but I already knew I'd somehow dampened the flames of this Dylan and April's passion for each other. As she kissed me, I expected that to be the moment I was yanked back to my own reality. Only, this parallel world I was in sped up instead. New memories lodging themselves in my brain haphazardly. Graduation, moving into a tiny flat in Manchester, a small garden wedding. A decade in seconds, leaving me nauseous.

It all came to a screaming halt with me sat in the pub again, across from Al. He looked older, his arms more muscular and the stubble across his chin thicker. Mostly though, he looked sad.

'How's Jodie?' I asked.

Al gave a one-shouldered shrug.

'Polite. Determined. You know Jodie. Once she's decided something, there's no going back. Divorce papers arrived last Monday.'

'Sorry, mate.'

'Yeah, me too. Can't blame her though.'

I conjured one of the memories settling itself into the folds of my mind. It was of Al, confessing to a six-month affair with a woman he'd met at a dentistry conference.

'She really won't forgive you then?' I asked.

Al shook his head and grabbed a handful of nuts, chucking one in the air and catching it in his mouth. An old nervous habit that'd re-emerged as he dealt with the fallout of his infidelity.

'I just keep wondering what the hell I was thinking. Jodie had returned to her law firm after back-to-back maternity leaves and was focused on making up for those lost years on the career ladder. She was co-sleeping with the kids to get enough sleep for work, leaving me alone in the spare room. When they weren't at nursery, the girls just wanted their mum. I felt like a spare part.' Al paused, lost in thought. 'Remember that Megan at uni?' he asked.

I nodded with creeping dread. To me, every memory was fresh and newly formed.

'Well, it was like that. I started wondering if I was living the right life. I love my family, but they were all in a stage where they didn't seem to need me much. I worried I'd missed out on being single. That I'd be happier now if I'd taken the time to date when I was younger, rather than marrying straight out of uni.' He chucked another nut in the air, before crunching it loudly.

'Obviously I wasn't thinking straight. But then I got chatting to Olivia at a work conference. She was a dentist too but reminded me of Jodie just after we graduated. Ambitious, but always up for a nightcap and a bit of mischief. I couldn't resist the temptation to just… see. I told myself it was a one-off, then a fling. But six months later, I knew I'd fucked my whole life up.'

Jodie had figured it out when Al stayed an extra night on a two-day conference. And he'd caved the second she'd asked questions. We all thought she'd forgive him. It was Al and

Jodie. We'd only ever known them together. But she didn't even entertain the idea. Kicked Al out immediately. He was still in Jonesy's spare room, much to Georgia's annoyance.

'Jodie says I betrayed her at the time she needed me to be strong and dependable most. Right when the kids were still babies, and she was trying to find a balance between being a lawyer and being a mum. She needed me to be there while she figured it all out. But I couldn't see beyond my own needs.'

Al sighed, staring at the ceiling. 'I dunno, Dyl. Sometimes I wish I could go back and have a fling with Megan in third year. Make my mistakes back then when I was young and there wasn't as much riding on it. Now I'll see my girls grow up in weekend snatches. And for what? A few seedy hotel room screws.'

His despair came off him in waves. It'd been me who'd warned him to stay away from Megan. Had my meddling in this timeline caused Al's divorce? Just thinking about losing April was unbearable.

Picturing her face triggered something, and Al's hunched form faded, replaced by more memories overwhelming my senses. Hundreds in quick succession. Another decade, two. Kids, first days at school, fish and chips on Whitby seafront, being best man at Adam's wedding, becoming an uncle several times over, supporting Jonesy through chemo then watching him give a speech at Al's second marriage. It gave me vertigo, and I was sure when it finally stopped, I'd vomit.

Only then, there she was. April, sitting in a rocking chair by a window I didn't recognise, staring into a garden slowly being soaked by drizzle.

'Dylan?'

How long had she been saying my name? I shook my head to order my thoughts. April's hair was almost blonde where she'd dyed it to cover the grey. Her eyes were crinkled round the edges, but they still shone like sunshine in a clear blue sky.

'It's just us again now.' She sighed.

I moved across the living room towards her, a twinge in my back making me flinch. I felt older, physically and emotionally. Years of being cooped up in an office chair had taken their toll on my bones. April's hands were flecked with yellow paint. She saw me notice.

'We did Van Gogh's Sunflowers in class today. Some of the kids were great, for twelve-year-olds.'

I let the memories trickle in before I said anything. April had spent the last twenty years teaching art at secondary school. Yet she'd got so sick of teaching the same old lessons to kids, most of whom had zero interest in art, that she'd stopped even doing it as a hobby.

I'd become a historic buildings inspector straight out of uni. It was supposed to be a stopgap while we worked out our grand plan to travel the world. Only, it'd stuck. I spent my days pouring over planning applications, compiling reports and advising on conservation projects.

Our lives had been busy for the last two decades as we'd brought up our children. Only, now they'd both left home for good, and life felt empty.

'Are you happy, April?' I asked suddenly.

She was taken aback. Standing up, she walked over and wrapped her arms around my neck. It was odd, looking into the face of this April, twenty-five-years older. Her skin less radiant, yet just as beautiful because it was her.

'I told you a long time ago, Dylan. You're everything I wanted. We've had a good life together so far. And we're not done yet.' She kissed me lightly on the lips, and I could feel the strength of our love. It'd never wavered all these years. But it hadn't enlivened us either.

This wasn't me; it wasn't us. Inside I was twenty-five-year-old Dylan, and catching sight of my reflection in the window, I exhaled. I'd stopped that hasty first kiss, and still, our lives hadn't been what we wanted.

'It was supposed to be great,' I murmured. The middle-aged man with a receding hairline staring back at me from the glass looked dull in his chinos and faded wool jumper. Boring. Tired from the mundanity of life.

Glancing round the living room, there wasn't a single sculpture of April's anywhere. There were no weird or wonderful historical artifacts. No photos from excavation sites in Peru or Egypt. No family photos of us hiking up to ancient ruins or seeking out little-known yet beautiful, centuries-old paintings. No memories of opening nights in indie galleries or sculpture unveilings. April had never sold or exhibited a single piece of art. Ever.

This life had given us each other yet taken everything else. Our hopes and dreams. Weren't they important too? Was contentedness the same as true happiness?

'Dylan? Dylan?' April said again.

This time, when I looked in her eyes, I saw something else. A sparkle I recognised.

'April?'

'Yes. It's me. I'm here.'

Suddenly, she was my April. Currently-in-a-coma April. Behind the wispy greys, crow's feet and faint lines on her forehead, my April shone through.

'I would take this if it got me you,' she said, reading my mind. 'But wait for me. I'm coming back to you. And it *will* be great. *We* will be great.'

She spoke quickly, before throwing her body onto mine, wrapping her arms around my neck. The warmth of her anchored me, tugging me back down to my reality.

My eyes flew open in the hospital armchair, and I could still smell her hair and feel the heat of her cheek on mine. Only, before I had a chance to catch my breath, I saw April. Looking right at me.

The Coma

SUMMER 2022

April

What was happening to me? To both of us? Somehow,
I'd managed to talk to Dylan. My Dylan, even though
he looked like a middle-aged man with some adorable
padding around his middle and grey in his stubble.

At first it was like the other times. I was there, but
not. Living snippets of another April's life in fast forward.
Dating Dylan, going to Rome, coming back and into his
arms before we zoomed through a life that was nothing but
ordinary.

But then, he'd asked if I was happy. As middle-aged
April answered, I could feel my Dylan's presence stronger
than ever before. He was there too; I knew it. The desperate
urge to talk to him surged through me until, suddenly, I
was in my body. In control.

Dylan only managed to say my name, but I could tell
he knew it was the real me.

As quickly as it'd happened, it was over. The second I
was in his arms, I experienced this sudden falling sensation,

my stomach dropping, air rushing past me until I slowed to a stop. Opening my eyes in my hospital bed, they found Dylan's staring back at me in shock. Then I was falling again, landing with a thud back in here.

I thought of the April from that alternative reality. The April who'd got Rome and Dylan but settled for a humdrum life working in a job she had no passion for. For some people, teaching gave them purpose. They spent a lifetime galvanising the next generation of talent, inspiring young minds to reach their own potential. But with no heartache, disappointment or challenge to drive her, that April had fallen short of hers. Becoming an art teacher was the backup plan to my backup plan, and she hadn't even been a very good one.

Then there was Dylan. He had no pizazz in that life. If I told my Dylan he'd spend decades doing a job with "inspector" in the title, he'd have taken his chances on the eccentric billionaire he worked for at eighteen.

I'd meant what I said though. I'd take that mediocre life with Dylan over one without him. I sensed the love in that house. Not just between us but for our children and the grandchild we had on the way. I'd choose building a family with him over travelling the world alone making art out of my misery.

My heart had chosen Dylan the moment he'd bumped into me in the library when I was twenty. And his had chosen me a few months later when I walked hungover into his kitchen.

I went there now, to that memory. Skipping through until I found the right one – the real one – like choosing an episode of a TV show on Netflix. It was odd – I was beginning to understand how to navigate this strange limbo I was trapped in. I could even feel the throb of the hangover as I was transported to that morning. The morning Dylan fell for me.

Coffee

JANUARY 2018

Carefully shutting the door behind her, April grimaced, trying not to make a sound. Creeping out of a student house at 6am the morning after letting some well-practised charmer chat her up had not been the plan. Then again, despite her banging head, parched mouth and the stomach-churning recollection of some questionable shots, it had felt good to let loose for once.

And Adam *had* been fun. April was new to the one-night stand thing. She was usually the "look for Prince Charming – head in the clouds" type. She did crave a shower and her own bed though so, leaving Adam sparko, she did an early morning flit.

No regrets, she thought, letting go of the handle and starting to tiptoe through the open-plan kitchen to the front door. Only, when she looked up, her eyes met his.

Dylan was leaning on the kitchen counter, scrolling through the football transfer news while the kettle boiled. Hearing the quiet clank of Adam's door, he looked up too.

With a sharp intake of breath, April suddenly did regret it. She regretted everything. After all this time, here he was. Her pulse began racing, her stomach sloshing as fervently as it had in the library three months earlier. OK, maybe that was the hangover too, but Dylan's deep brown eyes were staring into hers so intently she could hardly move a muscle.

Hyperaware that she stunk of booze, had a beer stain on her dress and the breath of a building site Portaloo, April wanted to cry. Oh, and there was the not-so-small matter that she was creeping out his friend's bedroom.

Why the hell did I listen to Lizzy? April thought, cursing herself.

'Hey.' Dylan smiled.

April was frozen to the spot, while Dylan's eyes still didn't move from hers. All April's hairs stood on end. Could a hangover do that? She didn't think so.

Did he feel it too? He looked taken aback. Then again, he was likely just embarrassed for her, being caught mid-walk of shame.

'Sorry, I thought everyone would still be asleep,' April stuttered, feeling the awkward tension crackle around her as some strange connection passed between them.

'They are. Unfortunately, my all-nighter was an overdue essay.'

April noticed the dark shadows under his eyes and the coffee jar on the counter. She also remembered Adam mentioning his absent wingman the previous night.

Dylan's gaze flicked to April's shoes, strewn by the front door. She had a flashback of stumbling in, kicking them off and giggling as Adam led her to his room.

'Well, I probably should get going,' April said, taking it as a hint to get moving and leave him alone to his breakfast.

'Coffee?' Dylan blurted, nodding to the still boiling kettle.

April's racing thoughts started hurdling over her hangover. He wanted her to stay for a coffee. Was he just being polite? Instinct told her to decline and scarper. But then she took in the playful smile that'd woken his dimples and the gold shining from his eyes. She'd spent months looking for him. Now she'd stumbled across him in quite frankly the worst possible scenario. But it didn't matter if he was just being friendly, she couldn't walk out that door without talking to him.

April looked over her shoulder at Adam's bedroom door.

'Oh, he won't be up until lunchtime. It's Saturday.' He laughed. 'And a coffee will definitely help get you through the journey home. I'm Dylan by the way.'

'April.' She smiled, walking towards the kitchen island and pulling up a stool. 'Adam mentioned you. Something about missing his wingman.'

Dylan laughed again. A wonderful laugh that sounded like leaves crackling underfoot on a crisp autumn morning.

'He obviously didn't need one in the end.'

Ouch, April thought, looking at the floor to hide her burning cheeks. Dylan's face fell as he saw his joke crash land.

'I don't normally…' she stammered.

'I'm teasing. Sugar?' Dylan asked, steamrolling the conversation forward. Thankfully, the kettle clicked, and the mundane task of making coffee gave them space to move into small talk. The tension eased, and before she knew it, Dylan was pouring her a second cup as they chatted like old friends having a catch-up.

'I nearly didn't bother with uni.' Dylan shrugged. He'd pulled up a stool to the other side of the island to face her. 'The summer after my A levels, I got a job for this super rich businessman who wanted to send an archaeological team to Peru. I was just doing logistics, research – boring stuff. But he offered me a spot on the team, to learn on the job from the best of the best, or so he said.'

Giggling, April rolled her eyes. It certainly sounded too good to be true. 'I'm guessing you've no regrets?'

'Nope. He promised me the world, then got bored within six months. Now he's talking about joining the space race. Bit of an Elon Musk groupie. Luckily my mum talked sense into me.'

Dylan confessed he'd been nursing a broken heart that summer too. His sixth form girlfriend had dumped him the day after they got their A level results.

'It stung,' Dylan said. 'Until I got to uni and realised it was much more fun being a fresher when you're single. Our housemate, Al, he's doing the whole long-distance thing with his school girlfriend and spends most of his time on the phone.'

She'd met Al the previous night and he seemed a friendly guy.

'So, what's your story, April Westbury?' Dylan asked.

'I want to be an artist.' April usually held that ambition back from people she'd just met. It was a pipe dream, like being a professional footballer or an actor, and she worried she sounded delusional. But for some reason, maybe it was the way he used her full name, she trusted Dylan wouldn't mock her.

'I know my chances of making a career from my art are slim. Most of my favourite artists weren't famous until they were dead,' she joked. 'Which is why I'm here, doing a history of art degree. It's a backup, as my parents would say. I can always manage a gallery or, at worst, teach it, if no one likes my sculptures.'

'Sculptures?' Dylan asked, pausing with his coffee cup to his lips.

People usually expected her to say paintings. But ever since her grandma bought her a box of plasticine for her fourth birthday, April had loved it. Sitting alone, moulding, carving and modelling differing structures and designs from the depths of her imagination.

'Like I said. Pipe dream,' she said.

'I'd love to see some of your stuff.' Dylan smiled like he meant it too, so she spent the rest of their second coffee showing him photos of her art on social media. Every piece represented a moment in her life. Her favourite was a fired clay model of a young woman cutting the strings of a silk parachute, because it signified her heading off to uni and living away from home for the first time.

'My journey alone into the big bad world.' She laughed. 'It's stupid, and I guess parachute girl would just plummet to the ground. But it's a start. I'm an artist in progress.'

Dylan watched the passion bring April alive. The pure unadulterated excitement running through her as she spoke about her art was the most stunning thing he'd ever seen. And the way she bowed her head bashfully after made him want her even more.

'You never know. Maybe she'll learn to fly,' he blurted, trying to shake any lustful thoughts out his mind.

It was Dylan's turn to blush and April burst out laughing.

'That's probably the cheesiest thing I've ever heard,' she teased. 'Most people just say, "yeah, it's pretty lame, April".'

'OK. You've made your point.' Dylan was chuckling too, and April enjoyed the way it made his dimples dance. A couple of hours had passed since she'd first walked out of Adam's room, yet when she put her empty mug down for a third time, she still didn't want to go.

'I'd offer you another, but we're both already way too wired with caffeine,' Dylan said, nibbling his bottom lip sexily. They'd run out of excuses to keep talking.

'I better go anyway,' April said, climbing off her stool. 'Before even more people are up and about to see my shame.' She grimaced at the thought of her journey home, even if she was far more buoyed after meeting Dylan.

Lizzy had almost convinced her library boy was nothing more than a whimsical fantasy, but if it was possible, Dylan was even more incredible than the picture she'd created in her imagination. Disarmingly funny, kind, with a sexy twinkle of mischief. He met her passion for art with his fascination with ancient cultures and civilisations. She could have talked to him forever.

She was about to tell him as much, not wanting to leave without knowing she'd see him again, when Dylan got there first.

'We're going to a house party tonight,' he blurted. 'I'm sure Adam would love to see you there.'

Adam. She'd almost forgotten about him. Shoving her

phone in her coat pocket, April opened her mouth to reply, but nothing came out. The awkwardness of hours earlier returned as the trickiness of their situation dawned on them both.

'Oh, well, maybe he could text me the address? I'll see if Lizzy fancies it.' April smiled tightly.

'I'll make sure he does,' Dylan said, walking her over to the door.

As April left, she didn't know what to think. Had Dylan asked her on a date? Or was he setting her up on one with his best mate? Either way, she sensed trouble ahead.

'You do seem in a bit of a pickle,' was all Lizzy could say when April finally rolled in the door. Even though it was mostly her fault, which April told her in no uncertain terms.

'I didn't take your knickers off,' Lizzy cried at April's shameless attempted blame-shifting. 'I just gently suggested *you* did.' She was sure it was just a hilarious coincidence April ended up at Dylan's house the night she finally agreed to stop searching for him. Yet, while she refused to accept any responsibility, Lizzy did agree to go to the house party.

'Just to see how this shit plays out.' She laughed, clicking play on whatever TV show she was in the middle of bingeing.

Typical, April thought.

Mid-afternoon, a message arrived from Adam.

Great time last night. Maybe see you later, he'd written, along with the address for the party. Concise. Casual.

Clearly not that keen on repeating it though, April thought. *Thankfully.*

Her creative brain began looping through the

possibilities for the coming party. Maybe they'd simply say hello, chat for five minutes before a frisky fresher caught Adam's eye?

Yes, that's probably what'll happen, April convinced herself. Neither of them had mentioned wanting more than a one-night thing anyway. Then she could chat to Dylan, they could become friends until a suitable amount of time passed to ask him out.

That was definitely the more likely scenario, she told Lizzy, who met her plan with an eye roll, knowing the likelihood of it blowing up in April's face. April chose to ignore her. For all her talk, Lizzy had never dated or had sex with anyone of any age, description or gender since they'd met at eighteen.

Deep down, April knew she should avoid the party. Trust fate to throw her and Dylan back together again. Follow him on social media until the whole "slept with his best friend thing" becomes a very distant memory. Then they'd both be free to explore whatever feelings were fizzing between them.

Only, Dylan was all she could think about, and every time she pictured his face, there was a furious flurry in her chest. If she were fourteen, she'd have been doodling "I heart Dylan" in her diary and planning their beach wedding in the Bahamas.

Dylan Rose.

April thought about his eyes looking seriously into hers and the smile that emerged from a teasing twitch at the corners of his mouth. She imagined those lips kissing her and his hands in her hair, before...

Oh God. What am I thinking? With a deep sigh, April

realised Lizzy wasn't being overdramatic. This wasn't going to end well at all.

*

'No party gets going until 10pm,' April told Lizzy when they arrived nearer 11pm. It was true. But April also secretly wanted to give Adam an hour or so to set his sights on someone who wasn't her.

It worked. When they walked into the lively living room, there were people sitting or standing on almost every inch of carpet. She spotted Adam in the dining room next to a group loudly playing beer pong. He was leaning over an eclectic-looking blonde sporting a pixie cut April could never pull off, one hand on the wall behind her.

Smiling to herself, she went looking for Dylan, quickly finding him getting a drink from the fridge.

'Dylan. Hi,' she said, hoping he couldn't hear the wobble in her voice. 'Do you exclusively hang around in kitchens?'

Spinning around, Dylan's face lit up. He looked at her as though he were studying a portrait.

'I worried you weren't coming,' he said. 'And yes, it's where the food is. The best room in the house.' Dylan looked about to offer her a drink when she heard a voice behind her.

'April.' It was Adam, slurring. 'Ye made it. Here, have a beer.'

Before April could even move, he leaned past Dylan to grab two bottles from the fridge, thrust one in her hand and slung his arm possessively round her shoulders. Dylan looked dismayed, while she visibly flinched. None of which Adam noticed. Clearly, he'd struck out with the pixie cut.

Not wanting to draw attention to the obvious atmosphere crackling between herself and Dylan, April gave a nervous hello, curling her hair behind her ear to try and dislodge Adam's arm. Still oblivious, Adam guided her to the living room sofa, where she could feel Lizzy watching them. Lizzy scrutinised April, Adam then Dylan in turn with her eyes narrowed, like they were a science experiment she was observing.

Party chatter soon took over, as April sat perched next to Adam. Al and Jonesy joined them, and she spent the next few hours trying not to look too long in Dylan's direction. But she felt his gaze linger on her, occasionally catching his eye and giving a shy smile.

'What am I supposed to do?' April hissed at Lizzy when she corned her coming out the toilet. 'Adam just pounced on me.'

'Make your excuses and leave. This is insane, April. Adam's fawning all over you while you're trying to chat up his best mate, who is looking increasingly confused by the way. It's a disaster in the making. Let's just go. You can "accidentally" bump into Dylan in a couple of months if you're still pining after him then.'

But April was incapable of listening to reason.

'And what if he meets someone else in those two months? I can't risk it.' April brushed past her, taking her seat back next to Adam.

By 2am, she was helping Dylan get a swaying Adam into bed, giggling as they got tangled up in their own feet.

'April, April,' Adam slurred. 'Get in. We can have shex

in the morning.'

April laughed to hide her embarrassment, but Adam was persistent.

'Seriously, April, staaaaay. Ye don't wanna get an Uber now. Pleeaase?' He sounded almost childlike, and April knew it was only because he was hoping for an easy lay come morning.

Still, she really didn't feel like waiting for an Uber. And then there was Dylan.

'OK, OK, I'll stay. But I need some water first.'

Adam was snoring on his back before they'd even closed the door. Al and Jonesy had disappeared to bed too. She was alone with Dylan for the second time in twenty-four-hours.

'Water?' Dylan smiled, getting them both a pint glass – obviously stolen from the pub – and sat on the sofa.

'Thanks. I hate being hungover two days in a row. Such a waste of the weekend,' she groaned, sinking into the armchair.

'What kind of lame student are you? Adam hates being sober two nights in a row,' Dylan joked.

The conversation picked up where they'd left off that morning, and they prattled away about everything and anything.

'My dad's not really around.' Dylan shrugged. 'Unless you count taking me for a birthday pint – usually a month late – since I was fifteen. I got lucky, though, because my stepdad Bryan is cool. He makes my mum happy and is a great dad to my twin sisters. Those two, however, are benevolent little dictators.'

His mouth twitched as he talked about his little sisters.

'IVF,' he added. 'I think the disappointment that my dad turned out to be such a shit weighed heavily on Mum, so she wanted a second chance to have a family. Ivy and Lola are five; she had them at forty-three. They're adorable, but the devil on each other's shoulder.'

April, on the other hand, was an only child.

'I don't mind,' she said. 'It does mean my parents are heavily invested in my future, though.' She was joking, but she couldn't deny she felt an element of pressure. 'I'm the only one that can make them proud, have a career, give them grandkids, look after them when they're old and decrepit, and they want that whole shebang. That's why they're so keen for me to have a degree as a backup to my sculptures. Don't get me wrong, they're massively supportive but also that annoying "voice of reason" as Mum calls it.'

Talking to Dylan was the first time April had ever felt truly comfortable with herself. Growing up, she always felt like the weird kid. The popular girls at school didn't think she saw their sniggers when she got overexcited about the latest boyband. Adults thought she was oblivious to their sidelong glances whenever she disappeared into a dreamworld. 'Ditsy April,' they'd say dismissively. Yet she was far more tuned in than it appeared.

Dylan automatically saw that about her. He listened with a genuine smile, enjoyed getting drawn into her whimsical ideas, especially when it came to her sculptures. He didn't make her feel silly; he made her feel seen. Even Lizzy, who would go to war for April, met a lot of her plans with an eyebrow raise and a word of caution. Dylan made April believe in herself because he believed in her.

'If you want to be an artist, then you'll get there, because you won't give up. Besides, I've seen parachute girl and I can't believe someone could make something so intricate out of clay with their bare hands. You're a visionary,' he said. 'Me, I'm just a bang average guy doing what everyone expects. A levels, uni, then I'll probably join some graduate scheme and do the same boring job all my life, get married and die in a worn-out armchair in a three-bed semi in Manchester.'

Dylan was laughing when he finished, his face flicking between serious and amused as that smile April already loved teased its way to his mouth.

He was wrong though. There was nothing average about Dylan.

'You're not stuck on life's treadmill, Dylan. No one studies archaeology if they don't have some sense of adventure. You nearly signed up to go to Peru based on the spurious promises of an eccentric billionaire for God's sake.'

Dylan suddenly looked thoughtful, like it'd only just dawned on him that his boring future wasn't all mapped out.

Their conversation wasn't always so philosophical. They teased each other about their music tastes too, or lack of in Dylan's case. He liked no discernible genre whatsoever. April could fall in love with a band or artist and play them on repeat, stalk them on social media and book a ticket to their next tour. He literally took music song by song and had never even downloaded a whole album or bothered to go to a gig, other than Glastonbury.

'Even that was for the non-stop party, not the headliners,' Dylan admitted.

Two hours flew, and by 4am, they were both yawning.

'I should say goodnight.' Dylan smiled clumsily, standing up and taking her long-empty glass.

'And I probably should make sure Adam's not choking on his own vomit.' April got up, cursing herself as soon as the words left her mouth. Why did she have to mention Adam? Going into his room had zero appeal, but she didn't know how to backtrack, especially as Dylan had to walk by Adam's door to get to his and was now more or less escorting her to it.

The situation was horrifying, and in those few short seconds, April agonised over how she'd possibly say goodnight to Dylan after sharing two intimate conversations with him that day, before sleeping in his best mate's bed.

'You're not average, Dylan, never think that,' she said, trying to diffuse the tension as she followed two steps behind him. 'You've definitely got a bit of Indiana Jones about you.'

Dylan laughed.

'Then perhaps you can be my sexy arty sidekick,' he chuckled, stopping dead outside Adam's door and turning abruptly to face her. April put her hands up to stop herself crashing into him. Her palms landed on his chest, just as his instinctively grabbed her shoulders.

Suddenly, their bodies were clumsily pressed together, faces inches apart as April looked up and into his eyes.

'Sorry,' Dylan uttered, and she could feel his warm breath on her cheek. A flush of heat rushed through her as their gaze lingered. Dylan leaned in, parting his lips as though about to kiss her when he suddenly stopped. Took a step back.

'Night, April,' he said, not looking at her again before

moving in what felt like slow motion towards his room and closing the door. It took April a whole minute to recover before she opened Adam's door and slunk inside.

Hating herself, she stripped to her underwear, climbing under the crumpled sheets and curling up as close to the edge as she were physically able.

This, she thought, *is the worst moment of my life so far.*

She slept fitfully, waking with a jerk every time one of Adam's long limbs brushed hers. When he reached over for her at 9am, she shrank so far away she almost fell out the bed.

'Morning.' He blinked. 'No 6am dash today?'

'No.' She smiled. 'I'd feel bad doing that two days running.'

'Aye, terribly rude not to even say goodbye after sleeping wi someone.' He winked. At some point in the last few hours, Adam had stripped off in his sleep and now thought they'd had sex again. April didn't correct him, worried he'd try for a morning session.

Pulling her clothes on, April made an excuse about unfinished coursework and left Adam snoozing.

'Dylan's gone for a run, said he couldn't sleep,' Al called from the sofa, clocking her scanning the room as she padded out into the kitchen.

Was I that obvious? she wondered, mortified, before scuttling off to curl up in bed in shame and despair, avoiding Lizzy and her judgemental lecture.

*

As predicted, Lizzy was just about ready to have April

committed for the mess she'd got herself in. Especially when she spent the following weekend repeating the mistakes of the first. At Dylan and Adam's. Joining them at the pub under the guise of seeing Adam, then staying up and chatting to Dylan all night before slinking off to sleep in Adam's bed.

'It's gross,' Lizzy chastised. And April knew she needed to extract herself from what was a precarious situation verging on disaster.

Only, Dylan started sending her funny memes from dodgy art shows over Instagram. April knew she wasn't helping things by replying with links to the weirdest archaeological discoveries. Like the one about the sex-crazed nuns she'd just sent.

They were in near constant contact. She wasn't following Adam on Instagram. She didn't know anything about his family, yet she felt like she knew Dylan's twin sisters almost like they were her own.

'You and Dylan need to admit what's really going on, so you can work out how to do this properly. What you're doing is cruel. What if Adam really likes you?' Lizzy said.

'Adam doesn't even know my last name,' April snapped. 'And I'm not sure how Dylan feels or what he's thinking. What if I end up humiliating myself? Adam will move on soon and won't care when Dylan and I stay friends. Then, well, then maybe we can start flirting more, and slowly...'

'Flirting *more*,' Lizzy roared. 'You're delusional and lucky Adam is too self-obsessed to notice that stupid laugh you do when his best mate makes a lame joke, or the way your eyes follow Dylan round the room. Flirting more, my arse.'

April had managed to dodge having sex with Adam

again and he'd started getting frustrated. Not being the easy lay he thought she'd be, April was certain her invites over, or to the pub, were going to dry up soon.

Then what? she worried. Never see Dylan again either? The very idea was unthinkable. She *needed* to see him.

*

It took three weeks of zero sex for Adam to finally get bored and ditch April. After a Friday happy hour at the student union, Dylan invited everyone back. Adam had barely spoken to April, even though he'd organised the entire night. He'd not even given her his usual peck on the cheek when she arrived in a barely there little black dress. April couldn't muster any affection either. As the night wore on, it became glaringly obvious nothing more was going to happen between them.

Then came the Uber dumping.

'I'm of te bed,' Adam announced, standing up and nodding over to April. 'I'll call ye an Uber.'

April shrank into the armchair. It was obvious to everyone in the room she was being kicked out. It was a loud, screaming "you're not invited into my room tonight" if ever there was one. Everyone averted their gaze in embarrassment for her. Everyone except Dylan.

They shared a brief look. Both knowing that this didn't just mean the end of April and Adam. It was the end of their late-night chats. Their secret messaging, their surreptitious glances when they thought no one was looking.

And what now?

Would Dylan forget about me too? April panicked.

As Adam's social life moved on to a different girl, would Dylan, too, resign April to the past? April started to feel pathetically desperate. She couldn't lose Dylan, not now she'd found him.

'Let the girl finish her drink,' Dylan said suddenly, to April's utmost relief. She was grateful she was still nursing a beer.

'Yes, I'll finish this then book my own cab.' She smiled, feigning total ignorance to Adam's instant dismissal.

'Suit yeself.' Adam sauntered into his room grunting goodnight. The others soon followed and once again she and Dylan were left in the living room. It was undeniable that they'd orchestrated it that way. A heavy silence sat between them as they weighed each other up.

Does he feel it too? she wondered. The importance of this moment? It was a turning point. The fork in the road April assured Lizzy was coming. Adam had made his feelings – or total lack of them – clear. So now what did they do?

The Coma

SUMMER 2022

April

For the first time, I made a conscious decision to leave a memory. I knew what happened next; I'd lived it already. I'd pull my phone out, ready to order an Uber, then Dylan would offer me that fateful lift home. We'd kiss for the first time.

I didn't need to see it again to feel it. It was always fresh in my mind. My go-to when I felt lonely or lost. Stepping back, I closed my eyes to Dylan's university living room and opened them again back in that hall of cinema screens.

The home page of my own personal streaming service. Suddenly, everything was crystal clear. I knew why I was there. Visiting my memories, following Dylan through an infinite universe of past, presents and futures.

It was love. Guiding us through time's ripple to help us find our way back to one another. And not only was love the trigger, it was also tethering me to our world. To Dylan.

April's Hospital Room

SUMMER 2022

Dylan

April had been there. Not whatever broken bits were left but all of her. I'd seen it in her eyes when she woke up in her hospital bed looking straight at me. Before she disappeared into her coma again. She'd only been awake a few seconds, yet she was there.

My hand had fallen from hers when I crashed back to reality. Reaching for it again, I shut everything out and willed myself back to her. It didn't work. I couldn't understand it. Perhaps April was too tired, or she'd moved on to another life of what-could've-beens.

Wherever she'd gone, I spent the next week sat by her bed, holding her hand, hoping I'd find her whenever I fell asleep. Desperately willing my mind to be transported into some world where we were together. A reality where I could kiss her again.

In the real world, April spent longer stretches awake but, apart from that one moment between us, so much of her was gone.

Her dad had taken on the task of telling April where she was and why. She never remembered though. Each time she woke up and her mind was a blank canvas, it was a fresh blow. Especially for her mum, who'd cry, distressing April even more. Ian began shielding Sarah from the brutal task of repeatedly telling their daughter she'd spent over a month in a coma.

'She cries every time,' he confided in me one morning. 'But it's the fear that kills me. She looks so scared. Especially when she asks if she can walk, and I have to tell her we're not sure.'

As expected, April had no memory of the crash, our fight, or even turning up on my driveway that day. And now she was sporadically awake, reality was hitting us all hard. When she'd been in the coma, we zoned in on any signs of life. A flicker of an eyelid or a twitch of the finger. Yet now we were learning her survival was only just the beginning. Twitches meant nothing when she couldn't recall her own name half the time.

Doctors suggested Ian and Sarah be April's main visitors when she was awake. The consistency would help April's memory recall, apparently. The rest of us could drop in briefly to say hello or longer if April specifically requested.

I mostly took the night shifts when April was sleeping. It gave me time alone with her, as well as hope that whatever supernatural power was at work would throw us together once more. Alas, so far, I'd stayed firmly in this nightmarish reality where April barely knew who she was, never mind what we were to each other.

Days, then weeks, passed. Then, one morning, Ian

called, just as I was climbing in my driver's seat hoping to get home for a few hours' sleep before work.

'It's April. She's asking for you,' he said. 'She's pretty insistent.'

I'd only left five minutes earlier. Steeling myself, I closed my driver door and jogged back to her room. April was propped up on pillows when I went inside, sipping on a cup of water. She'd only recently started drinking small amounts.

'Dylan,' she said. Nerves zipped through me when she said my name. Her parents quietly got up and hugged me before leaving the room.

'Be patient, please,' Sarah urged. I looked over at April, her forehead lined with worry and confusion.

'Hey, you.' I smiled, taking a seat. She stared at me a while. Unable to gauge what memories she had, I waited for her to speak.

'To me, this is the first time I've laid eyes on you in nearly four years,' she said. 'But I know that's not quite true.' Ian was right about the fear. I saw it now, sat behind her eyes as she rummaged for memories that simply weren't there anymore.

'My dad told me we had a fight. Before the crash. What happened that day, Dylan? Why did we argue?'

'April...' I took her hand, causing her to flinch. Pulling away, I moved my hands to my lap.

'Sorry,' I said. 'Habit.'

'No, it's OK, it's just... unfamiliar.'

Talking her through what happened that day, I looked her in the eye to make sure she was following.

'I said some shitty things,' I admitted. 'I called you

selfish for showing up out the blue. Accused you of using me to sell your art. I'll never forgive myself for it. It was emotional overload, seeing you again like that after so long. Although, your timing was terrible.'

April stared at the ceiling as I spoke.

'I asked you why you ran off to San Francisco, and you said it was because you were ashamed of how you'd acted over Rome. I got mad. It seemed such a trivial reason to throw everything we had away.'

Clearing my throat, I tried to control the anxiety rising in my chest.

'But I know the truth now. Why you left like you did. I know it was because...'

'The fresher.' April's voice was almost a whisper as she started to cry. 'I'm sorry, you must hate me.'

'April, you were depressed. I hate that I didn't see it then. I see it now. You were depressed and hiding it from everyone. And the way I treated you, with this saviour complex of mine, it only made things worse. Which I also hate because I only ever wanted to make you happy. I hate that my love wasn't enough to keep the darkness out. I hate that in a moment of self-destruction, you ended up in someone else's bed. But I could never hate you.'

April looked so defeated.

'I didn't know it was depression until after that valentine's night. I got help then.' Her voice was small. I had to suppress the urge to kiss her.

'And you'll never go through anything like that alone again. Besides, the fresher, Rome, the running away. None of that stuff matters. It's ancient history – the kind we dig up, learn from, then move the fuck on. Nearly losing you taught me we can't let our past mistakes get in the way again. Our love is stronger than that. It brought you to my driveway all this time later, and it had me physically unable to leave your side through all this.'

'Did I say why I just showed up like that? It seems rash,' she asked.

I laughed, and for the first time in years, we shared a joke.

'Do we really need to have the conversation about how you can be a bit impulsive? To answer your question though, I think you came for the same reason I'd been freaking out since I learned you were coming home. You still loved me. And if I'm honest, if you hadn't come to visit me, I'd have found myself wandering into your exhibition the day it opened. I can't shake you, April. Believe me, I've tried.'

'I do still love you,' she said. 'Just in case there was any confusion.'

'There has been a bit,' I admitted. 'There was this whole thing with Jen sending me a plane ticket...'

April's eyes widened. I told her again about Jen's invitation to the exhibition launch and the bit about me ending my engagement.

'I'm sure the nurses will fill you in on that too,' I said. 'But none of that is your fault. I was an idiot to think I could marry Kel. I knew that the second you appeared on my driveway. Instead of admitting it, I got angry at you. And scared of getting hurt again. But nothing was as scary as nearly losing you. Not even close.'

I tentatively took her hand again, stroking her forehead gently. April rubbed her eyes, her breaths beginning to deepen. Dread lodged in my gut when I thought of her going back to sleep. Forgetting again.

'Dylan, can I ask one more question? Everyone else gets cagey when I ask, but I think you'll be honest.' Her fear had returned, and April looked haunted. 'How many times have we had this conversation?'

I felt my own face darken as I contemplated my answer. She deserved the truth. To know what she was dealing with.

'A few,' I admitted.

'How many, Dylan? Please.'

'Five,' I relented. 'This is the fifth time we've spoken about that day. Our fight.'

April started gasping as the alarm rose inside her. I squeezed her hand, hoping it'd slow her breathing.

'Five?'

Not as many times as her dad had been forced to tell her about her crash. The coma. But enough to hurt. Each time I'd wiped her tears and tried to soothe her distress.

'Hey, doctors say five times is nothing. It's still early days. And that's the first time you've had any inkling this wasn't the first time we've spoken. I'm willing to have this conversation as many times as you need for it to stick. I'm not going anywhere. But if it comes down to it, we'll *50 First Dates* the shit out of this.'

April's eyes were already closing, but she smiled at my teasing.

I didn't tell her how hard it was, answering those difficult questions before watching her slip into a place that robbed her of the answers minutes later. Out here, we were living some nightmarish Groundhog Day. Inside our minds, it was a relentless *Sliding Doors* where nothing I tried put anything right.

'I'm scared,' she whispered, her face suddenly vulnerable. 'I don't want to fall asleep and forget. But I'm so tired.'

'I know. I'm here, and I'm not going anywhere.'

'Will you lie with me?' April's eyelids were drooping almost shut, but she managed to shuffle up to make room while I clambered onto her bed. Lying on my side next to her, I held her close as she buried her face in my neck, careful not to dislodge any wires or tubes.

'You smell like you.' She sighed softly, drifting off. Feeling her warmth, I was suddenly exhausted too. Letting drowsiness take me, I thought of how safe and comfortable I felt falling asleep with April in my arms.

Coffee

JANUARY 2018

AN ALTERNATIVE REALITY

Dylan

Suddenly I was awake again. My eyes still throbbed with tiredness, but I wasn't in hospital. I was younger Dylan in the middle of his second year, standing in the kitchen of my student house after pulling an all-nighter on an overdue essay.

Leaning on the counter, just waiting for the kettle to boil, I spotted a pair of red heels strewn by the front door. Kicked off on the way to Adam's bedroom.

Any minute now, Adam's door would creak open as April attempted to sneak out. My memories of it were four years old, but I could still recall hearing the lads arrive home around 3am just as I'd hit full flow. Writing about archaeological looters tunnelling illegally under Pompeii and the recent discovery of a ceremonial chariot buried under the volcanic ash.

I'd chastised myself for leaving the essay to the last minute as I heard their drunken banter through my bedroom door. Not only had I missed out on a Friday night booze-up with Adam, Jonesy and Al, but the essay subject fascinated me. I'd known I could do a much better job if I prioritised.

Now it was 6am, and I'd just finished. That's why I was in the kitchen – I needed a last coffee before I crashed out for several hours, ready to watch the Manchester football derby that afternoon.

Only standing there now, I realised something wasn't quite right.

Wasn't I scrolling through the football transfers? I thought. When April had snuck out of Adam's room, I'd been looking at the transfer news.

Patting my pockets, I realised my phone must still be on my desk. Nipping back to my bedroom to grab it, I got back just as the front door slammed. The shoes by the mat had gone. Out the window, I spotted the back of a brunette scurrying towards the bus stop barefoot, heels in hand.

I'd been thrown into the past, but before I'd had a chance to make a change, someone had made one for me. Had the Dylan of this alternative life been someone who didn't have his phone permanently glued to his hand? Or had it been April? Did she choose to scurry out ten seconds earlier?

It didn't matter. Either way, we missed our fateful meeting that day. Now, suddenly life was whooshing by again. I wasn't in control here, and in no time at all, it was twenty years later. I tried to cling onto the memories of my real life, but it was useless as new ones barrelled in like wrecking balls, smashing and erasing everything else that'd come before it like giant chalkboard rubbers.

Everything rolled to a stop in a car park I instinctively knew, as a boy I instinctively loved slammed the passenger door of a grey family minivan.

'Dad, just promise you won't pretend to be Indiana Jones again,' he said, as we walked towards the double doors of the local secondary school. I laughed, apparently understanding Indie wasn't cool to thirteen-year-old boys anymore. Especially when their dad tells their classmates he's like Indie minus the whip.

'OK, OK, but don't blame me if someone else brings it up.' I smiled, the life I'd landed in becoming the only one I knew. 'Indie is legendary.'

This was the second careers day I'd spoken at, and the head teacher always likened me to some film archaeologist, even though it was miles away from my historical consultant job.

I used to travel much more, before the kids were born. To historical sites across Europe and South America. These days, I mostly had artifacts sent to me for analysis, or I did remote research. My wife, Kel, preferred it when I wasn't off galivanting, as she put it.

'It's good you got it out your system in your twenties,' she always said. We'd married at twenty-five, and our daughter, Missy, had – accidentally – come along a year later. We'd not planned to start a family so soon, but the moment she arrived, I knew I was born to be a dad. I was happy to sacrifice the travelling to watch them grow up. Even if, now teenagers, they didn't leap into my arms like they used to. I'd gone from Alfie's hero to the cause of all his embarrassment as the clock struck midnight on his thirteenth birthday.

Walking through the school doors, Alfie almost let that one slam too, on the young girl behind him.

'Woah,' I cried, catching it just in time. 'Sorry about my rude son.' I turned to her mum, who was loaded down carrying some enormous, twisted pile of metal. A flash of royal blue looked up at me from under a bouncy brown bob and the world stopped turning.

'Don't worry, my fault for lugging in this monstrosity, but Isla insisted.' She was slightly out of breath yet a ball of smiling energy. Light shone from every pore as she gently steered her daughter through the door using her knee.

'Oh,' she cried, pulling up as the door banged shut behind her. 'It's you.'

Was it hot in here? I suddenly felt flushed. My legs had turned to jelly, and my heart was racing in a way it hadn't for two decades, which made me incredibly uncomfortable given I was happily married.

'I'm sorry, do I know you?' And what *was* this feeling going on inside me? Was it attraction? I'd not so much as glimpsed at another woman since meeting Kel. I prided myself on being a loyal husband, my eyes never wandering.

Yet this pull towards this beautiful stranger walking into my kids' school was entirely involuntary. Almost as though my world hadn't just stopped but tilted on its axis.

'Erm, we went to the same uni I think. Manchester, right?'

'Right.' Another parent was coming through the door, so we carried on moving through reception to the assembly hall. It struck me as odd, though, that she'd recognise someone she'd seen around campus twenty years earlier.

I'd definitely never met her; I knew without a doubt I'd remember if I had.

Watching her give her talk to a room full of first and second years thirty minutes later, I listened intently. Her name was April; she was an artist and mum to eleven-year-old Isla, who'd been born in San Francisco before they'd moved back to Manchester six years ago. April had then set up her own art gallery along the canal, but her speciality was custom-made sculptures.

'This,' she said, gesticulating to the giant mental sculpture I could now see was a rose bush in full bloom, 'is Isla's favourite. It's a copy of one I was paid to make for her favourite park in San Francisco.'

April told the kids how she'd studied in Rome in her third year of university, before taking an internship in America. She'd worked hard at a gallery for several years, exhibiting the odd bit of work, until she was commissioned to do a piece for a charity event.

'Being an artist takes dedication, and it's always good to have a backup plan,' she said, with a serious head nod that made me think she didn't truly believe in backup plans. 'But there are a lot of different ways to make a career out of art. With hard work, and some good fortune, you can create, exhibit and sell your own pieces. Or you can take on commissions like me, curate for a gallery or even teach it. The most important thing is not to limit yourself.'

She had the young students enthralled, especially Isla, who hadn't yet reached that age when anything her mother did was met with huff and a glower. Me, I was transfixed.

The way April smiled at everyone, all at once, made my pulse quicken. A second later, guilt crushed me, bringing the kind of sticky heat that made me feel uncomfortable in my own clothes.

When it was my turn to talk, I was painfully aware of her eyes on me, grateful I'd done careers day the previous year so could answer questions on autopilot.

As the morning ended and the kids went back to lessons, some of the parents arranged to go for lunch at the local pub. Most of us had taken the entire day off. That's how I found myself sitting next to April in a corner booth, talking about our time at Manchester uni.

With Alfie and Missy both going home to Kel, and April's mum picking up Isla, we decided to make an afternoon of it. I knew it was a terrible idea, but I couldn't help myself. I was intrigued by why April made me feel so alive.

'My friend Lizzy's going to pop in; she's a physio and her last client was at 2pm.'

As head of PE at our kids' school, Adam said he'd join us after the final bell, with Jonesy and Al arriving later.

'A uni reunion, of sorts.' April smiled, bringing over another round of drinks.

'Remind me how you knew I went to Manchester?' I asked, still struggling to believe she'd remember me all these years later. I barely recognised Jonesy sometimes.

April blushed and looked at the table, letting her hair fall in front of her face to hide her embarrassment. I had to fight the urge to tuck it back behind her ear.

'Actually, I sort of had a crush on you.'

A crush? On me?

'How is that possible?' I was baffled as well as amused. 'We didn't know each other, did we?'

333

'No. We only met once actually. Very briefly. In the library. It was my second year just after reading week. You were rushing across the foyer up to the old archives and you ran straight into me. I guess I thought you were cute and always hoped I'd run into you again. I didn't though.'

'Huh. And now all these years later, here I am.'

'Here you are.' April sipped her wine, clearly wishing she'd not said anything.

'I remember that night,' I admitted. 'Shame I was too preoccupied with my very late essay to be paying attention to any beautiful women I crashed into.'

My attempt to ease her embarrassment made April blush more. Luckily, I spotted Adam coming through the door in his hoody, jogging bottoms and trainers. Seconds later, he'd got himself a pint, a bag of crisps and was arriving at our table with an amused grin on his face.

'Well, well, well. It really is a uni reunion.' He plonked himself down opposite April and threw her his most charming smile.

'Hello, April. What's it been? Twenty years since ye snuck out ma bedroom at the crack of dawn?'

April frowned, before a flicker of recognition turned into a dawning realisation.

'Adam?' she squeaked. 'Sports science Adam?'

'The very same. I have to say, I had more than ma share of girls at uni, but ye were the only one who ghosted me. After we'd had so much fun, too.' Adam stuck out his bottom lip in mock sadness.

April looked like she wanted the pub floor to swallow her whole. I felt this unfamiliar twist in my gut. If I didn't know better, I'd have thought it was jealousy.

'So, you two...'

'Oh yeah.' Adam nodded, clearly enjoying torturing April with this story. 'Our first night out after the Christmas break in second year. You were pulling an all-nighter I think, Dylan. Late wi yer coursework as usual.'

I cringed as Adam continued.

'April was at the bar all heartbroken over some guy she'd met in the library and never seen again.'

Catching April's eye across the table, I realised he was talking about me.

'Luckily, I was there to console her wi some shots. Didn't hang around in the morning though, did ye. Bolted.' He winked at her now, oblivious that his teasing was mortifying April for a far deeper reason than their one-night stand.

'Your memory of that night is remarkable considering the amount of alcohol we threw down our necks.' April's teeth were almost gritted as she spoke.

'Always remember the ones that run out on me. Was usually the other way around.' Adam had recently married, but he'd been well into his thirties before he'd started dating anyone seriously.

'I was in the kitchen,' I cried, suddenly remembering the morning they were talking about. 'I nipped back to my room to get my phone, and when I came back, I saw you closing the door and walking down the street. Red shoes.'

April and I had been seconds from meeting all those years ago. I found myself wishing we had, before the crushing guilt returned and I thought of Kel back home cooking fishfingers for Missy and Alfie's tea.

'It was all a long time ago now,' April said, lifting her wine to her red lips. 'Another lifetime really.'

Her friend Lizzy arrived. Talk moved on to friends we'd had in common and uni reunions we'd been to.

April had briefly married an American artist named Blake, but after Isla was born, they realised they were more friends than lovers. She'd moved back here, and now Isla spent six weeks every summer with her dad.

'I couldn't ask for a better ex-husband if I'm honest,' she said.

I thought we'd blustered through any awkwardness when I overheard Lizzy chastising April at the bar.

'You told him about the library? He's married April. *Married*,' she cried.

'He asked, and I didn't want to lie. Anyway, it was decades ago. It's just a funny story now.'

Lizzy glowered at April. 'Is there or is there not still a scrap of paper in your purse with your name and number on it?'

'Yes,' April hissed. 'But that's just for sentimental reasons.'

'Sentimental my a…' At that point I cleared my throat to announce my arrival.

'Jonesy and Al just got here and technically it's my round.'

It was soon last orders, and by now, any earlier tension had vanished as we all laughed and chatted like old friends. But I couldn't deny I was inexplicably drawn to April. I knew I had to do something about this growing attraction, especially as I kept inadvertently catching her eye. Each glance more loaded than the last.

As everyone said goodbye outside, I quietly asked her to meet me by the canal.

Ten minutes later, we were standing under the stars by the moonlit water. It would have been romantic if I hadn't been so wracked with guilt.

'Hey.' She smiled, falling into step with me as I walked.

'Hey.' I didn't know where to start, so I launched into it.

'Meeting you today has been… surprising.' I was too old and too married to tiptoe around problems.

'I know. I'm sorry about that library stuff, should have kept that to myself.'

Dismissing her apology with a shake of my head, I smiled down at her.

'Not at all, it almost explained a few things to me. Why I was feeling so… intrigued by you.' It was clumsy but important I explained. 'There's no denying we have some connection. I can't really explain it, other than to say I do wonder what would have happened if we'd met back then. At uni. I probably always will.'

'Dylan, you don't have to do this. We can walk away just having had a nice night at the pub.'

'We can't though.' I sighed. Our kids attended the same school; we'd bump into each other every now and again and I needed there to be no lingering atmosphere Kel, or the children, could pick up on.

'I need to apologise because I can't be friends with you. We can't try and know each other after tonight. It's not a safe path to go down. I love my family, my marriage, and I have this gut feeling us being friends would eventually jeopardise that, as hard as I'd try for it not to.'

She smiled. 'I understand. Maybe in another life. It has

actually been nice to put a name to the face. I did always wonder about you.'

We came to a stop by the road where we'd go in different directions home.

'Goodnight, Dylan.' April held out her hand, and I shook it, grateful she didn't go in for a hug that'd cause my resolve to waiver. She had that pub smell of salt and vinegar crisps and Pinot Grigio, while the rose scent of her perfume clung to her coat.

'Goodnight, April.'

With relief and regret, I watched her walk away.

She only made it a few steps when she stopped and whipped around.

'Dylan? Dylan?' she whispered loudly. It was a question, not a statement. 'It's me, it's April. Your April.' It was like I regained consciousness, right there in the middle of the road under the glare of the streetlights.

'April?'

Suddenly we were us again in forty-year-old bodies. Rushing over, I embraced her, pulling her head into my shoulder.

'I've been trying to break through for hours,' April gasped. 'I knew you were in there somewhere too.'

'April, I have so much to say. So many questions to ask. Do you know what's happening to us?'

April shook her head, and her bob grazed her chin. Unable to resist, I ran my fingers through it. It suited her short.

'I want to kiss you. Can I kiss you?'

April shook her head again.

'We're just visitors here. If this April and Dylan do turn

out to be real, in a parallel universe somewhere, it wouldn't be fair to them. Their lives went in different directions to ours.'

It was impossible to hide my disappointment, but she was right. What if they remembered our kiss? Or worse, someone saw them and thought they'd been unfaithful? We couldn't risk it.

'I miss you. I need you to come back to me, April.'

'I'm trying, I promise. My body just needs time.' She looked around at the empty street. 'That's why I've been hanging out in here. It's like a cinema of my life, only some films I've seen before, others, like this one, are brand new. They belong to a different me in an alternative life. But I am starting to understand how this place works, which I think means I'll be ready to leave soon.'

'So why am I here too?' I asked.

'Love, silly.' April smiled, making the sun literally rise around us. 'You weren't ready to let me go, which kept me here, in limbo.'

I'd created this place?

'We both did,' April said, reading my mind. 'Our love for each other.'

'I'll never be ready to let you go.' It was the only thing I was certain of.

April cocked her head to the side and smiled again. 'I think that might be another reason you're here. There were a few things you needed to understand. But don't worry, we can speed this up. I've found the remote.'

My fingers tremored as April reached out and curled her hand around mine.

'There's one last life I need to show you. Close your eyes – this will be quite the ride.'

Before I could block out the light, the world started twisting. Images whizzed past me so quickly I couldn't make them out, like I was in fast forward on an old video tape.

It slowed briefly, and I saw April in a building that was so forebodingly familiar. The hospital. Only, she was cradling a tiny bundle in her arms. A baby with a full head of dark hair. Our baby? April looked besotted.

Everything sped up again, slowing sporadically to show images of April. She was always in the hospital. Carrying a car seat with a sleeping baby inside, holding the hand of a little boy as he toddled beside her, a small butterfly strip across his forehead, then dwarfed by a spotty teenager with floppy hair and his arm in a sling.

Then later, she looked middle-aged and was holding a baby again. Only this time she was sat next to the bed of a young woman who was the spitting image of her.

Older again, I saw April sat in one of the rooms her parents kept disappearing into with legions of doctors. Her head was on the shoulder of a grey-haired man. Me. We were both weeping.

It sped up again, before abruptly stopping in a room that was a carbon copy of the one Coma April currently occupied. Only we were on a different ward because the window didn't look out over the car park.

She had tubes up her nose and winding down her arm into her wrist. A mask hung close by for when she needed pain relief or help to breathe.

She was dying.

I felt it instantly as I landed in the body of the old man sitting next to her. My back hunched and twisted, my arthritic hands aching at the joints as I held hers. An inexorable sadness swallowed me whole.

The liver-spotted skin of April's hand felt papery to the touch. It slid across her bone as I squeezed. A halo of wispy white hair fanned out across her pillow, and she was so thin she was almost skeletal.

'April,' I whispered, that antiseptic stink worming its way down my throat, making old-man Dylan nauseous. The elderly lady remained perfectly still, and I was starting to fear she was already gone when her eyes flicked open. My April stared back at me, her piercing eyes even bluer against her pale complexion. Death was creeping up on her.

'You made it,' she croaked.

'Are you OK, are you in pain?' I asked, trying to whip round and look for a nurse, only to be held back by my own failing body.

'It doesn't hurt. Not anymore,' April said. She'd been here before. But I couldn't understand why she'd brought me there.

'I can't watch you die. Please, April, I can't do this one.' Holding my breath, I tried to pull myself out of this decaying body and back to my own. Will myself awake. Then April squeezed my hand.

'You won't. Stay calm. We'll leave before that happens.'

'What's wrong with you? Can we work it out? What hurts? We can stop this happening.' I was gasping for breath, trying to fend off a panic attack.

Yet OAP April burst into hysterical laughter.

'It's just one of a thousand illnesses that could eventually finish me off. And why would we stop it? Look at me. I'm not twenty-five here; I'm in my late eighties and pumped full of morphine. Dylan, let the memories in.'

Pausing, I let the old man's life click into place like pieces of a stained-glass window. I saw it clearly now. The eighty-ninth birthday we'd thrown April when doctors made it clear she wouldn't make it to ninety. The room full of kids, grandkids, great grandkids, nieces, nephews and beyond. April's legacy. Our legacy.

'Eighty-nine.' She smiled. 'I'll take that too. That's sixty-five years with you. Imagine the real memories we could make.'

'Right. Because these aren't real. Or they're not really mine at least.' It was hard to remember that when I could physically feel the fragility of my bones. Yet I was starting to understand.

'They *could* be, yet not necessarily,' April rasped. 'Our future is still unwritten. There are boundless possibilities ahead of us. Some will be magic, and we'll wonder how we ever got so lucky. Others will be testing, and we'll have to work hard to get through them. Together. It won't be perfect, but it'll be ours.' Her chest rose labouredly with the effort of speaking.

'When we do get here, or to a point like this, I'll need you to let me go, Dylan. And you'll be ready. So will I, if it ends up being me, hunched over your decaying old-man bod.'

Wiping my cheeks with my palm, I noticed my skin had that musty odour of age and was brittle and loose like April's. Touching my hand to my hair, it felt coarse, and for the first time, I looked down and noticed my six-pack had given way to a soft paunch. A dull ache stretched up my back, and my hip was stiff and alien, like it wasn't my own.

But this elderly Dylan's mind was swimming with beautiful memories. There was something else, too. He had no regrets. Through all the ups and downs of life, he didn't wish he'd done a single thing differently.

April's crepey hand lightly squeezed mine again as I nodded my understanding.

'We won't have to worry about this moment for decades. There's another memory I want to take you to, a real one this time. One of mine that you don't have. Let's get out of here, before one of us croaks it. Again.'

'But, how?' I asked.

Old-lady April chuckled. 'It's easy now I've figured it out. I *am* the remote.'

Then her eyes closed and, suddenly, my ears were ringing. Everything was tipping upside down. This time it felt like I was flung through space and time, until I landed with a jolt into a body sat at a laptop in the library at Manchester uni.

This wasn't another reality. This was the real me, with no memories of any possible futures. Just the now, and in the now, my own thoughts were overwhelmed by the stress of a looming deadline causing chaos in my brain.

Why do I always leave things last minute? I was thinking. I'd got away with missing a few deadlines in first year, but I'd promised myself I'd get my act together. Now, here I was again, my first big essay of the semester due in the morning and only half written.

Leaning forwards, I bashed on the keyboard a few more times when an email alert flashed up. A research paper I'd been desperately waiting for had finally been returned to the archives.

By someone who no doubt finished yesterday, I lambasted myself.

Still, I was relieved. I'd heavily – and lazily – relied on some of the historical archaeological methods outlined in an online summary of the paper. It was so ancient the library only had one hard copy and it was now upstairs in the archive returns pile.

Making a mental note of the author and journal volume, I leapt from my seat and hurried towards the stairs, muttering the vital information under my breath. I was hardly aware of anything else going on around me as I took huge strides through the foyer.

Out of nowhere, a girl stepped in my path, and before I could steer round her, she bounced off my chest, flying towards the ground. It was a good job my impending deadline already had my nerves on edge. A surge of adrenaline gave me feline reflexes, and I caught her before she hit the floor.

Grimacing, I scooped up her "I Heart Rome" bag and bundled it back into her arms.

'Phew, empty,' I whistled, passing her a bright pink reusable coffee cup and noticing her dark hair had spilled haphazardly over her face in the fall. All too aware I needed that research paper fast, I tried to make the quickest, but most sincere, apology I could. Pulling her close, I pushed the stray strands of hair from her face to look her in the eyes.

'I'm sorry. You OK?' I gasped. Her blue eyes widened as she looked back at me, but she nodded, so I turned and hightailed it up the stairs two at a time.

Only, with each step, everything started slowing down.
Dylan, pay attention.

I was just a voice in my own head, but somehow, I managed to get my message through.

Pay. Attention.

By the time I got to the top, I was struggling to remember the name of the author, or the volume, I needed. Instead, a flash of the girl's face crossed my mind, and I stopped in my tracks, thinking about her huge blue eyes as they met mine. The feel of her soft chocolate-brown hair was making me tingle. She'd smelled of fresh berries and rose petal shampoo, and the instant replay of our collision sent my heart into an Olympic sprint.

April.

Instinctively, I span around and rushed back to the balcony. Looking down, I breathed a sigh of relief. She was still there, looking shell-shocked and staring off in the direction I'd raced away from her.

'Hey,' I called down.

The beautiful library girl looked up and smiled the kind of smile that made me forget to breathe.

'Can I have your number?'

'Dylan!' she cried with annoyance. 'You can't change anything in this one.' April was laughing as I walked back down the stairs and stood in front of her. 'I was giving you the memory, seeing as you were too distracted the first time. It was a gift. But you can't change it. Have you learned nothing?'

'I couldn't help myself,' I teased. 'Don't you wonder? What would have happened if I'd been paying attention that day? I think about it a lot.'

'Not anymore.' April sighed. 'That's the point of all this, of limbo. I don't think we were supposed to make it through uni still together. We needed to find our own paths first. Reliving our past has helped me heal because it taught me to forgive myself.' She smiled and thought for a moment. 'It taught me not to give up.'

'And you, Mr Saviour Complex,' she said, looking at me sternly. 'You needed to learn that you can't mend everything.'

Biting my bottom lip, I thought about all those sliding doors I'd slipped through. At uni, I'd been so busy swooping in to fix everything, I'd made April feel broken. Then I'd been sent back in time only to do the same.

'You're not broken, April. You never were. It was all just bad timing, misaligned ambition, life.'

'Life.' April sighed, tilting her head at me. 'Just because we got everything wrong never meant we weren't right for each other. And, as I said, our future hasn't been written yet, so can we please get on with it? With no regrets.'

'No regrets.' I nodded. '*Now* can I kiss you?'

'No.'

Suppressing a whine, I pouted like a puppy she'd just kicked.

April giggled. 'Only because I'm fairly sure I won't remember it. Brain damage, remember? All this wipes from my memory whenever I wake up, and if you try explaining it to me, I'm going to think you're bonkers. But you'll remember. And you and your fully functioning brain will need to be prepared for what comes next.'

'What is next?'

'Rehab, physio, physical therapy and a whole lot more in-between. It's going to be rough. I've seen it seven hundred different ways and it's always rough. Don't try to make everything better for me.'

Holding one hand, she stroked my cheek with her other. 'Just love me, Dylan. Hold my hand, let my mum do the tough talking and my dad the heavy lifting. At some point, the darkness will creep in again. But if you promise just to love me, maybe lie with me in a dark room sometimes, I promise I won't give up when the going gets tough.'

'April, loving you has never been optional for me.' I wasn't allowed to kiss her, but she stepped forward and put her head on my chest. I enveloped her small frame in my arms, savouring the feel of her warm body against mine.

This was the April I remembered. It felt like coming home. And finally, I was ready. We both were.

April's Hospital Room

SUMMER 2022

Dylan

When I came to, April's mum was gently shaking me.

'Dylan. The nurses need to change April's sheets before their shift ends.' Her voice was a whisper even though it was still only late afternoon.

My head throbbed with the heaviness only a truly deep sleep could induce. My limbs were still wrapped round April, her hand clasped in mine on top of her chest.

'Sorry. She was scared about forgetting again. She asked me to lie with her.'

Sarah smiled.

'Every time she sees you, she wakes up calmer, less agitated and frightened. Even though she doesn't remember anything. I know it doesn't make sense, but it's true.'

I told her April knew we'd all been having the same conversations with her on repeat. Sarah agreed it had to be a good sign.

'I hope she starts remembering soon. Ian loses a piece of himself every time he tells her about the accident. He won't let the doctors do it even once in case that's the time she remembers. He wants it to come from someone she loves and trusts.'

As if hearing his name, Ian emerged at the door carrying a tray of coffees.

'Doctors are hopeful the confusion and memory loss will lift soon.'

But like April had warned me in limbo, we all knew there was still a long way to go. Until they could get April out of bed, we wouldn't know what physical effects she'd be suffering, other than muscle atrophy.

'We can deal with anything,' Sarah said, hugging me as I climbed off April's bed and shook my aching body. 'So long as she keeps waking up.'

April's Hospital Room

SUMMER 2022

April

Mummering voices wormed their way into my ears, getting louder as I slowly became aware I was awake. Their relaxed chatter was soothing and before I let the light in, I listened without looking.

Something was different.

Previously, whenever I'd woken, it'd been like wading through a desert of quicksand in a dense fog, my loved one's grainy shadows in the distance. This time, although it took a few seconds, the confusion had lifted slightly and I knew where I was and why.

Head injury. Car accident.

Images of Dylan and I in different realities spanning a hundred lifetimes slipped away, and I knew I was never going back to that chaotic cinema of the past, present and future.

Hospital. Surgery. Coma.

The new information rained down, washing away all recollection of limbo. Clearing the cache of my brain, ready to be replaced with fresh memories in the real world. I couldn't remember my car flipping over on the wet road. Footage of the whole week preceding that day had been permanently wiped too.

I had a vision of myself boarding a plane in San Francisco, smelling the dry, recycled air, taking a long last look out the window at the Californian sunshine. Closing my eyes as the thrust of the engines pushed me back in my seat and hearing a whoosh as the plane lifted off the ground. Then, nothing.

Snapshots of bright light. The smell of antiseptic and cleaning products. Sometimes a waft of coffee. People saying my name.

'April. April. April.'

Mostly it was Mum calling to me. And Dylan. I remembered Dylan telling me he wasn't going anywhere, no matter what.

He still loved me.

My eyes flew open at the thought, frantically searching the room for him. And there he was. Leaning forwards, saying my name.

'You're awake again.' He smiled gently. He was nibbling his bottom lip in a way that was so heart-flutteringly familiar. A zap of electricity blazed through me at the recollection. It was such a small memory, but it existed.

'You'll make your lip sore,' I croaked. Dylan's nervous smile morphed into a giant grin, and he started laughing.

'Yes, I will. You once bought me a ChapStick.'

'Mum. Dad.' I looked gratefully at my parents. 'How long was I asleep?'

I'd been out all day, but it was the first time I'd

remembered choosing sleep, rather than slipping back into unconsciousness.

A doctor came in and started asking questions. My parents' names, who the prime minister was, my date of birth. Then he pointed at Dylan and asked who he was.

'Dylan. My boyfriend.' As the words tumbled out, I cringed. 'I mean, he *was* my boyfriend. I don't know if he is now. But he's here, and he says he's not going anywhere.'

The sound of Dylan quietly chuckling soothed my soul.

'Let's just say we're figuring some things out. You'll start remembering more soon.'

As he spoke, his voice forced another memory in and I frowned, digging into my brain for the information.

'We had a fight.' I couldn't recall the argument. 'But you sat right there and told me about it.'

Dylan leaned further forwards, gently stroked my bandaged forehead and told me not to agonise over the details too much.

The doctor explained the muddle the coma had locked me in was lifting and that it didn't matter how many times I needed to ask things or how many times I had the same conversation. I was slowly remembering.

April's Hospital Room

LATE SUMMER 2022

Dylan

With every day, April remembered more.

Thankfully, my tutor gave me coursework and research extensions. Logged my exceptional circumstances for the trips I'd missed to excavation projects in Italy. It meant I could spend all the time I wasn't in university at the hospital.

April still slept most of the time. Her injuries and coma left her suffering severe fatigue and excruciating headaches. There were days she needed so much morphine she barely made sense.

'But she's lucky,' the neurologist assured us.

It took another week or so for her to remember why we'd fought the day of the crash.

'Just explain it once more; I'll remember tomorrow,' she'd say. Eventually, it stuck.

Yet it took several more difficult conversations before it sunk in that I knew about the fresher. The secret she'd kept so long, believing it would be the end of us.

I hated seeing her cry, which she always did. It didn't matter that I considered it insignificant after seeing her so close to death. For April it was a defining moment. A time when she let herself, and me, down. Stopped believing in true love for a split second too long.

Everything I'd been through had taught me I couldn't take away her pain, but I also knew, given time, she'd see it for what it was – a blip at the depths of her illness – and forgive herself. She didn't remember limbo, yet it'd kept her alive, and the lessons she'd learned were inside her.

'If you ever need to talk about it, I'm ready and willing. Otherwise, it's not something I'm going to agonise over or dwell on. Both our mistakes are in the rear-view mirror.' It was a well-practised speech, given I'd said it to her every day. Then, after a few weeks, she stopped bringing it up, and I guessed she was ready to move on.

April's day-to-day short-term memory was steadily improving. After a month, her initial trauma-related amnesia had gone. There'd be some things she'd never recall, yet they'd be small, comparatively. A childhood holiday she didn't remember going on, an old acquaintance she couldn't quite place or the smell of her favourite prawn cocktail crisps.

April suffered mood swings, too. Mostly down to the extreme fatigue, yet she had a slight temporary hormone imbalance thanks to the brain injury.

Every part of her was our April though. Sunshine flooded the room whenever she greeted a new visitor. Even if the sky outside was grey and cloudy. Her biggest smile was always reserved for me. Every time I arrived, she looked like she couldn't believe I was there. It took my breath away in the way only April ever could.

One evening, I arrived to find her sat up, giggling with Jen and Lizzy. They each had a plastic cup of smuggled in white wine.

'I'm only having a few sips,' April protested, rolling her eyes at my disapproving look. 'Jen's drunk most of it, and besides, we're celebrating.'

'Yep,' Jen giggled. 'I've decided to extend my trip. Permanently!' The Manchester gallery showing April's art exhibition needed someone to run the show while April focused on her recovery.

'Jen did such an excellent job setting everything up they decided to keep it in situ for six months. Then she'll take it on a UK tour for me. Hopefully I'll do guest appearances when I'm up to it.' The news – and wine – had brought a flush of colour to April's cheeks. She'd not said it, knowing how worried we all were about her survival, but she'd been worried the accident would derail her hard-won career.

'Wow, that is good news; I'm happy for you both.' I beamed, perching on the end of April's bed. It was astounding how quickly life picked back up at breakneck speed after almost ending altogether. April had hardly even skipped a beat. She'd even promised the gallery that, by the time the exhibit returned from tour, she'd have some new pieces.

'It'll be like a sequel. Or an epilogue. With the crash, the coma. And our first reunited kiss once you bother to give me it,' she added with a pout. Jen and Lizzy's cackles only deepened the burgundy of my blush.

'A few sips?' I asked. 'Then that coma has significantly damaged your wine tolerance, never mind anything else.'

April poked her tongue out. I shot her another amused scowl. Secretly, I was warmed by the return of her unrestrained wilfulness. An overexcited April was a welcome sound. The room, the atmosphere, everything seemed lighter and brighter with her happiness.

'You two look like you're getting on better.' I nodded to Jen and Lizzy, who were sat so close their thighs were touching. I'd watched Jen and Lizzy bicker and wholeheartedly disagree for the entire duration of April's coma. Jen had even decamped to an Airbnb after the first few weeks. I'd sensed some definite energy between them. Only now, they roared with laughter.

'Dylan, they're holding hands.' April laughed, seeing my baffled expression. 'It was that obvious, I clocked they'd got together almost while I was still unconscious.'

Apparently, it'd happened within days of Jen arriving. Your typical case of opposites attract, with the added push of them seeking solace in each other while their best friend was fighting for life. Jen had only moved out so they could explore their relationship without being on top of one another.

'I always fancied her.' Lizzy chuckled. 'Why else would I put up with you squawking away in the background of my video calls to April.' She kissed Jen lightly on the nose with an affection I'd never thought I'd see from Lizzy.

Watching them, it was suddenly immediately obvious. But I'd been so occupied by my trips into the past, I'd missed it all.

They complemented each other. Yin and Yang finding their perfect balance. Meeting in the middle thanks to their mutual love of April. I smiled to myself. April had that effect on people. She brightened their lives and made them better.

'I did wonder how you were tolerating Jen's Zoom invasions, Lizzy,' April confessed. 'No one else ever got invited to wine time.'

After the happy couple left for a dinner date, I climbed into April's bed and pulled her into me, wrapping her in my arms. It'd become our nightly routine.

'It was a serious question, by the way. How come you haven't kissed me yet?' she asked again. We were watching Netflix on her laptop, and the question took me by surprise.

'Because you told me you wanted to remember it.' I didn't mention the whole "while we were in limbo" bit. It sounded crazy, even to me. The fresh memory of bumping into April in the library foyer that October 2017 evening was the only clue I had that it had all happened.

April nodded and looked at the screen for a while. 'But I've been remembering most things for a while now. And I'm hardly going to forget you kissing me.'

She was right. I'd told myself it was because I wanted it to be private. There were still nurses wandering in and out of her room. But really, I was terrified.

'It's like a do-over of our first kiss,' I said, opting for a half-truth. 'I guess I just want to make sure I get it right.'

April tilted her head up to look at me, a sly grin appearing.

'You should keep waiting then. You took a run-up for our first kiss, and right now I can't even walk. I'll definitely need to be prepared.'

Laughing, I pecked her on the top of her head, being careful to avoid the dressings on her still-fresh scars. 'Perhaps that's what you can tell your physiotherapist. You're in training for one hell of a kiss.'

April's Hospital Room

AUTUMN 2022

April

'Careful with my cards,' I told Mum, sitting fully dressed in my bed and watching her pack up my things. 'I've already got a new sculpture in mind for them.' I'd had Jen press some of my flowers too, and Adam had taken some photos around the hospital for my next art project. We got on a lot better now I'd nearly died.

'And make sure my medication and treatment plan is at the top,' I insisted.

Mum smiled. 'I've been over everything five times with the doctor,' she assured. After three months – half of which I had no recollection of – I was going home.

I'd worked hard for this. Constant memory exercises. Hardcore physio because my leg muscles had atrophied, plus my brain had forgotten how to walk. Everything hurt, and I'd get relentlessly frustrated that my body wouldn't do what I wanted.

I was finally well enough for outpatient care. I couldn't wait to get to Mum and Dad's, yet the thought of being away from the team of nurses and doctors who'd saved my life multiple times was terrifying.

I was thankful to be going home at all, though.

'You're bloody lucky, Ms Westbury,' my favourite nurse had told me. 'There's a young lad in the next room who fell backwards off a wall and is going to need twenty-four-seven care for the rest of his life.' In hushed whispers between rounds, she'd also filled me in on Dylan's very public showdown with his fiancée. Which is why she was my favourite. I felt dreadful about it, especially as Dylan clammed up whenever I mentioned it. It was sort of none of my business really, and I didn't want to force him to talk about something he felt so terrible about.

'I was wrong to let things get that far when I knew I was still in love with you. It's not a nice feeling, hurting someone like that, and I'll always be disappointed at myself for it,' he admitted one afternoon, before changing the subject and insisting he wanted to focus on the future and my recovery.

'April? You're miles away.' Mum was looking at me curiously as she zipped up my suitcase. 'Penny for them? Your thoughts?'

I sighed. 'A lot has happened in this room in such a short space of time, that's all.' I'd nearly died, twice. Been in a coma, struggled through physio. Then there was Dylan. We'd spent hours talking. About the past, the future and the right now.

Mum nodded thoughtfully. 'It certainly has. But you can't be afraid of the future, darling. We're all just glad you have one. Especially Dylan.'

We'd all been surprised when he'd not battled Mum and Dad to let me go home with him. Taking personal responsibility for my recovery would have been a very Dylan thing to do.

'You two have always gone into things full swing.' Mum smiled, sitting on my bed as we waited for the nurse to bring me the wheelchair I'd be going home in. Mum was fond of Dylan. 'I'm glad he's being sensible about this.'

Mum was taking a sabbatical from work to care for me. Dylan had fallen behind on his PhD and was determined to get his doctorate before the end of the year. Everyone was glad he was allowing himself to focus on something other than me.

'I told him you wouldn't want him helping you on the loo, anyway,' Mum joked. 'Although I imagine he'd enjoy the sponge baths.'

'Mum,' I gasped, giggling. It wasn't that funny, though, as I was dreading even Mum having to do the personal stuff.

'I know it's scary, coming home, where it'll be mostly you and I battling through the difficult bits of this,' Mum said, taking my hand. 'But don't disappear on me. Four years ago, I should have noticed you were ill. I'm your mother. I knew things weren't right, yet because your light usually burns so brightly, I convinced myself it was a dip rather than depression.'

I shifted uncomfortably, wishing I could get up and walk away from this conversation. 'I know you got yourself out the other side of it in the end,' Mum continued, 'but you will not deal with it alone again. I'm on high alert, especially as this injury is bigger than a missed year abroad and a broken heart. Much bigger. You must tell me the moment you start feeling low.'

I knew there was no shame in my mental health struggles, but I dipped my head to hide my blush. 'I promise, Mum,' I muttered. I was already on the waiting list for counselling through a brain injury charity.

'It was Dylan's idea actually,' I said. He'd been very insistent.

'I'm glad. We're all in your corner, April. I've never seen someone fall apart like Dylan did on the night of your accident. Worse than me, almost. And I know him being here was the reason you fought back so strongly. If I hadn't been so terrified myself, I'd have enjoyed the romance of it all.'

Mum paused, and I could see she had something else she wanted to say.

'You're a very passionate woman, April, and Dylan lets his whole world revolve around you. You're both lucky to have found the other half of yourself; a lot of people end up settling for something that's only halfway there.'

I'd been expecting some Mum Advice at some point. Now it was here, I smiled.

'But love can never be perfect; not like you want it to be. Dylan will do the wrong thing sometimes. He might disagree with you, darn right piss you off or even bore you on occasion. But don't run or fight it. Ride it out; throw your hands in the air and enjoy the loops it throws you through.'

I suppressed a giggle, silently willing the nurse to hurry up with my wheelchair.

'Those intimate moments, grand romantic gestures and desperate bedside vigils are worth all the times he falls short,' Mum continued. 'Because he will. And so will you.

If love was perfect, it wouldn't be such a rush; it wouldn't invoke such passion inside you. You, my dear April, light a fire in that boy, and he takes all that fanciful magic you run on and somehow makes it real.'

She'd rehearsed this monologue.

'What exactly are you trying to say, Mum?' I asked.

'That this isn't a fairy tale. And this moment isn't your happily ever after. It's still just the beginning of one hell of a thrill ride, so buckle up.'

'Thanks for the pep talk, Mum.' I put my arms out so she'd shuffle in for a hug. 'But Dylan and I have finally managed to figure most of that out on our own, and something tells me we're both ready for it this time.'

April's Bedroom

Dylan

April's room was the same as it was when we were at uni.

'Dad wanted to turn it into an office, but Mum wouldn't let him.' She laughed. 'Although she reckoned it was mostly because she didn't know what to do with all my crap rather than sentimentality.'

Her parents lived in a sprawling bungalow so hadn't needed to make too many adaptions. They'd brought a futon into April's room so she could have somewhere to sit and watch TV. She was sick of sitting in bed.

I sat on it now, watching April practise getting around her room using a walker.

'I feel useless. It takes me forever to do anything,' she moaned. The April I'd known in uni wasn't one for exercise, but she'd toned up cycling the hills of San Francisco. 'I miss my iron thighs.'

'A month ago, we celebrated you walking ten tiny steps. Now you're only worried about being slow and a bit spongey,' I reminded her. We were all stunned at how far she'd come, relying on her wheelchair as little as she could. But then again, April always was determined once she put her mind to something. 'Don't tire yourself out though; sit with me.'

She eased herself down and half swung, half lifted her legs up and onto my lap. 'Mum gave me this big speech in hospital.' She smiled. 'You'd have cringed it was so cheesy.'

'What about?' I imagined Sarah cornering April for a mum-and-daughter moment.

'Love. Us. She warned me things wouldn't always be perfect and not to run away when they weren't. But I'm not going to run away.'

On impulse, I pulled her forward, so she was sat fully on my lap.

'You can't actually run anywhere anyway,' I said. 'Besides, I never needed perfect. I just needed you.' Curling her soft hair behind her ears, I gently caressed the bald patches that had been shaved for surgery. She tried to hide them, but it got harder as more new baby hair sprouted.

'There was something I wanted us to talk about one more time, before we never, ever mention it again,' April started.

The footballing fresher.

'I know you say none of that matters, and I've started to understand why it happened. I think I can even forgive myself for it. But when you tell our story, did I cheat on you?'

Rubbing my temples with the thumb and index finger of the hand not curled around April, I took a deep breath. 'Do we need to put a label on it?' I asked. 'I think it's far more complicated than that.'

We'd both taken an emotional battering when I went to Rome.

'I tried to force happiness on you then ghosted you when it didn't work. You rejected my quick fixes for self-sabotage. Our relationship had totally broken down, but I don't even think we can pinpoint when it was officially over. And we're the only two people who matter.'

I told her about Al and Megan. April was horrified, until I explained perhaps it was something Al had to go through to be the husband he is today.

'He loves Jodie, no question. Always has, always will. He just got lost for a second,' I said. 'And so did we. I used to be all churned up with regret about losing you, but not now. Since your accident, I've learned to accept the mistakes I made, because I'm damn sure I won't make them again. And you won't either.'

I thought back to old-man Dylan holding an eighty-nine-year-old April's hand in her final moments.

'Someone old and wise recently told me that just because we got everything wrong, doesn't mean we're not right for each other. Besides, we're still young, but we're not those kids anymore. We're different now. We needed that time apart to discover who we are without each other.'

'We're different but the same,' April said, staring at her ceiling. 'You're still the Dylan I fell in love with that day in the library. The history geek-next-door with the earth-shattering smile.'

'And you're still the same April, who daydreams as she walks, carrying the pinkest coffee cup possible and an adorable "I Heart Rome" bag I really should have paid more attention to.'

April whipped her head down, her eyes so wide I worried I'd fall in them.

'Dylan, the library? You remember?'

'Let's just say the recollection came to me while you were in a coma.' I laughed. 'But yes, I do. I remember you smelled of that shampoo you used to love. I remember slowing down as I got to the top of the stairs and realising how beautiful you were. For a split second, I almost turned back, but then I remember nearly forgetting the name of the paper I needed, panicking and forcing your face out my mind.'

April almost winded me as she launched her whole body at mine on the futon, her soft lips finding mine. It was like going back in time to that morning in her uni living room. My heart felt like it was going to explode as she kissed me. First it was ferocious, but then, in a way that always drove me wild, she pulled back. Her mouth moving tenderly over mine as we savoured the moment. Passion quickly took over again in a crescendo that left us both gasping for breath.

'That was even better than the first,' April murmured, her lips still grazing mine. 'And look… we're already in my bedroom.'

'Are you sure?' I asked.

'I promise I'm not going to break,' she breathed, leaning in to kiss me again. I felt my whole body give into hers. Every fibre of me jangled with nerves as I carried her over to her bed. Then, as our bodies found a rhythm, recognising that thrillingly familiar spark we shared, pure exhilaration slowly took over until all I could think about was how I'd survived this long without her.

The Library

SUMMER 2023

April

'You have to go inside alone.' Lizzy smiled, nodding towards the door of the University of Manchester library. To celebrate a year of being back in the UK, and the day I returned all my walking aids to the hospital, she'd lured me here for a "trip down memory lane". Only now she was abandoning me at the revolving door.

She was up to something.

Scrunching my nose up, I stepped into the foyer, my footsteps echoing in the emptiness.

'Hey,' a voice called, and I looked up to see Dylan standing on the balcony at the top of the stairs, his smile not quite reaching his dimples. He was nervous.

'Where it all began,' he said, spreading his arms out wide. He was dressed casually in jeans and a dark, long-sleeved T-shirt pushed up to his elbows but looked jittery.

'For me at least,' I said, looking up at him curiously. 'I'm still not sure how you suddenly remember bumping into me that night in minute detail.'

Dylan laughed, burying his hands in his pockets and making his way down the stairs towards me.

'April, you know better than anyone that memories can reappear even after the most convincing vanishing act.' He stood in front of me, his dimples finally awake. I counted the gold flecks in his irises as he ran his fingers through my hair.

'When you first got home from hospital, you asked me what I say when I tell people our story. I finally know the answer. I simply say we loved each other so much we tried again, even though we royally fucked it up the first time. We took another chance despite screwing it up so bad we barely survived it.' Dylan sighed, not tearing his eyes from mine. 'And if we thought it got tough at uni, then this last year, especially those months you were in hospital, have been on another level. At times, it even felt like I'd lost you for real.'

'It has been rather brutal,' I admitted. Dylan's gaze was so intense I couldn't look away.

'Yet here we are,' he said. 'Through it all, the one thing I was always sure about was you, April. I was sure the day you walked into my kitchen. The day you flew to San Francisco, the day you showed up on my driveway and every day in-between. And I'm sure as hell certain now.'

I wanted to tell him I was sure too, but Dylan was in full flow.

'There were times I wished I did things differently. Not anymore. Now I know all I have to do is keep choosing you and nothing else will matter. So that's why we're here. In the place you first knew we were the other half of each other. I'm asking you to choose me too.'

My hands started to tremble as I realised where this was going.

'Are you doing a speech?' I hissed.

Dylan bit his lip. 'Stop it. And no, not *a* speech, *the* speech. Let me finish.'

I pressed my lips together in silence while Dylan took a deep breath and carried on.

'My love for you burned even when I tried to lock it away. Since I stopped fighting it or fearing it, loving you has only made me stronger. Better. And this time, when I say all in, I mean it. Not just the lightning bolt moments and unstoppable kisses in libraries and living rooms, but the missteps, the unreturned voicemails, the angry outbursts, the comas. I'm here for all of it. So be here for all of it, too, April. Marry me so we can infuriate each other forever.'

Dylan had been so focused on his speech, he dropped to one knee almost like an afterthought, holding my hands.

'Marry me, April,' he said again, laughing this time.

'That's all I've ever really wanted,' I said, laughing too. 'I'd marry you tomorrow if I could.'

'That can be arranged.' He grinned. Suddenly, he looked dismayed. 'Fuck, I forgot the ring.' Scrabbling in his pocket, he produced a red velvet box and slid a band on my finger with shaky hands.

'It was still perfect,' I said, so lost in his smile I didn't look at the ring straightaway. When I did, I gasped.

'My grandma's!'

Tears welled as I admired the fifties diamond setting hugged by a cluster of sapphires.

'Your mum gave it to me. Told me I better make it good.'

Mum certainly was on team Dylan. Which was comforting, even though they'd spent the last nine months double-teaming me whenever I was too trodden down with the effort of physio or frustrated by the headaches that made it impossible to concentrate on anything but breathing.

On the days exhaustion trapped me in bed, Dylan climbed in with me and curled himself around me in the dark haven of my duvet. Mum would bring us comfort food that was somehow still healthy. Dad would busy himself with practical things like converting the bathroom into a wet room so I could shower by myself.

We all had our moments. But I was finally back in the studio at the gallery twice a week under the watchful eye of Jen. Lizzy kept my spirits up with some sardonic advice and plenty of wine. I felt shrouded in love in a way that made me feel cosy and safe.

'There may be some people waiting at the pub.' Dylan smiled, getting to his feet, my hands still in his. 'Just Lizzy, Jen and the guys. With champagne – to commiserate with if you'd said no. I wasn't being presumptuous. I've learnt with you, April, to always expect the unexpected.'

Poking Dylan in the ribs, I stuck my tongue out.

'Come on, you knew I'd say yes. In a thousand different lifetimes, I'd always say yes.' And somehow, I knew that to be true.

'Just one thing,' I added. 'You mentioned unstoppable kisses in libraries. There weren't any of those that I recall.'

'Not yet.' Dylan tucked my hair behind my ear, cupping my face and tilting my chin. 'But there's about to be.'

I giggled, leaning into his chest.

'Good. You've got to end it with a kiss.'

Dylan stopped, his lips mere millimetres from mine.

'No, April. The kiss is still only the beginning.'